QUEEN RISING

FALLEN REALM
BOOK THREE

JOLINE PEARCE

e-ISBN: 979-8201737870

ASIN: B09X4VYTJ3

Print ISBN: 9798344137698

READING ORDER & CONTENT NOTE

The *Fallen Realm* series is meant to be read in order. *Falling Princess* is the first book in the series.

Eternal Knight is the second book in the trilogy, and *Queen Rising* is the third.

Crimson Throne is a standalone parallel story that can be read independently of the main trilogy.

Please note that this series contains strong language, descriptions of violence including sexual assault, major character death, blood, and scenes that may be problematic for people with eating disorders (*Queen Rising*). It is intended for mature audiences.

GLOSSARY

Pronunciation guide & definitions:

Auralia (au-RAY-lee-uh): the name of the sun goddess who gave the Kingdom of Auralia its name. Means Golden One. Symbol is the celestia.

Astra (ah-STRUH): Star or stars.

Čhióni (che-ON-ee): Ice. Formal name of the Mountain of Ice.

Čovari (cho-VA-ri): A secretive sub-tribe of warrior-scholars loyal to the royal family.

Dael (Day-el): Auralian currency.

Myseč (MI-sech): "Moon"; moon person.

Myseči (MI-SECH-ee): plural form of Myseč; moon people. Symbol is a crescent moon.

Skía (skee-UH): Shadow gang dedicated to overthrowing the royal family. Any Auralian who wishes to join may do so. Symbol is an eclipsed sun.

Tenáho (ten-AH-ho): a village in the Mountain District. Means Hillside.

Tuli Bayne (tu-lee bān): Waterfall Town. Bayne is a common term for village or town.

Vatira (vah-TEE-ra): Fire. Formal name of the Mountain of Fire.

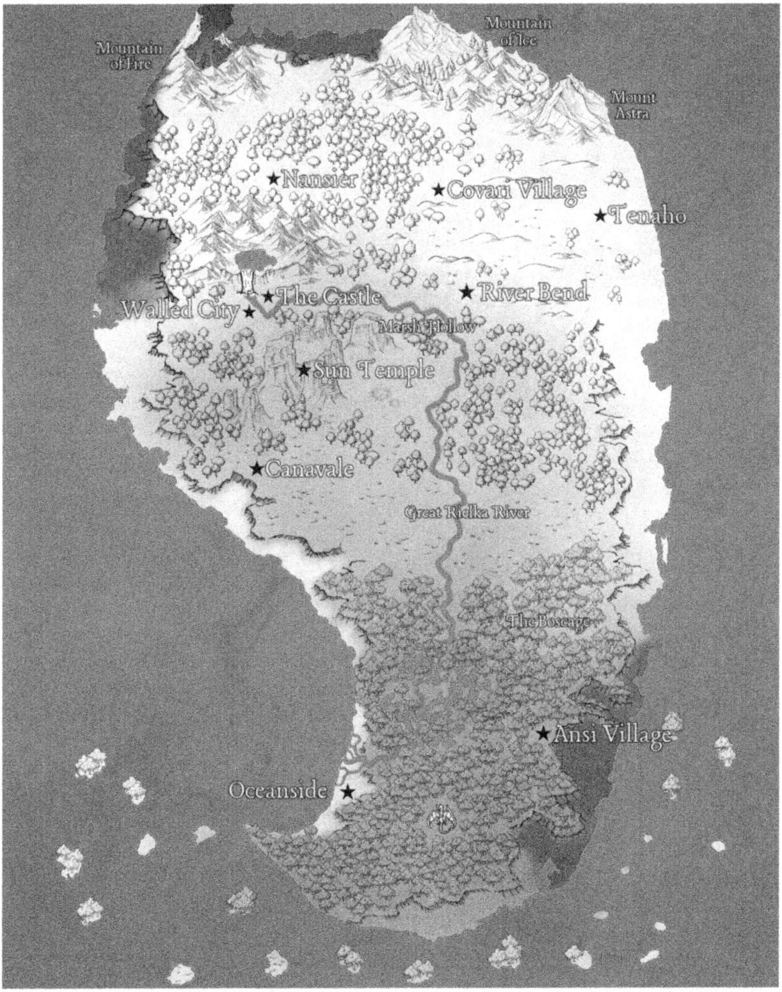

Mountain of Fire
Mountain of Ice
Mount Astra
Nansier
Covari Village
Tenaho
The Castle
River Bend
Walled City
Marsh Hollow
Sun Temple
Canavale
Great Rielka River
The Boscage
Ansi Village
Oceanside

SEED

CHAPTER ONE

This is a stupid way to die.

My final thought as I plunged to my death.

A split-second later, my arm nearly dislocated. Hard fingers grasped my hand and held, stopping my descent with a bone-rattling yank. I yelped.

Or, not. At least, not yet.

"You're all right," Lorcan called down from directly above me. My body twisted as I clutched his forearm. The torque broke my weakened grip. Sweat sent me slipping out of Lorcan's grasp with a panicked screech.

Another hard stop, this one marked by the bite of rope into my hips and thighs. Right. The makeshift harness Lorcan insisted I wear. He grunted and shifted as he took my weight. I landed hard against the steeply sloped Plateau and bounced off rock and dirt. Blood dripped from scratches on my forehead, shoulder, and knee, but I wasn't dead. I'll take it.

"I said, you're all right," he called out.

"How?" I demanded, plaintively.

How did he stay on that narrow path, with my weight falling upon him?

How are we not both dead?

Gravel rained down on my head. I squeezed my eyes closed, the better not to see the steep slope of the Plateau descending dizzily hundreds of meters below my dangling boots.

"Use your feet to brace yourself."

I detected a note of strain beneath his deliberate calm. Lorcan has a level head. My heart cracked, remembering the night we lay together in my study and Bashir tried the door, presumably to search for information about Auralia's war preparations.

It took me several tries, with my body failing to cooperate, until I got my boot soles planted, knees bent. There's a long, nearly vertical slope down with nothing but roots from long-dead trees and odd boulders embedded in the sheer face, to catch us if we fall.

"Can you climb?" he asked.

I tried, with an inelegant grunt. Arms burning, my hands claws of desperate strength, I kicked and scrambled up the surface. Lorcan had managed to loop the rope holding me around a protruding rock, and he used it to haul me up, centimeter by hard-won centimeter. His entire body leaned out almost perpendicular to the Plateau.

What did I notice? Was it the breeze kicking dust into my face? The terrifying splendor of dangling from a thread between earth and sky? The way my heart hammered as though to break right through my ribcage?

No. It was Lorcan's straining muscles, crisscrossed with the evidence of a life lived in violence. It was the intensity in his blue eyes and the way the wind ruffled his light brown, sun-bleached hair. The precise slant of his nose between sharp cheekbones.

The familiar thin white scar was still there, barely visible beneath a smudge of dirt. One small thing remains unchanged. Familiar. *Hello, my friend.*

Our gazes clashed and locked for the briefest moment. Then I grasped the rock and found my footing on the trail again, panting against the dirt.

"Are you okay?" he asked, breathing hard. Sweat gathered in the hollow of his throat, that place I liked to run my fingers over for comfort. Touching him there used to make me feel so safe. If he could relax, so could I.

Never again. Not knowing what I know now.

"I think so," I gasped, almost burying my face in the sun-warmed earth, shaking from head to toe. I clutched a root and held on, trembling.

"Pivot your feet like this." Lorcan brought himself back to a normal standing position and demonstrated, placing one boot before the other. "That way you won't be on your toes all the time. Use the inset stepping stones and avoid the dirt sections in between. It's unstable."

He's told me this several times already, but I keep forgetting. It's hard to walk sideways. It's hard to creep uphill on the balls of your feet. It would be hard for a woman who wasn't half-dead from starvation, like I am.

"We're close, Princess. Can you make it?"

I nodded, though I wasn't entirely sure. I had no other choice but to press on. Having started this mission of dubious importance, there was no way but forward now.

By the time we reached the top of the Plateau, I ached from neck to ankle and had a headache to boot. We made it, rolling over the top onto the grass. In a final indignity, my pack slapped the back of my head.

Alive, though. That was worth celebrating. A year of isolation with a violent madman had given me a new appreciation for living—if I could figure out how to do it.

I clinked water cans with Lorcan and drained what was left in mine.

The vista spread out below us almost made the climb worth it. Waterfalls sparkled in the distance. From here you can't see the ravaged fields, or the ruined villages. Only a sea of bright green grasses that have cropped up to replace what once was agricultural abundance. You'd hardly know there'd been a war. Far off into the distance you can see the Three Sisters...

Which reminds me.

"I need to make the annual pilgrimage at some point this summer."

Lorcan stiffened. "Last time, you nearly froze."

"You remember that?" I asked pointedly, not looking at him.

He scowled. "I remember now. I didn't for a while." He pushed up from the ground in a fluid motion. "Come on. I'll show you the way to the bunker."

"I've been into Saskaya's hidden lab before, Lorcan."

He gave me an inscrutable glance. Might be annoyance. I almost hoped it was. My unease at being alone—truly alone—with him, was back. Arguing keeps an invisible wall between us, and I need him to stay on the other side of it. Lorcan betrayed me. Broke my heart, cheated, and lied about it. I can't afford to let him get close again.

Assuming he'd want that. He says he wants to restore my trust in him, but what he really wants is the stupid crown. Using me—just like everyone does. Like he's done from the moment we met. I should have heeded that warning voice.

My title and birthright are nothing but a curse.

I followed him into the broken Sun Temple—for one thing, he's my only way to get back down. For another, he has the box with my father's remains.

In the center of the Temple lay a large pile of rubble from a hole in the roof. The carved stone interior seemed relatively undamaged, apart from the loss of the Goddess Auralia's arm.

"I should probably think about giving a speech for the Midsummer festival," I mused, my voice echoing from the stone walls and what's left of the ceiling.

"If you're launching right back into tradition," Lorcan said over his shoulder, bypassing a scattering of broken wood and slate, "you might want to hold festivities somewhere else."

True enough.

"Probably at the castle." My footfalls echoed on the stone. "For Ifran's workers, at least." As badly damaged as it is, The Walled City is rubble. If anything can be built this summer, it will be a testament to his dedication and skill. I can give his workers one measly speech on a high holiday.

I brushed past him and started down the stairs to the lower chamber of the Temple to the Hall of Ancestors. Lorcan's quick, quiet steps caught up to me almost immediately, as though we haven't just spent hours climbing a sheer rock face. I trudged on sore legs. My stomach growled. Today has involved a lot of physical exertion. He's so fit that he's hardly winded.

Halfway down the stairway, as the light from above dimmed, tiny lights embedded into the stone walls began to glow. The effect is similar to candlelight, powered by the supply of liquid energy in the secret laboratory at the opposite end of the Temple chamber. These lights don't go out. Ever. It's the eternal sun of the Goddess Auralia.

A light in the darkness.

I have never needed one so badly as I do now.

"I hope I'm not keeping you from plans back at the camp." My tart insult echoed off the limestone. Lorcan's step faltered. All right, that was unnecessary of me. *You're supposed to be the descendant of the goddess. Act like it, Zosh.*

Yet I need to keep him at bay. It would be too easy to fall back in love with him—if I ever fell out of it.

Tonight, we will be very alone. More alone than while sharing a small apartment at the castle.

More than when we were at River Bend, where I learned of his betrayal.

When he didn't respond to my goading, I added, "By tradition, the royal family spends the first night of internment in vigil inside the Hall of Ancestors. I mean to do so tonight."

After tonight, and my final visit to the Sky Temple, I'm done with tradition. I'll break them and make my own.

And then, Auralia's line dies with me.

Tonight, I'll bid farewell to history. Tomorrow, I start claiming my power. My crown. My throne. My country.

The last Auralian queen.

We emerged from the stairway into the soft glow of the hall. It reminds me of the way exhibit halls were lit at Edinburgh Castle, and in parts of the Louvre. A long stone bench faces the high wall with neat squares of stone. On it, taking up most of the space, was a roughly constructed wooden box. Most of the squares were carved with names. The most recent is my mother's.

Five millennia of my ancestors' bones lie here. This is my family's crypt.

"There should be a tool to pry open the vault," I said, searching for it.

"Zosia. Wait a bit. Let's eat before diving straight into the next task."

"Right."

He would harass me to eat, even without considering my state of starvation. Yet it's true that I'm famished and filthy, and there's no need to rush this. We aren't returning to the castle tonight. By the time we get Cata and my father into the burial vault it will be dark, and I intend to honor them properly.

Lorcan led me to the rear of the Hall, opposite the mausoleum, with the ease of someone who knows this place intimately. A section of rock, the seams invisible to the naked eye, swung silently open. Pale violet light spilled out.

Inside was a control panel, a large bed-like structure with clear crystal walls on three sides, and a rudimentary living area. It's meant to be a refuge of last resort for the queen or princess, should she become ill or injured. The construction is Čovari, made of the same strange material as the Sentinels, inscribed with ancient Auralian.

As far as anyone knows, Lorcan is the only one who's ever used it.

Two bunks occupied the darkest corner of the room. Lorcan placed his pack on one. I took the other.

"I'd like to wash up, if I may."

The look he gave me was sharp and unreadable. Did he expect me to ask him about his recovery here? I probably should. Yet knowing what he did afterward, I'm reluctant to inquire about any aspect of that time in his life.

"By all means, Princess."

He showed me the way. I was taken aback to find his

soap and a razor in the washroom, along with a clean towel. "Have you been staying here?"

"It's a convenient waypoint. I'm in and out," Lorcan replied. "Or, was." There's no real door, only a partition. "Not a lot of privacy. Saskaya and I were here together for months." Glancing around, he huffed a quiet laugh. "No wonder she shoved a sword into my hand and told me to get moving."

He did—away from me. Chasing the invaders out of our country and organizing resistance fighters, leaving me to starve, trapped in the castle alone with a monster, for over a year—while he slept with every woman who lifted her skirts or dropped her trousers. Lorcan claims he didn't remember me. I'd write it off as one more lie, but even Raina assures me it's true.

Once he came and fetched me, I tried to strike a bargain with an outsider. We need money. But Lorcan couldn't bear to see me wed to another man.

Now, we're publicly engaged. I'm stuck with him through the Autumn Harvest, when I'll be formally crowned. Three and a half months of torturous forced proximity.

Again.

This time, it was my idea. An attempt to save face after I ran away from a political marriage I myself had negotiated.

All he had to do was say, *I remember every day with you.*

Lies. He remembers tattered bits and pieces and none of the important moments. He doesn't remember us. He remembered he wanted what I represent. Nothing more.

He exploited my heartbreak.

I let him, to the detriment of my country. I was a lovesick fool, never imagining that Lorcan, of all people, would break my trust so coldly.

I had a few minutes to rue my idiocy while I quickly showered away the dirt and sweat from my climb. Avoiding my reflection in the fogged mirror, I pulled on a clean white shift and the new violet gown. It swallowed my thin frame. The belt helped a bit, the bunched fabric giving an illusion of curves where I used to have them. Short hair had the advantage of drying quickly. I held it back from my face with the gold diadem I brought with me. I didn't think to bring a brush, though the leather sandals were a relief after hours in my boots.

Lorcan did a double take when I come back out into the main room ten minutes later.

I glared, even as my heart leaped at the memory of him doing precisely the same thing when I wore my green gown in Paris eighteen months ago.

"My father would appreciate the formality," I cut him off before he said anything about my unnecessarily fancy clothing.

"It's a nice dress."

"It is." Too bad I won't be needing another one in white. The one I'm wearing was presented to me as an example of the maker's skill, in hopes that I would grant her the honor of crafting my wedding gown, but the giver couldn't have known our engagement is a sham.

Lorcan saved my country from conquest, but he cost us the money we needed to rebuild. Money I would have obtained for marrying Prince Sohrab. Maybe it wasn't much to the rest of the world, but Auralia is bankrupt. All I had to offer was myself and the title that casts a shadow over my entire life.

Then I leaped at the chance to have Lorcan back, and ruined my best chance of setting Auralia right in the process.

Catastrophic princess fail.

I placed my sweat-stained clothes into the steam washer while Lorcan took his turn in the shower. It all felt quite domestic—reminiscent of life in our shared dormitory at university in Scotland. Before I knew Bashir was a power-hungry murderer and aspiring rapist, back when my biggest problem was concealing the nature of my feelings for Lorcan lest I hurt those of our mutual best friend, Raina. I dragged my fingertip along the contents of Saskaya's messy desk, remembering.

A folder of Cata's press clippings lay open. I flipped through it for a moment, remembering the way she kept these articles on hand to show me what they wanted me to be. But that wasn't me, then, and they're not me, now. They're sad reminders of how badly I've already failed at the most basic tasks of being a princess.

At the sound of Lorcan's return, I closed the folder. There's no reason to hide that I was looking at it. In the photographs I look impossibly young, and more beautiful than I have ever actually felt. I'm inexplicably embarrassed by them.

I didn't appreciate my good fortune then. I'm not sure I deserve it now. What a foolish girl I was. Yearning for things I was never going to have. An education. Freedom. Respect and love, most of all.

All proved elusive. Now there's nothing left but the dreary weight of ruling.

"Sas used those to try and jog my memory." Lorcan's voice, so close by, jolted me. I sensed him rather than looking up—the clean scent of his freshly-washed skin, the warmth of his body at my back.

"It didn't work," I said, flatly.

"Not really." Lorcan reached past me to flip it open

again. He paged to one of the later entries in the stack. Us at the Louvre. Me in a backless emerald dress that hid nothing. I looked like a Hollywood movie star, and Lorcan was mind-numbingly handsome in his suit. He, too, looks impossibly young. That life seems so long ago, now. "This one. I remembered that night, a little."

"A little?"

Does he remember how boldly he undressed me from neck to navel? It didn't take much. The bodice was held up with two pieces of silk tied at the back of my neck. Lorcan took advantage of a dark corner of the museum to touch me, when there was no other way for us to be together privately.

He glanced at me then, and my insides erupted with flutters. "Pieces. Fragments. Things I didn't trust or believe. It was very confusing."

Stupidly, I remained rooted to the spot. "How so?"

"I would have these...episodes. Not dreams; I wasn't asleep when they happened. Right on the edge, though." His hand came to my back. I flinched at the contact but didn't move away. "I would be kissing you, or touching you. There was this crushing sense of longing. I'd wake up then—or become fully conscious, I guess—and remember you yelling at me in the snow after that party. Running away in Princes Street Gardens. Now I know you were running away from the men I killed, not me. But at the time..." He trailed off. "I couldn't put the pieces together to figure out the truth. I was sure you despised me, but Raina insisted I was wrong. Saskaya didn't know either way. Suspected there were feelings, but didn't know how much they'd changed."

Because we hid everything we were, back then. Too afraid of being separated, only to have it happen anyway.

We should've claimed the time we had together. Like Scarlett and Kenton did.

My heart pinches at the memory of Kenton's playful roughhousing and sometimes brutal honesty.

The warm press of Lorcan's palm left an imprint on my back when he removed it. I exhaled through parted lips, staring without focus. As long as he doesn't know how he still affects me, I can get through the next few months of this façade.

"You weren't entirely wrong," I said when I could breathe normally again. "I did despise you, at first."

I can't quite despise him now, though. He's lost so much. Part of me believes that when he confessed to remembering me after pretending not to for weeks, he was reaching for that shared past, hoping we could reclaim what had been taken from us.

That's the part of me that needs to hold him at a distance. The danger is that he'll betray me all over again. I can't afford any more false starts to my shaky rule, and he's already made a fool of me once.

Lorcan set out two bowls. I tucked my skirts beneath my bottom and sat. I glanced up to find his flinty eyes crinkled with mirth.

"I thought you never hated me."

"Never too late to start." I smiled sweetly. His answering smirk was simultaneously familiar and rage-inducing.

I'm starting to suspect that Lorcan knows exactly what effect he has on me, and that Raina was right: he will try to worm his way back into my good graces. I cannot allow that to happen. The only thing more humiliating than being cheated on by the man I spent a year waiting for, would be giving him a chance to do it twice.

Or marrying him, and setting myself up for a lifetime of infidelity.

There are many things I need to bury tonight. My father. Cata. The love I once shared with Lorcan.

All my hope.

Nothing good ever comes from hope.

CHAPTER TWO

" **A** re you sure this is going to fit?"

The square of stone came off easily. The interior of my mother's grave smells dusty but not dank. Dry and old. I had no difficulty sliding my father's ashes inside. Cata's body, however, was a different story.

"No." Unlike my father, Cata's body is partially intact and sealed inside the rough-made box. Said wood box does not want to go inside the crypt. I'm not sure what the rules are as to giving her a vault of her own. As the last living representative of Auralia I suppose I can make my own rules. Letting my father, mother, and their closest friend lie separately for eternity was not quite what I had in mind—but the damn box will not go in.

"What if we take her out?" I asked.

Lorcan, who has been hoisting the box mostly alone for the past twenty minutes, dropped it onto the bench, breathing hard. He must be feeling the climb, and my fall surely strained even his seemingly limitless endurance. Not that I noticed the rise and fall of his chest or the way his shirt pulled across his shoulders.

I totally noticed, and promptly felt both stupid and ashamed. Disrespectful of the dead, and of myself.

"The box must go." I contemplated seeing Cata's remains for a few seconds, then added, "In. It must go into the hole. Without opening it. I've seen enough dead bodies in one lifetime."

Lorcan chuckled mirthlessly and scanned the wall. "What about relocating her over one?"

"It's not quite what I had in mind, but it will do."

"It doesn't have to be forever."

"Um. Lorcan. The point of burial is that it's final."

How are we finding humor in this grim process? I don't understand. Nor can I imagine trying to make this work without him. It's morbid, it's miserable...and yet I'm not sinking into overwhelming despair over it, either. His presence is more of a comfort than I want to admit.

"What I mean, Princess, is that we'll have to come back with a stonecutter to carve their names anyway."

"True." Assuming there are any skilled tradesmen left alive.

"What if Cata takes this slightly larger space for a while, and when the time comes, we can move her in with your parents? Or, ideally, have someone else do it for us?" Lorcan patted the fractionally larger square one column over. "I have had enough of death and dying, too. I want to get on with living. I can't imagine Cata would protest."

"My father would."

Nothing I did was ever good enough for him.

Lorcan was already popping the face off the niche next to my parents'. Not ideal, perhaps, but better than the alternative.

Together, we wedged Cata's makeshift coffin inside, not that I was much help. Lorcan did most of the work. I dusted my hands and sat back while Lorcan fastened the stone facings into place. I can hardly lift them. I doubt I could have when I was in my prime; they're very heavy. Ordinarily this is a task that falls to the temple priests, but most of them have been slaughtered, and none lived up here before the war.

"What now?" Lorcan asked me when he finished.

"Now I sit here and wait until dawn."

His face falls. "You won't sleep? At all?"

I shook my head. The diadem pinched my temples. I rubbed them and adjusted its position. "It's a night of quiet contemplation for the surviving family. Which, at this moment in our history, consists solely of me."

"Your father didn't make you do this when your mother died." He phrased it as a sentence, but I heard the question in his voice.

"Of course. He stayed with me. I wasn't alone." It was the last time I ever wept. *Nobody wants a queen who cries, Zosia. A goddess doesn't weep. She is strong. You must be strong for your people.*

I was nine years old.

I spread my deep violet skirt over my knees and knelt on bare stone, muscles screaming in protest. I'm hardly going to be able to walk tomorrow, much less climb back down the Plateau.

"You don't have to stay out here. Go ahead. Get some sleep, Lorcan. I'm fine. The dead can't hurt me."

Only the living do that.

"I said I wasn't leaving you. I meant it." He sat on the bench behind me. He must be exhausted after hauling me and my father's remains up a flat-topped mountain, and then lifting a heavy box and trying to jam it into a hole.

I wished I didn't find so much solace in his presence.

After all, the next time I come down here for the night, it will be me going into a stone niche, with no one to sit and mourn my death. Mine will be the last name inscribed upon this wall, unless I change my stance on having a daughter.

Fear of one's own demise is not a good reason to inflict this life on someone else, though. Besides, I would need a partner if I decided to do it, and I don't have one.

All I have is one broken knight and a shattered heart.

"When you came here for your grandmother, what did you do?" Lorcan asked, softly, from behind me.

I shrugged. "I was younger then. My mother was with me. She told me stories until I fell asleep."

"About?"

"My grandmother." I wish he'd shut up and let me contemplate my failings, but I can't bring myself to ask him to be quiet. "About...about her adventures when she was a girl. Mariel was very spirited, even after she had my mother and my aunt. Just...you know. Memories."

All I have left of my family, now. Memories. Dust. This mausoleum in a broken temple. A ruined castle and a demoralized kingdom. Freedom, for as long as I can hold onto our independence. It all feels so precarious. An impossible task lies ahead, and I am already so weary.

I wonder whether I would feel more alone, or less, if I were engaged to Sohrab right now. Whether it's possible to feel lonelier than I do in this moment.

"Tell me a memory of your father. A good one," Lorcan clarified, and the weight of loneliness lifted fractionally.

"I..." A good memory of my father. Gods know we had our battles, two stubborn people who loved one another but couldn't get along. I had to search back. Years.

"Tell me about the bicycle," he prompted.

I couldn't restrain the tiny laugh that burst out of me.

Inappropriate. My father would be appalled. If my father hadn't brought me a bicycle from one of his early trips to the outside world, Lorcan and I wouldn't be alive now.

"I would have been six, maybe seven. He had it carried all the way up the pass between Chioni and Vatira, then strapped to the back of his coach for the trip home. You could see it shining as he drove through The Walled City. My mother took me up to the ramparts to watch him coming home. I was so excited."

Swallowing, I let the memory take me. It hurt, but it helped a little to remember, like lancing a boil. "He was so proud of his gift. He—he..." I shifted my weight on aching knees. "He liked me better, then."

Lorcan said nothing for a moment. "Because you were little."

"Because he could control me. And because...because I was happy then. Easier. More like my mother. Not so"—*sullen and sad*—"difficult." Before Lorcan could say anything, I continued, "He stopped the coach in the middle of the castle courtyard and had the bicycle brought down. He tried to show me how it worked, but he was too big. It made my mother laugh to see him try to demonstrate how to use the pedals and the brakes. I loved that bike. Rode it until I was too tall to ride it anymore. He always..." I swallowed. "He always said he would bring me another one, someday. But instead, he gave me a horse."

"Sky."

The horse I rode in the Olympics three years ago, in Beijing.

I nodded. "When I was twelve. I think he hoped the horse would give me something positive to focus on, since nothing else was going well for me, and it did. For a while."

"I'll get Sky back for you, if you want."

It's a nice offer. A nod to what we once were to one another. I'm sure he's sincere. But when my lips parted, what came out of my mouth was, "Let him be free."

Subtext: *I can't be, so let my horse roam.* Sky escaped during the sacking of The Walled City, and he seems happy enough with his herd. At least one of us should have a good life. It won't be me.

"The offer stands, Princess."

"Thank you."

Together, we sit in vigil to await the dawn.

WE RETURNED to the castle late the next day, once again covered in dirt and sweat, but without incident. Lorcan and I retired to the makeshift royal living quarters. Immediately after I bathed and changed, Ifran arrived.

"We found this in the throne room." He handed me the carcass of my father's satellite phone. "I thought you might want to have it."

"Yes, thanks. Saskaya might be able to salvage some of the data."

I turned the broken device over in my hand. I believed it crushed beyond use, but while the screen is a web of cracks, the body seems undamaged. I might have been able to make it work, had I been brave enough to venture into the murder scene. I could have called for help. Maybe. I never heard it ring, after that night.

Still, the bitter possibility that I suffered pointlessly remains.

Just how pointlessly was driven home not two minutes later.

"Your Highness, I brought you and your knight—oh." The maid's eyes widened. I swear she batted her eyelashes as if I, Lorcan's ostensible fiancée and her sovereign, weren't standing right there. Slowly, she turned to place the tray she was carrying on the table near the window. Staring, she breathily continued, "Sir Lorcan, I wouldn't have come in had I known."

Rubbish. Complete and utter shite, as Scarlett might say.

My knight stood there, bare-chested. There's no way he's oblivious to her gawping. Ignoring it, yes. But he's not stopping her, either.

"Dismissed," I snapped. The woman pulled herself together and bustled out the door. Which I slammed.

Lorcan shrugged into a shirt, eyeing me warily. I helped myself to an apple from the lunch plate and stalked out.

I can't stay here.

We'll expose our sham of an engagement within days, at this rate. He and I might still get along when we're alone in private, but whenever the real world intrudes, the divide between us remains a cavernous gap. At least my absurd display of jealousy will bolster the illusion that we're really together, if not quite in a way I would like.

THE RIFT between us deepened upon our return to Čovari Village the next afternoon. I led my horse into the stable, followed by Lorcan, who was in turn followed by Sethi's nanny, Tahra.

I was briefly tempted to raise the Auralian legal age of adulthood, because seventeen is way too young to be making consequential decisions like sleeping with engaged men—as though laws have ever stopped people from having sex with whomever they wish. (Except me. Lucky me, I always get to be the exception. At least some things never change—and it's always the shittiest parts of being a princess.)

In a tacit admission that flinging my reins at Lorcan and stomping away the way I did the last time we arrived in town, hadn't been the nicest thing to do, I brought my gelding into his stall to untack him. Unbuckling leather and grooming my horse gave me plenty of time to listen in on Tahra's attempts to flirt with Lorcan.

He promised he wouldn't embarrass me publicly before we part ways in the fall. Three more months of pretense.

Lorcan couldn't even make it three weeks.

Apparently, it's harder to bury seeds of hope than it is to bury your own father and surrogate mother. The stuff is a weed, popping up no matter how often I think I've eradicated it from the fallow garden of my heart.

I'll grant that the woman at the camp was only expressing friendly admiration, if you squint hard enough. Arguably, the maid who accidentally walked in on Lorcan's semi-nudity was taken aback by his stunningly masculine form (sarcasm font) and meant no offense. It's true that his scars are arresting, and he is very attractive. I'm sure people stare at him a lot. I did.

But this? There's just no excuse.

Even if Tahra miraculously suffered a failure of vision when I came into the stable, Lorcan damn well knows I'm right here. Anger made my fingers unsteady as I loosened leather straps.

"I'll help you with your horse." Brazenly, she followed

him into the cramped stall. "I wouldn't mind some person-alized riding lessons myself."

Ridiculous. The Čovari are all accomplished equestri-ans, taught from childhood. Better than me, and I competed in Olympic jumping. I didn't bring home a medal but I scored decently high among the best riders in the world.

No. Tahra is asking for another kind of ride altogether.

Did Lorcan tell her to get lost? Give any indication that he understands what she's after?

He did not. Lorcan played dumb, precisely like he used to do with Raina.

"I could give you a few pointers. Although I've seen you on a horse." Leather slapping as he unsaddled his mount. "You don't need any—"

I latched my horse's stall door, slung my pack cross-ways over my body, picked up the saddle, and strode up the center aisle toward the tack room.

"Princess, you shouldn't be—"

"You seem busy, Lorcan." My frostiness came from pure hurt. He's not dense. Tahra guiltily dropped her gaze. Yeah. I'm not imagining what she's after. It's common knowledge that we're betrothed yet she's acting as if I'm not here. Because she, like every other woman (except those of Hallie's persuasion, of course) old enough to entertain romantic notions, would love to spend a night or more in Lorcan's arms.

And he's been perfectly happy to oblige them.

He doesn't see it. Willfully, or through sheer thickhead-edness, I have no idea. But in that moment, I understood with crystal clarity that the dynamic of our union, were I foolish enough to go through with it, would be me chasing away his admirers while he stood idly by, pretending not to see the problem. Because he says he wouldn't take them to bed, and that should be enough for me. His word as his honor.

But he has no honor in this regard.

I could turn a blind eye, and if one of them gets Lorcan into a compromising situation, I would have to pretend not to see it, thus encouraging the next, and the next.

Or I can keep chasing women off and let my people paint me as a jealous wife. That is the position Lorcan has placed me in, and he seems either unable to see why it's a problem or that every time this happens, it feels like that moment at River Bend when I *knew*, all over again. There's no winning, and it is energy better spent serving my people. I could never say yes to that.

Perhaps I'm not being fair to him or Tahra, but this is the place where I am the most broken and Lorcan constantly presses on it.

"Zosia, wait."

I kept walking. I deposited my saddle and bridle in the tack room without cleaning them and headed for Saskaya's house. Convenient, how easily he forgets his promises to me when there is any other woman's attention to be had. If he wants to win back my trust, he's going to have to do better than this.

The arrangement I insisted upon is making me crazy.

I should try and find another solution to our predicament. One that sends him far away from me. And yet...

There was the moment near dawn in the Hall of Ancestors when I forgot he was there, lost in morbid thoughts about my own mortality. When I couldn't feel my legs anymore from hours of kneeling on cold stone, and stumbled getting up. Lorcan caught me before I fell. A shadow at my elbow, a warm presence at my back. A reminder I wasn't alone. I turned into him and buried my face in his shoulder while he held me. It felt like he cared. I wanted to believe it.

Perhaps he does, on some level. But not enough to give up the adoration of any pretty girl who walks by.

I don't know who this new Lorcan is. Yet I can't stop loving the old version of him. The one I knew before the invasion of Auralia changed everything we might once have been together.

CHAPTER THREE

I found Raghnall supervising my brother as he splashed in a mud puddle with a couple of shepherd puppies, gleefully making a terrific mess. The sight made me smile.

"Welcome back, Princess."

"How is my little bro—"

"Shh!"

Right. I can't acknowledge my only living relation.

"Mudlark," I finished, substituting an English word for the secret I had nearly betrayed. I can't cost Sethi membership in his mother's tribe. That's his choice to make, someday. I have no doubt that he will choose to remain with the Čovari. Who would give it up to be known as the half-brother to the last princess?

Gods. He's eighteen months old. I'm writing off a *toddler*. I can't continue like this. I don't know what else to do to distract myself from my deepening embitterment. Stay focused on rebuilding—although every decision I make reminds me of how badly I messed up with Sohrab.

"Happy as a pig in..." Raghnall hesitated. "Poop."

"I see that."

"Sas is upstairs in the lab. Do you need help carrying things inside?"

"No. Thank you. I have it."

I'm sore and aching in more ways than just the physical. I spotted Lorcan coming out of the stable. He started coming toward me, but hard on his heels was Tahra. I hefted my bag and turned away.

"You've stalled out." Saskaya frowns at the scale. "The trip to the castle was a mistake."

"It was unavoidable. I needed to take care of my father."

Saskaya rolled her eyes. "Your father is dead. You need to take care of yourself. At this rate, you're not going to recover until sometime next year. Let's see...you need to gain another 10-12 kilos before you're back where you were before the invasion. That's the minimum weight for your height, by the way. You went in there without much to lose."

"I feel as though all I do is stuff my face."

"No, what you do is play with your food and eat half of what you're served. The shredding is a normal response to starvation, Zosia, but you need to actually put the food into your mouth and consume it for this to work. Not run around expending energy on things like climbing cliffs."

Saskaya was pissed about my visit to the Temple, which compounded my sense that I could not do anything right. I hoped that giving my father a proper send-off might alleviate some of the guilt I've carried for months. If anything, it's made my internal chaos worse—a state compounded by the standoff with Lorcan.

"The dirt bikes were fun, though," I joked. My heart isn't in it. I dropped my head onto my chin and sighed.

"Are things any better with your knight?"

"No." I sat up again and pushed away the notebook Saskaya is using to record my health progress. I see she spoke with Raina about Dr. Wen, recently. I wonder what she makes of the antidepressants I'm taking. They don't seem to do much, although the doctor said it could take a few weeks for them to start working.

"Sas. What was it like when Lorcan first came out of his coma?"

I don't know what prompted my question. The thought of him being trapped in that eerie bunker for months weighs on me, that's all. Waking up to that weird blue light, and trying to put himself together like a puzzle missing pieces.

"Poor kid flopped out of that fishbowl barely strong enough to stand," Saskaya replied, absently. She'd gone back to tinkering with a small screw on a vial of concentrated violet energy liquid.

"Fishbowl?"

"The crystal-sided bed in the Temple. When the fourth wall comes up, it's leak-proof. Put your patient inside, fill it, set the temperature, and you have cryogenic therapy. It can also maintain stable body temperatures, or act as a warming tank."

Why didn't they build it on top of Mount Astra, near the Sky Temple? Surely, freezing representatives of the goddess to nearly death isn't a great long-term strategy for survival. I really wonder about my ancestors, sometimes. Wise women, my royal posterior.

"Wasn't the water pretty gross after months of him floating in it?"

"It's an amazing piece of machinery, Zosh. There's a filtration system in the base. Diluting this stuff"—she shook the vial of concentrated energy liquid—"sterilizes the water. The risk of infection with a head wound like that was very high. I strapped him into one of Raina's intravenous lines with antibiotics as a precaution. Waste of valuable resources. The Čovari elders were smart people." She tapped her silvery temple. "Speaking of smart, how's your test prep coming along?"

"It's not." I haven't told her that I won't be finishing my degree. I've authorized a partial payment to settle Kenton and Bashir's accounts. When—if—money becomes more readily available, I'll pay mine, Lorcan's, and Raina's, so they can complete their studies if they so choose. I know Raina is working on hers. For me, there are too many other pressing priorities. My degree remains ever out of reach. "Tell me honestly. Did Lorcan really forget me? Or has he been using it as an excuse for his behavior?"

It's confusing to me, the way he claims not to remember me, but then recalls details from events I was sure he'd forgotten.

Sas set aside her project, sat back in her chair, and crossed her arms. "Zosia, that kid was a mess."

I arched one eyebrow. My friend sighed and returned her attention to the disassembled dirt bike engine on her desk.

"Your boy," Saskaya continued, tilting the piece of machinery to get a different angle—

"He's not 'my boy.'"

She shot me a look. My cheeks heated. "I mean, beyond publicly."

My friend glared with pure skepticism.

"He could barely stand up when he came out of the tank. Didn't recognize me. Mistook me for my sister for a solid week. It was like having another baby on my hands." Saskaya blows a strand of hair out of her eyes. "I never even wanted one. Suddenly I was raising Cata's son and trying to put my sister's protégé back together. To say I was grumpy about the situation is the understatement of a century."

I laughed at that. "So, Lorcan was trapped in an underground bunker with a grouchy technologist for six months."

"Three of which he was unconscious. That was fine, other than the chaos unfolding below. I was pinned down and in no position to fight off invaders, so I took the precaution of detonating the entrance to the Plateau to prevent the invaders from getting up to the top." Saskaya cast me a lopsided grin. "Bored, but free to focus on my research. Which at that point consisted entirely of trying to override the hacked control system on the Sentinels." Her grin faded. "What a nightmare. Zosia, I feel so responsible for—"

"Shh. Sas. You're no more responsible for the invasion than I was."

I know what she's feeling though. The kind of guilt that cannot be reasoned away, only endured.

"No, but I'm the one who spent my entire adult life assembling five-hundred-year-old robot soldiers, only to have them malfunction and hunt us down."

Saskaya pinched the bridge of her nose.

"Sas. It wasn't your fault."

"I built the thing that killed my own sister, Zosia. I will own that forever."

"I know." I lurched out of my seat to embrace her. "I know."

Saskaya patted me on the back and let go. Demonstrative emotion isn't her style. I released her reluctantly, craving physical contact. Sethi is such a gift in this sense. My brother will climb into my lap and smack my cheeks with his pudgy hands and giggle when I protest. He's a bit like Kenton was, in this sense. No sense of propriety.

Gods, I miss Kenton. I need to get in touch with Scarlett, but I'm dreading it and keep putting it off.

"To answer your earlier question—what I think you were getting at—yes, Lorcan was genuinely messed up. We all hoped Lorcan was going to pop up just as he was before the accident. That didn't happen. We're all changed, Zosia, including you. You can't hold him to old standards."

My foot tapped the air. No one is giving me a pass. For me, standards of conduct are higher than ever.

"Does that mean I can't hold him to any standards?" I briefly described what happened in the stable earlier. Saskaya's sigh was not encouraging.

"I'm too old for this romantic turmoil. Never had the patience for it anyway. You're the princess, Zosia. A boy-crazy seventeen-year-old isn't a threat to you."

I mulled this while she kept talking.

"Lorcan has practically been a resident of this town since he was twelve. Girls have always liked him, and I include my own sister in that statement."

I closed my eyes in horror. "Please tell me they weren't—"

Saskaya cut me off with a groan. "No, not like that. Gods, you're suspicious. I mean the day he stumbled into town thinking he was on his way to River Bend, Cata lit up. She always wanted a kid, and here was this winsome boy with a burr under his saddle to be a knight for the princess. She got word to his mother that he was safe and took him under her wing. And I'll be damned if the one thing that hasn't changed in the eleven years since is his dedication to you."

"And his appeal to women."

"Two things, then." Saskaya cut me a look. "I don't know what happened to put your confidence in the gutter like this, Zosia. Whatever it was, get a handle on it. There's nobody in Auralia like you. Lorcan is not stupid enough to throw away the chance to be with the crown princess for a teenager with more hormones than sense. Watch for a few days if you don't believe me. He's patient with her. With everyone." She poked my shoulder. "Especially with you."

Not that I deserve it.

I tried to follow Saskaya's advice that evening. I sat back and observed Lorcan, who hung around the house on the pretext of helping with Sethi instead of retreating to Cata's cottage. Tahra followed him around like a lovesick puppy. As far as I could tell, he neither discouraged nor encouraged her. He was friendly, without giving any indication that his feelings were at all romantic. Exactly like he did with Raina.

Saskaya might be right. I needed to get over this crisis of confidence where Lorcan is concerned. It didn't mean I had to forgive him, but I couldn't continue letting it weigh on me constantly. I don't know how to handle any of this.

Princess fail. As always.

SPROUT

CHAPTER FOUR

Saskaya didn't understand why I was upset with Lorcan, and that had me second-guessing myself. Was I being foolish, or was I justifiably wary of his motives?

A call with Raina clarified nothing.

"He hasn't tried to propose, has he?" she demanded.

I snorted. "To the chambermaid at the castle, to Tahra, or to one of his other conquests?"

"To you. I take that as a no."

"No."

"Good."

Briefly, I gave her a summary of our trip to the Plateau —fall and all—along with a description of what happened afterward at the castle.

"Do you feel better?" Raina asked, surprising me by sidestepping the opportunity to drag Lorcan.

"Not really. I just feel..." I trailed off.

"Feel?" Raina prompted.

"Empty. Alone."

"You have Tovian and me. Hallie, too."

Except that I couldn't go back to River Bend and poison their happiness with my flailing. Being around their joy only makes me feel worse than I already do.

Nor could I stay here and risk betraying my brother. Avoiding the castle as much as possible was necessary to maintaining the fiction that Lorcan and I were to be wed in a few months. We can't withstand the scrutiny and the constant come-ons from women who still believe he's fair game.

I had nowhere to go.

I don't belong anywhere, even within my own country. *Especially* within my own country.

That evening, the others laughed and joked while cooking supper, passing Sethi from one to another. Tahra shyly tried to flirt with Lorcan, who was more relaxed than I'm used to seeing him. He's always opened up a bit in kitchens, around food. Apparently, that hasn't changed. It's an echo of the years we spent in Scotland, when I would hide in my rooms while Lorcan cooked and the other suite mates socialized.

But while everything else had changed, I remained the outcast. Isolated and unwanted. The sister who can't even speak the word "brother" aloud. A bride with no marriage on the horizon.

My thoughts were toxic and my heart ached.

Everything I meant to leave at my father's grave followed me down the hillside. I've never been very good at walling myself off emotionally, no matter how hard I tried not to feel. It's always been pretense.

What will I do when my princess fails become queen fails?

Horrifying, mortifying thought.

I slipped outside onto the deck. No one followed me. I listened to the crickets and let the warm evening soothe my frayed nerves. When I glanced inside through the window, I saw the four of them gathered around the table. Not yet eating, but close. Laughing.

Why can't I belong?

Why can't anyone love me, as I am? Forget the titles and the stupid legends. Once I wanted freedom. I wanted to explore and test myself. I wanted sex. (I still do, though it seems unlikely anyone will ever want that with me, now.) But deep down, I just wanted to feel like someone cared about me for a little while. I knew I wasn't going to find those things at home.

Now, I have no home. Nowhere to go, nowhere to be.

Lorcan glanced up. A moment later, Tahra glanced over at him, then followed his gaze, and frowned when she saw me.

Yeah. I'm not wanted here.

I waited for them to lose interest in watching me, then made my way down the deck and toward the path up the hill overlooking the village. Above the cave where Sas once concealed her rebuilt Sentinel army, before the war. At the top, I sat against the boulder near a twisted old tree, watching the waterfall glint in the setting sun. It's so peaceful here. I wish I could stay with Saskaya and Sethi, and lose myself in studying. Tinker with machines. Grow a garden.

I wish there weren't bridges and towns to rebuild, a castle to restore, stone to quarry, roads to repair...outside countries to convince we still have a viable independent government, despite being an entire country in need of rebirth.

I threw a stone down the hillside. Plucked a blade of grass and watched the shadows lengthen. Fireflies danced in the deepening twilight. The time to eat came and went. I ignored the hollow grumble of my stomach, something I've gotten good at doing over the past year.

I should go. But where?

Lorcan once warned me there's nowhere I can run that he can't find me. I was therefore unsurprised to see a small figure coming up the path toward me, growing larger with each step. I was only surprised it took him so long to seek me out.

Busy with Tahra, probably.

When he approached, I cast him a warning glare. He halted a few feet away, leaning one hand against the tree trunk, his expression tight and troubled. Lorcan is no longer quite as good at concealing his emotions as he once was.

"You missed supper."

I shrugged. "I find I don't have much appetite these days."

My voice hitched oddly. It was hard to form words around the tight ball of hurt lodged in my throat. I tried to swallow it, but the feeling lodged in my chest and grew.

"I didn't touch her. Tahra."

"It doesn't matter anymore, Lorcan. Do whatever you want. I'm not your keeper." I tossed the pebble I was idly toying with.

"It does matter." He exhaled in a huff of frustration. "I want to win your trust again, Zosia."

Not Princess. Not Highness. Zosia. Stupidly, this softened my resistance toward him a tiny bit.

"You have it. I trust you with my life, Lorcan." Not with my heart, though. He had it once and didn't value it. Doesn't need it. He won't let me die, though; I can count on that. He came close, but if not for him, I wouldn't be alive now.

"That isn't what I mean, and you know it."

I rested my chin on my knees, arms tight around my shins, my body curled into a ball. "If we were to marry and you chose to take up with a lady at court—assuming I am successful at reestablishing the nobility and restoring the castle—or a maid, or the governess of our children, I would have no choice but to look the other way and pretend I didn't see it. I can't accept a life of humiliation."

The one I'm forced to lead is hard enough, without knowingly adding to the burden.

Lorcan edged closer to me. Cautiously, he dropped to the earth, sitting straight-backed a few feet away.

"I won't do that. I still love you, Zosia. I couldn't let you go. I should have told you in Trissau. Confessed everything. I wish I'd handled it differently."

Events had unfurled at breakneck speed, in part because of me racing to save my country. I'm responsible for how things played out between us, too, which makes me feel even worse.

"I can't do this," I muttered, throwing another pebble.

"Do what?"

"I am not equal to the task of rebuilding this country."

"Shh. You don't have to do it alone, or all at once."

"My mother would be so ashamed of me right now." I almost choked on the words.

"No, Zosia. Why would you think that?"

I haven't cried since I was nine years old. Not when my father was murdered. Not when my friends were shot down before my eyes, or the man I loved nearly died, or I found out the depths of his betrayal, or when I learned I had a half-brother.

I didn't understand, at first, why my face was wet. The hot, itchy tightness in my chest was nothing new, nor the burning sensation in my eyes, but the liquid on my cheeks? That was unfamiliar. I swiped my cheek and stared at my hand in disbelief.

To my absolute horror, I sniffled.

"No one wants a princess who cries, Lorcan," I whispered. "Much less a queen."

"Did you ever think that your father was wrong, Zosh?"

"Constantly."

"Then why do you accept that as truth?"

"Because he was right. People want..." I stopped short, sniffling again, feeling the wall I've painstakingly erected around my emotions crumbling. Panic rising to replace it. I don't know what my people want. I'm not my mother, who spent as much time as she could outside the castle. Listening to her people. Approachable.

Whereas I've been hidden away, learning my father's approach to governance, which was capable as far as it went. But while he was respected, my mother was adored.

Raina cries, and no one thinks less of her for it.

Lorcan might have a point, the bastard.

"After everything you've been through, you didn't snap your fingers and right the world overnight? No one expects that of you. Least of all anyone who cares about you."

Cares about me. Is it possible I've had what I wanted all along, and couldn't see it?

My face crumpled. I could feel my chin wobble and my eyes swelling. Lorcan leaned over and gently turned my face to his. I jerked away.

Don't look at me.

He let me go, but didn't give up, and hauled me into his lap instead. I stiffened at the contact, hating how much I needed it, before my resistance broke and I burrowed into him. He kissed my forehead. My cheek. My lips. Softly. Gently.

"No matter what happens, I'll be with you every step of the way. I'm not leaving your side, Princess. Never again."

I clutched him with every ounce of my meager strength. I want to believe it. Part of me does. If it hadn't been for what I've seen in the past few weeks, I would, whole-heartedly.

But he's lying to himself as much as he is to me.

"I'm sorry it took me so long," Lorcan whispered against my hair. "I lost my way for a while."

I buried my face in the crook of his neck, wracked by harsh sobs that shred my lungs, feeling pathetic for needing this, but unable to give it up quite yet.

We both stumbled. Him, I might be able to forgive, with time.

Myself...that's a different question. I'm falling apart when my country needs me most. The thought ripped through me, sharper than a tiger's claws.

I've been set up to fail in every conceivable way, and I am. Nothing I've done has worked. Everything I try backfires.

I want nothing more than to do right by my people. I'm such a catastrophe of a princess; I should probably step down. Should have let Bashir kill me. I certainly don't deserve this...this...

Lorcan stroked circles on my back and held me tight. A long time passed before my tears subsided. Even after I could breathe properly again, I remained entwined around him. Like it's the last time I'll ever get to hold him this way. He stroked my hair and kissed my temple.

"I've never seen you break like this, Zosh."

I made a sound against his neck. It's humid and dark

there. The moon is bright enough to pierce my eyes when I finally cracked them open and loosened my grip, putting space between our bodies.

"I've always respected that about you. The way you get back up every time you're knocked down. Resilient."

"Me?" I sat up. There was a horrifying amount of snot in my nose. Crying is every bit as horrible as I remembered; I'll never give in to this urge again. Wordlessly, Lorcan offered me a handkerchief, which I soiled. Thoroughly. I stuffed the disgusting rag into my pocket for laundering.

"I've been hanging by a thread for years, Lorcan."

"I know." He continued to rub my back. "You were dealt a lot of shitty cards, Princess. We asked a lot of you, and you always gave your best." He faltered. "I've thought a lot about the way we all treated you back then. Closing you in while shutting you out. It's a wonder you didn't rebel more."

I drank water from his canteen and splashed some on my face for good measure. I wish I felt better, but I just feel empty. Hollowed out. I will not be making a habit of crying.

"Where do I go from here?" I asked, plaintively. I will have to return to the castle for good, one day, but I'm not ready for that, yet. Visiting was bad enough. Besides, if I go there, Ifran and his crew will ask me about every little detail. It will slow down their work. My fake engagement won't withstand the scrutiny, either. So that's not an option unless Lorcan and I become better actors, or work out our disagreements in truth.

Lorcan offered me a hand. I stumbled, rising to my feet. I seem to do that a lot these days. My balance is off. He steadied me and said, "Come home with me."

It took a few seconds to process his suggestion. It's a terrible idea. Yet, I have no better ones.

"To Tenáho?"

"I have a house there." He ducked his chin a little sheep-ishly. "It isn't much, just a cottage. It sits empty when I'm away. You can stay as long as you want to. Rest."

When I didn't immediately respond, he added, "I need to go back and see my family. People will expect you to have met them, if we are to be wed."

There are public optics to consider. This evening has not changed my mind about marrying him. Publicly, we're still romantically linked, but it's a ruse.

"Yes. Okay. Sure. We'll go to Tenáho."

Where else is there for me, now?

Lorcan smiled and touched the tip of my nose. I've given him the answer he wanted, even though I'm not sure this is a good idea. It almost certainly isn't, but I can't think of a better plan.

"My mother and sister will be glad to finally meet you."

He took my hand and led me back down the hill, meek as a lost lamb.

CHAPTER FIVE

L orcan's house was as small as he promised. The kind of cottage an elderly spinster might occupy, or a bachelor planning to move up in the world. Large enough for two people at the most, as currently configured.

A single bed sat in the airy loft at the top of the stairs, overlooking an open room below, which was dominated by a dining table and a fireplace flanked by mismatched chairs. He indicated that the kitchen was beneath the loft, and when I peeked in, I saw an ancient wood stove, a cracked ceramic sink and gleaming new wood counters. He's done work on this place.

The privy was located outside—inconvenient, but common in older homes in this part of Auralia. Beneath the stairs to the loft was a small nook with a rough wooden trunk.

The only decorations are sharp and shiny. Blades. Bows. There are even a few guns in the mix, though they were placed for convenient reach rather than displayed with pride. I found an empty hook and added Raina's dagger to the collection. It seemed to fit there. A memory for later. I didn't need it anymore, and it was never really mine.

My reflection in the blade showed my lips pulled up at the corners in a sad smile. He gave me a knife; I gave him one in return. According to Raina's tradition, that makes us betrothed.

Medals, carefully framed, from his athletic achievements. Reminders from another life. It seems so remote now. Before he became my knight, he was regularly featured in the global press. I know it was cover for his spying, but it's undeniable that Lorcan could have chased stardom abroad. Instead, he stayed to protect a princess who didn't appreciate his efforts.

Looking at these reminders of a lifetime ago was humbling. I can see what he gave up to serve me. I'm disappointed in myself to remember how little I deserved it.

How little I deserve it now.

"You can take the bed," Lorcan offered, carrying my small pack up the stairs for me as though I were incapable of doing so myself. I'm fatigued after the day-long ride. I haven't fully recovered from our climb to the Sun Temple. Nor from the ordeal before that.

I need rest. Ostensibly, that is the purpose of my stay here. Enforced idleness.

"Where will you sleep?"

I couldn't see his reaction to my perfectly reasonable question because he was up in the loft. I don't know if he was hoping we would magically fall into bed together, but if so, I needed to head him off at the pass. This is already too much physical closeness. If I had known there wasn't even a bedroom door, I wouldn't have come. I'm sure that's why he didn't warn me. Conniving man.

The ride here from Čovari Village was quiet. We

encountered few other travelers, no attackers, and Lorcan has never been one to chat idly. I lost myself in thought for most of the journey, mostly ruminating on the trip we took to the Sky Shrine. Upon crossing the bridge into Tenáho, a young boy shouted to his friends, "It's Lorcan, with the princess!" and ran to spread the news. You'd hardly know there had been a war. The children chased us until Lorcan dismounted and produced a bag of honey candies. This, at least, had not changed.

My smile faltered. Lorcan will, one day, want children. If he doesn't have a few already.

Coming here was a mistake.

"I'll make a pallet on the boxes under the stairs," he called down.

It's the only logical place to put a bed, unless you were to move the table up against the wall in the main room, or put a bedroll on the floor of the loft, which defeats the point of creating privacy in a small space.

"You won't fit. You're too tall."

Lorcan chuckled. "That is not often said about me."

I gave a long exhale. He isn't short. Taller than me, and easily a stone heavier than when I last saw him before the war. All of his newly-acquired growth is pure muscle. I would barely fit within the scant space.

"It's your house. I'll sleep beneath the stairs."

Lorcan's footfalls were light and quick as he came back down from the loft, took my chin between his thumb and forefinger, and tipped my face up to meet his eyes. It's a shock to look at him now. I hadn't realized how much I'd been avoiding it.

"No princess sleeps beneath the stairs in my house."

I jerked my chin away. He let me go.

"I've slept worse places."

An echo of what he used to say, in Scotland. We both know that now, I am the one who has slept in the worst place imaginable.

"No guest, for that matter," he responded lightly, dispersing the sudden tension. "Go ahead and settle in. You can put your belongings anywhere there's space. I don't mind if you move things around to make room."

This could have been our honeymoon, had we married upon our return from Trissau.

As it is not, I unpacked my extra sets of clothing, my new red Converse shoes, my notebook and glitter pens, my hairbrush, and a few small personal belongings, leaving one item in my bag, which I stashed beneath the bed. I spied nowhere to hang my one violet dress, and I didn't want to go searching for a closet, so I left it in its pouch and placed it on the shelf next to the desk. The shoes I tucked beneath the bed.

I will be washing laundry frequently, owning so few clothes, and all of them borrowed from either Raina or Saskaya. I might need to suck it up and buy some that actually fit. A small expenditure won't make much difference in the overall state of the Treasury.

Idly, I scanned the book spines. Lorcan, as always, surprises me. Tucked in between his beloved tomes on Auralian lore was *A History of Tax Policy and Collection.*

He never gives up, does he? A wry smile twisted my mouth. I can't imagine he's actually read such a dreadful book, but as Cata used to say, he's full of surprises.

Farther down the line, a small red book titled, *A Compendium of Auralian Amphibians.*

What a shock, seeing that. I wonder what happened to my little mossy frogs. Probably dead, by now. I paged through it, remembering. What a brat I was at eighteen.

Yearning for a freedom I couldn't quite define, without recognizing the lengths my friends and family went to trying to give it to me.

I snapped the book closed and set it back on the shelf.

"Are you hungry?" Lorcan asked from below. There's no real privacy to be had in this house.

"Yes," I called down, partly because it's true and partly because if I don't eat, Sas will lecture me about it. I went downstairs to find Lorcan in his kitchen. "What can I do to be useful?"

"Nothing." He cast me a lopsided smile. "There is nothing for you to do here except read, if you want to, and rest. Tenáho is the most boring place in the world."

"I highly doubt that." I took a couple of plates down, intending to set the table. "What do you do when you're here?"

"Fix things around the house, catch up on village gossip, make sure my mother and sister have what they need, and when I start going out of my mind, I leave."

I smiled at that. He's working so hard to win me over.

Lorcan must have made an appealing target for so many women facing bleak postwar romantic prospects: a proven provider and excellent protector, with a home of his own, and a prestigious job defending the princess, which takes him out of your hair for much of the time. No wonder they queued up to spend a night with him, hoping he might stay.

Yet here I am, again, the odd one out. I could have him but I refuse to claim him.

This situation is so awkward. I wonder if he remembers that day in Cata's kitchen. In Trissau, he claimed to remember every day with me, but it's hard to tell what's true and what's he's conveniently not telling me. He is, after all, a trained assassin. Spies with loose lips don't live long. Like Cata, he's selective about what he chooses to reveal. It's not helping his supposed quest to win my trust.

"Shouldn't you let your family know you're back?" I asked. I admit I'm curious about the woman who allowed her twelve-year-old son to leave home and seek his fortune.

"They know. Trust me." Lorcan chuckled ruefully. "Word has gotten around. By now, the entire village knows I'm here and who I'm with."

My cheeks went warm. This trip will be great cover for our fake engagement.

But Raina was right. Lorcan is trying to win me back. The question is whether I can withstand three more months of his efforts to worm his way back into my heart.

THE MAKESHIFT BED-BENEATH-THE-STAIRS arrangement didn't last one full night. I was startled awake by a loud thump followed by a low moan, and lay in the warm covers, with my heart racing, trying to remember where I was. Listening, while Lorcan cursed under his breath. Relieved to remember that I wasn't in a fetid jail cell and Bashir wasn't two meters away, with nothing but a few iron bars to protect me from his wrath if he escaped.

"Are you all right?"

I held the oil lamp high. His rumpled hair sticks up endearingly, casting shadows like a hedgehog's quills. It still manages to half-conceal one blue eye. His hair is a haystack; it makes me want to run my fingers through it. Always has, no matter how much I try to hate him.

Lorcan sat upright, with one knee bent and his foot propped on the opposite one, examining his swelling ankle.

"Kicked the wall," he said ruefully. "Hard."

"I told you, you're too tall for this space."

His gaze met mine. "Do you have another idea, Princess?"

I'm going to have to relent on the bed issue. Devious, scheming man. He knew there was only one place to sleep when he asked me to come here.

"Let's get you a cold compress." I took the lamp into the kitchen, leaving him in darkness, and rummaged around looking for a tea towel. I checked the icebox, a literal padded box with a block of ice inside, used the pick to chop off a chunk, and wrapped it in the towel.

"Do you think it's broken?" I asked, returning to him.

Lorcan shook his head as he tied the towel tightly around his injured ankle. "Might be. Wouldn't be the first time I've broken a bone, although this might be the dumbest way."

"Here. Take these." I handed him two tablets from the outside world and a glass of water.

"What are they?"

"Advil. Ibuprofen. You took them after Manchester."

"So, you're not trying to poison me."

I huffed a laugh. "I've considered it, but no."

After examining them, he tossed the pills into his mouth and swallowed them. I pulled his hand, encouraging him to get up, and put his arm around my shoulders.

"Come on. You can't sleep down here anymore."

"I'm not going to try anything. If you don't want me to touch you, I won't. I'll stay on my side of the bed."

I was too busy navigating the stairs with him leaning on me to glower properly.

"But if I did, you'll be happy to oblige me."

"Of course, Princess. Say the word." Lorcan dared to buss a kiss against my hair.

I rolled my eyes. "This is only because I feel bad about forcing you to sleep beneath the stairs in your own home."

"You always know how to flatter a man's ego, Zosia."

I pinched his waist. Flutters in my stomach. Teasing, like old times.

"You don't need me to flatter your ego, Knight. You have Tahra for that."

"She's a good kid. It's hard for them. A lot of the boys her age either died fighting or are away defending Oceanside. She's harmless."

Every comment I could make would reveal my insecurities, so I kept my lips sealed. *Good kid* doesn't sound like something he'd say about a woman he was sleeping with. I don't know this man anymore, though. I doubt I ever knew him as well as I thought.

We made it awkwardly up the stairway and over to the bed. Lorcan's hair spiked the moonlight coming in through the window, throwing his features into shadow, sharp and beautiful. He laid back with a groan.

"This is so much better. I can stretch my legs all the way."

I indicated that he should lift his leg so I could elevate his injured foot with a pillow. Lorcan seemed to find this fussy of me. He also clearly enjoyed it. Once he was tucked in properly, I had to figure out how to get into the bed. He's taken the side closest to the edge. Lorcan yawned and patted the place next to him, nearer to the wall.

"Come on, Zosh."

There's no help for it. I clambered inelegantly over him,

momentarily straddling his waist with my nightgown hiked up around my thighs.

He enjoyed that, too. Scheming man, as well as blind. I might not be quite as emaciated as I was a month ago, but I'm a long way from recovered. There's nothing to ogle. Or desire.

Before my head hit the pillow, he snaked an arm around my torso and pulled me close against his side.

"What was that noise about not touching me?" I complained, but I already had my head on his shoulder and my palm flat in the center of his chest, near his heart.

"Indulge me. I sleep better if I know you're safe." He yawned. "I haven't slept well in a long time."

"You're not being remotely subtle." I burrowed closer to his side. "I'm onto you, Lorcan. I know what you're trying to do."

"Is it working?"

Yes.

"No. Now, go to sleep."

CHAPTER SIX

I was again awakened rudely, this time to bright sunlight and too much warmth, by the opening and closing of the front door. An intruder.

"Lorcan?"

A woman's voice. Dismay spiked through me, even as I registered Lorcan's arm around my waist. Someone is familiar enough to walk into his home without notice—

Lorcan rolled onto his back and rubbed his eyes.

"Mother? Have you heard of knocking?"

"Oh! What are you doing asleep at this hour?"

My foolish jealousy ebbed instantly, with embarrassment filling its vacated space.

"I can't meet your mother like this. Do something!" I hissed. Lorcan's bright eyes danced with mischief. He's not wearing a shirt. I'm in nothing but a nightgown. We're sharing a bed. There will be no pretending this wedding isn't happening. Devious, scheming man.

"Sprained my ankle on the stairs last night," he fibbed easily. "We were up late."

There was a beat of silence. "Princess Zosia? She's here?"

"I don't know where else she'd be. Then again, she's been known to run off."

I propped my head on one hand and poked him in the ribs. Lorcan flinched, grinning. Unrepentant.

"I brought you bread. Baked extra this morning. I'll leave it here on the sideboard and check back later. Come and see me today; I want to discuss your birthday party."

The door clicked closed. Lorcan covered his face with his hands and groaned.

"Birthday, huh?" I prodded him in the ribs again, right beneath the long white scar from his visit to Manchester. He came so close to dying that day, and many other times, too. A celebration of his life—of surviving one more year—seems in order. "When is it?"

He once said that living to twenty-five seemed ambitious. He came very close to not making it.

I know he's turning twenty-three, but not the specific day in July. It's a travesty that I don't know these basic details about him.

"End of July. She's going to invite the entire village." He groaned again.

I'll miss the Midsummer festival at the castle if I remain here. On the plus side, I won't have to give any speeches until October. I should probably make an announcement about my coronation ceremony. Give the people something to look forward to. I can write something short on the satellite phone and send it to Saskaya to hand off to the priests—what few survived. They were easy targets. Killing them was a quick way to demoralize the population, and raid the smaller temples of gold and jewels. Priceless antiquities, looted and lost.

"Old man," I teased, poking him again while he lazily attempted to brush away my hand. "Ancient."

"Definitely. It's past time I settled down. As my mother often reminds me."

Before I could make a smart remark, Lorcan rolled up and pinned me to the bed, tickling viciously. I screamed and struggled, but he held me down until I was breathless and surely red-faced. When he finally relented, I swiped the tangle of hair out of my face and peered up at him.

The kiss hangs in the air between us, there to claim if either of us moved.

"How's your leg?" I asked him, deliberately turning away from that dangerous shoal. I saw his disappointment.

But I can't let myself get hurt like that again. No matter how sweet this has been, or how wrong I was about Tahra, all I can do is clutch the scraps of what's left of my dignity. I'm not the one who strayed.

I'm the one who waited, even if I had little choice in the matter.

Bat wings fluttered over the bright morning. *Bashir. The cell.* Part of me is still there. Part of me will never escape.

WE WALKED into town to have lunch with Lorcan's mother. I was inexplicably nervous about the excursion. I don't want to lie to the nice woman who brought us the bread we ate with butter and jam on the patio behind his cottage. Yet here I am, acting as though I intend to marry her son.

"You and Lorcan have a busy summer ahead." Rya's eyes are exactly like Lorcan's—blue that appears to shift from wintry ice chips to cerulean, depending on the light, yielding no hint of emotion. "If the rumors flying around have any truth to them."

I delicately took a slice of bread and began tearing it into tiny pieces. Lorcan captured my hands to stop me.

I asked for this pretense. It was my idea. I cannot afford to be unnerved now.

"The rumors are true," he lied easily.

"Which ones?" I blurted out, freeing my hand. "Forgive me; people usually refrain from gossiping about me in my presence. I don't know what is being said."

"That there will be a wedding alongside your coronation ceremony," Rya replied evenly. I know she caught the bread exchange a moment ago. Nothing gets past this woman. Lorcan gets his talent for observation from her. I'm fidgeting and avoiding eye contact—not exactly subtle, either.

Come on, Zosia, you know how to keep yourself in check.

Ever since that last night in Čovari Village, when I lost control of myself, I haven't quite been able to get it back again. This holiday is exactly what I needed to try and get my head on straight before I make another attempt to lead my country out of crisis.

If such a thing is possible. Fear of failing yet again might keep me pinned here indefinitely.

"We'll make an announcement when it's time," Lorcan lied smoothly. "Zosia is still recovering from a lengthy ordeal. As I know you can see, Mum."

The hilarity of my assassin knight trying to fool his own mother was almost more than I could bear. I ducked my chin to hide a smile.

"Another subject of wild rumors." Rya propped her chin on her hand and her elbow on the table. "Were you really in the castle alone for an entire year?"

I glanced at Lorcan. "More or less." I don't want to discuss Bashir. I changed the subject. "I understand you were a cook there at one point?"

"While his father was in service to your mother, the late Queen." Rya nods. "Fantastic kitchens. It was quite an operation, keeping the castle residents fed."

She clearly relished the challenge.

"Destroyed, unfortunately. The roof caved in with the late snowfall last winter. The Sentinels shot out a supporting wall. Once it collapsed, the food stores were ruined with dirt and mold. It was a near thing for me when Lorcan finally showed up." I smiled and gestured vaguely to my body. "I'm supposed to be resting. Yet there's so much to be done. I could work twenty-four hours a day and hardly make a dent in it all."

"Which is why you're not working any more than strictly necessary," Lorcan interjected. "Limited physical exercise, as much food as possible, and rest. Rebuilding will wait." He folded his forearms flat on the table. Wiry muscle and tanned, scarred skin covered with a light dusting of hair. "Fortunately, Tenáho is the least exciting place in all of Auralia. The perfect place to rest and recover."

Rya scoffed.

"How would you know? You never spend any time here," she asked. To me: "My son, as I am sure you're aware, spent a few months in this town before running off to seek his fortune. I nearly had a heart attack when I found him missing. Sent out search parties to look for him. Thought he'd been eaten by a wolf-bear or a maned tiger." Pinning Lorcan with a glare, she added, "The population of which are out of control after feasting on all the lost sheep and escaped horses from last year. The city is on me to do something. As if I can go out and kill wild beasts."

She raised one eyebrow and looked expectantly at Lorcan. He smirked.

"So, this is my problem now?"

"Why is the city asking you to take action?" I asked, bewildered.

"I am the city manager," said Rya.

"Ah."

City managers are typically elected officials who oversee the day-to-day administrative functions of a village. Need to apply for a permit, record the sale of a property, or pay your tax bill? The city manager's office is where you'll go. It's a testament to her competence that Tenáho is peaceful and prosperous after a year of war. It helps that the town is located in a remote part of the country with no strategic military value—to the northwest is Mount Astra, and to the east and south are sheer rock cliffs facing the sea.

The city manager's office is also where you go to file a complaint about public nuisances. Such as your sheep being attacked by maned tigers.

"It's a pity about your mentor," Rya said softly, reaching across the table to pat Lorcan's arm. "She was a good woman." To me, "You knew her?"

"Cata was a second mother to me." I sipped the glass of cider before me. If the alcohol content is more than three percent, I'd be surprised, yet after drinking less than a quarter of it I'm feeling buzzed. I haven't touched alcohol since before the war. I helped myself to one of the cookies Rya put out for dessert, hoping it will blunt the impact. They remind me of the ones Lorcan brought to Cata's house after our falling out in Scotland.

"Tragic loss." Rya took a cookie, too. "Had anyone else found my son, I'd have demanded he come home and stay in school here in this boring town, which he loathes so much he bought a house here."

Lorcan rolled his eyes.

Excellent trolling, Mum. I smiled.

"But she was convinced of his talent, even that young. I knew he missed castle life and wasn't happy here, so I let him stay with the Čovari. And now look at him." She smiled with satisfaction. "Poised to be the next king of Auralia."

The cookie turned to dust on my tongue.

AFTER LUNCH, Rya walked us to the town square where her office was located. Shops lined each side, with a fountain in the center. People stared openly at me, which I ignored.

"Is this where your birthday celebration will be held?" I asked Lorcan sweetly, having foolishly consumed all my cider.

He side-eyed me.

"Probably. The town hall is available to rent for celebrations."

"I assume your mother, as city manager, has secured the venue." I hiccupped.

"You're cute when you try to be haughty and tipsy at the same time."

In a display of maturity, I stuck out my tongue at him. Lorcan squeezed my hand as we continued past a row of shops and back toward his home.

The clearest sign of war is the emptiness of the shop windows.

One, however, caught my eye. Dresses. Simple ones, in the local style—apron-like with a square neck, lacing at the waist to fit the wearer. They were displayed on dress forms, over lightweight ivory shifts. It's nothing compared to the slinky modern gowns I used to wear in the outside world, but as I said, was a little drunk, and I haven't shopped for anything in forever.

"Do you want to go in?" Lorcan asked, following my gaze.

"No, no. The Treasury's finances couldn't withstand the blow." I stumbled. Drunk. He propped me up. Again. What an apt metaphor. Constantly picking me up and setting me on my feet like I'm Sethi's age and not twenty. Twenty-one, rather. Two birthdays missed, not that I much care. Celebrations were never much fun for me. They were always a performance for the populace, so it's amusing to see Lorcan suffering through a similar predicament. "Thank you. I might need to avoid cider for the foreseeable future."

He slanted me a grin.

"One reason to get you back to full health."

I cast him a questioning glance. "I'm not following."

"So you can drink wine at our wedding banquet without falling over."

I elbowed him in the ribs. I can't contradict him publicly. Someone might overhear. I'll argue with him back at the cottage—if I remember to.

"Were you always this conniving?" I demanded.

He lifted one shoulder and let it fall.

"Never worked on you, Princess. You've always seen right through me."

I wonder if that's true, or whether it's more flattery. I rather like the idea that he's never been able to fool me, but I think I'm giving myself too much credit.

The sky overhead shifted to a darker hue as clouds gathered. By the time we arrived back at his cottage on the outskirts of town, fat raindrops thudded against the ground. We made it indoors just in time to avoid a crash of thunder and pounding rain.

"Mountain weather," Lorcan moved about, closing the windows. "Sneaks up on you."

I yawned. It's barely mid-afternoon and I think I'm hungover. Rain is the perfect excuse to crawl into bed with a book. Lorcan changed into loose pants and takes the space next to me.

"You know we're not getting married," I mumbled.

"So, you say." He flipped the page on his own book.

"Excellent work maintaining the public image though." Our knees fell against one another, mine covered by the blanket, his outside it. Rain pattered against the window above us.

"My life in service to the crown."

Okay, that is him being annoying on purpose. I pushed his knee with mine. He pushed back. We came back to the center, still touching through layers of fabric. My stomach fluttered, because hormones have no damn sense.

"If you want the dress—or anything else—you should buy it." Lorcan didn't look at me. He turned a page. Lightning briefly turned his face a ghastly green.

"Scarlett is coming at the end of summer, after her internship in New York with the United Nations ends. She'll bring our belongings from Scotland. I don't need much to get through the next few weeks."

Nothing from my former life will fit, though. It'll be nice to get back my laptop with notes from school stored on it, not that I'll ever finish that damn degree, now.

Our shoulders touched, too. I laid my head on his bicep. Oh, this is bad. Very, very bad. But it feels so good. I'm tired, a bit chilled and craving human contact. Why overthink it?

Lorcan kissed the top of my head.

"Anything you need, Princess. I'll pay for it. If the Treasury needs a loan, I can cover it."

"Keep your money. You've more than earned it."

He chuckled softly. "Stubborn."

"I am often told so."

"My wallet in service to the—"

"Shht." The words on the page aren't really sinking in. My eyelids kept trying to close on me. "How is your ankle?"

"Better."

"Not broken, then." I bit my lower lip to keep from smiling. I don't doubt the injury was real, but do I think he was milking it? Yes. Do I mind? Not terribly. Should I? Probably more than I do.

A soft *hm*. He flipped the page. I drifted off.

Hours later, in full darkness, when the rain had diminished to a gentle sprinkling of drops against the windowpane, I awakened with a full bladder. Lorcan's body was wrapped around me like a child holding a favorite stuffed toy. The tops of his thighs pressed against the backs of mine. His arm weighed heavily on my waist. I wriggled out of his grasp and clambered out of bed.

Downstairs, I stuffed my feet into my boots and grabbed a cloak from the hook beside the door.

I hope he got a discount on this house, considering the plumbing situation.

When I came back, shivering, Lorcan was where I left him. I crawled back into bed, shoved him onto his back, and stretched myself against his side. He stirred long enough to hug me close.

"Bad dreams?" I murmured. He shook his head, sleepily.

"Good ones."

CHAPTER SEVEN

"Does she always talk this much?" I asked Lorcan under my breath forty-five minutes into a hike into the forested slope leading up to the cliffs outside Tenáho.

It wasn't supposed to be a strenuous trek. For Arya, it isn't. Lorcan is so fit it's hard to imagine a physical challenge he couldn't meet. I, however, am dying. How I climbed all the way up to the Temple, and then back down, is a mystery. It's possible that I'm fatigued more from his sister's incessant chatter than from the actual hike.

"Pretty much." His eyes crinkled at the corners. "She's been curious about you for years. Now she has you as a captive audience. Sorry."

"It's fine." For once, I actually meant it.

Unlike her mother and brother, Arya is a hotheaded chatterbox. Physically, she looks like a younger replica of her mother: same light brown hair, slight stature, full mouth and high cheekbones. Beyond that, they are nothing alike.

"Did you get to go clubbing?" Arya asks me. "I can't

decide whether it looks fun or terrifying. I'd love to have the chance to find out."

"No." I haul myself up a switchback, lungs burning. I'm starting to think my companions are part mountain goat.

"Pity. Probably my brother's fault."

"No comment." I gasped. Lorcan glanced back at me, half-concerned, half exasperated.

"It's not very fair that my brother has been out traveling the world while I'm stuck here in boring old Tenáho. I'd have enjoyed being outside Auralia. Unlike my stick-in-the-mud brother."

"I thought you liked it here," Lorcan said.

"It's okay. I didn't run away screaming from it like you did. Not that you ever invited me anywhere. After we moved here, I never even got to see Midwinter at the Sun Temple, or the Midsummer bacchanal, much less Paris. The Louvre," she sighed. "London."

"By all means, come to the Harvest Festival," I panted, before remembering her presence there would be a given if we were, in fact, marrying. Lorcan caught my slip.

"If you miss it, I'll never forgive you," he added.

"Ha. Fat chance of that. Can I be one of your ladies in waiting, Princess?"

"You'd have to be a lady, Arya," Lorcan teased.

I let the siblings snipe at one another and focused on putting one foot in front of the other. The thickly wooded forest blocks most of the sunlight. It's still hot and I'm sweating through my last clean top and trousers.

"Hold up." Lorcan stopped abruptly and tilted his head, listening.

"What is it?" Arya asked.

"I might be able to figure that out if you'd be quiet."

I hid my grin by taking a drink of water. Arya gave a

long-suffering sigh. Thirty seconds later, Lorcan was back, crouching low to stay out of sight. I put one finger to my lips. Arya nodded.

"Maned tiger with two cubs. We'd better take a different path."

"You're not going to shoot them?" Arya asked.

"No."

"Mum won't like that."

"Which is why we aren't going to tell her what we saw today, right?" Lorcan's exasperation was countered with an affectionate ruffling of his sister's hair. He and Arya led me down a side path.

Not long after that incident, we came to our destination: a lake nestled in a depression of rock. The view out over the valley below is spectacular.

"Worth the climb?" Lorcan asked, dropping down beside me on a section of the grassy bank.

"Ask me tomorrow." I caught his quicksilver flash of disappointment from the corner of my eye and squeezed his arm. "It's beautiful up here."

He looked at me, not at the vista. "Gorgeous."

It's a good thing I'm already a sweaty mess—my face is already flushed from exertion. I don't know how I managed the climb to the Temple, in retrospect. Pure determination. Or desperation to not feel so guilt-ridden and sad. It didn't quite work as I'd hoped.

"Are you coming in or not?" Arya popped out from behind a bush wearing nothing but undergarments under a thin shift. She flung her clothes over a bush and splashed into the water.

"Is this why you brought me all the way up here?" I asked. "If I'd known, I'd have brought clothes to swim in."

"Don't need clothes." Lorcan stripped off his shirt, toed

off his boots and unbelted his trousers. My face went from warm to scalding as I dragged my gaze away.

At the cottage, we're careful not to undress in front of one another. Still walking on eggshells. Partially, it's because I don't want him to see me looking so wasted. If I go into the water, the way my bones jut out beneath my skin will be clearly visible. It's not as bad as it was a month ago, but my sense of shame is inescapable. He's already seen me like that once.

I remained on shore. I kicked off my boots and rolled up my trousers to my knees, wading in the shallows. One small concession to the heat. My calves are like sticks. The belt clings to my hipbones for dear life.

"Come in, Princess!" Arya called from the deeper end of the lake where it abuts the cliffs. "You'll feel so much better."

I shook my head. Nobody needs to see that.

She squeaked. Her head disappeared beneath the surface of the water. Alarmed, I looked around for Lorcan but didn't find him. Seconds later, the siblings popped out of the water, one head after the other. Arya sputtered, kicking and splashing as she lunged after her brother in a futile attempt to get revenge.

I waded a little deeper into the water. A mistake, in retrospect. While I wasn't paying attention, the two of them ganged up on me and pulled me into the middle of the lake, kicking and screaming.

"What part of 'I am not coming in the water' did you fail to understand?" I chastised them when I got my feet under me again. "What if I couldn't swim?"

I can, though I'm no Olympian. That's not the point.

"I'd have saved you," Lorcan cast me a grin. I splashed water at his smug face. He dove under, easily avoiding it.

"If you want your clothes to dry before we go back down, I recommend hanging them in the sun," Arya said.

If I stay in the deeper part of the lake, they won't be able to see what I look like. The water is clear and clean, cool enough to be refreshing without giving me too much of a chill. I went behind a stand of trees to strip off my top and trousers, wrung them out as best I could and draped them over a branch in a patch of sunlight.

There's no way they'll be dry by the time we leave. Curse them. Those were my last clean clothes, too.

I tied a knot in my undershirt to keep it from floating up and scrambled back into the water as quickly as I could. I didn't swim so much as I sat on submerged rocks and watched Lorcan and Arya play. It reminds me of the way Kenton used to roughhouse with me. He was the only one who ever did that. I swallowed past the lump in my throat, remembering.

"You okay?" Lorcan swam over, broad shoulders cutting easily through the water.

"Fine. Thinking."

"Sorry we dragged you in."

I waved him off.

"It's fine." I pushed off the rock and dog-paddled a short distance away. "I don't really want to be exposed while looking like this. I don't feel like myself anymore."

I can't point to a single moment since puberty where I felt like I inhabited my own body. What self am I even talking about? I closed my eyes, opening them when Lorcan said, "Yeah. I know how that is. Disorienting."

I forgot he's been through a similar experience. We are alike in this way.

"Yes. That's exactly it. With so many people watching me..."

He leaned over to kiss my temple. "No one is watching you here, Princess."

No one but him, the one person I feel most uncomfortable being naked around. Especially given what happened at River Bend. A shudder rocked me at the memory.

He wants this to be a reset. Start over, as we are now, not who we were before the war. Lorcan is trying. It's impossible not to see how hard.

The nightly cuddling is lovely, but I can't imagine being with him that way again. Or rather, I can imagine it, but I only see my old self enjoying it, and that's because when I envision it, we're both bumbling virgins back on that thin dorm mattress in Scotland.

Now, it's all fraught and poisoned. I want to, with him, but I know I'd spend the entire time worried I was doing things wrong. Knowing that he's already experienced so much only makes me feel more inadequate than I already did—on top of feeling bitterly jealous and rejected.

Every time I try to grasp at hope it wilts in my hand. I don't dare take the sprouts Lorcan keeps offering me.

That part of my life is over. Ended before I ever had a chance to begin. I'll be mourning the loss for the rest of my life.

Damn Lorcan. Damn everything.

On the way back down the mountain, we all stop abruptly as the maned tiger and her cubs slink across our path. Breathlessly, we wait for them to pass in a silent shadow of orange and brown stripes.

Ours are similar to Sunda tigers, only with thicker manes, with males topping out at around 100 kilograms—more than twice what I weigh right now.

"Majestic," I said on an exhale. "I've never seen one before."

"Never?" asked Arya, curiously.

I shook my head. "I didn't get out of the castle as much as I would have liked to. You know. Before."

"Because of your mother?"

My chest went tight and hollow. I haven't felt like that since the night on the hillside before we left Čovari Village. Less than a week ago; a lifetime. "Can't risk the last remaining princess. Everyone knows the legend. If Auralia's line falls, so will the country."

And fall, it will. Nobody knows that, though, except possibly Lorcan. Depending upon how much he overheard of what I told Dr. Wen in Trissau. But the country doesn't have to. The legends are stories, not fact. I'll set Auralia up as best I can to continue long after I'm gone. Assuming I can ever figure out how to get my feet under me.

"Talk about pressure," Arya interjected. "I always thought being a princess would be fun. You get everything you want, don't have to do anything except wear nice clothes and attend fancy parties."

"A common misperception." I plucked my wet clothing away from my skin. "Not many would sign up for this life, knowing what it entails."

"My brother would," Arya said, pointing. "He's wanted it since he was a kid."

Lorcan has gotten ahead of us, scanning the path for any threats.

"You mean, since he was twelve."

Arya shook her head emphatically. Strands of damp brown hair stick to her neck and her cheek. "Younger. It's practically my first memory. Our father had just been promoted to the head of your mother's guard, so we went into The Walled City to see them ride out. Lorcan took one look at you and said 'I'm going to marry Princess Zosia.' He would have been nine or ten. Tops." She grinned. "Our father nearly tanned his backside when Mum told him what Lorcan said. It did absolutely nothing to deter him. All he did was get quiet about it."

"I had no idea it went that far back."

I had no idea he remembered that day, too. It was such a small moment. Riding with my mother, I clambered up on the seat to look back at him, and waved.

Those bright eyes boring into mine like fate. Unforgettable.

What a pity he's gone and ruined everything, when his lifelong ambition was within reach. It's a loss for us both. Though...if I were to change my stance on continuing Auralia's line, possibly not a total one.

BUD

CHAPTER EIGHT

Upon our return to the cottage, Lorcan lent me a soft old sweater and threadbare wool pants that I wouldn't have been able to pull over my ass if I were my old self. He plied me with a bowl of hot stew over rice and went out back to do the laundry.

"This place came with one of those old-fashioned hand crank machines. It'll be a few minutes." He kissed my forehead. I should be helping out more. I'm neither incapable of doing chores, nor unwilling to do them, but Lorcan won't let me lift a finger.

I used the time to call Raina and get the latest on her ongoing efforts to stop pirates from sending reinforcements to our southern beach.

It's better now, but they still make regular attempts to land. I can't blame them for trying to find a better life—these pirates are poor and desperate. Yet I am not obligated to sacrifice my country to people who intend to take what they want through murder and violence, no matter how much I sympathize with their poverty. They can seek a better life without destroying ours. They chose not to.

And I certainly hold the Skía responsible for exploiting them.

"Let me help," I interjected. "What can I do?"

"Sit on your ass, eat, and don't fuck Lorcan," Raina shot back.

"I wasn't planning to." I watched him through the window of the kitchen as we talked. "But there's only one bed."

Raina groaned. "Romance novels are fiction, Zosia. Not dating advice."

I chuckled. "Wouldn't know. Never got around to reading the one you loaned me." Exhaling, I explained about the stairs, his ankle, and how we came to be sharing his bed. Chastely. My friend was unconvinced.

"Fine. Sleep with him if you absolutely must, but do not marry him, for the love of everything holy."

"I won't. He hasn't asked, anyway."

"You could ask him. I did. Don't recommend it."

"I already tried that once," I admitted. In King Humayun's antechamber. "In Trissau."

"Unbelievable that he didn't jump at the chance," Raina said. "Idiot."

"Lorcan wanted to be the one to ask me." With a flash of panic, I remembered telling him he could ask me whenever he wanted and the answer would always be yes. Obviously, that's changed. "It was only supposed to be a formality. It was before I knew about... about..."

I can't even say the words. *His cheating.*

Raina made a disgusted sound. "Was he always a control freak?"

"Yes. Didn't you notice?"

"I guess I brushed it off when I fancied myself in love

with him. Besides, his possessiveness was all directed at you, not me." She pretended to retch.

"Hey, now. That's my temporary, sham fiancé you're fake-vomiting about."

"Oh, no." Raina groaned. "More romance tropes."

"What?"

"I was certain you were smart enough not to let Lorcan back into your life."

No wonder I'm so confused about what to do and how to feel: Saskaya thinks I should marry him. Raina says I'd be a fool to trust him again.

When I asked him what he wanted from life, he said: *Save the country. Rescue the princess. Marry her, and live happily ever after.*

I laughed and said I didn't need saving. I'm not sure that was ever strictly true, though. My life has been in jeopardy since the day I was born and will be until the day I die —hopefully, not from murderous Skía, but one way or another, it's coming. My death is as inevitable as anyone's. The question is how I use the time I have left to me. I've always known it might not be very much.

It was that fact that drove me into the night in Beijing. The need to experience a taste of freedom. Something. Even if no one else understood why or how badly I wanted it.

And the one night we were together physically, in River Bend, he said, *you have no idea how sexy it is to have you, Princess, panting and begging me to fuck you. None.*

I think he meant it as a compliment—he was turned on by it, despite my starvation—but remembering it now feels like the bright sun going behind a shadow. Lowering to know that all he ever wanted was the princess. Though he as good as told me, had I but listened.

If I needed any more evidence, Arya gave it to me earlier today. *I'm going to marry Princess Zosia.* A child's oath. I was always on a pedestal, an object to acquire on his personal quest. Perhaps at one point he came to appreciate me, Zosia, as a person, but it wasn't enough to make him come for me when I needed him most.

He didn't put me first, any more than anyone else ever has, and nothing about his behavior since our reunion indicates he ever will.

I watched Lorcan turn the crank of the barrel with our clothing inside. I don't quite understand how both Raina and Saskaya are both right despite giving me opposite advice. The one opinion I don't trust is my own. If I can't even trust my own judgment where my own guard is concerned, how can I lead an entire country?

Maybe I can't. Everything I've tried since getting out of the castle has gone wrong. I admit I'm hiding here in this mountainside village. Shirking responsibility. I resolved to be more diligent about submitting the applications for international aid Saskaya sent me to fill out. Having failed to bring in money through marriage, begging for money is the least I can do.

Just like my father did.

"Raina, is it possible he's lying about his memories?" I asked, pushing aside my rumination about all the things I've done wrong.

"In what way?"

"I can never tell when he's not telling me the entire truth, when he genuinely doesn't remember, or when he's lying outright."

Raina sighed. "He's never been an outright liar. He's always had a...how to phrase it?"

"A relationship of convenience with the truth?"

My friend laughed. "That's a great way to put it, Zosia. Yeah, he's changed a lot. I didn't really want to see it. He was hurting, and acting out from a place of pain, not that it excuses anything he did. I wasn't there when he woke up, but Sas and I were in touch regularly. I almost didn't believe how screwed up he was until I saw him again around Midwinter."

I wasn't there when he woke up. I suppose it's possible he resented me for not being there for him at his weakest moment—reasonably or not. Feelings aren't rational.

"Can you send me an article or two about head trauma? Something accessible to a layperson?"

Studying always helps me understand things better. I'm still academic-minded, even if there's no chance I'll ever get to pursue my intellectual bent now.

"Sure. But I hope you're not thinking about forgiving him."

"Why, Raina? What happened?"

"Ask him first." A long pause. "If he tells you the truth, I'll consider forgiving him. *Consider.*"

"It was bad?"

"Really bad. Not to change topics on you—I know this is important, and I want to talk you out of doing anything stupid—but we could really use you and Lorcan in Ocean-side for a bit, once you're ready."

"Why?"

"Saskaya has new weapons for us to test out on pirate ships."

I grinned at the cackle of excitement in Raina's voice, though the mention of Saskaya and weapons sent a shiver up my spine. Her track record is...not great. It isn't her fault, but I'm surprised she was willing to work on weapons development again.

"Not that it's so difficult to sink the shitty boats they use, but they're fast, and we have a chronic ammunition supply problem. This could solve it, if it works," Raina continued. "I also need someone reliable to get medical supplies down to them. Tovian will meet up with you."

"We can leave right after Lorcan's birthday next week."

"Great. Take a couple of weeks to rest, and then get ready to work your butt off."

Raina didn't need to ask which day it is; they've known one another forever. I wonder if I'll ever work up the courage to get the true story of what happened between two once-close friends.

I might prefer not knowing.

IT RAINS DURING THE NIGHT. My clothes weren't dry the next morning, placing me in something of a predicament. Nor were Lorcan's, but that was less of a pressing matter as he had plenty of alternative options to choose from.

Rather than confront this extremely minor setback when I first awoke, I rolled over and went back to sleep.

"I have something for you," Lorcan said when I finally came down from the loft, still wearing his pants and a threadbare tunic that probably last fit him when he was training with Cata. On me, it hangs off one shoulder and my nipples are clearly visible—as are my lack of breasts. I was never well-endowed but I had more than mosquito bites. I folded my arms over my chest self-consciously and examined the package. It was wrapped in plain brown paper and tied with string.

"Go on. Open it." He smiled lopsidedly. You'd think it was a Midwinter gift for him as a little boy. I worked the knot out of the string and untied it. When I saw the contents, I gasped.

"Lorcan, this is too much." There were not one, but *three* dresses inside, one green checked, one white with embroidery at the hem, and one solid blue. Beneath them was a soft brown sweater lined with linen, two elbow-length linen shifts, and a yellow petticoat. It's an entire wardrobe. Twice as much clothing as I owned before. He must have cleaned out the shop.

"Do you like them?"

"They're beautiful. I don't know how to thank you." Impulsively, I kissed his cheek. Embarrassment bloomed within my chest. Lorcan has been dropping affectionate little kisses on me here and there. This is the first time I've reciprocated.

I ducked my chin. When I look up at him again, a faint pink tinge is visible beneath his tanned skin. "So, you still do that."

"What?"

"Blush."

"I do not." Lorcan's indignation was adorable. "Assassins don't blush. We're incapable of it."

"Ha. You always have." I poked him in the chest. "Wait a minute. Does this mean you had these clothes around yesterday when we came back from swimming?"

"Maybe." He squeezed my waist gently.

"Schemer," I complained. Gods, he's not even pretending to hide it. "Feed me; I might forgive you."

Lorcan chuckled and set about making breakfast while I

changed into the green checkered dress. I layered it over a white shift, since I get cold easily. Although it's warm now, the weather patterns can shift quickly here in the foothills of Mount Astra.

The lacing at the waist makes it almost look as though I have a normal woman's shape. Still thin, but not so starved. Perhaps going around in a warrior's castoff clothing hasn't been doing my self-image any favors. Not to mention that the tunics Raina lent me are so short they leave my bony wrists exposed.

We ate, as usual, outside on the patio. I propped my bare feet on one of the unoccupied chairs, my skirt falling up my legs and pooling above my knees.

"I remember you sitting on your balcony like that," Lorcan says. "Early. When you didn't like me."

"I still can't figure out how you got onto the roof to spy on me." I picked up an apple and handed it to him, wondering if he remembers. He took it and bit. His expression precisely the same as it was that day, if not quite so boyish anymore. The sight stole my breath.

He shrugged. "Your father wanted to see you. But you looked so content reading about frogs on your balcony. I didn't want to interrupt." Lorcan's mouth curved into a grin. "Besides, the view was spectacular," he adds, indicating my legs.

I mock-gasped and pressed my palm over my heart. "Are you telling me that my sworn knight was ogling his charge?"

"There weren't many perks to guarding the world's grumpiest princess," he teased.

"You wanted that task and you know it."

"Of course, I did. I still do."

A shadow from a passing cloud fell over the fields below

us. Our relationship as princess and knight will end soon. Neither of us said anything for a moment.

"How are preparations for your birthday celebration proceeding?" I asked, to break the uncomfortable silence. I know perfectly well that Rya has rented out the town meeting hall for the afternoon and evening, ordered casks of beer and cider, and hired vendors to serve food. I also know Lorcan is only tolerating all of her fuss because last summer, his family believed he was one breath from death.

As far as Rya and Arya know, this will be his last summer as a resident of Tenáho. I dislike lying to them, but that decision was made before we came here.

Lorcan scrubbed his face. "Extravagantly."

"Are we still to meet your mother for lunch?"

"Yes. Which means we should probably get going."

We washed up the dishes and made our way into town. I chose my new Converse instead of boots. Arya about went out of her mind with envy when she saw them. Not the reaction I was trying to provoke, but amusing nonetheless.

"What are these? Where can I get some?" she asked, examining my shoes. "You know my brother almost never brought me things from the outside world? No mobile phone, no camera, no clothes—"

"How much money do you think knights earned?" Lorcan said with exasperation. "And what would you do with a phone, anyway? There's no service here. Not unless you want to spend all your wages on satellite service."

Arya pouted. "Instagram. TikTok."

I groaned. The last thing I need is Lorcan's sister creating mood boards or whatever and becoming an Auralia influencer.

"How do you even know what that is?" he demanded.

"You told me about it, Lorcan. You showed me pictures of you and Princess Zosia one year."

He frowned. "I'd forgotten that."

"There were a lot of embarrassing memes about us going around for a while," I added gently. "Scarlett says there still are. Something about 'shipping'?"

"Boats?" Lorcan's confusion echoed my own.

"I don't know what it involves, but I don't get the sense it means boats. We'll have to ask her about it when she arrives."

"When is she coming?"

"End of August. I'll have to arrange transportation for her and all of our belongings."

Another item for my endless to-do list. Saskaya and Raina are working hard to take the pressure off me, but I felt guilty for continuing to dump my responsibilities on them. I need to start picking up the slack.

After lunch, we walked Arya back to her job at the local paper shop. She manages the inventory and the front counter, and was supposed to be learning how to make paper from agricultural byproducts like rice leaves, or sturdier stuff from palm leaves harvested in the south. Currently, that stock is exorbitantly priced due to how many palms were razed during the war, and the difficulty of transporting raw materials. Arya never envisioned herself as a papermaker, though.

This would be a great time to hint that she should make preparations to join my court in the fall, if I intended to marry her brother. Since I don't, the omission hangs uncomfortably in the air.

I purchased a small quantity of brown sketch paper, not unlike the stuff used to wrap my new clothes. The cost didn't deplete my meager purse too much. It doesn't feel like much of a gift for Lorcan—especially considering his generosity in hosting me and buying me too much clothing—but it will round out the better one I brought from the castle.

I have owed him a birthday gift for several years, now. His party will be an opportunity to even the scales.

CHAPTER NINE

By the time we noticed the thickening cloud cover outside, it was too late to dash home and avoid the rain. Lorcan and I stood outside the shop beneath the roof overhang. A gust of cold wind blew through the town, flapping my skirt around my knees and whipping my hair into my eyes. I shivered.

Lorcan took me in his arms. "We should have left sooner. This will go on for a while."

"Mmm." I leaned back against his chest. "I'll bring my new sweater next time."

He kissed my cheek. "Why? You have me."

For now. I didn't spoil the moment by giving voice to my thoughts.

A canvas-topped wagon pulled by a determined-looking pony trudged up the hill and into view.

"Lorcan," called the driver. "Are you and the lady stranded? Want a lift?"

"Melcan." He waved. "If you have space."

"The princess can sit next to me; I don't bite."

Melcan is at least seventy, with a weather-beaten face

and uneven tufts of hair protruding from beneath his cap and the insides of his ears. I took his proffered hand and hopped into the box next to him, tucking my skirt around my legs, shivering. Lorcan jumped into the back of the wagon alongside dirt-crusted farming implements.

"It's no royal coach, Princess, but I hope you'll tolerate my humble conveyance."

"We appreciate your generosity, Melcan." I used the royal we to speak for Lorcan and myself. Glancing back at him, I smiled. Poor Lorcan's knees are bent up to his chin. Alone, he probably would have risked getting wet. Or hung about his sister's shop, or gone to his mother's. Anyone in this town would open their doors to him.

And many of the women would invite him into their beds. A fact I'd best keep in mind. I still don't trust him on that score.

"I thought I left in time to get back before the rain started. Pickles here doesn't like getting wet much," Melcan said. The pony flicked her ears with irritation. "Water gets inside. We were down in the fields tending my daughter's plot."

"What have you planted?"

"Squash, rice, and beans," Melcan turned to me. "Hoping it will be enough to get through the winter. Two daughters, both widows, and five children to feed between them. Never thought I'd be the only man in the house at my age."

"I'm so sorry for your losses." Trite, but true.

"It's been a difficult time for everyone. We're all tickled to have you staying with us. The last time royalty set foot in Tenáho Village would have been in your grandmother's time. She was a great traveler. Loved to be out in the countryside."

I smile. "I barely knew her. I was little when she passed."

"Wonderful lady. Unpretentious, like you. I bet your mother, the late queen, was the same way."

A sharp pang of longing in my chest. "I remember she liked to be out among her people. My father preferred to remain in the castle. Let people bring their problems to him, if they're so important."

A frisson of shock went through me, as if I'd spoken too bluntly.

"Aye," Melcan nodded. "Good king, but a bit removed from village life, if I may speak so freely. It's how the Skía got such a hold in the country."

"What do you mean?" A crash of thunder overhead sends Pickles lurching into a trot. "I thought they've always been a threat."

"They have. To you, especially. But it's hard to recruit when the population is prosperous and content. Your father's approach lacked the human touch, you know? It was easy for those criminals to peel off sons and daughters who felt the modern world had more to offer them. Ever since your father opened the border, it's been building. A lot of young ones felt cut off from the new. The older ones resented it."

I pondered this information. Arya's fascination with the outside world isn't an outlier. She's like me, at that age. Obsessed with all things modern. I assumed I was the only one, but I was normal. Utterly normal. I just didn't know it. Had no context for comparison.

"Me, I'm too old for change," Melcan laughed. "I have my house and my family and my Pickles. Life isn't so bad. I don't need modern problems."

"Is this a common attitude amongst the people?" I asked.

"Common enough. Now that us oldsters account for more of the Auralian population you'll likely find resistance to new technologies. Course, the younger ones like your knight back there don't listen. Want all the gadgets they can get. You've an unenviable task ahead of you, Princess. But I like what I've seen so far. You'll manage fine."

I can't imagine what he's seen to give him that impression, after a quarter-hour of conversation. Platitudes, but I'll take the crumb of positive feedback. Goddess knows I never had any from my father.

He dropped us at the door to Lorcan's cottage. We waved him off.

I've long said that I didn't want to follow in my father's footsteps when I ascended to the throne. When I thought of what my rule would look like, I imagined it as the Gaol, only colder, darker, and more frightening. An endless wasteland. But now I have a guide, of sorts. I want to follow my mother and grandmother's approach to governance.

I understand why my father wouldn't let me leave the castle. He'd already lost his wife. His primary job was to keep her alive and support her, or their daughter, and he failed on both counts. The danger was too great, so he kept me clutched so firmly in his grasp that I couldn't breathe.

With Lorcan, I could roam freely...as long as I keep him at my side.

Which is not currently the plan.

Maybe Saskaya was right. I should try again with him. This visit has been wonderful, giving me insight into parts of his life I've only glimpsed before. Now, I get to see it every day. He's patient and funny, kind and generous, even when his sister is driving him crazy or his mother insists upon honoring him in ways that Lorcan would prefer to avoid. He's a good man. Haunted and scarred, but he tries not to let it show.

Plus, I have Raina's (begrudging) permission to fuck him. Not that I need it, but considering how little I trust my own judgment anymore, I appreciate having it.

Inside the cottage, Lorcan toweled my hair gently. I changed into his old woolen trousers again and helped myself to one of his sweaters. It hangs off one shoulder. Everything still hangs off me. I'm a human clothes rack.

"Do you want tea?" he asked when I came into the kitchen. The kettle was already emitting a high, uneven whine.

"I'd love some." Leaning my hip against the counter, I watched him pour the water into a pot and set out two mismatched cups. I shouldn't do it. I'll only get my heart broken again. And yet...I want to.

At night, we sleep curled around one another, but it's been chaste. Not even a hint of sexual interest from him. It would be impossible for him to hide it.

"You look thoughtful." Lorcan placed one cup beside me. "Melcan didn't bother you, did he? Bit of a character."

"No. He didn't bother me." *You do, though. I can't decide what to do about you.* My head says to leave the past in the past. My heart...No. It's not my heart. It's everything from the neck down, wanting to try what I've been denied. If I'm still capable of feeling those things. After River Bend, I'm not sure. I hadn't felt desire in so long, and then to have the first attempt end so disastrously...

"Interesting guy," I said, keeping my thoughts to myself.

"I see you stole my sweater." Lorcan tugged my sleeve.

I ducked my chin.

"Didn't I give you your own sweater just this morning?" Lorcan smiled over the top of his mug.

"I like this one better." I smiled back. "Feels like wearing your hug."

"That, you can have any time, Princess." Lorcan set his tea aside and took me in his arms. My heart battered against my ribs. I felt his pulse beating hard, through layers of fabric, as I traced the line of his throat with my fingertips and brought them higher, tangling them in the hair at the nape of his neck. Always in need of a haircut. That's never changed in three years, several continents, and one war.

"I love you," he murmured against my temple. My remaining resistance breaks. I tipped my face up to kiss his lips. Gentle. Chaste. Our first real kiss since the disaster of our arrival back in Auralia a month ago. The one at the castle was for show. For others.

This one is only for us, and it's as tentative as you can imagine.

A flash of lightning from outside highlighted every lash, every striation in his iris. *What have I done?* It's my last coherent thought before the next kiss.

This one is not chaste. It's hungry and unyielding. My lips parted on a gasp, and memories flooded through me, only to be erased with each press of his tongue, every hot breath against my cheek. Past and present became a confusing blur in my mind.

Lorcan picked me up and placed me on the countertop. I wrapped my legs around his hips, locking my ankles. He nipped that place beneath my ear that makes everything south of my navel clench, hard. His erection pressed against my thigh, not quite where I wanted it. I inched forward, seeking blindly.

"Zosia. I've missed this."

How can he miss it when we never really had it in the first place?

I tried to shove doubt away. I want this. I want him. I just want something to go right between us, for once.

He worked one hot, callused hand beneath the hem of the sweater I wore. I clutched his muscular shoulders. Afraid he won't like what he finds there—or doesn't find—terrified it will be like last time. Breathing him in, when I can inhale at all. It's one dizzying sip of air after another. Lorcan traced my new shape, bumping over my ribs and my spine, working his way up toward my nonexistent breasts—

Thunder crashed overhead. I flinched.

He's done this before. It's not me he misses.

I can't do this.

Uncontrollable panic surged through me, sending my heart rate galloping. The last time we did this I *knew*. I'm not special. Just one more in an apparently endless line—

My thoughts tumble uselessly. It's all mixed up. *I'm* mixed up. Broken.

That night in Čovari Village, I was like a bottle of champagne that had been shaken until its cork popped. There's emptiness now, but the dregs of everything wrong with me are still inside.

I pushed him away, hard. I couldn't get enough air, but I managed to say, "Stop."

Did I whisper? Was it a shout?

Lorcan let go. I took in his kiss-bruised lips, his disheveled hair, one eye barely visible beneath the fall of his unkempt mane. Pupils dilated until the blue was only bright sapphire slivers. The frustration and worry written on his face.

"Too much, too soon." He nodded slightly, frowning.

"It's okay. We'll stop." He stroked my hair. "Zosia. It's okay. It's okay."

It's not okay.

I'm shaking so hard the lid of the teapot rattled audibly. When I hopped down from the counter, my knees gave out. So wired and jittery I can hardly stand. The world looks too bright, too dark, too much. Wrong. All wrong.

"I've got you." Lorcan tried to brace me upright, the way he's done so many times when I'm off-balance. "It's okay."

It's not. I thrust him away and run, wobbling, bumping into the dining room chair, scrambling up the stairs to the loft as though Bashir were on my heels, one second away from grabbing me. Skinning my shin on the step. I stumbled to the bed and burrowed into the blankets.

So much for fuck him and get it out of your system. One more failure compounding all the rest. I wonder if I'll ever be able to have sex with anyone, without having a panic attack.

Probably not. Bashir made sure of that. What he didn't poison, Lorcan did.

I lay curled in a tight ball, trembling. After a while, Lorcan came and sat next to me on the bed. I don't know how we'll share it after this mess. But he was gentle with me, just sitting there quietly, stroking my hair until my trembling subsided and my shallow breathing slowed. I faced the wall as my spirits sank through the floor. Fat tears welled and slid down my nose, wetting the pillow. A different kind of crying. Not so snot-filled, but somehow even lonelier than the last time.

"Do you want to talk about it?" he asked what felt like hours later, though it probably wasn't that long. Rain drummed against the window. Other memories surfaced.

Better ones. The way we lay here reading side-by-side the last time a storm rolled through.

"No."

What would I say? That I think I'm broken beyond repair? We're good together when it's the two of us with no outside pressure, but it will never work because that is not, and cannot be, my life? I feel unwanted on every conceivable level, and it's partly his doing?

Inexplicably, I missed Sethi. Things are so simple with him. Except for being unable to acknowledge him.

Lorcan's hesitation told me this was just as awful for him as it was for me. I doubt he's ever been in a situation he can't fight, strategize or charm his way out of. The only equivalent for him I can think of would be when his father died by suicide. There was no way to fix it, though his twelve-year-old self tried to.

That night, I'm the one who clings to Lorcan like a frightened child to a favorite stuffed toy. In the morning, we picked up as though nothing had happened. Yet the tension was back, an invisible stain on what had been a lovely respite.

CHAPTER TEN

The morning before Lorcan's birthday celebration, we were sitting out back on the patio. I had finished my perfunctory, somewhat freeform Midsummer speech and sent it off to Saskaya for editing. I spent the previous afternoon trying to negotiate lumber prices from the Timberlands, and after securing one-third of what Ifran had requested at twice the price I was prepared to pay, decided to distract myself by looking at the edits to the joint paper with Lorcan. It's not going well.

I have no vision for what my country needs, apart from: jumpstart the economy, re-establish our postal service, figure out an export product, negotiate trade relations...a to-do list is not a statement of my leadership goals. Anyone could do them. I don't know where best to direct my energy.

I'm afraid to try anything. Afraid of failing again— publicly. I wish my father was here, or Cata, to guide me. Yet they'd both probably try to do it for me. It might be for the best that I have to figure this out for myself.

I threw the pile of papers aside. Lorcan cut me a side-long glance.

"Everything okay?"

"Frustrated." I sat up. Today, I wore the solid blue dress with the brown sweater, even though it's warm outside. "Not making headway on anything useful."

"Take a break."

"I thought this whole visit was a break." I got up from my chair.

"Where are you going?" he asked. Lorcan has kept an even closer eye on me than usual, if such a thing is even possible, since I freaked out on his kitchen counter the other day.

"Your birthday is tomorrow—"

"It's today, actually. The celebration is tomorrow. More people can attend on a rest day." He made a face.

"Even better." I kept going, calling back over my shoulder, "I have a gift for you."

It looked pathetically small. Then again, that's partly the point. It's portable. Still, when I think of his extravagance toward me, it feels petty in comparison.

"Go on. Open it."

Lorcan ripped into the paper. The sketchbook he of course recognizes, having been in the shop with me when I bought it. Making purchases in secret is hardly feasible when you spend every moment together. But the black zippered case marked Castle Art Supplies momentarily baffled him.

"What's this?"

"You'll have to unzip it to find out." I propped my chin on my hand. "It's not brand-new, unfortunately, but it's only slightly used. You can't get them here in Auralia."

He brightened at the sight of colored pencils. 72 of them, with a few worn at the tips.

"My father brought them back for me on one of his early trips to the outside world. Unlike you, I'm not much of an artist. Ifran's workers found them in the rubble of my old rooms."

"I can't believe you remember my doodles." Lorcan examined the rainbow array of colors.

"Your sketch of mossy frogs remains my most prized possession." And always will, no matter what happens between us. "Saskaya is holding onto it for me until I move back into the castle."

"I'll have to take it up again." He kissed my cheek. "Thank you, Princess."

"Lorcan. What happened with you and Raina?" I'm not sure what prompted my question—I hadn't intended to ask it, though it's been kicking around in the back of my mind ever since the call. The instant it's out in the air between us, I knew it was a mistake.

He zipped the case closed and set it on the table. "Are you sure you want to know?"

No. I am fairly certain I would rather not hear this. But I asked for the truth, even when it was hard or hurtful, so I can't exactly back out now. I nodded.

"Raina caught one of her maids coming out of my room. It was clear that we had been..." He trailed off uncomfortably. "Together. She was furious with me. I said things I am appalled to remember now."

"Such as?" A queasy sensation settles into my stomach.

"Essentially that we were consenting adults and she had no right to criticize."

"Which was true," I said, trying to be clear-headed about it. He didn't remember me. So he claims. Remembered nothing of our promises to wait for one another. It hurts that he did that, but Hallie wasn't wrong.

He stared out into the fields below. "She accused me of stalling in my mission to rescue you. I told her I didn't care."

It's a fist to my solar plexus. "Didn't...care?" I repeated incredulously.

He nodded tightly. "I didn't care about much at that point. I was sick of all the killing and yet it was all anyone valued me for. I was good at it, but I hated it."

I tried to breathe past the tightening of my chest.

"You once said you were afraid that all you were was an assassin. That there was nothing more to you than the ability to take lives." My voice sounds strained even to my own ears.

"The period between when Saskaya sent me out of the Temple to fight until the day I found you was my worst nightmare. That's all I did. Kill pirates. Kill Skía. Take down encampments, steal or destroy their supplies, and repeat the process all the way from Central Auralia to Oceanside." He lifted one shoulder and let it fall, but I could see how tormented he is about what we asked him to do for us. "I thought the least my supposed friend could do was stay out of the way while I...blew off steam. I was unrepentant and rude. We fought. Physically."

I closed my eyes.

"I didn't hurt her," Lorcan hastened to reassure me. "She tried to hit me, and I wouldn't let her. Raina is stronger than I thought. We fell onto the bed. I think she was scared I would—" He paled slightly beneath his tan. "She didn't know what I would do. If I meant to hurt her. I didn't know she was pregnant at the time. They were keeping it a secret. Tovian found us like that and nearly murdered me. If she'd given the word, I wouldn't be sitting here with you."

"You didn't care whether you lived or died," I whispered.

"No." Lorcan examined his hands. "I had lost my way. I'd lost you, and despite everyone telling me that was the way I needed to go, I didn't believe them."

Birds sang. Grasshoppers whirred. I waited.

"Raina ordered me to get my ass to the castle and not to come back to River Bend unless it was with you. I told her I wasn't...I wasn't in any rush to save a spoiled brat of a princess."

Twist my guts and rip them out through my throat, why don't you. Then again, is he wrong? "When was this?"

"April."

"You left me sitting in the castle for all that time? Knowingly?" I gaped at him, aghast. The details clicked into place instantly. "If you'd come right after you woke up, I wouldn't have starved. The kitchen roof caved sometime in March. It was the last heavy snow of the season."

"I remember it. Melting snow made the roads almost impossible to get through for weeks." He blew out a sigh. "I'm sorry, Zosia, I'm so sorry."

I stared at my hands, wishing I'd left the past in the past.

"Raina fired the maid on the spot."

Why he offered this information, I don't know. He got a servant fired. It's not his fault entirely—I'm sure she was willing—but without him, it wouldn't have happened. It makes what he did worse, not better, that a maid suffered the consequences.

"As she should." If you tolerate staff sleeping around on the job, you don't have a properly run castle; you have a brothel with a vicious gossip problem. Who's sleeping with whom, which nobles are the easiest to lure away from their spouses, questions about the paternity of every child born to the nobility. Infidelity is highly frowned upon here, for good reason. A queen who permits that kind of behavior quickly loses the respect of her people. Eventually you have to fire almost everyone and hire new workers—a task made more difficult when most of the population refuses to work for you. It can take years for the nobility to recover standing among the people.

It's why the castle manager is so important. It's the most visible expression of the queen's ability to maintain order and justice. Setting expectations and enforcing them fairly is vital.

One more reason our engagement is, and must remain, a sham.

Lorcan's expression turned stony. "I disagreed. To Raina's face. Thinking back, that was an incredibly stupid thing to do. I didn't like being the reason the maid was fired. I wanted to help her but didn't even know her name. Raina threw me off the premises before I could ask around. After that, I started to wonder how many other women I'd gotten into trouble with my selfish behavior. I swear I stopped after that."

"That was three months ago, Lorcan. Half that time, you've been with me."

I sipped shallow breaths. I really *don't* mean anything to him. He'd have happily gone off to rescue a maid whose name he didn't know, but me? I could rot in my castle for all he cared.

Until he conveniently remembered that he had a shot at becoming king. Then, suddenly, he's all sweet and loving again.

I pushed out of my chair and slammed into the house. It's not the way to react if I want him to be honest in the future, but Auralia help me; it hurts.

I'm glad I didn't see things through with him the other day. Something inside me was telling me not to go through with it, and when I didn't listen, it hijacked my entire nervous system to shut things down. My instincts might not be so terrible after all, if I simply listen to them. Stop pining for what I know I can't have, focus on what I need. What my people need.

My knuckles turned white where I clutched the countertop. I observed this dispassionately, as though from a great distance. The bright sky and bucolic countryside visible through the window frame were as unreal to me as the first time I landed in Scotland.

I don't belong here any more than I do at River Bend, or Čovari Village. I need to leave this place. Soon. I can't go without Lorcan—the Skía might be diminished but they're still lurking in the shadows, biding their time. I don't know where to go, though.

Adrift, again.

Raina mentioned something about going to Oceanside the other day. A long trip might be what I need. See my country. Take stock. Be more visible. I doubt my mother or grandmother would have wasted weeks sulking in the mountains.

Lorcan came in quietly, carrying my birthday gift. We eyed one another warily. "You said you wanted the truth."

"I did." I have regrets. "I appreciate your honesty. I just don't understand how you can claim you love me when you left me to starve for months." I swallow hard. "Or how you could race off to help a woman you only know by her vagina—"

"Stop it."

I see it then. The hard, dark part of him that he tries to keep hidden. It's not as easy for him to conceal emotions now. There's too much pain written on his body and in his psyche to ever be that boy on the rooftop again. But he chose this path.

"To help a woman you only know by her vagina," I repeated, enunciating each syllable like a proper fucking lady. No commoner tells me to stop speaking in that tone. No one tells me to stop speaking at all. Ever again. "But you left me trapped with a monster. Do you know why Bashir was naked when you killed him?"

I glimpsed a quicksilver beat of fear in his eyes. Good. I want him to know the full depth of what he's done to us.

"Since we're in the business of honesty this morning." I held his gaze. "He wanted me to know exactly how much it would hurt when he got out of his cell and raped me."

No reaction. I kept going.

"Bashir liked to talk to me. Night and day. If I was in that cell, he would stop trying to batter the door open and tell me how he would force me until I was bred, then after I had the baby, he would rip my head off with his bare hands, throw it into the throne room with my father, and keep violating my corpse until it disintegrated—"

"Stop." Not a command this time. A plea. "I don't want to hear this."

"I don't want to talk about it, either. I haven't told anyone. Not Raina. Not Saskaya. No one, until now. I need you to know what you left me to face alone." I just need to tell someone. He had a hand in making me go through that nightmare, so he can live with the knowledge, too. "I went to the castle to buy time so you could heal. I led the Sentinels to The Walled City so that Raina and the Čovari had a chance of getting you to the Temple to recover. I locked myself in with a madman for you."

"I know."

"For the first few days we were trapped together, Bashir hunted me down every corridor of the castle. I slept in the dumbwaiter until I felt it moving, and barely made it out before he caught me. Once I captured him in that cell, I could get away from him for a few hours every day. But eventually those hinges were going to give way. I didn't have much more time when you finally showed up. The only question was how painful my death would be."

His gaze cuts away from mine.

"I locked myself inside the cell at night because I would rather starve to death than endure what Bashir vowed to do to me."

Lorcan said nothing.

"We asked a great deal of you, Lorcan. Raina, Saskaya, Tovian, Keryn. All of them, on my behalf. You will always have my gratitude for that."

"I don't want your gratitude, Zosia."

"No, you want to be king." I scoffed. "That's what you cared about all along. The princess. Not me."

My words were a slap in the face. He recoiled.

"That is pure *bullshit*."

"Is it?" I asked softly, raising one eyebrow. "Didn't you tell me that to my face? I once asked you what you wanted from life. You said: Save the country. Rescue the princess. Marry her, and live happily ever after."

His throat moved.

"I used to wonder what it would have been like" —used to, as in, last week; good thing I was never dumb enough to say it out loud— "if I had been born someone else. A village girl here in Tenáho, for example. If we would have had a chance at happiness then. But now I know. Another woman would be the princess, and you would have gone off chasing her instead. It was never me you wanted. Zosia."

"It's. Not. True."

My brows lifted. Waiting. Listening.

"Are you imagining there's any daylight between who you are and what you are?"

I regarded him warily.

"Zosia. Yes, the fact that you're the princess is part of it, because it's part of you. If all I wanted was a princess, I could have dated Raina. I could have been her Prince Consort years ago if a title was all I cared about. I want you. Everything you are. I wanted you in that stupid nightclub you sneaked out to, dancing in a top that left your entire back exposed. I've loved you since that morning on your balcony when you were reading about frogs in your nightgown with your bare legs propped on the wall."

I don't know what to say. This truth-telling business is more than I bargained for. I cut my gaze to the floor, feeling small and petty in blaming him for Bashir's violent threats. He didn't know.

Yet he abandoned me. Everyone does. My mother. My father. Even Cata. She abandoned her own son in the name of duty.

"You have a strange way of showing it," I said with eerie calm. Disassociating from myself the way I used to do all the time, the way I haven't been able to do since that night on the hillside.

"As I've said—repeatedly—I didn't remember. What I did remember was bad."

"But people told you. You just didn't care."

"Are we done with this?" Lorcan demanded hoarsely. "I can't go back and change what happened. Wishing I had done everything differently doesn't make it different. I want to make amends, Zosia, but I can't if you're too embittered to ever forgive me."

He turned his back and walked out. Down the hill into the fields, sunlight glinting on his hair the way it did that day in the Colosseum, three years ago.

Leaving me alone for the first time since my rescue.

CHAPTER ELEVEN

I pottered aimlessly around the house. Organizing my belongings. Preparing for my departure the day after Lorcan's birthday celebration—with or without him. I'm no longer sure which it will be.

When evening came and went without his return, I fixed myself a simple meal and finally downloaded those articles about head injuries Raina sent me. It took a while for the satellite connection to transfer all the file data.

It's not an ideal reading situation, but since I didn't have anything better to do, I curled up on Lorcan's side of the bed to read on the screen. While I was online, I fired off a few emails to Saskaya—a long form she sent a while ago for me to fill out and submit to a charitable organization, in hopes of securing funding—and to Scarlett: *can you please bring computer printer paper, and three pairs of size 36 Converse in different colors? They're a gift. I'll reimburse you.*

With what money, I don't know. Arya will like them, though it hardly makes up for the fact that I'm not going to marry her brother, thus stranding her here in Tenáho when she's been looking forward to getting away.

While I was messing around with my device, I noticed a new email pinging my inbox.

Dear Princess Zosia,

Last year, my husband and I had the honor of winning a charity auction held at the Louvre for a visit to your country. I have hesitated to contact you after reading reports about the precariousness of your political situation. However, I understand that the problem has since been resolved. We are keen to visit Auralia. My daughter is a tremendous admirer. Her birthday is coming up this fall. We would like to claim our prize if it is safe to do so.

-Mrs. Knauss

Oh, fuck. Forgot all about that obligation. I forwarded it to Raina with a quick *what do you think?*

Then I settled in to read about traumatic brain injuries, which is a thoroughly depressing way to spend a pleasant summer evening.

Everything supports Lorcan's assertions. TBI, as it was abbreviated in the articles Raina sent, can be associated with memory loss, personality changes, poor impulse control, and anger—all of which Lorcan has demonstrated. Memory problems in particular tend to be centered around a period of time near the injury. Nothing he says he experienced is implausible.

Yet he made a remarkable recovery. Physically, he's stronger than ever. Psychologically, it's amazing he came out of the experience as undamaged as he did. It was about as good an outcome as we could have hoped for.

Lorcan isn't gone. He's different. The man I knew before is someone I am still getting to know. There are definitely parts I don't like. His carelessness in sleeping around, of course. His open disregard for my well-being from when he woke up until a few weeks ago.

But there are elements that I do prefer over his old, silent self. He's freer with his affections. I don't wonder what he's thinking all the time anymore. He's emotionally more available than he was before his accident, and to me, that's an improvement.

The phone ran low on battery. I didn't have a way to recharge it, for now, so I set it aside and went for a short walk. Fireflies lit the path into the town. I choose the opposite direction, going down the hill, around the fields, and then looping past the apple orchard back to Lorcan's cottage.

He was there when I got back. Watching me from the window, ready to intervene if anyone attacked—even here, it's a risk. I doubt he went very far away today. Just enough to give us both some space. Always watching over me.

I have to admit that the first sight of him jolted me. I was so on edge about our fight that I didn't know how to react.

"You came back."

"It's my house."

He was sitting on the unmade bed where I spent the afternoon. Changed and ready to sleep. His bed. Asserting his ownership.

"Do you want me to leave?"

Lorcan held out one hand. "No, Zosia. I want you to stay."

For how long, though?

I took his proffered hand and sat on the edge of the bed. "I don't want to live in the past, Lorcan. I don't know how to move forward, but there is one thing I know for certain: I do not want to remember the past year any more than absolutely necessary."

"Neither do I." We looked at one another. Lorcan

reached out and brushed his thumb over my cheek. "Sorry does not touch the surface. I wish I had better words, Princess. I promise you will never have to go through anything like that again."

"I'd have done it anyway." I sniffled. Still not a crier. Yet, I, too, have lost the ability to hide my emotions. Perhaps that's for the best. There is one more truth I need to tell him, an apology of sorts, for bludgeoning him with it earlier. "Knowing what I do now about how things would play out, I would do everything the same if it meant saving your life."

I meant it to be kind, but Lorcan's shoulders slumped. "I don't deserve it."

"Deserve it or not, I love you and it was worth it to have you in this world with me. Even if you might not always thank me for it." I kissed his forehead. "Happy birthday, Lorcan. I'm sorry I ruined it. Thank you for being truthful with me. Truth is a rare and valuable commodity for a queen-to-be."

"You didn't ruin anything. I did. Long before today." He pulled me down, into his arms, rolling us onto the mattress and tugging the blankets up. I breathed into the crook of his neck. Traced the dip and rise at the base of his throat with my fingertips.

Goddesses, I'm going to miss him so much when we part for good this fall. For now, I have this. It will have to be enough.

Unless...

I'll think about that later.

"Cute jacket, Arya," I tugged on her sleeve. "Why aren't you wearing a dress?"

I WORE my white one with embroidery at the hem, and the blue underskirt peeking out the bottom.

"Some of the girls said we'd go as boys so there's enough dancing partners."

She gestured vaguely to the open hall lined with wooden tables and benches. Perhaps one-third of the people assembled are men. Most of them are old, like Melcan, helping move furniture out of the way to accommodate the musicians. The rest appeared to be younger than Arya. One young man was missing his leg beneath the knee. A middle-aged man wore an eye patch and limped.

War has not left Tenáho unscathed.

"Where's the birthday boy?" I asked.

"Hiding." Arya grinned. "Lorcan hates this kind of thing."

I found him in the back of the event space where the kitchen is located—where else. Rya baked a massive cake. They were trying to figure out how to transport it into the main room.

"What if we bring a table to the door, put the cake on the table, and carry the table over to the wall?" A large sign read, *Happy Birthday—23—Hero of Auralia*. Lorcan just loves that last part. I've been teasing him about it all day.

Things are mostly patched up between us. Again. A bond neither of us can quit, built on a foundation too crumbled to support the weight of more than a fragile friendship. We can't work as lovers. But I might be able to keep a part of him with me, if I revise my stance on having children.

If I can have children. The next few months with him are my only chance to try.

I could do it. Queens have gone without King Protectors before. A few, anyway. Lorcan could have the freedom he wants, and I'd have a family of my own. A small one. Me and my daughter. But mine to love.

I will never send her into the frozen pool at Mount Astra. If she wants to get an education abroad, I'll encourage her to fulfill her dreams. If she wants to lead, I'll step down. I'll play the role of High Priestess for as long as I must to take that weight from her. I wouldn't be alone ever again, if it worked.

Having a baby would be a way to carry Lorcan with me once he's out of my life for good. If I'm capable of it. Between my mother's infertility and my emaciation, it's hardly guaranteed.

Saskaya was right that I'm in no position to be raising a baby right now, but in a year or so? With the country hopefully more stable, the castle livable again, my rule as Queen established? Then, it could work.

He can't know. Maybe he'll guess. Probably. Almost certainly. Lorcan is capable of counting nine months. The obvious solution would be to take up with another man as soon as we split, at least publicly. But that's messy and I don't know where I would find one, anyway. I don't have the energy for another public deception. This one has been hard enough.

Everything depends upon getting my weight up far enough to be physically capable of bearing a child, and not flipping out the next time I'm intimate with Lorcan. If there is a next time. I'm willing to try, but is he?

The thought of going through the rest of my life as an

untouched virgin—ugh, how did it come to this?—isn't appealing to me, either.

I have plenty of doubts about my plan, but I can't think of any better solutions.

"Are you ready for this?"

Lorcan's palm rested lightly on my back, startling me.

"I think so. Are you?" I grinned at his pained expression. He dressed up for the occasion in a dark-blue jacket not dissimilar to the one his sister wore, and light brown trousers.

"As ready as I'll ever be," he said darkly.

"Oh, come on now. It's good practice for you to be the center of attention." That feels dishonest. I'm implying I'll marry him, when nothing has changed. *It's a general statement,* I tell myself, ignoring the flurry of butterflies in my stomach.

I patted his arm. "Go on. Think how I feel every holiday when I have to pretend I'm a goddess."

"You are a goddess," he said, kissing my cheek.

"Flatterer."

Rya may be a small woman, but she has a big voice when she wants to get people's attention.

"A year ago, we thought Lorcan was dead. We knew he had been taken to a secret location to recuperate from severe injuries sustained while defending Princess Zosia and Princess Raina of the Myseči." Applause. I bowed acknowledgment, briefly meeting Lorcan's eye. A warm flutter in my stomach. "After his near-miraculous recovery, my son turned South to fight the Skía-led invaders." Applause; boos for the Skía.

"We lost many beloved villagers," Rya continued. "Brave fighters fought valiantly to hold back the invasion until he could turn the tide. I am immensely proud of my son and beyond grateful for his return."

More applause.

From the corner of my eye, I noticed a woman watching me. A visiting princess, no matter how she tries to blend in, is going to be a curiosity—but there was a vague hostility about her that caught my attention. She had dark brown hair and full lips. An even fuller bosom. Green eyes, like mine, but more emerald. She's strikingly beautiful.

Her gaze slid away from me and to Lorcan, who'd taken over from his mother to say a few words. He's so habitually quiet that I was surprised how well his voice carried when he wanted it to.

"You did well," I complimented Lorcan when he returned to my side. "I don't get to see you give very many speeches."

"I suppose that will change soon." He looked out over the crowd, sparing me a response. I didn't want another fight, much less at his birthday celebration. "We're to open the first dance."

"At least this time I won't be reprimanded for choosing you as my partner." Lorcan looked at me askance. "The last Midwinter ball before the war. You were on duty. I tried to convince you to dance with me, toward the end. I was tipsy and tired and I exercised poor judgment. I was supposed to be choosing a husband, but you were the only one I wanted. My father had a fit."

He frowned.

"I thought you were trying to get me into trouble."

Shaking my head, I said, "One of your mixed-up memories. Ask—"

I broke off. There is no one to ask. Kenton and Cata were

the only ones to witness it. I could be lying to him and there's no way he could confirm it. "I guess I can't corroborate my story. Everyone is dead."

"I'll take your word for it, Zosia."

Trust, so easily given. I was humbled.

Lorcan took my hand and led me into the center of the empty dance floor. I've opened hundreds of dances in my lifetime, but that night I swear I felt every single gaze upon me. It was a country dance, fast and tricky. We got about three steps in before people started joining us on the floor, which was good because I only knew the steps from the castle version, and the local variety was a bit different. After one set, I bowed to Lorcan and then to the next partner. Knowing my actions will be scrutinized this evening, I have a plan.

"Will you do me the honor, sir?" I asked the man with one leg. His entire face lit up. His forehead is marked by a long scar from center to the edge of his eyebrow, though he tries to cover it by wearing his hair long and brushed forward. Not unlike Lorcan's preferred style.

"I'd be delighted, Highness, if you don't mind adapting the steps."

"Not at all. Show me how it works."

He did, and we moved to the edge of the dance floor. The man, whose name I never quite caught, was unexpectedly adept with his crutch and one working limb. After several minutes he released me and took up with one of the girls in a brightly-colored frock like the one I wore. I move on to the man with one eye. Then to the older gents.

Get the men dancing. Honor the veterans. Make my people happy, for once.

A pale shade of the happiness I felt on that boat while

fleeing Trissau enveloped me. The first real joy I've felt since that moment.

I don't trust it. But oh, how I needed to feel it.

CHAPTER TWELVE

Dancers spilled out into the town square. Evening painted the sky in shades of coral and aquamarine. I edged out onto the cobblestone streets for a breath of fresh air.

"That was a canny move," Rya offered me a waxed paper cup of cider. "Dancing with the injured veterans, and then handing them off to the others."

I curtsied. "Many years of training. Reassuring that I remember how to read a crowd."

Rya smiled. We touched paper cups.

"You'll make a good queen."

Good or not, I have no choice in the matter.

"I hope so. Much depends upon my ability to steer us through the winter. No one will think much of my leadership if I let famine set in. Or a resurgent invasion."

We wouldn't win this time. Auralia's fighting forces have been decimated for a generation. The world remains curious about us, but not one country has been willing to offer aid. Even now.

I realized my error too late. *I*, not *we*.

"There won't be a wedding announcement forthcoming, will there?" Rya's gaze rested on the statuesque brunette who regarded me with such hostility earlier. Warmth leached out of me.

I sipped my cider before responding quietly, "No."

"Does Lorcan know?"

"Yes."

"Pity. He came so close to achieving his dream." Rya contemplated the dancers. Jars with candles inside were strung between the main hall and the fountain in the center of the town square. "I shall tell Arya not to quit her job at the paper store, yet."

"Who is she?" I asked abruptly, indicating the dark-haired woman. She'd come outside, hips swinging, and posed prettily beneath the string lights. It's difficult to imagine her doing anything other than prettily.

"Masika." Rya's tone was neutral. "She was married to a shopkeeper here in town. A war widow, now. She and her in-laws run the general store. That's her daughter playing in the fountain."

A cluster of children have waded into the water, all splashes and giggles. One, with glossy dark hair like a seal's fur, is unmistakably Masika's offspring.

"She isn't happy living with her husband's family. Lorcan raised her hopes briefly when he first returned."

Raised her hopes, and likely her skirts, too. Masika wouldn't bolt if he kissed her in his kitchen, like I did. I hope they didn't share the bed I've been sleeping in. The thought sent a shiver of revulsion down my spine.

"Masika and I have that in common." I tipped the rest of my cider down my throat and crumpled the cup. Rya slanted me a thoughtful look. I decided it was time to change the subject.

"If you ever tire of Tenáho, I could use a competent Treasurer. Especially one who can work miracles."

Rya chuckled. "The crown's accounts are that depleted?"

"You have no idea." I remembered myself and put one finger to my lips. "It's a secret. I trust you not to let word get around."

"Your trust is not easily earned. I'd be a fool to lose it over gossip. However, if we weren't in dire straits, you wouldn't have gone seeking a rich husband so quickly after your rescue."

I can't believe I'd nearly forgotten about Sohrab, Hallie, Cyrus and Humayun. It feels like a lifetime ago. "Right. Of course."

Not much of a secret, after all.

"Your coronation ceremony will be a good source of revenue."

"In what way?"

I've been fretting about the expense.

"People will come from all over to witness it. You'll have to provide shelter...or you can sell the privilege, and the hassle, of providing it. That late in the season only hardy souls will want to sleep on the ground."

"I knew I admired you." With a wink, I turned on the ball of my foot and waved. "See? Your talents would be very useful to the crown." I displayed my crumpled cup. "I think I'll have another. Spill more state secrets, you know?"

Rya laughed.

While I was making my way toward the cart with the cider barrel, Arya came bouncing over to me, her eyes bright with excitement.

"Seen Lorcan?"

"Not recently."

"Huh. Still dancing, probably."

"A hazard of being the guest of honor," I grinned. "Oh, there he is."

Lorcan was framed by one side of the open event hall, looking out into the square. My grin faded when Masika approached and took his arm. My stomach sank when he followed without protest.

Arya's indignant gaze bounced between her brother's retreating back and me. "You're not going to intervene?"

"No."

"She's not...Why not?" Arya demanded.

"Everyone in this room is watching me, Arya. If I go after them, I look like I don't trust my own fiancé"—which I don't, but I'm not saying that to his little sister—"whereas if I don't, people will think I don't care what they do. I can't win, either way. It's best not to draw attention."

Her eyes were wide and serious. So similar to her brother's, it pinched my heart.

"I won't ruin his birthday party by making a scene," I added, gently.

"Well, that doesn't mean I can't intervene." Arya's eyes narrowed with determination. It's so familiar I wanted to laugh, despite the hollow in my stomach. She's as fierce as her brother. "Get me a cider, will you?"

I shook my head, chuckling, despite the despair clawing at my heart. A few minutes later I had two cups in hand. Arya was back, dragging Lorcan behind her. He stopped short when he saw me, frowning.

"She wanted to talk. That's all."

"It's not my affair." Literally. I handed Arya her drink. Then I took Lorcan by the elbow. "I'm not interested in fighting again. Or publicly. You created this situation. You figure out how to handle it."

Then I released him and slid into the crowd. One of the few advantages of resembling a twig in skirts is being able to thread easily between bodies. More easily than I did in Beijing, back when I still had hips. I made my way out of the stifling hall and back into the night air.

Masika was standing nearby when I popped out of the crowd, talking in low tones with another woman. She glared at me. Seeing her, I stopped short.

I do not have the time, energy, or patience for this shit.

"Lovely evening," I said brightly, continuing past them. I drained my second cup of cider and tossed the wax paper into a provided bin.

He was so quick I didn't even hear his footfalls. Lorcan caught my arm, spun me around, and kissed me.

"What are you doing?" I protested.

"Handling a situation." He smiled against my mouth and didn't release me.

"Feels more like you're handling me." I freed my arms and wound them around his neck.

"There's my grumpy princess," Lorcan said affectionately. He bent to kiss my nose. Laughter bubbled out of me. "You don't have to worry about me, Zosia. All of that is behind me."

He doesn't need to be specific—I know he means about the other women.

But I worry that he doesn't understand how quickly innuendo can progress into rumors. Or appreciate how quickly subtle advances can turn into expectations. The years he spent with me were mostly away from court. I may have hated it, but I was always closely guarded for a reason, even within the castle walls.

I worry, most of all, that he doesn't understand how

much of a public figure he's become, or how that makes you a target.

Then again, it won't be an issue after October. It's not worth spoiling the time we do have together. We'll soon be gone from here. I won't be returning. Lorcan can make his own choices. Masika won't have cause to glare at me for long.

A pang in my midsection. *Mine.*

He isn't, though. Never really was.

It's been delightful to play at being ordinary people for a while. To forget, as far as possible, that we are Princess and Knight, not two villagers like Masika and Lorcan would have been, if he hadn't gone off on his quest to restore honor to his father's name.

The past few weeks have been a taste of a life we were never going to lead. I sighed wistfully.

"We should go home." Lorcan kissed me, softly. We barely moved, swaying to the music without moving our feet. It's more of an excuse to hold one another. I laid my head on his shoulder, wishing this could last. If not forever, then at least longer than we have left.

"The birthday boy cannot sneak off before the cake is served," I reminded him.

Lorcan groaned. "Are you sure?"

"Positive." I poked the spot on his ribs where he's ticklish. Flinching, he set me free.

"Come on, let's get that cake served so we can get out of here."

After the huge dessert was sliced and served to several hundred people—no small undertaking—we made our escape. It wasn't late, barely ten o'clock, but it's more partying than I've done in a long time.

Lorcan took my hand as we walked along the unlit path

in silence. Moonlight and stars dotted the wide dark sky above.

Immediately inside the cottage, he was on me. Or I was on him—it came from both directions. He pulled me close, brushed his thumb over my cheek and leaned in. Our lips met softly, and for several minutes, I thought it might be all right this time. The panic attack might have been a one-off.

He splayed his fingers around my ear, tangled in my short hair. I opened to him, welcoming the gentle intrusion of his tongue, skimming my hands up his muscular back. Lorcan made a greedy sound. I smiled against his mouth. He moved down, nipping that spot beneath my ear that weakens my knees and sends a hot pulse of need through my core.

Lorcan backed me up a step. Another. The edge of the table bumped my bottom. I hesitated. Anxiety swelled when he brought his hands to the laces at my waist.

"Wait."

Lorcan froze.

"Let's...get ready for bed first?"

I needed a moment to quell my unease. I want this. I do. It's just that I can't stop reliving that moment of searing shame when I had my shirt off and my mouth on his—

You don't ever have to do that again.

I was so eager for him the time we were together in River Bend. Desperate for anything familiar, for love, for acceptance. For sex, too. Now, I associate that excitement with shame and disgust for my body. It's confusing and frustrating for me, and I have no idea how to explain it to him. My reaction isn't coming from a rational place.

Though my reasoning isn't always on point, I am, at heart, a logical thinker. A scientist. I am controlled. Or I thought I was.

Nothing about this is logical.

"Sure." He kissed my forehead. "Everything okay, Princess?"

No. I'm trying to seduce you and I don't know if I can go through with it.

"Fine," I mumbled. "Be right back."

I changed into my nightgown and washed up. *Come on, Zosia. Get it together. Fuck your boyfriend for his birthday.* Perhaps I can muscle through this if I don't let him see me naked.

When I came back in, Lorcan followed me upstairs. I can tell I've worried him. He folded himself into the bed next to me and took me into his arms. "We don't have to—"

"I want to," I said quickly. It's true. We're leaving soon. After this, opportunities for privacy might be few and far between.

We resumed where we left off, and it's nice, so nice. But the instant Lorcan worked his hand beneath the hem of my nightgown and touched my skin, I jerked back with a harsh, "Stop. Wait."

I pushed the fabric down and held it there.

Fuck, fuck, fuck.

This is such bullshit.

I'm so angry with myself I might cry. It's my boyfriend's birthday and I can't bring myself to have sex with him, even though I've wanted to for literally years. I pushed back to sit cross-legged on my half of his bed.

"Zosh. It's okay."

But it's not. *I'm* not. I really *am* irreparably broken.

He put one arm behind his head the way he did that first night we were together, eighteen months ago now. The way he did that night at River Bend, when I found out he hadn't waited. It's a sexy pose. He's not wearing a shirt. I can see every sculpted muscle and so many of his scars. The thick one across his low belly. The neatly stitched one curving up along his ribcage. Many others, most faded and indistinct. A few new ones.

"Bashir?" he asked frowning.

"Yes." I lunged at the excuse he offered me. Anyone would be traumatized by the shit Bashir said and did, but for me, it's been manageable. I knew he was out of his mind by the end, and pitied him as much as I feared him. So, no, Bashir is not the reason I can't do this.

Lorcan pieced it together immediately, though.

"You didn't panic when we were together after Trissau. At River Bend." His features slowly tightened as though in great pain. I've seen him in acute pain before; this is worse. "It's me. I did this to you. To us."

Several responses flitted through my mind. I discarded each one as inadequate or unkind. I don't know what to say. Lorcan rubbed my arm gently with his free hand. "Zosia. I'll fix it. I'll do anything it takes. The past couple of weeks have been the best weeks of my life. I want you to trust me again."

I do. With my life. Not with my heart. "I meant what I said last night. I love you. I would have done it—"

"You shouldn't have had to do it. I should have been more careful that night. I should have listened to the people around me when I woke up, instead of resenting them for making me fight." He swallowed. The muscles in his throat work. "Most of all, I should have stayed when I brought you to Saskaya's. I should have told you everything."

"We both had a hand in making this." I don't blame him. I mean, I do. Part of me always will. But there's nothing either of us can do to change the past. I'm holding onto my bitterness and resentment because it isn't safe to let go. I don't know how to.

"We'll start over. Let this be a new beginning, okay?" I whispered.

I'd like the time we have remaining to us to be good. But then, I have a lousy track record of getting things I want. And Lorcan and I have a terrible knack for new beginnings.

"Sure, Princess."

Lorcan pulled me down. I nestled against his body. We kiss and hold one another for a long time; I don't think either of us slept.

We both know better.

There is no starting over. No fresh beginning. We carry all the broken bits with us. All we can do is pick up the pieces and try to mend them.

Try not to fracture further.

CHAPTER THIRTEEN

Lorcan kissed my shoulder the next morning, his front was pressed flush against my back. He likes to sleep this way, with one arm beneath my neck and the other over my waist.

This morning, as rain drizzled against the window, his hand drifted lower to where my nightgown had gotten twisted around my hips. He traced lazy circles on my thigh right below the hem of my underwear. Rough stubble scraped pleasantly along my neck. Drowsily, I snuggled closer. I'll miss this so much.

"Okay?" he asked in a warm puff of air against my earlobe. I entwined my fingers with his left hand, the one trapped beneath my neck, and leaned my torso back against his bare chest. Heat from his skin warmed mine. I'm never cold when he holds me like this.

Lorcan gently worked his right hand beneath my night-dress. My breath hitched when he flattened his palm over my low belly, shockingly warm and tough-skinned, covering my navel.

Anxiety is right there, waiting to see what he'll do.

Ready to shut things down. I closed my eyes and listened to the rain. Stretched my hand up behind me to play with his hair. More lazy circles with the tips of his fingers at my sternum. Embarrassment when he runs his palm over my ribs. I exhaled and made myself stay still, only jerking in protest when his thumb skimmed the underside of what used to be my breast. He stilled, but didn't move his hand away.

"Okay?"

I said nothing, trying to decide. He brushed his thumb over my nipple. It reverberated through me. Softening resistance. An ache between my thighs.

He did it again.

"Okay," I whispered, belatedly. I do want this. I always have. But it's hard not to be mixed up when people tell you that you're the hot girl on campus, yet your experience is that men who seem to like you at best, don't care, and at worst, want to hurt you. Like that boy who kissed me at the party, or the one at the dance who pinched my thigh when I didn't let him grope me. Bashir is his own category.

Or, they turn me down flat, like Kenton did. Like Lorcan did that night in Scotland.

When they do say yes, they lie about their motives. Lorcan, especially.

So how foolish is it that I still want to feel this?

I can't stop bracing for the backlash, though. Nothing good has ever come from wanting this. Not for me.

Lorcan kept lazily touching me. Teasing my nipples, running his thumb over my breast. Neither advancing nor pressing me for anything more. He didn't seem to mind that I only entwined my fingers with those of his free hand. Toyed with strands of his hair.

We're supposed to be packing up the house. Preparing

to leave. Instead, we stayed in bed, listening to the rain until the clouds passed and the sun came out.

WE STAYED THE NEXT DAY, too, doing nothing in particular. Reading. Cooking. Minor chores. My pack remained on the floor beneath his bed, empty.

That night, we slept as usual. Like a couple of abandoned kittens curled together for warmth. Early in the morning, Lorcan picked up where we had left off the day before. He slowly hiked up the hem of my nightdress, stroking my thighs, my hips, carefully avoiding the sharp jut of my hipbone as he moved up to my stomach. When I stiffened, he waited until I relaxed again. Neither of us spoke.

Instead of continuing up to my breasts, he moved downward, south of my navel to the tops of my thighs, and back up to play at the waistband of my shorts. Nothing like modern panties. Čovari made, given to me by Sas when I had nothing, made of a blend of spidersilk and linen that stretches just enough to fit comfortably snug to the body. A different kind of tension sets in; a low thrum in my core. Dampness between my legs.

Lorcan kissed that spot beneath my ear. At the same moment, he slips his hand inside my underwear. It worked. Instead of giving in to panic, I gasped and tilted my hips to press against his palm.

"Fuck," he muttered against my neck. There's nothing tentative about the way he touches me. A slick glide of rough fingers through my swollen folds. I exhaled in a low moan. Lorcan's cock twitched against my ass. He's been

careful not to press against me, trying to conceal his erec-
tions. At first, I thought he didn't have them. Then he
wasn't quite as careful, and I attributed them to ordinary
male bodily functions. Awkward every time, until now. He
ground against my bottom and stroked my center. Crooked
his fingers to hit a place inside me, hard enough to make me
see stars. I made a choked sound and went stiff, rocking
into his hand.

Before it completely subsided, he withdrew. I lay there,
bewildered and breathing hard.

"Next time, leave these off," he murmured against my
cheek, tracing the outline of my undershorts. Then, Lorcan
rolled away and out of bed.

It took me a long time to gather myself and go downstairs. I found him in the kitchen—where else?—making
breakfast.

"Morning."

Oh, didn't he look pleased with himself. I couldn't
exactly blame him. Clever man, figuring out how to get
around my hang-up so quickly. Probably spent all night
thinking about it, which is flattering, in a way.

"Morning, yourself. How can I help?"

"You can't." He kissed my head. "Make yourself useless.
Rest while you can."

We took our breakfast out onto the patio one last time.
Lorcan did laundry while I washed the dishes. It's the last
day of our sweet domesticity. I'll miss this cottage. Tenáho,
too. He might think it's boring here, but I loved every
minute of my stay. (Almost.)

I found a nook in Lorcan's loft with a peg for hanging
clothes, covered by a curtain. While he was outside, I hung
the white dress with embroidery I'd worn to his party. I

won't be coming back to wear it again, but I like the idea of making a small claim to his space.

My satellite phone, now recharged with an energy stick, buzzed. Raina.

Uh, we have a situation.

I texted a question mark back to her.

Raina: Hallie's father is pissed. He wants her and Laila back. We've been trying to deal with it so as not to bother you while you're resting, but the situation has reached a boiling point. I'll forward you the emails.

Wonderful.

Me: If they don't want to go, I won't make them.

Raina: Then we might be at war again.

Me: Welp. That sucks.

It more than sucks. I was being flippant because of the terror that shot through me. People will not send their few remaining men to fight for a couple of foreign women who came here seeking safety. Who barely speak the language. This is a crisis of my own making.

Raina: [crying emoji] Why can't people leave us alone?

I have no response to that. Instead, I texted, **We'll be in Čovari Village tomorrow evening, will Tovian be there?**

Raina: Yes. Keryn, too.

Interesting. The leader of the Mountain Folk doesn't usually come down to the lowlands. Politically, ties have been strained ever since word about Bashir's betrayal got out. I should be doing more to manage the situation.

I should be doing more, period. Rest time is over. I'm as recovered as I'll ever be.

Raina: I can arrange a charter plane for that family that wants to visit. Will the castle be in decent enough condition to house fancy rich outsiders by then?

"Fucking hell," I whispered. "Where will we get the money for a charter plane?"

Of all the stupid things to spend our daels on, right now. Past me was writing cheques that present me can't cash.

Me: Who knows? Maybe we'll be at war again and I can put them off for another year.

Raina: Gallows humor, Zosh.

Me: Sorry. Gotta take the laughs where you can, you know? I'll check with Ifran.

"Everything alright?" Lorcan asked, glancing at my phone, then at me, as he came inside carrying a basket.

"King Humayun wants Hallie and Laila back." I set my phone aside, face down. "They're threatening to attack if we don't give them up willingly."

Lorcan's jaw tightened. "I was afraid of that."

"Then why did you let them come with us?'

He shrugged. "You didn't want to leave them behind, either."

"True." This will be my first major test as a leader. "I won't risk any more lives. Not for this. Not for anything." I sighed. "Assuming I can avoid it."

Lorcan stroked my cheek. "I've been hanging onto something for you."

"Oh?"

"Might come in handy." Lorcan led me up to the loft. He withdrew a small metal chest from the locked lower drawer of his desk—an astonishing lack of security considering what was inside. Placing it on the scuffed wood surface, he opened it.

Inside were stacks of U.S. currency in fifty- and hundred-dollar denominations, alongside a large pile of euros. Scattered around are smaller denominations of other banknotes, some of which I didn't recognize. Yuan, I think. I wasn't allowed to handle money in China. There was also a fair amount of gold and gems in varying forms, from uncut rocks to finished jewelry. I gasped.

"Where did you get all this?"

"Pirates and Skía. Individuals usually didn't carry much. Take out a few encampments, though, and it adds up." Lorcan locked the unassuming metal container and handed it and the key to me. "For the Treasury." A small smile. "It's not fifty million dollars, but it will help ease immediate pressures."

"I don't know what to say. It's yours. You should keep it." The thought of how many lives Lorcan took in order to amass that much money over a few short months is sickening. We have always asked too much of him. "You more than earned it."

"I have plenty of money." He glanced around the tidy cottage. "I bought an entire house out of the proceeds, Princess. You have workers to pay, supplies to purchase, wounded fighters with families to support..."

You. Not, we. Nor does he mention the expenses of the wedding that won't be happening. I inhaled. He seems to have accepted that I'm not going to marry him.

My relief came mixed with sorrow. No good can come of trying to build a future on foundations as crumbled as ours. I have to focus on the bigger picture and not get distracted by personal temptation. Do what's right for my country, not chase empty promises of happiness.

We spent the rest of the day packing up our belongings and closing up the house. Rya and Arya came for dinner so we could use up our food, to thank them for hosting the party and to say our goodbyes.

Tomorrow, we face the real test. Can we put aside our

personal problems long enough to work together effectively for the next few months? Or will they continue to bubble up as arguments and impede Auralia's progress?

The success or failure of my reign rests on whether I can guide my ravaged country through the next few months. Whether I can give my people hope for the future when I, personally, don't have much.

Tovian waved as we rode down the path into Čovari Village.

"You're late," he grinned, his white teeth flashing. Although they look very different from one another, Tovian reminds me of Lorcan in many ways. Tovian is all easygoing good humor, while Lorcan is—or used to be—shy and quiet. Yet both men maintain a somewhat bewildering sense of optimism, despite projecting an air of casual lethality.

"Royalty is always on time," Lorcan clasped his friend's hand.

"Not when she's keeping other royals waiting," Tovian replied, bowing slightly to me. He, too, is a prince, or the equivalent of one in the Ansi tradition. As I understand it. I'm keen to learn more about his people. "If it were you and I, Lorcan, we could leave tonight. I doubt Sas will let us make the princess sleep outside, though."

"I've done it before," I informed him loftily, untying my pack and loosening the saddle on my horse.

"Even if Saskaya approves, I want Zosia to rest properly," Lorcan said. "It'll be a rough ride down to Oceanside. The others are here?"

"Keryn arrived two days ago. We've been waiting on you two."

Tahra came darting out of the barn and offered to help untack his horse. I bit back a smile and tried to remember Saskaya's admonishment that a seventeen-year-old is no threat to me. It's easier to keep that in mind after our break-through in Tenáho.

It won't matter in a few months, anyway. Once I relin-quish my public claim on Lorcan, Tahra can have him.

Mine, a little voice whispered.

He isn't, though. He never really was, any more than I've belonged to myself.

The toddler climbed down the steps, leading with the same foot each time, and darted toward me. My heart swelled.

"Sethi!" I scooped up my brother's small body. He giggled and patted my cheeks with sticky hands, squealing, "Zozo!"

Apparently, Zosia is too much of a mouthful for a toddler. I officially have a nickname. It's unexpectedly charming.

"Where's Mama?" I asked, not expecting a response, nor getting one. Instead, he wriggled out of my arms and ran over to Lorcan and Tovian.

"I see where I stand." Pretending to pout, I hoisted my pack. The sight of Lorcan holding my little brother squeezes my insides every time. It's a pang of loss for what can't be, and for the gross unfairness of my plan. He might hate me for what I've done, when he finds out. But he will have other children, with other women—for all either of us know, he might already have a few.

If he's been that careless with other women, there is no

rational reason for him to be upset about me joining the queue.

Our daughter will be mine alone. Assuming I can bear one.

"Tenáho was good for you," Saskaya remarked upon noting my new weight, squarely in the *underweight* category instead of *severely underweight*, where I was before I left, and well above *very severely underweight* as I was when I first arrived.

"It was."

"You look happier."

"I am."

"Did you work things out with your knight?" Saskaya asked, setting aside her notes.

"More or less." Nothing concrete. Only a vague plan to seduce him, which Lorcan is thus far cheerfully going along with, and get pregnant, which he doesn't know about.

"When will you announce the wedding?" My friend tapped the air with one foot. "I noticed there was no mention of it in the announcement about your coronation ceremony. A lot of people did."

"When we're ready." Meaning, never. But Lorcan gave me the perfect excuse. "Lorcan hasn't technically proposed to me. He says he's waiting for me to 'stop running', whatever that means."

Saskaya huffed. "Have you two ever considered not fighting for five minutes? Agree on a plan, and execute it?"

"Where's the fun in that, Sas?" I winked, but she's right. Lorcan and I have never really been on the same page. As I keep reminding myself, the foundation of our relationship has never been solid enough to build upon.

"Must keep the sex exciting," Saskaya muttered.

I arranged my face into careful neutrality. How to

even start explaining what's (not) happening there? I walked away from an advantageous engagement to be with him. We shared a house for weeks. Of course, everyone thinks we're together that way. Hopefully soon, we finally will be. Otherwise, my succession plan is doomed to fail.

Another sex-related failure might break me for good.

For propriety's sake—ridiculous, considering Lorcan and I have been cohabiting for weeks and are publicly betrothed—Lorcan stayed at Cata's empty house with Tovian and Keryn. I missed sleeping next to him.

In what I chose to interpret as cosmic approval of my succession plan, that night, I got my first cycle in months. I've tipped the scale far enough into a healthy weight range to resume menstruating. Yay, I guess.

Now it's a matter of convincing my temporary boyfriend to do his part.

Judging from the way Lorcan has been transparently campaigning to seduce me for weeks, that doesn't sound too difficult.

See? We can plan, or at least I can. All that's left is the execution.

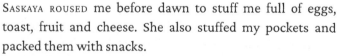

Saskaya roused me before dawn to stuff me full of eggs, toast, fruit and cheese. She also stuffed my pockets and packed them with snacks.

"No backsliding," she warned.

"This recovery thing is tedious."

"You're telling me? Seriously, let's get you healthy so I can get back to my real work. I'm a scientist, not a nurse."

I flung my arms around her. "Keep my box hidden until I can get it to the Treasury."

"Please. This is Čovari Village. We don't have crime." Saskaya held me by the shoulders. "Your box is safe. Lorcan is under orders to keep feeding you."

"You give him orders?"

"He takes direction well." Sas grinned. "Try it sometime."

Except when it comes to rescuing spoiled princesses, apparently. I'm trying not to hold that against him, but part of me will never quite forgive him for leaving me until the very last possible moment.

"Oh, and Tahra is coming with you."

I blinked at Sas for a minute. It's too early for this. The sun has barely cracked over the horizon. "Why?"

Saskaya tilted her head and gave me a lopsided smile. "Why do you think?"

I rolled my eyes. "Wonderful."

"She's young, bored, and a good fighter. Tahra volunteered immediately. Give her a chance, Zosia."

To do what? Fuck Lorcan? That's supposed to be my job. I get him until October, and then let women fight over him. That was the deal. It was on the tip of my tongue to say it, but then I would have to explain things I prefer keeping to myself, so I didn't.

We mounted and set off, haphazardly. Keryn's huge gelding dwarfed the rest of our horses. Seventeen hands tall, the spirited animal didn't like Tovian's mount, a dark chestnut stallion with blond mane, tail, and fetlocks. Therefore, I rode in the middle. Lorcan led, with Keryn in between us, Tahra behind me, and Tovian bringing up the rear, to his mount's profound frustration. We picked our way down the mountainside. It's an excruciatingly slow process. Keryn's charger hated the slow downward trudge and kept trying to pass Lorcan's bay mare. Tovian had his hands full trying to keep his horse in the back.

By the time we came down the pass into Marsh Hollow, everyone was hot and grouchy. I was the only one who seemed bothered by this cursed place—and then I remembered why. Lorcan has been past the site of his near-death many times since his recovery.

Stopping in the marshes didn't appeal, so it was early afternoon before we took a break near a stream at the edge of the Great Central River.

"Is that my horse?" I gestured to a large white stallion surrounded by a cluster of mares. "It is. It's Sky."

Lorcan rested his hand on my back. "I can catch him for you. Not now. But eventually."

Keryn's laughter boomed like thunder. "Good luck. That stallion is living his best life." They pointed to the half-grown colts and fillies bearing the clear stamp of Sky's paternity. They're not wrong. Sky has been to Beijing and carried my royal backside over endless jumps. Yet he's clearly happier with his many mares and his progeny than he ever was in the royal stables.

I feel the same way.

"You might have to catch the entire herd while you're at it." I wrapped one arm around Lorcan's waist.

"I'll help you," Tahra piped up. "If I can have one of the foals."

Lorcan caught my eye and smiled faintly. It's a bold thing to ask for the offspring of a royal stallion, even if he has been running wild for more than a year. In one sense, Saskaya was right. The distance between Tahra and me cannot be measured in years or in social status.

The threat she represents is in her youthful optimism

and willing availability. I cannot compete with undimmed hopes for the future. That has to appeal to a man who's been through as much as Lorcan has.

Storm clouds gathered in my thoughts.

The threat isn't from her. It's from Lorcan. What he says he values and wants versus what his actions show. Whether I believe he'll be true to me, were I to go through with the wedding.

I don't.

Once he married me, there would be nothing to stop him from taking as many women to bed as he wished. I'd have no more leverage over him than I did the year I was trapped in my castle. I shouldn't need it; I should be able to count on his loyalty as surely as he can count on mine. Without that, it's hopeless.

At least I'm clear-eyed about where we stand, now, even if part of me yearns for a scrap of hope.

"Lorcan can handle things, Tahra," I said gently, "when the time comes."

BLOOM

CHAPTER FOURTEEN

We spent the night in an abandoned cottage. Tahra and I took the bed. Keryn, Tovian and Lorcan placed their bedrolls on the floor.

Tahra snores; that's all I'll say. I would rather share a bed with Lorcan, but for now, we are maintaining decorum out of respect for our companions.

Too much scrutiny would quickly reveal that while our friendship is real, the romance is mostly pretense. I wonder how long we'll be able to conceal the truth. What Tahra will do if she suspects.

The second and third days of our journey brought a slow evolution to the landscape as we moved down through the Central Valley, following the Great Rielka River through the Grasslands District and then skirting the Boscage. Along the way we passed burned-out farms, the ruins of which were overgrown with vines and moss. An inordinate number of sheep skeletons dotted the landscape.

"Set free during the pirate rampages. Most didn't survive. What did, have been rounded up by surviving villagers," Tahra explained. "The predator population exploded."

An ecological disaster, alongside an economic one.

We encountered numerous wolf-bear packs on our journey. The scientist in me was delighted. The environmentalist wanted to document every sighting. The pragmatic part of me wanted to keep moving.

Pragmatism won out. I took as many photos as I could with my satellite phone. No one will ever be able to confiscate the device from me again. I may not be queen yet, but I may as well be.

This desolate world unnerved me. A little more than a year ago, ours was a thriving population. Now? We came across burned-out wagons and skeletons every few kilometers. Some are dead pirates left to rot in the sun, their modern clothing distinctive for the bright dyes and synthetic fabrics unavailable here.

The rest are my people. We don't have the time to stop and bury everyone. We're fortunate not to have been hit with cholera, considering all the bodies.

On the fourth day, I was increasingly overheated and slowly being driven insane by a combination of Tahra's dogged attempts to flirt with Lorcan and my horse's constant efforts to graze instead of walk. Only Tovian perked up as we moved deeper into the Grasslands District.

Lorcan took it all in stride. Ever solicitous of me, tolerant of Tahra, and friendly with Tovian and Keryn. He was disgustingly perfect.

I remained Auralia's reluctant royal. I also remained alive despite one unexpected run-in with a pack of wolf-bears, which Tovian, Lorcan and Keryn handled easily. Tahra did not appreciate the honor of being told to stay back and guard me.

Thanks, kid.

"It's not you," Lorcan told me upon their return. "She's tired of being told to stay behind."

I had my doubts. Everyone keeps telling me they're unwarranted, and maybe they are. She's smitten with Lorcan, though, and it grates on me, the way he ignores it.

Or maybe it's their friendship I envy, wanting to keep all of him to myself. That is not healthy. I've never had a boyfriend before, so I'm not sure how I'm supposed to act.

We set the horses free once we came to the entrance to a narrow trailhead.

"From here, we go on foot," said Tovian. "The horses will wander off to graze."

"If this is too much, we can take a slower route," Lorcan offered. I am the weak link in this group. Everyone else is warrior-fit. Me? I am as strong as you'd expect a half-starved princess to be after four days of travel over rugged terrain. I'm slow and keep asking for rest breaks, though I try hard to keep up. No one seems to mind waiting for me, though.

It's hot and sticky in the jungle. I wanted nothing more than to take off every stitch of clothing, which I briefly considered, only to realize there was no way to do so without others seeing me naked.

I haven't seen myself full-length in a mirror since that awful night at River Bend. Lorcan's cottage only had a small one in the outdoor privy and makeshift shower. I know I am not quite as knobby as I was immediately after my rescue, but I also know I'm far from what I was before the war.

Leaves shook noisily overhead.

"What's that?" Tahra asked, apprehensively.

"Dragons." Tovian scanned the canopy. "They're harmless. We keep them as pets."

"Pets," I repeated incredulously.

Dragons are not harmless. They bite. They lash their tails like whips, when provoked. If you get scratched by one, the wound is prone to infection. Fortunately, the winged lizards native to Auralia also mostly avoid humans. Larger specimens, like the one that flew overhead a moment ago, can grow to nearly four meters long.

"Yes. They're intelligent and easy to train. Children like them." Tovian was bemused by my skepticism. Lorcan stifled a smile. He knows something that I don't.

"Does Raina know about this?" I asked, panting as I hauled myself up over a root-gnarled, muddy hillside. I'm the only one not carrying a pack, only a small bag of personal essentials, yet I'm the laggard of the group.

"She has one."

"She does *not*."

"It lives with the Ansi, but it's hers. Garnet. I even made a silver collar for it."

"This, I cannot wait to see." I would love to arrive at Ansi Village—or whatever it's called—town, city, hamlet, I don't care as long as there's a bath and proper bed available. We're all pretty ripe. Biting gnats are getting the better of me. I keep walking into clouds of tiny insects. One even got into my eye. I'm itching like crazy. Keryn and Tahra are, too.

"Soon, Princess. There."

Bewilderingly, Tovian pointed across the fast-moving river at a sheer rock face. Right. There was literally nothing ahead except volcanic rock, eroded and pock-marked, with occasional trees valiantly clinging to crevices. I saw nothing to indicate a civilization of thousands of people lived nearby—which, I assume, is the point.

We soon came to a large fallen tree across the river raging several meters below. The top has been flattened to make it suitable for walking, with a rope strung across beside it. Apart from that, there was nothing to prevent you from slipping over the edge. Keryn eyed it warily.

"It's strong enough to support you," Tovian reassured them.

"Aye, perhaps. But am I nimble enough to get across without toppling over the side?" Keryn's eyes narrowed. "Only one way to find out."

They edged out onto the log bridge, gripping the rope with white knuckles, moving slowly at first, then fast enough to make the tree bounce alarmingly.

"See?" Tovian called out, laughing.

"You next, Princess." Lorcan gestured at me to cross. When I hesitated, Tahra barged ahead.

"I'll go."

She moved fast, skimming one hand along the rope. Showing off. A third of the way across, however, she slipped and went flying out over the river below, clutching the guideline with desperate strength. I gasped. Lorcan darted out onto the bridge and pulled Tahra back to safety.

Tovian shook his head disapprovingly. "Go slow, Princess. A little momentum helps you keep your balance, but don't rush."

"I won't." Once the other two reached the other side, I carefully picked my way across. The surface of the bridge was slippery from the humidity and spray from the churning river. My small pack shifted, pulling me off-balance for one terrifying moment, but I made it safely to the other side.

Tahra sat slumped against a tree, a pallor beneath her flushed face, still breathing heavily. I dropped onto the ground next to her.

"Are you okay?"

She nodded. Judging from the way she glanced past me, I'd say her crush on my knight just morphed into a case of outright hero worship. I bit back a smile. *I know that feeling. Been there.*

Lorcan waited for Tovian to cross, then went back for his pack. His hair curled at the nape of his neck and around his ears. Mine stuck to my forehead and cheeks in irritating tendrils. Everyone was ready to be done with this journey.

Tovian led us straight toward the cliffs. I was on the verge of asking whether he expected us to scale the sheer rock face, when a harsh hissing and flapping sound overhead caused me to bring my head up sharply. My mouth fell open and hung there as I gawped.

An optical illusion. This island is full of them—the most notable being that from the exterior, we appear to be nothing but a lot of rock topped by an active volcano, surrounded by dangerous shoals.

This particular illusion is a huge archway guarded by hundreds of dragons. Green, crimson, black and yellow—all sizes and colors. They hissed and whipped their tails until Tovian made a high-pitched whistle. A signal of some kind. The lizards settled back into their sunny crevices, tails lashing irritably, as we passed beneath their perch.

Inside the archway was a huge cavern dotted with dwellings carved into the stone. A fast-moving, needle-thin river that had cut a deep gouge into the ground, topped by a sturdy stone bridge. We crossed over it to what are, clearly, Tovian's people.

Predominantly darker-skinned with black hair, they

favored brightly-colored leather garments or, in deference to the sultry weather, none at all. Handprints in a chalky white substance covered their exposed skin, of which, there was a substantial amount. Our impractical linen and wool clothing were rumpled and out of place.

An old woman with thick gray braids and tiger teeth on a string around her neck came forward.

"Princess Zosia," she said in a commanding voice. "Welcome. We have heard a great deal about you. It's a pleasure to welcome you to the Ansi tribe."

Unsure what to do or who she was—clearly a leader—I bowed.

"Great to see you, too, Mum," Tovian teased. A man who bore a strong resemblance to him came forward to clasp his hand. "My brother, Tomar. This is my mother, Queen Brenica." To his mother, "The Auralian princess is exhausted. We can catch up this evening."

Goddess bless Tovian for noticing—a phrase I rarely use. Every muscle was sore from days of hard travel. I itched everywhere from gnat bites. There was dirt crusted in every crevice from my scalp to my toes, and all I wanted was a bath and a nap. Instead, I had to put on my best diplomatic face and go meet with the intimidating leader of a tribe that has chosen to remain hidden away from the rest of Auralia for at least five hundred years, emerging only to play a pivotal role in the battle.

Dragons rattled their wings. The vile creatures deserve to be leather. I only like these animals intellectually; give me plants any day. Plants don't bite.

Tovian led Lorcan and me up a steep incline to a spacious rock chamber lined with scraped animal hides. The floor was covered in a woven grass mat. A bed frame of wood and stretched leather was piled with furs. Spidersilk doesn't seem to be a thing amongst the Ansi.

"You can use my room. I'll share my brother's while we're here." He tapped the wall hangings. "Noise reduction. Sound carries against the rock. Keep that in mind."

Hollow grasses formed a sort of exterior plumbing system. The rushing water above the door provided white noise. Despite this, our voices echoed faintly, even though we weren't talking loudly.

"Fair warning," Lorcan's smile was knowing. "Thanks."

My already-hot face steamed with embarrassment. Hopefully I can finally get reality to match widely prevalent assumptions. The men clasped hands, and Tovian made his departure.

This is no different from sharing Lorcan's cottage in Tenáho. Or a dormitory suite in Scotland, or adjoining hotel rooms, or a small apartment in a castle that houses hundreds of other people. Yet one small cave felt infinitely more intimate.

What bothers me is that there's no privacy for changing. He'll see me naked. I can't even look at myself without cringing. I suppose I was going to have to confront that challenge at some point. Still, my anxiety spiked. I avoided looking at Lorcan as I unpacked.

I flinch when he touches me, gently, on the shoulder.

"Leave that for now."

Five days since we've been alone together. It feels like a lifetime. Each minute and passing kilometer took us farther from the tentative accord we reached in Tenáho. Starting over, again.

"Would you mind giving me a moment?" I ask, hating my shyness. Unsure how to change it.

He nodded and, after hesitating, departed. Huh. I should take Saskaya's advice—he does take direction well. I don't think that was the context she meant though.

My phone went off.

Raina: heard you made it to Ansi Town okay. How do you like it?

Me: Cool place. Arrived about half an hour ago.

Raina: Tovi told me. Brenica's amazing. You'll love her once you get to know her.

Raina, typing fast and making mistakes: Listen, you're about to get dragged into an Ansi thing, just trust me, go with it. They do it to all new arrivals. You'll be a lot more comfortable if you let them dress you and paint you.

Me: ?

Raina: it's a little strange and invasive the first time

Me: Strange, how?

Raina: Especially the hair removal part. Think of it as a spa! Waxing!

Me, panicking: WHAT

Raina: Just go with it!

Me: WHY DIDN'T YOU WARN ME

Me: WHY DIDN'T *ANYONE* WARN ME?!

Me: I'm going to kill Lorcan for this. Tovian, too. Hope you're ready to be a widow.

Raina: Reception inside the village is crap call me when you're out in the field tomorrow—whatever you do

The text message cuts off as though she hit send prematurely.

"Zosia?"

I tossed the phone onto the bed. *Fuck, fuck, fuck.* "Yes?"

"Queen Brenica is asking for you," Lorcan called through the covered entrance. I smoothed my hair away from my face, gathered my courage, and descended the walkway to meet my fellow queen.

CHAPTER FIFTEEN

"Princess Zosia. Your presence here is an honor."

I bowed. "It is an honor to be your guest."

I may be the future queen of Auralia, but here, I am a foreign dignitary. An itchy, grumpy, tired, smelly one who isn't in the mood for formalities.

"According to our custom, everyone who comes from the outside must wash away the scent. The Ansi go out into the world but, until recently, we did not invite the outside world in. You have Princess Raina to thank for our newfound openness, as well as the Skía and their pirate army." Her smile faded. "The work of ridding our shores of that scourge is not yet finished. My ladies will prepare you and your companions for the next phase of your journey."

Oh, great. Here we go.

"Each step has a purpose, Princess. I understand you may find our methods intrusive but they are necessary. We will scrub you clean" —the queen's nose flared delicately— "and make your skin smooth so that our paint sticks properly. The paint keeps away bothersome gnats" —*I am sold*— "and other discomforts, as well as providing camouflage.

You will be given clothing appropriate to protect you in this environment. My sons will show you how it works tomorrow. Your knight is already familiar with this process."

I cast him a withering glare. *Thanks for the heads up.* Lorcan's eyes crinkled at the corners.

"When my son said you were small, I assumed you were short as well, like his wife. As you are considerably taller than expected, the clothes we have might be a little... skimpy."

Auralia, kill me now. I am begging you. I forced a smile. "I'm sure I'll manage."

The queen's dark eyes danced with humor. "I doubt your knight will mind. Will he be painting you?"

"I...uh, as opposed to?"

"The ladies."

"Yes. Sure." Better to have Lorcan do it than strangers, right? How do I get into these situations, anyway?

My answer apparently sufficed, for Queen Brenica abruptly turned and indicated that I should follow her down to where Keryn and Tahra were looking bedraggled and skeptical. It's on me to set an example. I followed our hostess back over the stone bridge with my head high, back straight, and heart in my throat.

She took us, and a crowd of around twenty Ansi women, down a path into another horseshoe-shaped canyon with a waterfall at the opposite end.

"Great, just what I was looking forward to," Keryn grumbled. "A cold bath."

"The water is warm," one of our attendants said, smiling. "Hot springs." She pointed to the top of the cliffs, hazed by a cloud of steam. The waterfall must cool to a comfortable temperature on the way down.

The Ansi dialect is to Auralian like North African or

Canadian French is to Parisians—different, though still the same language. It takes concentration. Concentration is tiring, and I was already at my limit. I gritted my teeth and stripped my clothes off when indicated. Covering the essentials as best I could with both hands, I jumped into the water.

Anything to avoid seeing myself naked.

As promised, the warm water is a delight. Almost enough to make up for the fact that three women instantly grabbed me and started scrubbing. Back. Shoulders. Hair. While I usually enjoy physical contact more than I probably should, this was too much. As embarrassing as it was, I was so overwhelmed with trying to process who was touching what part of me that I had no extra energy to focus on my self-consciousness about my body—until they started with the hair removal, like Raina warned me. (Barely.)

"Is this strictly necessary?" I demanded. The women shrugged.

"If you want the paint to stick," one said.

"The hair is itchy," said the woman holding my knee angled against the rock. "We don't have to take it all off, but the men like it better if you do."

Men liked this? Would Lorcan? I'll endure *any* indignity if it finally gets me laid.

"Whatever you think is best," I mumbled.

Keryn objected vociferously to the depilation process. Tahra's silver hair apparently extended to below the waist, to the fascination of the women yanking it out at the roots. She endured this stoically in true Čovari fashion.

I was red from head to toe by the time the women helped me out of the bathing pool, not only because of having every hair painfully plucked out from places I didn't think I grew any. I cannot believe Raina put up with this treatment. What was she thinking, letting me walk into this situation without warning? She had almost a week to send word!

The herbal-scented creams they smoothed onto my skin were nice, though. Even Keryn rubbed their forearms appreciatively.

"That was an experience," they commented.

"You liked it?" asked one of the Ansi women. I wish I knew them by name, but that will take more than a single afternoon. Right now, I'm doing my best to memorize their features.

"Parts of it," Keryn answered, grinning. "Could do without being plucked like a duck."

"It was an experience, wasn't it?" I laughed. Now that it's over, I can admit it wasn't so bad. The Ansi are even less fussed about nudity than the Čovari. I, however, remained deeply self-conscious.

The instant I was out of the pool, I draped a rough-woven towel around my torso.

"Why do you hide?" one woman asked, cocking her head.

I shrugged and turned away. My breasts aren't as flat as they were a few weeks ago, and my stomach isn't concave between my hip bones, but I'm not me.

Then again, my body has never felt like mine. This isn't so different from the way my father used to stuff me into formal robes, or how I had to dress up for photographers and black-tie events in the outside world. I didn't recognize myself in those images, either. Whatever is happening to me in the aftermath of my recovery is part of a long history of never feeling like I belong to myself.

"You should be painted before you dress," a woman with stripes on her face and palm prints over her naked breasts stated. Apparently, this paint does not wash off. Fabulous.

"Clothes, please."

Such as they are. The top was little more than two pieces of green dragonskin leather held in place by straps at the neck and around my back. The skirt was supposed to cover my ass, but since Tovian neglected to specify that I am quite a bit taller than Raina, it only does so when the side laces are loosened enough to ride low on my hips.

At least there's a fur shrug to conceal my shoulders and sandals with a laced-up covering for my lower legs. If the skirt actually hit mid-thigh like it's supposed to—as Tahra's does—my lower body would be well-protected from stray branches and thorny undergrowth. I wouldn't feel so obscenely naked.

"You look..." Tahra trailed off. Her silver hair had dried in a long braid down her back. Mine, after much discussion, was corralled into two thin braids from my temples to behind my ears and tied with tiny pieces of leather.

"Absurd?"

"Incredible."

It's a nice thing of her to say. I really should give Tahra the benefit of the doubt more often.

"Same difference." With a sidelong glance at her, I reluctantly added, "You look fantastic."

She does. Full of robust youthful health. Ready to kill pirates with her bare hands—and that's before she's been painted. The women approached with two bowls, one full of chalky white and the other with muddy violet paste. Both smelled strong but not unpleasantly herbal.

"Lorcan is painting you?" asked Tahra, wistfully.

"Yes."

I strode away. It's not well done of me. I have something

she wants—or she thinks I do. The truth is a lot more complicated.

Begrudgingly, I can admit that this getup is cooler than the clothes I arrived in, and I haven't been bitten by a single gnat since the bath. I'll take it. My nether parts might never recover from the indignity of being stripped nearly bare, though.

As long as I can have a nap, I'll recover.

BACK IN THE dim rock-walled bedroom, I found Lorcan sitting on the bed, cross-legged. Waiting for me.

"Feel better?" He didn't attempt to hide his smile. Even in the dim light filtering in through the leather privacy closure, I could see his reaction to my getup. His gaze skimmed down my body, then—slowly—up again to meet my eyes. Pupils blown between a narrowed, possessive glance. Heat and nervousness coursed through my blood.

I bit my lower lip and glanced shyly away. *This is it. Finally.*

A twinge of guilt over what I hoped the outcome would be.

"You might have warned me about the bathing process."

"Why? So you could worry about it for the entire trip?" He rolled off the bed. I take in his outfit. It's basically leather shorts with shoulder and shin guards like mine. It should look absurd, but it instead accentuates his lean muscularity—and leaves most of him bare.

"I said I wanted to be told the truth."

Why am I pressing this point, now?

"I didn't lie to you, Princess." Lorcan dipped his thumb in a bowl of pungent purple paste. He drew a cool, wet line down the bridge of my nose. Then he took my chin between his forefinger and thumb, tipped my face to his, and kissed me.

"This is the fun part," he said, lips brushing against mine as he spoke.

My insides turned warm and soft.

I wanted adventures. This is definitely an adventure, and it seems like it might lead to other things I want, too, if I can keep my anxiety under control. There was no hint of a looming panic attack.

"I like fun. What should I do?"

"Paint me." Lorcan held out the bowl. When I didn't immediately dip my hand in, he took a fingerful and traced a line along the part on the top of my skull.

"Like this?" I put both hands in the paint, squelched it, and made handprints on his pectorals. The heat of his skin was a pleasant contrast to the temperature of the purple stuff. When I pulled them away there were two perfect marks in deep violet on his chest. He chuckled.

"You always were a quick study, Zosia." He set the bowl aside and perched on the edge of the bed, drawing me between his knees. Lorcan scanned me from head to toe. "You look—"

"I look ridiculous, and so do you, Knight."

I should be tired, but my fatigue is secondary to the newness of this odd process and my growing excitement that this might finally happen. Sex. I'd all but given up hope.

I took more of the paste and squished it between my palms. Lorcan tucked his hands behind my thighs and brought me onto his lap, straddling him as far as I could

with my skirt restricting my movement. It felt kind of sexy,
with the leather digging into my skin that way. I wasn't
wearing a stitch of clothing beneath the tiny skirt, and I
didn't know how Lorcan would react when he found out.

I clasped his shoulders, leaving handprints on his
biceps. Next, I smeared purple along the ridges of his
cheekbones with my thumbs, covering the thin scar
beneath his eye. *Mine.* Only I get to see it, now.

The banked fire in his eyes smoldered, turning his eyes
darker than I've ever seen them.

I took his face in my hands and kissed him hard and
open-mouthed, leaving marks on his jaw. Lorcan made a
sound in the back of his throat, grabbed my ass and ground
me against his erection. I liked that. A lot.

"Painting is fun," I murmured against his mouth.

"See?" Lorcan fumbled with the side laces on my skirt. I
stopped him.

A disturbing thought quelled my ardor. "How often
have you done this?"

He shook his head. "Never. It has..." He hesitated, then
scooped up a palmful of paint. "Implications."

The cool press of paint on the backs of my upper thighs
made me exhale against his face. We kiss, and kiss again.

"Implications, in what way?" I asked when I could
breathe again.

Is this what Raina was trying to warn me about? If so,
she didn't seem overly concerned by whatever they are, or
she would've tried harder. It seemed kind of like an
afterthought. Can't be that serious.

Lorcan returned his attention to the laces of my skirt,
which were biting into my hips as my knees moved farther
apart. A current of air wafted between my thighs, and I
shivered slightly when it caressed the wet, newly exposed

part of me. He got it undone and slid the garment away. I couldn't decide whether I was more embarrassed or aroused to be naked from knee to sternum. Either way, I kept my eyes on him as heat crawled down my throat and spread over my chest. My nipples were tight points against the butter-soft leather.

Lorcan glanced down. His eyes widened. "Holy fuck, Zosia—"

His cock twitched inside the ridiculous shorts. His clothes weren't so easy to remove, sadly for me.

"Yes, please," I whispered, and sank my teeth into his earlobe.

So nervous. Too nervous. I don't know what I'm supposed to do. *Why doesn't he hurry? Please, finally, let's get this over with.*

That wasn't quite the approach he wanted to take, though. Lorcan wanted to take things slow. I should probably be grateful for that, but I can't be. I want it done. I want to know what it feels like to have sex. I want the best chance of getting pregnant possible, given the short time we have left together.

If I push for it, though, he'll suspect, and that will raise questions I don't want to answer.

So once again, I must temper my enthusiasm and *wait*.

CHAPTER SIXTEEN

There's a squish of paint as he takes up more. His palms landed on my back and slid messily upward, making me gasp. I inched closer on his lap. He dug his fingers into my buttocks and rocked my newly depilated sex hard against his erection, grinding hard. I exhaled against his neck. *Oh, yes.* I've needed this.

He didn't ask before untying my top. I didn't protest. The triangles fall to the floor. I'm grateful for the low light. It's the first time he's seen me naked since the fiasco in June. I braced. But instead of recoiling, Lorcan takes me in with hot blue eyes that devour me whole.

I squirmed, wanting him to look yet not wanting to be seen as I am.

"Zosia." He breathed my name on an exhale. I scooped more paint and traced it along his collar bones, noting the nicks and scars visible in the dimness. Placing a fingerprint at the hollow of his throat where I like to stroke him. *Mine.*

The wet press of his hands against my ribs made me flinch closer, arching upward. Lorcan took this as an invitation to draw a purple line from the hollow at the base of my throat to the end of my sternum. He bent his head to nip that spot beneath my ear, while circling one nipple with his thumb. I clutched his hair. He moved down, sucking my skin, rolling the other between his thumb and forefinger. My mind blanked out. Good. Minds are useless in these situations anyway. Who needs to think?

Just deflower me already. For a moment, I thought he might. Lorcan shifted, depositing me on the surface of the bed. I scrambled for the furs provided as bedding, feeling shy again. Trying to cover myself before panic set in.

"You okay, Princess?"

I can't believe he picked up on it so quickly. The feeling eased.

If we stop now, I might not get another opportunity to try with him.

"Yes. Everything's okay."

I lay propped on my elbows with a skin draped over me, torn between wanting to continue this and fear that it would all go sideways again. Lorcan settled himself beside me and moved the bowl to where it was less likely to get spilled.

He scooped a thick glop and kept tracing the line of my sternum between the modest rise of my breasts, down to my navel. Painting the hollow. Drawing a sun around it, a reference to the Sun Goddess from whom I am supposedly descended. I'd have rolled my eyes, but he bent lower to press an open-mouthed kiss to my stomach. My insides lurched with each new touch.

I watched with fascination. Being exposed this way wasn't so terrible. With all the purple paint streaking my body, I don't feel quite so naked. Which doesn't make much sense, but then again, neither do I, lately.

"I—Lorcan?"

"Mm?"

He was taking his sweet time with this. I hope we're not keeping Queen Brenica waiting. "What implications?"

"It means that in the eyes of the Ansi, I'm yours."

He leaned down and put his entire palm flat into the bowl. Then he pressed it carefully, tenderly to my low belly, leaving a perfect palm print right above my pubic area. Claiming ownership. "And you're mine."

I should not like this. I do, though. I love it. My secret thoughts on his lips. There was a pulse between my legs. A rush of wetness dampened my inner thighs.

Lorcan removed the paint from his hands with an astringent-smelling rag. It takes the purple stain right off. Reassuring to know that if I don't like the markings, I can get rid of them. Then he adjusted his position and skimmed one hand up the inside of my thighs. Obligingly, I parted for him.

"If you want to stop, say so. At any point."

Mutely, I nodded. Stop? When I'm finally getting what I want? That will not be happening. Still no sign of an impending freak-out. Maybe he was right: the attack in his kitchen happened because it was too much, too soon. This slow, sensual seduction doesn't seem to be setting off alarm.

Maybe I'm not irreparably broken. That would be nice.

I adopted his pose from the couple of times we've been together like this before, with one arm behind my head, bunching furs behind me so I was propped high enough to look at him.

Lorcan's gaze met mine, then fell back to where I am totally exposed. This is simultaneously the hottest and the most embarrassing thing anyone has ever done to me.

He traced one finger through the slickness at my center.

I gasped. The other times he's touched me there, it was dark and we were covered up, whether by clothes or by blankets or both. Lorcan exhaled a low groan as he parted me. Looking. Studying me. More wetness as he traced a path through my folds.

At least that's one part of me that can't look different than I did before. Not that he ever saw me like this. Back then, Lorcan was so shy, he needed encouragement to touch me.

No longer. This new Lorcan is bold. I think I like it?

My hips shifted upward, seeking, when he circled my clit. I couldn't tear my gaze away from his face, watching while he examined me wonderingly, as though I am the rarest treasure and he alone gets to see it. I might pass out from sheer embarrassment; it's hotter than being thrown into the Mountain of Fire.

He bent his head and licked straight up my center.

I hissed with surprise. It feels so much better than I ever imagined, and I have imagined this a *lot* over the years.

"Okay?" he asked.

"Yes."

Goddesses, yes.

I inched down the bed toward him.

Lorcan brought his hands up around the outsides of my thighs and went to work, a slow glide building gentle pressure within me. Down to dip inside me, then upward to draw lazy patterns on my clit. Each pass made me writhe. Airless, panting moans escaped my lips no matter how I tried to keep them in. They kept spilling out of me, which Lorcan seemed to particularly enjoy. When his gaze flicked to mine, I swear there were crinkles at the corners. Laughing at me? I'll never recover if he's mocking me at this vulnerable moment.

Needing to hold onto something solid, I grasped the side of the bed, and when that wasn't enough, his hair.

He flattened his tongue against my clit and bore down. I cried out, convulsing as he licked me through the crest. The sound echoed off the walls. When I came back to myself, I decided to never leave this room. Everyone will know what we've been doing.

They already presumed we were doing this, so I'm not sure why it matters. Logic is not my strong suit right at this moment. It's bewildering to go from having to hide this side of me to engaging in sex with nothing more than a thin curtain between my nakedness and the entire world. Tenáho didn't count. We weren't doing anything much, until the very end.

My breathing slowly returned to normal. Lorcan rolled up and unlaced the leather tie from my leather skirt. He took my limp arm, made a loop, and secured my wrist to the side of the bed. Then he did the same with the other side. I watched him do this without resistance.

"What are you doing?"

"Experimenting." Lorcan's bemusement was etched in the corners of his mouth, a secret, knowing smile that does things to my insides. "Stopping you from pulling my hair out. Not that I minded, but I'm not looking to be plucked bald."

Satisfied with his handiwork, he sat back. "Still okay?"

"I...you're not going to leave me here, are you?" I could probably get out of this but I'd rather not test it. He's asking a lot of me right now. Feeling captive isn't something I ever thought I'd enjoy after last year.

"Ask and I'll untie you. We can stop at any point."

I guess he really means it.

Then he slid between my thighs and went back to work.

I've heard of tying people up during sex as a thing that exists but I never once thought about it happening to me. It's as though everyone else has been taking advanced calculus while I'm still trying to master basic arithmetic.

I have to give myself entirely over to him. Trust him to find the ways I enjoy being touched—which, thus far, is everything he's doing.

Fuck, I've needed this for *so* long.

Lorcan dragged his finger downward, trailing my wetness into the space below my sex. I shivered and let my knees fall open wider.

"That's it, Princess," he growled, and I realized how tense I was. Lorcan dipped his fingers inside me, monitoring my reaction.

"What am I supposed to do?" I whispered hoarsely.

"Nothing. You don't have to do anything. This is my time to learn you." He brought his fingers up to my clit again, circling. "Figure you out."

The way he did in Scotland. When we weren't getting along. I've been perpetually behind the curve in learning what makes him tick.

Lorcan erased all thought from my mind when he stroked down the sensitive skin between my sex and the pucker of my ass, trailing my own moisture. He wouldn't *dare*.

He didn't, but he looked intently as he drove me to the edge, then left me hanging there while he explored a new area of interest with his tongue and his fingers. I've never been handled so intimately before. Not unless you count Dr. Wen, which wasn't quite the same experience.

I moaned and tried to wriggle closer. Seeking what I needed while he teasingly denied me a second climax. I might technically still be a virgin but this is sex, no mistake about it, and I loved it.

"Lorcan, we don't have all afternoon. Quit playing around." I gave up hinting at what I wanted from him with wordless sounds of pleasure and tried the direct approach. Maybe Sas was right. "Make me come."

Get inside of me, already. Give me the full experience.

He chuckled. "If that's what you want."

"What I do not want is to be left hanging like this when Queen Brenica comes back for me," I pant.

"She won't."

"You sound very sure of that."

"Tovian mentioned the soundproofing for a reason, Zosia. They know what we're doing. Being reunited is celebrated among the Ansi." Lorcan held my gaze as he moved back, licking gently and thrusting two fingers inside me. I whimpered, struggling against my restraints. I wanted to demand that he get naked and fuck me already, but I was too turned on to form words. When I come, I'm going to break in two. I'll be wrecked and useless. I want it so badly —and he knows it.

I can command and plead all I want to, but here, I'm subject to his whims, not the other way around.

He really does get off on having the most powerful woman in Auralia yielding to him. Having me in his control.

The thought hits like a match strike, flaring and gone but leaving a brightening glow. Is he scheming to wield this kind of power over me all the time? How would he use it?

Lorcan wants me to trust him, and I do—but only so far. Not with the most vulnerable parts of myself.

"Come back to me, Zosh," he murmured, crawling up my body and sucking my nipple between his teeth. I can't clutch his hair. All I can do is arch into his mouth. My entire breast fits inside.

Once he decided to let me have what I needed, he gave it abruptly, with crooked fingers and short, hard thrusts. My vision blurred and sounds I'd never made before came out of me as successive waves crashed through my body. Spasms clenched my abdomen in ripples. I let go, falling into nothingness as my body pulsed around him.

When I could breathe again and my vision hazed back into focus, I was exactly where I started—lying on a bed frame padded with animal skins, the fur sticking to my sweaty skin, wrists bound. Naked, mostly. Too limp to care.

Lorcan kissed my temple.

"How are you feeling now?"

"Unh." What I meant to say is utterly demolished, but that's too many syllables. Lorcan freed my hands. I rubbed my wrists, which bore dark, indented rings. He hadn't tied them very tight. I pulled against my restraints while in the process of losing my mind.

He dropped one arm over my stomach. I rolled onto my side, facing him, draping one leg over his waist. We're doing this now, right? Finally?

Lorcan skimmed one hand down my body from shoulder to knee. He buried his face against my neck and sighed. Tangling my fingers in his hair, I held him close like this. Anticipation rose. I couldn't be more ready to lose my virginity, at long last.

"You still have to finish painting me," he murmured.

"I am not capable of a commensurate performance, Knight."

Painting was nice, but it wasn't what I wanted. His laughter puffed warmly over my skin.

"It's not a competition." He kissed me and rolled onto

his back. It's interesting to have my face above his, to be the one bending down. He tasted like me. I shifted to get a better angle on an open-mouthed kiss. Lorcan palmed my ass, pressing down, until I was straddling his waist, on my knees and elbows.

"Please," I whispered.

"Later, Princess."

Disappointment leached into my arousal, killing it. Always later. Never now.

"Why?" I whined.

"So we can do things right. Take our time."

Take our time? The fuck? What have we been doing for the past few years? What have we been doing all afternoon?

Lorcan, annoyingly, was serious. He took my hips and shifted me off him. *Damn, double damn, triple damn.*

Sitting up, he offered me the bowl of paint. "You missed a few spots."

The head of his cock protruded from the insufficient coverage of his Ansi shorts. I ignored the bowl and reached for his erection, squeezing through the thin leather. Lorcan's eyes screwed shut. "Fuck, Zosia—"

"Please?"

"Not now. You can touch me if you want to. No more."

There's something wrong with me. Whether it's how I look now, or something else, I don't know, but there has to be a reason he continues to refuse me.

Shame lanced through me.

I don't want to think about this right now. I don't want to be angry or sad. It's probably nothing fixable, but I hate not knowing what the problem is. It's me. I'm the problem.

Once might be enough, I told myself, *if I time it right*. Maybe I can put a blindfold on him and he can think about whatever kind of woman he does want to fuck, since I'm not it. Tahra, or Masika. That maid at River Bend, perhaps.

Lorcan turned his back. I straddled his hips from behind, on my knees, all of my front pressed to his entire back. Not bad, actually. I can touch all of him while still hiding. Starting in the center of his chest, I worked my way down. The texture of his skin over taut muscle, interrupted in places by scar tissue, made me ache with want. Again. Already. Nothing seems to change that. I kissed the nape of his neck.

With a fortifying inhale, I carefully extracted him. There's not much room for me to to stroke. His whole body tightened as I worked my hand up and down as best I could.

I'm grateful for the low light. He can't see anything other than my hands and arms. Touching him like this, however, made me feel the depth of my inexperience. I can't possibly do it right. I faltered.

"You—you should take over." I released him.

"Okay, Princess?" he asked, half-turning to me.

Not really. "Fine."

His refusal rattled me. I'd rather have him inside me than pretend I can please him like this. I held back, watching with interest in hopes I might learn something. Ever the diligent student.

Lorcan didn't take long. A few strokes, a tensing of his body, his breath harsh. I keep myself out of the way, plastered against his back, peeking over his shoulder. Milky liquid gleamed in the crevices and planes of his abdomen.

I kissed his shoulder. Lorcan blew out a long breath.

"Is there a reason you don't want to...with me?" I asked, because if so, I need to stop pretending my plan will work. Any plan. All of them.

Failure clawed at me.

"Want to, what?"

"Have sex. With me. Am I too"—*what's the right word? Ugly?*—"unappealing?"

I squeezed my eyes closed against the memory of myself in the mirror at River Bend.

He slumped, pinning me against the rock wall of the cave.

"Please don't tell me you think that."

I didn't say anything. I wish I had my real clothes on. I wish my eyes didn't sting. I wish a lot of things.

"It's just that you keep saying no."

Only to me. Not to anyone else.

"Zosia, a couple of weeks ago, you had a panic attack in my kitchen when we tried to do this. Today was good progress."

Good progress is not going to get me pregnant, though. This is my one shot at having a family, securing my succession, and keeping a piece of him with me, before Lorcan is out of my life for good. There's no time for incremental progress.

It's not lost on me that what I want to do to him—use him for breeding stock—wasn't so different from what Bashir would have done to me. Except I won't hurt Lorcan in the process. He doesn't even have to know. All I need is for him to be as careless as he was all last winter. I know he's not taking contraceptive teas. I'd have seen them at his house. Assuming he overheard Dr. Wen, there's no reason for him to be worried about getting me pregnant.

Gods damn it all, at least let me *try*. If it doesn't work, I can accept that. But I can't accept not making an attempt. My vision swam.

Lorcan ran one hand down my arm and kissed my shoulder.

"Let's end this on a high note? Try again tomorrow?"

I swallowed my disappointment and tried to ignore my growing suspicion that there's something he isn't telling me. I'm sick of doubting him, and of feeling like the last woman in Auralia who hasn't had sex.

I should just find someone else to do this with.

Except, now I'm painted. If I understand the significance right, it's akin to being married. I'm sure that would be frowned upon.

He totally planned this. Lorcan is uncannily good at cutting off every exit before I think to look for them.

"You haven't finished painting me," he said with a soft smile.

I laughed, relieved that he hadn't told me outright that I was too hideous to want to fuck properly. There was hope for me yet. "True."

Finding the paint bowl, I advancing at him, pretending to attack. As if I would stand a chance against a trained assassin.

Lorcan feinted, picked me up and threw me onto the bed. I smeared paint everywhere and came up giggling. Ten minutes later, he had my handprints on his hips, disappearing into his pants. On his thighs. On his forearms. They look so small.

Marks of possession. *Mine.* For a little while. My heart squeezed.

None of this is real.

There will always be another Masika leading Lorcan off into a dark corner, a Tahra he won't send away, a maid in our chambers willing to lift her skirts. He belongs to everyone, now. One argument between us—hardly an uncommon occurrence—and he'd have a hundred women lining up to comfort the poor beleaguered Auralian king, no matter how much infidelity is frowned upon.

Whatever it is about me that he finds too off-putting to complete the act, hasn't been a problem for him with anyone else. It's me. I'm the problem, which is why no matter how hard he's been trying to convince me otherwise, I remain certain he would stray in a heartbeat. I have no trust for him to win.

CHAPTER SEVENTEEN

We emerged from our dwelling a little before sundown. The sky above the rim of the horseshoe hazed gold. Below, the horseshoe gathering area was thrown into shadow lit only by the fire in the center. Dragons scurried along the warm black rocks.

"Good nap?" Keryn asked when we came down to the circle. They plucked a morsel of fish and rice from a plate. My stomach rumbled.

I nodded. No sleeping involved, but they don't need to know that.

"How did you get painted?" I eyed the handprints in purple on their skin.

"Ran a gauntlet, got slapped by every woman in this dragon den," they chortled. "Took all of ten minutes. You two were gone for hours."

Embarrassed heat crept over my face at their knowing grin. There are no secrets amongst the Ansi, apparently.

Queen Brenica waved me over. "I trust you are rested from your journey?" Her eyes were bright with amusement.

"Not exactly."

"Pity. You have an early morning ahead of you, if you intend to accompany your friends." She passed me a bowl with salted fish balls. I took one, then another. Completely uncouth. They were delicious and I was ravenous. Too hungry to process what she'd said about tomorrow morning.

"You like those. Take them." She nudged the bowl closer. "Ordinarily, Ansi do not involve ourselves with the affairs of Oceanside. We trade our goods in the city under the pretense of being traveling merchants. We fish in the rocky shallows with our small skiffs, like other Auralians, but we do not concern ourselves with their problems, nor they with ours."

I helped myself to grilled palm fruit in tamarind sauce, listening.

"Since the war, our preference for privacy is no longer feasible. The grasslands we depended upon for raw materials are decimated. We can live on fruits that grow here in the Boscage and on meat we hunt or fish, but we depend upon the Grasslands District for grain. The sea is infested with pirates who shoot, rape and maim without mercy. Without Oceanside and access to the water, we cannot feed our people.

"Tomorrow, my sons will show you how pirates continue to plague us despite our efforts to chase them off. We need more than a tentative alliance between the people of Oceanside and the Myseči. Our ammunition supplies dwindle by the day. We need a strategy, and we need it soon. Tovian and Raina have looked for every possible solution and nothing has worked to drive them off for good. If you can secure outside assistance, or more powerful weapons, we stand a chance. If not..."

"I understand. I will find a solution." Somehow.

Projecting confidence I don't feel. "Saskaya has sent us with an experimental weapon to test."

I could tell it wasn't the answer Queen Brenica was hoping for. I can't blame her. Saskaya's last weapons killed her own sister and trapped me in the castle for a year. I'm skeptical, too.

"Your father made connections among powerful people in the outside world. Politicians. Bankers. People who could help us."

I take more food—who knew being tied up and licked for hours worked up such an appetite—partly to delay responding.

My father believed that if we could cultivate the right allies, Auralia would be saved. But we are a small island in the middle of a large ocean, with no geopolitical importance, no economy to speak of, and no trade partners. Pirates are everyone and no one's problem. It's always someone else's waters. Another politician's responsibility. No one was ever coming to rescue us.

We saved ourselves. What made a difference was how the different tribes worked together.

Čovari technology set us back. It also saved our best warrior's life.

Lorcan was right all along. Auralia doesn't need outsiders. We need to rely on one another.

Saskaya's people blunted the initial attack, at great cost to their tribe.

Myseč leadership filled the vacuum while I was incapacitated. Raina's medical training bought time to heal Lorcan, while she and King Myseči coordinated a defense that contained the invaders long enough for him to awaken and physically recover. She and Saskaya saved my life, too.

The Mountain Folk kept the northern end of the island

from becoming a second beachhead for the Skía, driving them away from the only other access point.

Ansi knowledge of Oceanside's terrain enabled our fighters to get close enough to the Skía and their army of pirates, blunting the impact of their technical superiority. Dirt bikes are faster than horses. Guns are deadlier than swords and spears, but if they couldn't see us, they couldn't shoot us.

Once we stole enough of their technology to turn the tide, thanks to Lorcan's daring raids on enemy encampments, our fighters pushed the pirates down the peninsula and back out to sea. The Skía slunk into the shadows once again.

Now, it's my job to hold this alliance together, ensuring my country is not perceived as a weak mark ripe for opportunists to pluck. To find ways for everyone to prosper. To mend what was broken in the fighting.

I thought about the application for international assistance sitting partially completed in my pack. About the electronic applications for aid I submitted while I was on bed rest and bored, or in Tenáho. A handful of rejections have trickled in.

Outside influences can help, if we use them wisely, but ultimately it was us, working together, that carried the day. Dependence upon foreigners is not the way.

We have everything we need right here.

"My father had great faith in diplomacy," I said slowly. Queen Brenica leaned in to listen. Belatedly, I realized I was mimicking Lorcan's habit of speaking quietly, so as not to be overheard, and to ensure others paid close attention to what I said. "Diplomacy has its uses. We will need it to forge new agreements with other countries. But we don't need it to finish this war."

I sipped fermented palm juice, sweet and tart and slightly fizzy.

The queen looked skeptical.

"Once I understand the scope of the problem, I will have a better answer for you." Which meant that tomorrow, I needed to see Saskaya's newest invention. I had the outline of a plan, a dot on a map to aim for while I tried to figure out a route to get there. I wasn't signing off on her latest innovation without seeing it in action, though, which meant I needed to sleep. I bowed, stifling a yawn. "If you'll excuse me, I need rest."

"Go," the queen grinned. "Your knight won't be far behind, I am certain."

Presently, my knight was seated between Tahra and Keryn, near Tovian and his brother. For once, I didn't feel a stab of envy. I'm tired, sated, and content to let him socialize without me.

Up in the rock-walled room, I washed for bed and put on one of Cata's old undershirts. It bags out around my body but it's long enough to cover my painted rear end. I can't get over how odd this painting thing is—which reminded me of my interrupted text conversation with Raina.

The rest of her text message reads: **DON'T LET LORCAN paint you, it has all kinds of connotations—**

I could've used that information a little earlier.

Raina, several minutes later: **Zosh? Still there?**

Raina: If he paints you, and you paint him, you're basically considered married. So don't be an idiot! Don't make the mistake I did!

Raina: The painting process can be pretty hot [sweating emoji, water emoji] which is part of how I ended up [pregnant emoji], just FYI. So watch out. I bet

Lorcan is devious enough not to tell you what it means.
Tovi was, damn him. I swear those men are colluding.

Me: [takes a selfie of me scowling and painted] Too late.

Raina, who was apparently still awake: [gif of baby laughing and falling over] You look great, but you better not make me lose this bet with Hallie. Speaking of whom, call me or check your emails, the situation is *bad.*

Me: yay

Me: will check in tomorrow, gotta go

If painting worked to get Raina knocked up, maybe it will work for me, too.

I fell asleep while checking my emails, dropping my phone on my face before conceding that I was too tired to focus and setting it aside. I'll deal with Hallie's irate father in the morning.

There are times when I wonder whether engaging with the outside world was ever a good idea.

LORCAN ROUSED me well before dawn. I didn't remember him coming to bed, though I did remember him rearranging my body so he could hold me the way he did in Tenáho. Apart from that? Blankness.

Still only half-awake, I opened my eyes to find him dressed in leathers and a tiger skull with fangs on either side of his blue eyes.

I'm dreaming, right? This is too weird to be real.

"Didn't mean to wake you up, Princess." He bent to kiss me. A tooth scraped my temple.

"Where are you going?"

"To test Saskaya's new weapon."

"Not without me, you're not." I kicked back the furs and sat up.

"It's a long, hard climb. Dangerous, too. You're safer here."

I wanted to ask whether Tahra was going. Whether this was an excuse to go off and spend time with other women —I'm not blind to the way some of the Ansi women look at him. If my frailty is an excuse.

"Lorcan. I love Sas, but I am not signing off on any weapon without seeing it in action."

I laced up my sandals and leg warmers, tied on my skimpy skirt and the excuse for a top. Lorcan held up that fur shrug thing, which I obediently shrugged into. It's not so different from how Cata used to hand me a dress and tell me to put it on. Boob tape wasn't any weirder to wear. He handed me a pair of thin leather gloves and a—

I dropped the wolf-bear skull with a thud.

"What the—Lorcan, it's too early for practical jokes."

He chuckled, picked it up and set it on my head, tying the straps beneath my chin. "Camouflage and head protection. You'll need it where we're going."

"I thought yours was just for show."

He shook his head, and said, "You're safer staying here."

"Will it be as dangerous as the climb to the Plateau?" He shook his head. "Then I'm coming with you." I tapped his bicep. "You can keep me safe."

His expression was halfway between pleased and concerned.

Tovian and Keryn met us at the stone bridge.

"Where's Tahra?" I asked.

"Sleeping. Couldn't rouse her." Keryn shook their head affectionately. "Teenagers. Need their rest."

My earlier doubts dissipated like early morning mist. I'm still trying to get out of the habit of mistrusting Lorcan.

"Drink this," he said, handing me a rough ceramic mug. Hot tea. I took a tongue-scalding sip. Lightly sweetened with honey, exactly how I like it.

"You remember." I couldn't keep from smiling.

"It's just like the old days when I made you get up early for swim practice." He leaned in for a kiss. Our skull helmets bumped, thwarting us. "Never been a morning person, have you, Zosia?"

"No. Whereas you're both a night owl and a lark. I don't know how you get by on so little sleep."

He winked. "I've had you next to me for weeks. Never slept better. I can go a while without."

"Flatterer."

He really is appallingly charming, when he wants to be.

We made our way through the dark jungle. Leaves shake overhead. Dragons, following us. They don't fly so much as glide, leaping from high rocks and trees. Occasionally they come running after you on the ground. The critters even swim if the current isn't too strong.

"We're taking the long way. I doubt the princess could manage the climb," Tovian told Keryn.

"I heard that. I'm stronger than you think," I called out. I climbed to the top of the Sun Temple Plateau. One day, I would really like it if people stopped underestimating me. That day won't be today.

"If you think you can manage, Zosia, the shortcut is right ahead." Tovian pointed, grinning.

I took one look at the rock wall rising a hundred feet into the air and quickly rethought my bravado.

"The long way, it is. Lead on."

We continued walking for a long time. The terrain rose slowly, then all at once.

"I thought this was supposed to be the easy way," I huffed.

"It is." Lorcan offered me a hand. I took it.

Around midmorning, we arrived at the top of the cliffs. Climbing the steep trail took the wind out of me. My legs will ache tomorrow. We climbed to the top of the black volcanic rock rim surrounding our island. From here, the churning blue waves stretch far into the distance. Directly below, you could see each tiny atoll surrounding the main island. Some of them were dotted with the unmistakable signs of pirates. Jagged rocks were clearly visible in the shallows, like teeth ready to bite out the bottom of your ship. Only the smallest vessels can navigate these waters.

"We don't want to give away our position until the last possible second," Tovian informed Keryn and me. Lorcan seemed to already know the plan. "All of us need to cross the open space between here and that rock formation." He pointed. "While crossing, we can be seen by the pirates camped at Summertide Atoll. Go slow, stay low. If I whistle"—he demonstrated; it sounds exactly like a bird call—"freeze. Understand?"

"Yes."

Lorcan produced a pair of binoculars and laid stomach-down on the cliff, glasses pointed at the largest rocky outcropping in the shoals off the shore of Auralia. Keryn and I crouched down. I placed my small day pack aside.

Tovian pointed to the opposite rise.

"I'll go first. We're close enough to the water that they could hit us with a machine gun. Watch what I do."

Tovian slid down the rock face in a scuff of dust. No

reaction from the pirates. Lorcan scanned the atoll below with a pair of binoculars. Keryn had theirs out, too.

"Raina will never forgive us if she's widowed," I muttered, eyeing the tiny figures moving around on the island below.

"He knows what he's doing," Lorcan said. A second later, he dropped his binoculars and made the same bird-like whistle. Tovian stopped—and disappeared.

I blinked. There was nothing on the dark rocks except a bleached skull and the carcass of a long-dead animal. Bits of hair, scattered bones.

Lorcan whistled again. Tovian moved. Like magic, he became visible again.

"Amazing," I said breathlessly. "The handprints break up his outline. The dark parts blend with the rocks so all you see is the lighter markings."

"When the Ansi don't want to be seen, they're impossible to spot." Lorcan tucked his binoculars away and said to Keryn, "Ready, Leader?"

"Aye, I'll show you how it's done." They scrambled down the ravine, kicking rocks everywhere. A whistle from the other side. Keryn froze. Again, I blinked, trying to pick out their form. Again, I failed.

Lorcan rubbed my arm. "Enjoying this?"

"I know this is serious work, but it's also so much fun. I never got to go on adventures. Only that one summer trip to Mount Astra with you." I prodded his chest with one finger. "You've been running around Auralia like this since you were twelve?"

He shrugged. "When I wasn't training, which was a lot of the time."

"Not fair. Not remotely fair."

Lifting my hand, he kissed the back and said, "It's past

time you got out of your castle and saw the country you're meant to rule, Princess."

Which I can do, for a while, thanks to him. Could continue to do, if I kept him around after our agreed-upon end date.

Not so much agreed, as decreed. We've come a long way toward reconciling, since then.

Releasing me, he made a different whistle. "Your turn. Go slow. Freeze if you hear the signal."

Even at full health, I wouldn't have been as strong or as fast as the others. I got signaled twice. Once I was across the exposed section, I kicked and pulled my body up over the steep rise on the other side of the pass, panting hard. Tovian dropped his binoculars and hauled me up over the lip, then tucked me behind an outcropping. Keryn was pulling long metal tubes out of their pack and screwing them together. Lorcan began his journey across the gap. When Tovian whistled, he went still.

Lorcan moved gracefully upon the second signal. Tovian glanced over at me. "Now you know our secrets. Where we live, our alarm dragons, how we move around without being seen."

"I'll guard the Ansi people's secrets with my life."

Tovian smiled faintly, the only indication he heard me.

CHAPTER EIGHTEEN

L orcan braced his hands on the edge and hauled himself up easily. Every corded muscle flexed. If my mouth weren't so dry, I'd be drooling. He caught me openly ogling him and smirked.

I bit my lower lip and dropped my gaze to the ground. Then I made a show of uncapping my water skin and drinking. I offered it to him, thinking about where that mouth had been yesterday afternoon. Wondering when he might do that again.

"Thanks."

Sparks skittered along my nerves. Lorcan passed it back to me and rummaged in his pack, removing a black drawstring bag.

"What's this?"

"Saskaya's new weapon."

"Oh?"

"When I was destroying Sentinels in The Walled City ruins, Saskaya asked me to pry out the laser eyes and anything attached to them."

"I imagine that was harrowing. Considering one nearly killed you."

He feigned indifference, yet I know how much courage that task required of him. Was this part of his reluctance to come and rescue me? He was afraid of the machines, and couldn't admit it to himself? If the kitchens hadn't been destroyed, and Bashir hadn't spent every day for a year trying to smash his way out of a cell, I might have been safer than any other Auralian. I can see the logic, from a certain angle.

If he hadn't slept around and then tried to conceal the fact, and if I hadn't starved, I might be able to forgive him for leaving me there. But he did, and I did, and there's no changing what happened, now.

"Sas adapted the beam. One of the old rocket launchers we stole from the pirates has a similar diameter bore. If this works, we'll have the firepower of a Sentinel, but without the hackable automation."

"Incredible. Why are we testing it here?"

Lorcan peered around the rock formation we're hiding behind. "Pirates have been using Summertide Atoll as a base of operations. We're a thousand kilometers from the closest place for them to resupply. There's no fresh water source other than rain. No food apart from what you can pull from the sea or shoot down from the sky. Everything has to be brought in. Can't swim. The water's full of sharks. Can't use large boats because of the shoals." He gestured to the northeast. "Skía bring in supplies and new recruits every few days. Used to be every day. Now it's more sporadic. We think they're running out of money and easy recruits. If we can stop them from bringing in any more supplies—"

"Then the ones already here will leave. Or die, trying." I

squeezed his shoulder. Partly as an excuse to touch him. "Excellent work."

"Let's see if Saskaya's invention fires or explodes, first."

"Has it been tested?"

"At Marsh Hollow. We shot at the cliffs to cover the Sentinel bodies with rocks." He indicated that I should follow him over to where Keryn and Tovian were examining the dull green tube of the launcher. This isn't my area of expertise, so I hung back while Lorcan added the lens. When he finished, a blue light flicked on from inside the tube.

Keryn knelt to check the aim. Then Tovian. Lorcan made an adjustment.

"Now what?"

"Now, we wait."

The sun rose high in the sky. It's not as humid out here on the cliffs but I'm taking a lot of sun. I tucked myself under patch of shade to call Raina. "Hi."

"I'm so glad you finally called."

Uh-oh.

"What's going on?"

"King Humayun wants Laila back. He's sending Hallie's cousin, the one with the yacht and the helicopter. They'll be here any day. If we don't surrender Laila, he'll send warships."

"Shit, indeed."

"He's super pissed that he's only dealing with me. I'm not queen enough for him." I could practically hear Raina's eyes rolling, all the way from River Bend.

"The guy doesn't like dealing with women as human beings, much less authority figures. What does Laila want to do?"

"She's fourteen."

"So? She's not brainless."

"Laila wants to stay with her sister for not-great reasons. She doesn't have to go to formal school, and she has this titanic crush on my brother."

I rubbed my temple with my free hand. My knuckles scraped against the teeth of my skull helmet. I took it off so I could press the phone more comfortably to my ear. "I'm sure Humayun loves that."

Raina snorted.

"Fortunately, he doesn't know. Yet. He's cut off Hallie without a cent. Same thing he did to her mother when she left," Raina said. "If Laila goes back, she'll never see her mother or sister again. If she stays, her father will disown her. It's not an easy choice. She'll probably be married off within the year if she goes home, though, and not to Damir, of course."

"What does Hallie have to say about it?"

"She wants Laila to stay here. Not that Humayun has any interest in her opinion." Raina snorted. "Being forced to negotiate with a pregnant princess has Humayun *riled*. He keeps asking to talk to my father or my husband. I keep telling him he can deal with me, or with you. Women are powerful here."

"I have no husband or father for him to appeal to. He'll have to deal directly with me. Which is going to be so delightful after I turned down his offer of marriage and then walked away from marrying one of his sons."

"Ran away, more like." Raina laughed. "I am so glad you did, too. What a catastrophe that would have been, in the long run."

I glanced over at Lorcan. Saving my ass yet again. I know his reasons for speaking up that day were driven by self-interest. He couldn't stand the thought of anyone else touching me. Our interests aligned that day. Despite everything, I'm glad he spoke up.

Now, I have to fix the mistake I made. If it winds up helping Hallie and Laila, the whole disaster will have been worth it.

"Humayun is threatening to file complaints with Interpol and other international organizations classifying us as a haven for pirates and child sex trafficking—"

"He what?!" I gasped. "That is underhanded as fuck—"

"Whoa. When did you start swearing?"

"In my head? Years ago. Out loud? Since the war." Nobody wants a princess who curses, but that's what they're going to get. I paced the length of the shadow, trying to walk off my surging anger and anxiety. "I'm not sending Laila back unless she wants to go."

"Great. Another war. Plus, we'll be international pariahs." Raina blew out a sigh. "Hallie should change her name to Helen of Troy. Hallie of Trissau."

I snorted.

"Plus, Scarlett arrives next week with all our stuff from Scotland. And the charity auction winners are coming in the first week of October," Raina added.

"Wonderful."

Two kinds of outside aggressors, plus civilians, arriving close together. How am I going to fend off Humayun and the pirates, without getting my friend or a bunch of strangers with more personal wealth than my entire nation, killed?

"Hallie and Laila's mother. What's her stance?"

"She wants Laila to come to Switzerland and live with her and her girlfriend," Raina replied instantly.

My father, for all his faults, bequeathed me with a global reputation for intelligence and problem-solving. He never meant to. He wanted to highlight my beauty (since diminished), dedication to duty (questionable, considering my atheism and reluctance to play princess). Despite my doubts and failings, I cannot deny that I inherited a deep pool of popularity among the denizens of the internet.

This is a tool I can leverage.

"Would she consider coming to live here? Both of them?"

"I can ask."

"Do it. If you have a few minutes, send me anything damning you can find out about Humayun, especially his country's human rights record."

"You want to go on the offensive?"

"Not militarily. PR. I'll call King Humayun as soon as I can. This afternoon or tomorrow. I need his direct line."

"Great. I'll text you the asshole's number. I'm sick of dealing with him; you can take a crack at it."

Tovian popped into view. "Someone wants to talk to you." I held out the phone.

He plugged one finger into his ear and wandered away, seeking privacy, smiling softly.

True love. I don't need to see that. My heart pinched in a painful reminder that for me, such things are out of reach. I love it for them. It's never going to happen for me; I need to let go of the fantasy.

I am a scientist; I deal in facts. The reality is that I love Lorcan, and Lorcan loves a version of me that never truly existed. He always wanted the princess. I live in this body but it's not really mine; time and history will claim my corpse. The only thing left of me will be my bones and whatever I achieve in the time I have left alive. Given my mother didn't live to see thirty, it might not be much.

Better get cracking.

"Zosia."

I snapped out of my maudlin thoughts and buckled my skull helmet back on. Lorcan and Keryn waved me over.

"Look at this." Lorcan handed me the binoculars. The creamy outline of a yacht swam into view. I adjusted the glasses and looked again.

"That's our boat!" I popped my head up. Lorcan put his hand on top of my skull helmet to bring me back down behind the safety of the rock formation. "Why didn't it crash? Every boat that size goes down in these shoals!"

The yacht we used to escape from Trissau, then sent out into the ocean without a captain, has been commandeered by the pirates. Bastards. It's enraging.

"Want me to shoot it?" Keryn offered, lining up the ship in their sights.

"No."

"No?" Keryn and Lorcan both look at me as though I've lost my mind.

"Keep it from landing. But don't sink it yet. I need that boat."

I scrambled back. There might be a way to point the pirates at Humayun, and vice versa, thus ridding me of two problems at once.

There came a familiar high-pitched beeping. It set my teeth on edge. I glanced at Lorcan. His mouth was tight and tense, his face focused and serious. The beeping became a solid whine. Keryn's finger moved. Blue light shot out of the tube into the water right in front of the ship's hull. A massive wave swamped its triangular front. The vessel jerked so hard to the side that it nearly capsized.

A warning shot. Keryn fired a second one. The boat completed its turn and sped into the distance.

Irate figures ran out onto the rocky atoll, shaking fists

and yelling. Whatever was on that boat, they needed it. Badly.

"Nice work, Leader." I patted Keryn on the shoulder. "You're a good shot."

"Had some practice." Their lips stretched wide around broad, slightly crooked teeth. Red hair semi-corralled in braids fluttered beneath the huge maned tiger skull they wore as a helmet.

Popping sounds as the pirates shot at us.

We moved to a new position and waited for the boat to return. It made a second attempt to land. Keryn drove it away once more. Eventually, it sped back out into the open sea.

Now, we just need to alert Humayun to its existence. As soon as I have Laila and Hallie's mother's backing, I'll call the king we both jilted and inform him that his daughters prefer to stay with me. I saved them from pirates. Take back your boat and go home with your consolation prize. If it works, I'll have decommissioned the Skía's delivery ship.

In the meantime, a global PR campaign highlighting Auralia's record of peace and equality, in contrast to Tris-sau's record of gender-based violence, ought to discredit any trafficking accusations the scorned king might make—especially if his own wife is willing to go publicly on the record as to why she left.

It's time I proved my worth as leader of this country.

CHAPTER NINETEEN

Back at the Ansi village, I briefly outlined my plan to Brenica. She seemed skeptical, which I admit unnerved me. My confidence might be marginally higher than it was when Sakaya scolded me (except where Lorcan and everything sex-related is concerned), but only because I doubt I could make the situation worse.

After our brief discussion, I went up to our room to clean up. I removed my leather top and skirt and put on one of Cata's old undershirts and a pair of underwear, which are more than sufficient coverage for this sultry place. The leather is more practical. It doesn't stick and wrinkle the way fabric does, and in this humidity, washing and drying is difficult. With thin leather, all you do is wipe it with a damp cloth and hang it from the piping. Easy to maintain.

Sweat curled the hair at the nape of my neck. It's grown a bit longer in the weeks since I was first rescued. When I get back to Čovari Village, I'll have to ask Saskaya for a trim. I rinsed away the grime with a cloth dampened with cold water from the pipe system. The purple paint on my body didn't budge.

Through the partially open flap covering, I caught sight of Lorcan and Tovian talking with a clearly upset Tahra. Poor girl. She didn't like being left behind this morning.

When she wrapped her arms around Lorcan's neck, my empathy evaporated. He didn't push her away. Instead, he hugged her back.

I waited. The longer Lorcan let her linger in his arms, the lower my stomach sank. Tovian glanced uneasily at me. I met his eyes for a brief second before tugging the entrance flap closed.

I have bigger things to worry about. But this is exactly why I cannot marry Lorcan. I always hated my father's focus on optics. Now, I understand their importance. Look perfect. Be unemotional. Never let anyone rattle you, no matter how rude or how deeply their words and actions cut. I don't want to stick a cork back inside my emotional champagne bottle, but I can't go around letting everything bubble out, either.

By tolerating Tahra's overt affections, he's giving the impression that he isn't faithful to me. Tovian saw it. Even if Lorcan is only begrudgingly humoring her the way he did Raina all those years—and after weeks of observation, I've come to believe that's all there is to it—Lorcan's behavior invites questions. I know he's been with women from this village, overheard whispers about his first visit here. Will they try again, now, thinking that he doesn't honor his commitment to me?

Lorcan doesn't seem to understand this, and I don't feel as though I can bring it up. He'll brush my concerns aside as unwarranted envy. I *am* jealous. But that doesn't mean my worries are unfounded.

Not to mention how much it hurts to have his infidelity

constantly thrust in my face. A fact I will have to contend with for the duration of our agreement.

It's not perfect, but my plan is the right one. He can capitalize on his popularity for as long as he likes. Hopefully, I'll get a daughter to love. If not, at least I'll get to try something I've wanted to do with someone I've wanted to do it with, for a very long time.

My phone beeped. Raina, with Humayun's direct number. This is what I need to focus on. Not the way Lorcan's behavior presses on my worst insecurities.

I settled onto the bed with my notebook and a pen, sifting through the news articles and reports Raina gathered for me about Trissau. It didn't take me long to outline my basic argument: Auralia's record on human rights speaks for itself. So does Humayun's. His wife—one of many—ran away. Is it so bizarre that his daughters made the same choice?

"What are you up to?" Lorcan ducked through the flap.

"Writing."

"The article?" he asked. The one we started together a lifetime ago. The one that's done, save for our edits and my vision statement of how Auralia will move forward into the future. I accept that finishing my degree is out of the question, but I could achieve that one small thing before relinquishing my academic aspirations entirely. But that isn't what I'm working on right now.

"Press releases." Briefly, I explained my plan. "I miss Cata. She would have known how to manage the PR angle." I miss her for other reasons, too. She would have been a good sounding board for this mess I'm in with Lorcan.

We have truly made a hash out of everything. Tenáho was lovely, and desperately needed, but it didn't change the fundamentals.

Lorcan slid onto the bed frame, unlaced his sandals and kicked them underneath. "You'll rebuild your team. In the meantime, if I can help, Princess, tell me how."

I touched my forehead to his. "You do help me."

He skimmed his fingertips along my temple. I tipped my face up to kiss him. This is what he wants to hear. It's no lie. He's the cornerstone of my life for a few more months. After my coronation ceremony, according to our agreement, Lorcan will resign from my service and go back to Tenáho to live in his sweet cottage, making a life for himself with Masika. Or he could leave Auralia and capitalize upon his global fame. By the time he departs, I need to be pregnant, if it's possible.

Rolling onto my side, I tangled my fingers in his hair and drew him down for a kiss. "I wish I knew if I'm doing the right thing."

"In standing up to Humayun?"

That, too.

"How I'm going about it. If Laila wanted to go back, I would send her, over Hallie's objections, if necessary. She doesn't want to go. Her reasons aren't great, but they are hers and I respect them. She'll get an education here, just like I did, and Raina, too."

"Zosia. You're doing fine." Lorcan lay on the bed with his body parallel to mine. Humid air in the scant space between our bodies. He smelled of earth and dust and that subtle note that's solely his. I played with the lacings on his Ansi garment, wishing I had the courage to push it down. I don't. The bulge in his shorts grew heavy and long. It provokes a confusing mixture of shame and longing within me. Shame because it's not me who does this to him; shame because I can't stop wanting him this way.

But he doesn't want me like that, as he keeps proving.

There's a core of real affection—desire, on my part—but for him it's duty and ambition. Nothing more.

"Where did you go, Princess?"

I brought my gaze back up to his chest. "Thinking." Planes of beautifully delineated muscle, covered with smooth skin marred by scars. I traced the one on his low belly with the tip of my finger.

Lorcan pressed his hand to my low abdomen, matching his fingers to the purple marks on my belly. He sighed. "I've been looking at these all day."

"I know." The marks peep out of the waistband of my skirt, when I'm wearing it. Now, they're visible over the waistband of my underwear. It's cute. More than cute—it's sexy, knowing his palm print rests over my womb, just out of sight. Sure enough, Lorcan tugged the waist of my shorts down to expose the rest of it. He inched down to kiss it reverently. My entire body tightened.

What if I just...told him what I wanted?

I backed hastily away from the idea. Then Lorcan would insist upon getting married, and there is *no* way. We agreed on the plan; we are executing it. Like Saskaya said we should do. I happen to have a small side plan, that's all. It's mine.

One person in my life will be for me, at least when she's young. I'm not marrying Lorcan when all I'd be signing up for is a lifetime of misery. Yet I don't want anyone else's child, either. He would protect our daughter if I'm taken out of the world prematurely. When, more like. Once Lorcan resigns from my service, I won't be able to roam my country as freely. Not without risking my neck every time I leave the castle. Eventually, the Skía will find me and he won't be there to save my life. It has to be him, or no one, so our daughter survives.

"You're gone again." Lorcan slid back up my body, working my loose white linen shirt up. I had to fight the impulse to yank it back down. I pushed him onto his back and lay on top of him, bent knees on either side of his, feet in the air, braced on my forearms.

"I'm right here."

"You were thinking, Princess. What about?" Warm, tough-skinned hands skimmed my ribs. Warmer than the air. Hot enough to burn. Gentle strokes of his thumb into the ridges of my ribs. I felt the rise and fall of his chest beneath me. He is a bit larger than he was before the war, and I am considerably smaller. We fit together differently than we did before.

"I think about a lot of things." Deflecting.

"Good thoughts?"

"Mostly." Not really. Sad thoughts. I never wanted this to become my life. I knew my chances of happiness were always slim. It's just the reality of being born a princess. There was a time when I fought that fate, for all the good it did me. "Trying to think of ways I could please you."

Preferably without letting him see me too much. Or having another panic attack.

Lorcan combed my hair away from my temple with gentle fingers. His breath against the shell of my ear sent a shudder through me.

"You vastly overestimate the extent of my experience, and you underestimate my determination to find every single way I can make you moan my name."

He sucked my earlobe between his lips and applied his teeth. Everything inside me turned liquid. Blindly, my hips ground down over his, seeking. Finding him rigid. Two layers of fabric separating me from what I want.

"The old you wouldn't have used a line like that," I managed to gasp in between panting breaths.

"It's not a line." He worked his way down my throat, sucking, grazing my skin with his teeth, incinerating me from the inside out. "Completely sincere."

I wonder what it would take to make him moan my name. More than I have to offer, certainly. Despair clutched at me. I mentally slapped it away but it barely subsided. I want to get this over with.

"Fuck me," I whispered. "Please."

Lorcan's arm tightened around my waist. He nuzzled my neck, pressing open-mouthed kisses along my throat, his hand flat against my lower back. And then, with one devastating word, the monster *ruins it*.

"No."

All I can see from this angle is his jaw and one ear. The oil lamp flickered.

"No?"

"Not yet."

"Excuse me?" This is ridiculous. He's been seducing me for weeks. Now, he refuses to follow through? Infuriating man. At least one thing remains unchanged despite the passage of time and a war: Lorcan can always be counted upon to drive me insane.

"I said, we're not doing this tonight."

I rolled off him and sat up, tugging my shirt back down. Again, that searing sense of shame. This is too similar to that night in River Bend.

"Why?"

I can't keep the brokenness out of my voice.

He propped his head on one hand, laying on his side, wearing nothing more than his ridiculous leather shorts that shouldn't be sexy, but somehow are, and an unbearably smug expression.

"I'm not ready."

Hurt explodes in my chest. He'll sleep with half of Auralia, but not with me? What about me is so repulsive to him? I don't understand.

What am I going to do about it, though? I can be upset later, when I understand his thinking. I bet I'll still want to strangle him once he explains himself, but for now, I swallowed my pride long enough to listen.

"Not ready," I echoed blankly. "If not tonight, when?"

"When we're married. Not before."

He's got to be joking.

Crinkles at the corners of his eyes. Conniving man. He planned this. Did he guess my plans to have his baby? Probably. Lorcan is one wily piece of shit. I'm so angry, I could smack the pleased smile off his face.

"We discussed this. We pretend to be together until the fall. Then we part ways."

"Things have changed since June."

I caught the tiniest bit of hesitation: *Haven't they?*

They haven't. He thinks it's enough to tell me he'll never betray me again. Yet he's never told Tahra that her attempts to monopolize his attention are inappropriate and need to stop. He does nothing to deter the women who make eyes at him here in the village. I don't know whether he was still taking them to bed the last time he was here, and I don't want to think about it, either.

His response to Masika, back in his home village, was to make a show out of dancing with me.

It's the same question I never answered when we were back in Scotland: does he enjoy having the attention of multiple women—then, it was Raina and me—or does he genuinely not know what they're after? Am I being overly suspicious?

That's what he would say. There's no point in asking him. He'd take offense and all I would get is an argument—as though we can avoid one now.

I can't trust him, whatever the answer. I love him; I know he loves me. Love isn't the problem. It's not enough. I'm not enough. Never have been. Never will be.

I pulled on a clean pair of trousers, quickly, with my back turned to him. His four fingerprints visible above the waistband, below my navel, aren't quite so charming, now.

"Where are you going?" Lorcan asked when I tried to get up.

"To ask Queen Brenica to perform the honors." *Calling your bluff, Knight.* I know he won't go through with it. He wants the princess. Me? I'm nothing. "You want to get married? Let's do this."

CHAPTER TWENTY

Lorcan shook his head. A vehement no.

"I intend to marry you in front of the whole world, Zosia. Nothing hidden or secret. I've had enough of that." Lorcan dragged me in for an attempted kiss. I turned away, and he said in my ear, "If you want to get laid, announce our wedding to coincide with your coronation ceremony. Everyone expects us to do both at once. Make your people happy."

I did hit him, then. I managed one good slap to his shoulder, which made him laugh, which in turn made me growl. He's so much stronger than I am that I couldn't immediately get away. He held my arms easily, pinning me against him while I ranted.

"You're the most conniving, unfaithful knight ever to plague a princess—"

"I knew you were going to hate it," he chuckled, though hurt flashed over his face.

"Then, why are you doing it? Why are you so manipulative?" I shoved hard against his chest. He finally let go.

"Why do I keep falling for it? I hate this. I hate *you*. Why do I keep letting you get away with this shit?"

I stalked toward the opening of our cave.

"Zosh."

He's on his feet, with a look that's halfway between pity and contrition. Not good enough.

"Don't 'Zosh' me!" I smacked his hand away when he tried to touch me, disgusted by my own cliché. "I am sick and tired of the way you tease and promise and *never fucking follow through*. Three years we've been doing this stupid dance. I'm done with it. I'm done with you!"

I took two steps forward. He pulled me back hard enough to spin me around to face him. Lorcan took my face in his hands and spoke low and urgently into my ear.

"You have every right to be angry with me. I will regret not waiting for you every single day of the rest of my life. I would far rather have shared that memory with you, than strangers whose names and faces I don't remember."

"Gods, Lorcan, how many were there?" I groaned, then hastened to add, "Don't answer that. I don't want to know."

It doesn't matter. Can't unring that bell. That's not the point. The point is that he is holding me to an artificial standard he doesn't feel compelled to meet for himself. He's costing me my one chance at a future that's worth living. It's unfair. It's bullshit. I'm fucking furious. I don't have time for this crap.

He took me in his arms again, though I resisted, fists planted on his chest, holding him at bay.

"I can't undo it. All I can do is prove to you that I can and will resist temptation. The highest temptation. You. Think of it as a wedding gift, because if I don't find a way to prove to you that I won't ever seek out anyone else, I know you'll always harbor doubts about me. It will eat you alive. I am doing this to earn your trust."

"That is the most twisted logic I've ever heard, Lorcan. You refuse to have sex with me to prove to me that I can trust you not to have sex with other people? You've never had any trouble saying no to me. You said yes to plenty of others. Make it make sense."

He was still smiling. The bastard thinks he's clever. I pushed harder against the wall of his chest. He didn't budge.

"I know I deprived you of the experiences you wanted to have when we were abroad, Zosia."

"You're doing it again now." Tears scratched my eyelids, but I refused to let them fall.

"Temporarily. For a good reason."

"The only time I was ever going to have a chance to date anyone without public scrutiny was in Scotland, and you, *selfish idiot*, took that opportunity from me."

"I did."

"And then you claimed that same privilege for yourself, you fucking hypocrite." *Let me go.* I need him to stop touching me. I feel too raw for this. Five minutes ago, I thought I was finally going to get something out of this horrible push-pull. Now, I just feel tricked. Angry, and deceived. Again.

"I did. And I'm sorry."

He's not sorry. I can hear it in his voice, which is still full of amusement.

"No, you're not. You'd do it all over again."

"I would change several things. I wouldn't have left you so nobly that night we were together."

"Which means you'd have fucked your way through Auralia after having been with me." I attempted one of the hold-breaks Cata taught me. Remembering her makes my eyes water. He stopped me easily; Lorcan trained with her, too. "You're delusional if you think there's any way we'd have come back from that."

"There wouldn't have been anyone else. I'd have married you the instant you were willing. Scotland has a tradition of eloping; I should have taken advantage of it. I should have claimed you when your father tried to pressure you into an engagement you didn't want."

"You're assuming I'd have married you, then."

I totally would have, and he knows it. I exhaled in a harsh, angry sob.

That, finally, made him loosen his grip. I shoved hard and gained my freedom, stumbling back a couple of steps. I stared him down, waiting for an apology I knew wasn't coming.

"You're right, Zosia. I should have let you go in Trissau, but I couldn't do it. I wanted to be your first everything. I still do—"

I cut him off. "You wanted to be my first everything, and yet you saved no first for me. I have—"

"First love." He touched his forehead to mine, clasping my hair, stroking it. I felt his tremble. Heard the desperate truth. "You've always had that. First love. Last love. Only love. No one else will ever have that Zosia. Only you."

For several seconds, only the sound of our breath filled the rock cave.

"I never saw myself as your jailer, Princess. I saw myself giving you the freedom you craved." He swallowed hard. "I thought we would go to Scotland—to Europe—and have those adventures together. I never thought you would despise me on sight."

"Because you traded my freedom for your own advancement!"

He flinched. "I didn't—"

I growled.

"See? If we do this now, you'll always doubt me. If you can think of another way I can prove myself to you, say it. Tell me. You name it, I'll do it."

"Stop playing games with me, Lorcan. That would be a great start."

He winced. "I'm not playing games. I'm serious. I know how badly you want sex, and I want that, too. But if I give you what you want now, you'll put off a wedding indefinitely. You'll delay it because you're busy with rebuilding. With finishing your degree—"

"As if that'll ever happen now—" I scoffed.

"—with ruling. There will be a hundred reasons, and to me, they'll feel like excuses. I don't want to be the knight you fuck on the side, Princess." Lorcan's gaze never left mine. "I want to stand at your side forever. I want you to choose me."

I took a deep breath, turned on my heel, and walked out.

Getting down from the ledge was easy. I simply hopped down and landed with bent knees. I wanted to crawl out of my skin with outrage. Hundreds of pairs of eyes followed me as I stalked toward the women's bathing pool. I know they heard us shouting. I'm too much in my feelings to care.

I want Lorcan's handprints off my body. Now.

I should find someone else to sleep with. If I could, in this state. Just to show I can. But it wouldn't drive him away. He as good as told me that. And then we'd both have to live with the guilt.

To be a good, rational leader, I can't make decisions

from high feelings. That's been Lorcan's unwitting lesson to me this summer.

In a basket beside the waterfall was a jar of that astringent stuff that removes the paint. I shucked my clothes, doused a cloth and started scrubbing his handprints away. It took forever. Lorcan laid claim to every part of my exterior he could touch. It's the inside of me he won't go near.

Once I was free of purple stains, I rinsed off in the warm water.

I admit I was not best pleased at the sight of Tahra coming around the corner. She's always been a bit wary of me, and no wonder. I've made little secret of the fact that I barely tolerate her presence. I got out of the water and wrapped a drying cloth around me.

"Yes?" I asked, imperiously. As imperiously as one can while naked, wet, and wrapped in a towel.

"Queen Brenica asked me to bring this to you. She said it was a better fit than what you've been wearing."

Tahra held up a dress crafted of blue and yellow dragonskin, cut to follow the body. Over the breasts and hips, it was a solid sheen of blue scales, connected by a matching seamless strip from navel to sternum. The straps around the neck and the back were intricately braided. Contrasting laces secured the skirt at the sacrum. I did need help lacing it. When it was on, the fringe of cut leather from mid-thigh to knee twitched with every step.

It is stunning. A dress befitting a queen, rivaling anything I'd worn in Paris, London, New York, or Beijing.

When it was on, I asked Tahra to fetch the purple paint. I squished handprints on my exposed shoulders, my waist, down my arms as though giving myself a hug. I painted thin stripes along my cheekbones and daubed a spot in the hollow of my throat. Reclaiming this body.

Like everything else after the war, it is different, and I am still adjusting to it. But for as long as I live, it's mine.

So attired, I returned to the circular gathering area with Tahra following a few steps behind. The sky above the rock rim was painted red with sunset.

One of the Ansi women flagged me down. "No man?" she asked, gesturing to the quarters I shared with Lorcan until an hour ago. Not all the Ansi are as conversant in the main Auralian dialect as Tovian and Queen Brenica are. Many of the women rarely leave the village.

"No man."

I'm done. Let Lorcan play his games with someone more receptive to constantly having her pride trampled.

Besides, that asshole hasn't even proposed yet. If he thinks I'll ever say yes now, he's got a rude awakening coming. Let him try.

BLOSSOM

CHAPTER TWENTY-ONE

That evening, I sat with Brenica and Tovian near the fire until the moon rose high overhead.

"Things are finished between you and your knight?" Brenica asked.

"Yes."

I saw the way women kept slipping up to our room where Lorcan was camped out, waiting for me to return. Each one came padding back down the ramp a few minutes later, avoiding my eyes.

"There will be no wedding?"

"No."

"Raina will be relieved," Tovian interjected.

"She objects to the match?" his mother asked.

"Raina thinks Lorcan has changed too much since his accident."

He's like Raina. They both show emotion so easily. The only royals I know who don't keep everything bottled up.

"And you? What do you think?" Brenica asked her son. "Is he so different?"

"I didn't know him before." His face was serious. "He

has changed since we first met last January. There was a point where I nearly killed him myself, not so long ago. Lorcan was like a tiger with a thorn in its paw. Angry at the world. Reckless. It fueled some of his more dangerous and impressive accomplishments.

"Since you've come back, Princess, he's been calmer. More of a housecat, content to purr in the sun." Tovian smiled.

I snorted. "A pet tiger, perhaps." There's a legend about a man who tried to keep a maned tiger for a pet. It ate him. I don't intend to make the same mistake.

Speaking of pets, a small red dragon comes waddling up to us. Around its neck is a silver collar.

"Your wife's?" I asked, and the Ansi prince nodded.

"Garnet." Tovian offered the lizard a piece of fruit. Dragons are omnivorous. Garnet sniffed the offering and delicately plucked it from his fingertips, flapping a short distance away to eat it while eyeing us suspiciously. Can't blame her, really. Humans are overrated.

Tahra, who has been sitting several feet away, rose silently. I exchanged glances with Tovian. Garnet wandered over again. I offered her another piece of citrus. Tahra's silver hair gleamed in the moonlight as she strode determinedly to our room.

Minutes passed. She didn't return. Tovian frowned and said, "I'll speak with him. Lorcan isn't thinking about how this looks to others."

"It'll be a fight." I got up. "Consider whether it's an argument worth having. I have decided that it isn't."

"At some point you'll have to stop pretending that there will be a wedding."

"I know. We planned to part ways in October." I sigh. "Our deception might not last that long. At least we had our falling out here, amongst your people, where it will remain a secret for a while longer."

"Thinking like a queen," Tovian said, softly.

"Do I have another choice?"

"You always have a choice, Zosia."

"Even if they're all bad ones."

I can't stand his pity. I got up. Garnet followed me, hoping for more food. I offered her another bite and popped one into my mouth, too. She flapped hard and landed on my shoulder, to my surprise, her claws digging into my flesh.

"You're surprisingly heavy for a flying lizard."

I ducked through the flap and into the room I shared with Lorcan, bracing to find them naked in one another's arms. At least then I'd know, once and for all.

The scene that greeted me was far more innocent. Tahra sat on one end of the bed, arms around her knees. She startled when I came in, glancing at me warily.

Lorcan was leaning against the wall with his notebook in his lap, and the colored pencils I gave him for his birthday open on the floor beside him. He carefully replaced the one he was using and closed his sketchbook. Both were fully dressed, not touching, just talking. Friends.

I felt like an ass. Lorcan always had female friends. Tovian might be his first male one, and given the tensions with Raina, there's a limit to how close they could be.

He took in my repainted body and new dress. Tightness around his eyes.

"Don't let me interrupt you," I said, grateful for every bit of my princess training. My voice was steady; outwardly, I am the embodiment of calm. Garnet wrapped her tail around my throat for balance, which felt a bit weird, but I didn't react.

"I need my papers." I bent at the knee. The fringe of my skirt touched the woven mat. The dragon hopped down while I scooped up the papers I was writing on before Lorcan came in and we argued. I put them inside my pack and shoved the clothes I discarded earlier inside, too. Shouldering the bag, I turned to leave. "Carry on."

Garnet followed me out of the rock dwelling. So did my knight.

"Zosia."

"I have work to do."

"Come back. Please."

"We leave in the morning. I need to assess the situation in Oceanside." I didn't stop. I didn't turn back.

"You're still running away."

"I'm doing my job, Lorcan. Fulfilling my duty."

"Fine. If you want to have this discussion publicly, we will."

Everyone below in the center of the village was watching us. So many eyes upon us, all the time. Tiresome.

"I don't want to discuss anything at all, Lorcan. You've made your position clear. Let me make mine similarly explicit: we're done."

"I'm not—" Lorcan was smart enough to stop talking mid-sentence when I raised one eyebrow. "I don't want to fight."

"I don't either. So, let's not fight." Again, I walked away.

"You're not queen, yet, Zosia," he called after me, in English. I shot him the middle finger without looking back. No one here will know what it means, except possibly Tovian. The gesture has no significance in Auralia.

Lorcan's soft chuckle trailed me down the rest of the ramp.

I loathe him.

I SPENT the night on a pallet in Brenica's rooms, working until the queen complained about the hour and I had to douse the lamp.

In the morning, I assessed my accomplishments: Press releases sent to Raina and Saskaya for editing, notes for the conversation with Humayun ready, indifference to Lorcan clutched like a cloak of ice around my shoulders. He doesn't want to have sex with me. Fine. That's his right. But then stop toying with me. Enough rejection. I can't take it anymore.

And I'm sick of clinging to my hurts. Let me move on.

I could find another man. Maybe. But when I thought of having a baby with anyone else, the idea lost all appeal. So, it's back to Plan A. When it's my bones in the Hall of Ancestors, there will be no one to sit in vigil for me. I shall be the last princess. The last queen.

Bashir wins, after all.

Our little group departed the Ansi village in a cloud of tension the next morning. Tovian and Keryn both took Tahra to task for being too forward with Lorcan. She sulked at the back of our spread-out line, leaving Lorcan and me behind Tovian. Arguing.

"You're the one who should've sent Tahra away yesterday." I didn't look at my knight as I spoke in a sidelong hiss of frustration. "Instead of leaving it to your friends to chastise her."

They didn't speak to Lorcan about it, leaving that to me.

"There was nothing to chastise either of us for. We didn't do anything. You know that, Zosia. You saw us. She was the only person who came to ask how I was after our fight. She's a friend. I wouldn't—"

"But you did." I cut him off because he may be right but he's still refusing to accept that Tahra's behavior was out of line.

He shook his head. "Not with her."

Relief loosens a bit of my resentment.

"You know perfectly well how she feels about you."

His jaw worked. "We covered this back in Tenáho. I don't want to keep arguing about what I did last year. I was wrong, I know it, I'm sorry. I'm trying to make it up in any way I can."

"By sitting with Tahra alone in our room?"

"We. Didn't. Do. Anything."

"It looked bad."

He scowled. "For someone who always hated her father's obsession with appearances, you sure seem to be concerned with them all of a sudden."

The truth hit home. Hard.

"Yes, well, now I understand why he was so adamant that I look and behave a certain way. My father was right."

I stalked away before Lorcan could respond.

I, alone, wore ordinary traveler's clothing. Brenica's dress was too beautiful to risk ruining it, so I stuck with my white linen top, brown pants, boots. Sweat ringed my underarms and dripped down my face. The Ansi know how to live comfortably in this environment. Lost in thought, I followed Keryn across a narrow vine-and-wood-planks bridge.

"Princess, wait—"

Lorcan's hand landed roughly on my shoulder, yanking me back. Trees rustled. Tovian and Keryn brought their weapons up. He carried a long spear; they held a frighteningly large blade. I shoved Lorcan away and took two steps forward before dropping into nothing.

I didn't have time to scream. My pack snagged on something and my fall stopped short, a jerk that left me dangling over the open jaws of a very, very large dragon. Its tail thrashed.

Should've kept the paint and Ansi clothes.

Keryn's massive sword swung in a blurry arc. The huge dragon shrieked, its fetid breath rattling the foliage. The pack gave way with a rip. Earth and greenery rushed up at me. I landed with an *oof* in the berm below. On the bridge above me was a flurry of activity—silver blades flashing, a spear poking at the creature's snapping mouth. I scrambled away, grabbing the strap of my pack as I tried to avoid being trampled or whipped by its tail.

Gasping, I kicked backward, right into Lorcan's chest.

Lorcan got one arm around my waist and dragged me into the brush while the other three drove the animal away. I'm not sure how he got down from the bridge. Jumped, probably.

As furiously as we'd been arguing, he didn't hesitate to come after me.

"It's all right," he murmured, but he was as rattled as I was, his arm an iron band around my middle and his breath an unsteady pant against my temple.

Tovian reached one hand down and yanked me up the steep bank. Lorcan needed no such assistance.

"That was a big dragon," I said, inanely, chest heaving, trying to recover my composure. My white clothing is now streaked with dirt and greenery. I picked a piece of fern out of my hair.

"Big Ada. He's been around since my mother was a child," Tovian said by way of explanation. I realized belatedly that he actually said "eater," like *ate-uh*. Not Ada. Still, the name stuck in my mind.

Tahra watched the trees for any sign of movement, bowstring taut.

"You're not hurt?" Lorcan asked. He hasn't budged from my side. This is a mirror to the day in Edinburgh when he fended off my attackers. That day brought us closer together. Today, his reassuring presence at my back only reminded me that we have months more of this to get through, before he'll be gone.

For good.

I refuse to admit to how hollow that makes me feel.

I'm not the one screwing this up. It's him. All him.

"A few bruises. I'll be feeling my own carelessness."

Okay, maybe it's not entirely him. Had I attempted to blend in with my environment instead of standing out, none of it would have happened. I let my bruised feelings endanger a rare animal; I vowed to get a handle on them for good.

"Let's keep moving," I said, shouldering my pack by the one usable strap. I wish I didn't need Lorcan so badly. Once October comes, and he's gone, I'll be trapped back in my castle. Again.

"Zosia."

I paused, waiting.

"If you want me to give up all my female friends, I'll do it."

He meant Tahra.

As though it would solve anything. If I can't trust him any time he's out of my sight, then this won't work. Ever.

Yet, he didn't do anything, no matter what Tahra wanted. I saw that with my own eyes.

I hated the way my father watched me, and yet I'm doing the same thing Lorcan.

"That isn't what I want," I said, turning away. "Please use more discretion. That's all."

I don't want to make my father's mistakes. Clinging to my old hurts because I can't figure out how not to. We're both screwing up this second chance at a life together. It took nearly being eaten by a dragon to realize that.

"I will. Zosia. I'll speak with Tahra myself."

When we reached the edge of the jungle, my four companions took several minutes to scrub the handprints from their skin with the astringent. They dressed in ordinary travelers' clothing. As much as I despise being the weak link in this highly-skilled group of warriors, there is no mistaking the fact that I can barely wield a weapon, and I am the only person in soiled garments.

Pride: take a hike.

CHAPTER TWENTY-TWO

T raveling on foot made for slow progress. We arrived in Oceanside as the sky turned pink and orange over the sea.

The last time I visited here, it was a thriving city. Now, it's a war zone.

Scorched husks of wooden dwellings dot the landscape for a hundred meters between the inner township and the beach. Before, the primary location of commerce was close to the beachfront. Now, it's behind a hastily constructed stone wall. It looks as though people dumped a lot of rocks and rubble in an attempt to protect the buildings further back from the water.

My stomach sank. Oceanside District accounted for thirty percent of the Auralian population before the war. If it still does...I have lost a huge number of my citizens. I knew this, intellectually, but here, I felt it.

It drove home for me how little margin for error I have. These people are survivors. They've been through a lot. As much as I have, if not more. They won't accept platitudes or bumbling in place of true leadership.

We attracted notice when coming into town, as expected. Lorcan hovered close to me. I would rather die than admit how comforting it is to have him nearby. We've barely spoken since the run-in with Big Ada. I changed my shirt after the dragon attack but there's no hiding the fact that I arrived looking less than regal.

We took rooms above the local tavern. Rustic is a kind way to describe it, but unless we wanted to camp in an abandoned shell of a house without running water, it was all that's available. A hole had been blasted into the wall. Some enterprising soul filled the gap with woven palm fronds nailed over it. Similar mats cover the windows, and can be rolled up or down to block out light. I couldn't figure out why one was placed near the floor until I investigated.

Noise from the public house below carried up into the cramped quarters.

I washed and changed into the purple gown with its gold belt and trim, my white slippers, and the white finger-less gloves with the celestia symbol embroidered on the backs of my hands. The belt loops twice around my middle and hangs down from my hip almost to my knee. The loose fit is comfortable. I felt reassuringly like my old self as I placed the diadem on my forehead.

Without a mirror, I cannot know how I look, but for once, I have an excuse not to care. Maybe I'll never replace all the broken mirrors in the castle. I can be like one of those witches in old fairy tales. A vampire.

Lorcan awaited me when I came out into the shabby hallway, his hair still damp. A white linen shirt clung in places to his torso. My breath caught.

No feelings, I reminded myself. Because that always works so well.

"Are you hungry, Princess?"

"No." I am, but food can wait. I doubt I've made progress toward my recovery but Saskaya will simply have to accept it. As long as I don't backslide too much, it'll be fine. I hope. Not that it matters, anymore. Lorcan made it clear he's not sleeping with me unless I make an honest man out of him, and I have no intention of doing that. "I'd like to meet with the district leadership."

I lifted my chin, daring him to question my decision to assert my authority here. He didn't. Lorcan led me out into the streets of what was once a relaxed seaside town, and is now the site of a tense, ongoing standoff.

The mayor, Ephram, was a grizzled man with an eyepatch, ironically enough.

"I wish we had better accommodations for you, Your Highness," he said. Keryn is in their Leader regalia, Tovian in ordinary clothing, like Lorcan, and Tahra in traditional Čovari attire. Black and gray, padding at the knee, shoulder and elbow, tall boots.

"I've slept in worse places."

"I find that impossible to believe, Highness."

Smiling faintly, I exchanged a glance with Lorcan. He knows where I spent the past year. His gaze slid uneasily away. My smile faded.

"Please, Ephram, show me what you have achieved in Oceanside."

For the next hour we toured the town on foot. I learned the origin of the stone wall—indeed, dumped there in a bid to deflect bullets from the pirates' machine guns—and visited the local school. Too many children; not enough teachers. Or parents. So many orphans.

We visited one of the towers where Auralian lookouts keep watch night and day over the beach. They've developed an alarm system. The Skía-led pirates keep changing up their tactics—attacking at night, at dawn, in the middle of the day. Sneaking onto the beaches and trying to creep along the rocky exterior wall. Coming at us with machine guns whenever they have supplies.

"The ammunition we captured from Skía warehouses and pirate encampments earlier this year is running out. We haven't been able to fish beyond the bay. There isn't enough food stored for the winter." Ephram showed me the empty caves at the base of the cliffs, hollowed out with time and weather. "The Grasslands District is effectively depopulated. We used the grain stores last winter."

Lorcan, of course, has seen this before. He helped to push back the invaders. The tour was for my benefit. He nonetheless stayed close to my side.

"How can I best help you?" I asked Ephram.

"We need to drive the pirates away for good, stop them from bringing reinforcements, clear the camp on Summertide Atoll, and obtain food to get through the winter. Next summer we can begin rebuilding, assuming we can get the materials."

I nodded. "I can assist you with that."

How, I don't know. We need every stick and log we can get to rebuild The Walled City. Perhaps we can construct buildings out of another material. Concrete isn't a viable option, stone requires quarrying, but bricks might be a possibility. Saskaya might have some ideas. Ifran will, too.

Lorcan slanted me a look. Ephram's lone eye bounces between us.

"I understand congratulations are in order." For the first time during our visit, he smiled. "Rumor has it that your nuptials will be celebrated this Harvest."

I smiled tightly and thanked him. Ephram moved on without further comment. Lorcan caught my arm and leaned close to whisper, "Announce the wedding, Zosia. Order the gown." His breath was warm against my cheek, followed by the warmer press of his lips. "Give your people a reason to celebrate."

Being an idiot, I mumbled, "You haven't asked me yet, Knight."

I strode away, following our guide, my violet skirts billowing behind me in the ocean breeze. Lorcan caught up with me in two strides.

"If I do, will you say yes? Because I was pretty sure the answer would have been no this summer, despite what you said on the boat."

Before I knew what he'd done. What he's become. How he'd changed, in some ways for the better, but all I'd registered was the loss.

"Ask me and find out, Lorcan."

Maybe, I've been thinking about this all wrong. I'm tired of clinging to old hurts. What might happen if I let them go? Choose not to let them plague me, as much as I can?

Trying to turn off my emotions never worked. My father's approach was wrong; why do I continue trying to replicate it? Raina and Tovian embrace theirs, and it makes them better leaders. Not worse.

I love Lorcan enough to want a baby with him. I know that when—not if—he found out, Lorcan would never rest until he had a formal role in her life. What if I've been lying to myself as an excuse to keep him close, even while holding him at bay because I'm scared to trust...myself, mostly. Afraid I'm not good enough to keep him.

His reasons for not being with me fully are illogical, but at least he's been consistent. He's never been willing to go that far. His attitude changed with regard to other women. Not me. His regret on that score is sincere.

Lorcan is capable of fidelity. I believe in my heart that he wants nothing more than to live a happy life with me. What if I chose him, the way he wants me to? He's been consistent about wanting that, too, ever since we were at school.

My fear that I would go into an unwanted marriage, never claiming some part of my own body for myself—that won't be an issue if I married him. Isn't resigning myself to a lifetime of celibacy a punishment I inflict upon myself?

What is waiting a few more months, if it means we'll finally finish what we started in Scotland?

I'm tired of uprooting every seedling of hope that keeps trying to sprout in every crevice of my heart. I'd like to water it, cultivate it, and make a little garden. Being a princess is lonely enough without forsaking everything that makes life worth living.

Do I want it enough to take the risk that he'll betray me again, though?

Inhaling deeply, I trailed Ephram onto the safe part of the beach, where there were small wooden boats lined neatly along the sand. I kicked off my slippers and walked barefoot.

Raina is going to kill me when I say yes.

CHAPTER TWENTY-THREE

We dined with Ephram in his home, precluding any further discussion of whether or not I will be a besotted dumbass and accept Lorcan's proposal. If he makes one. I could be overestimating the chances of that happening.

Afterward, I changed into my nightgown and sat up responding to Raina and Saskaya's messages—text, phone, email—and checked in with Scarlett, who has begun her journey back to Scotland from New York. I fell asleep working at the table by lantern, using my satellite phone and scribbling notes on paper.

At some point, Lorcan carried me to bed. He did not get in with me, which I became startlingly aware of just before dawn when an explosion made me sit straight up.

Lorcan rushed in a moment later.

"What is it?" I asked.

"The boat we scared off must have gotten through. Pirate attack."

He bundled me into a dark-brown cloak and out into the night, leading me through the streets to a shelter in one of the empty storage caves. Hundreds of pairs of eyes shine back at me. Children. Old people. Mothers with babies. Everyone who can be spared has rushed to the beach. The ones who cannot fight are here.

"Tahra will guard you," Lorcan said, taking me by the shoulders.

"No. Take her, too. I'll be fine."

I'm not useless. I have no idea what to do with children but surely a show of courage will comfort them.

Tahra darted away, in the direction of fire and smoke, clearly thrilled to be part of the action.

"Go, Lorcan. I'll be safe enough here."

After a beat of hesitation, he ran after Tahra.

We waited. Dawn stained the sky gray, then pale blue. The alarm bells stopped ringing. I bade the rest of the women stay and ventured out into the town, surveying the damage, alone. Dead bodies were piled in the center of the city, awaiting burial. Two houses and a tower aflame, though the blaze was controlled by a line of men and women passing buckets. The fires presented no danger to the rest of the village. Lorcan was nowhere to be seen.

"Out with Tovian," Keryn informed me when I came across them near the rock wall, breaking down Saskaya's new gun.

Alive—this time. How many more chances will we have before our luck runs out?

Squinting at a bit of metal that refused to come free, Keryn said, "They're plotting how to get onto that island and drive the pirates out of the encampment. Problem is they can see you coming, and these waters are filled with sharks. As long as the pirates are resupplied, we're in a stalemate."

"He's solved worse problems," I murmured, thinking of the Sentinels in The Walled City.

"Patched things up, have you?"

"Not really."

They glanced at me, skeptically. "Suit yourself, then."

I moved down the beach, seeking a private spot, satellite phone in hand.

Time for me to implement my plan. I send a few messages to my friends, to get them out into the world ahead of my discussion with King Humayun.

I hit the call button to reach Humayun's direct line. The time zones were favorable. Humayun was by turns insulting and cajoling, demanding to speak with the king (what king?) and then deriding my kingdom as, quote, "an antidemocratic theocracy led by a girl," (apparently antidemocratic theocracies led by men are fine) and not just any girl, but an "unfaithful girl who breaks her word."

Fair. I did that. I own it. Although, technically, I hadn't promised anything when I left. Sohrab and I negotiated an agreement but nothing was formally signed. I didn't quite apologize, though I did make a few conciliatory noises which did nothing to dampen Humayun's ire.

I let the king rant and rave at me for some time before gently but firmly informing him, in a tone I might use with Sethi, that Laila wished to remain here, that her sister, mother, and the ship's captain would all attest to the fact that she left of her own volition, and that I had, in fact, saved them from a pirate attack, though we lost the ship. Lying about that last part, but no one can prove it. Since his son's well-armed, helicopter-toting yacht is in the vicinity of my island anyway, how about he come and reclaim his fancy boat?

Cursing; threats. Humayun disconnected the call.

I spotted Lorcan loping up the beach with Tovian, backlit by the rising sun. Lorcan peeled off and dropped onto the ground beside me. There was soot smudged on his forehead and cheek. His knuckles bled. The knee of his pants had a hole. His eyes are bright, but I can see he's tired.

Weary of fighting, though it's all he's ever known.

I tossed my phone aside and rubbed my temples.

"That bad?" He kissed my shoulder through the nightgown.

"It went better than I expected it to." I couldn't hide my despondency. This is my life, forever, now. Dealing with international leaders, half of whom are, frankly, egotistical lunatics on a power trip. Coming up with ideas to fend off disaster. I've trained for it, but I, too, am weary of the responsibility. "I expect the pirates will be missing their prized resupply ship by this evening."

"Nicely done, Princess. Clever."

"If it works. I've sent out the press releases, too. Getting ahead of the inevitable messaging war in the global press."

We sat on the sand, together, watching the waves. Watching the sun rise over the churning ocean with the past at our backs and an uncertain future ahead. A fleet of pelicans dipped into the water, one at a time.

"Zosia?"

"Hm?"

"Marry me?"

I glanced sharply at him. I don't know why I was surprised to see him holding a ring. The timing, probably— I'm in my rumpled nightdress; he's filthy with battle. Yet it's right, somehow. The past twenty-four hours have been a culmination of everything that has brought us to this point. We'll fight together to save this country. Side by side.

Blue eyes full of hope and fear. They closed when I

leaned in to kiss him, my heart fluttering like a bird's wings beating air to rise.

"Yes," I breathed against his cheek. Lorcan's hand closed over mine. I felt his slight tremble. Hard metal and sharp stone dug into my palm.

"Thank the gods," he exhaled against my temple.

"You don't have to give me anything. You already gave me a betrothal gift. Several of them, in fact." Dresses. A knife. His life.

"Those were just gifts, Princess. Ordinary things. This is...more."

I opened my palm. An emerald and an amethyst in a gold band winked in the brightening sunlight. I gasped. It's too much. Betrothal gifts are often jewelry, but I can tell this ring cost a fortune, which is not part of our usual traditions. "Where did you get this?"

"I found the raw stones when I was out adventuring. I had them cut and set in a modern style, which I thought you'd like. It matches your crown." He's nervous. Lorcan is never nervous. By contrast, my hands were steady when I slipped the ring onto the fourth finger of my left hand. I admired it for a moment, then pulled him in for an embrace. His arms tightened around my back. He smelled of sulfur and sea.

"I love you."

"I love you, Knight." I brushed back his hair, smiling. "I suppose I'll have to get used to your new title in a couple of months."

He blushed. It's barely visible beneath the grime and his tanned skin, but I'm close enough to see the pink tinge creep over his cheeks. The white line of his scar stood out. I ran my thumb along the mark and kissed him again.

"We should get back." Already, there's a list of things I need to do running through my head.

"One more."

Lorcan kissed me senseless. There were many more than one. When we finally parted, I retrieved my phone and typed out one more message as we walked.

"What are you doing?" he asked, a bit apprehensively.

"Sending out one more announcement." I smirked.

My phone immediately started pinging with incoming messages. Lorcan's went off, too.

Raina: Fuck you! How dare you! I lost a thousand dael, Zosh!

Me: Your gambling problem is not my concern, Raina.

Raina: [middle finger emoji] There'll be no living with Tovian after this. He was sure you'd relent.

Raina: Are you happy?

Me: Yes.

I snapped a picture of the ring and sent it to her.

Raina: Not very Auralian, coming from the man who's the Goddess' biggest believer.

Raina: Pretty, though.

Lorcan reached over and took my hand. Together, we made our way back up the beach.

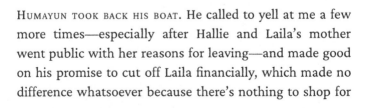

HUMAYUN TOOK BACK HIS BOAT. He called to yell at me a few more times—especially after Hallie and Laila's mother went public with her reasons for leaving—and made good on his promise to cut off Laila financially, which made no difference whatsoever because there's nothing to shop for here. It will matter if and when she wants to return to the outside world. Until then, she and her sister are permanent guests of the Auralian crown.

Keryn, Lorcan and Tovian blew up the next couple of supply ships; dilapidated, barely-seaworthy things. The sea turned red for a few minutes as sharks feasted. I found myself oddly dispassionate about it. They came here to kill us. The sharks were only behaving according to their nature. I didn't mourn the loss of such men, though I pitied them.

The last of the pirates packed up camp and departed the way they'd come: slinking away in the middle of the night on tiny boats with loud motors, the only reason we knew when they left.

The standoff was over.

By the time of our departure from Oceanside I was feeling pretty good about my fledgling leadership. I made a brief speech to the remaining residents. I haven't had to speak publicly in so long that I was a bit rusty.

I promised Ephram to be in touch often. I would not forget how hard his people have fought to save our country. They've been reinforced by fighters from as far away as Tenáho and Nansier, but Oceanside took the brunt of the initial invasion, and it has been the ongoing front ever since Lorcan routed the invaders from the interior.

For our return trip, we took a parallel route through what used to be the more arid and formerly more popu-lated side of the country. On the first day, moving north-ward, we passed burned-out farmhouses, many kilometers of broken fences, and of course, skeletons. We need a proper burial for all the unclaimed bodies. What a task that will be.

The first day passed uneventfully. We spent the night at a homestead where Lorcan and Tovian knew the owners,

Elia and Iacov. From the warm way she greeted him, I momentarily wondered whether Elia was one of Lorcan's conquests. My discomfort must have shown, because Tovian took me aside and explained that my betrothed had reunited the husband and wife after Iacov was injured at Oceanside.

After that, I vowed to give Lorcan more credit.

"We have never hosted royalty before," Elia told me, uncertainly, as Iacov herded their children to bed on a makeshift pallet in their parents' room. She was visibly pregnant. A fourth child.

"Your generosity is more than sufficient," I told her, meaning it. Lorcan and I would have a double bed to share. Tovian and Keryn would take the children's beds, with Tahra sleeping on the floor between them.

"I highly doubt a princess finds a worn-out guest room 'sufficient.'" Elia said ruefully.

"I spent several months in the Gaol at the castle," I quietly informed her. "A bed is a luxury beyond compare."

Elia looked stricken. Later, when I was sitting on the edge of the bed in my nightdress, I overheard her speaking in low tones with Lorcan in the hallway.

"The Gaol. She wasn't serious."

"She was. Half-starved when I found her."

I suppose it's no secret. Still. To me, he sounded unrepentant about the time he wasted gallivanting around. Taking pride in my rescue. It *was* a remarkable feat; no one else even made an attempt. Yet it struck the wrong note. I didn't catch what they said next, until Elia said, "—grateful for you returning him to us."

Fixing everyone else's life, basking in his glory. Alone.

Are you sure that in marrying Lorcan, you aren't marrying a man precisely like your father?

I don't want to believe that. And yet, the possibility is there, that he will slowly confine me to my castle prison again in the name of safety. Only allow me to leave on approved occasions, under heavy guard, leaving me to chafe under the restrictions necessary to keep me alive.

Quietly usurp the power that is rightfully mine.

He could do it, easily. Lorcan has a deep well of popular support to draw from. I don't. Not at home. Only abroad, which hardly signifies to people who have been fighting for their very lives. In theory, marrying him means I, too, will benefit from that support. In practice, I feel uneasy about the imbalance.

We were more equal, oddly enough, when we were the princess and the knight. Both of us consigned to roles we might rather not play, but must. Now, he is free to be whomever he wishes, while I'm as shackled to destiny as ever. I'm more envious of that fact than I am of the women.

What if this is my biggest princess fail yet?

"Princess," he said, coming into our shared guest room.

"Knight," I shot back.

He took his place on the bed beside me. "Zosia."

"That's better, Lorcan."

"Old habits die hard."

"I won't be a princess for much longer."

"No. I suppose not."

I don't want to fight. I wanted these fissures of doubt to stop eroding our relationship before it gets traction. It's easier to ignore them when I'm lying in his arms, but we don't have that luxury. We're on the move back to my castle.

Late that afternoon, we came to the burned-out, silent shell of a hamlet beside the Great Rielka River.

"What is this place?" I whispered. I didn't need to pitch

my voice so low, but the sight of so many broken buildings gave me shivers.

"It was Fennigal Bayne," Lorcan said. "Before the pirates took it over. Killed most of the inhabitants, the ones who didn't flee."

"Where did the ones who fled, go?"

His horse shook its mane, as though the animal was unnerved by the quiet, too. "Some of them joined the fighting. Others took shelter in nearby villages, or went north in search of family. A lot of refugees ended up in Cannavale."

Before the war, many Auralians rarely traveled far from their home villages. Now, Auralian cultural life is scrambled. Broken. Like everything else.

I am tasked with reassembling the pieces into a whole. I can't even manage that for myself. How will I do it for anyone else?

"Stay back."

Lorcan's arm like an iron bar across my abdomen. I stopped in my tracks.

"What's wrong?"

"I saw something move." He exchanged a look with Tovian. "Stay with Tahra."

"Why do I always have to watch the princess?" she complained.

Thanks, kid. I should probably stop thinking of her as a child, but I can't help it. She reminds me of myself a few years ago, in some ways. Anxious for adult experiences, without adult wisdom.

Lorcan whipped around. "You want to go see whatever's out there? Be my guest." His gaze cut sharply to me. "I'll be more than happy to guard the princess."

Tahra's gaze dropped. I couldn't believe it. Maybe Tovian and I were finally getting through to him.

"Probably a stray dog," Tovian said, inching forward. His eyes scanned the ruined houses restlessly. Lorcan moved along the side of a building, blade in hand, a pistol strapped to his side. He said something I couldn't hear.

This is how they worked. As a team. A unit. I wish I'd been there to see it.

A motion from the corner of my eye made me whip my head around.

Not a stray dog. A child.

I rushed forward, only to be brought up short when a stone-faced, dirt-smudged girl pointed a sharp knife at my throat.

CHAPTER TWENTY-FOUR

Lorcan was at my side in an instant. I motioned for him to stand down.

"It's all right."

"Who are you?" someone behind her demanded.

"The princess."

"The fuck you are," a young male voice said, angrily, from the shadows behind the girl. I could barely discern his outline in the deep gloom of the hovel they were hiding in. He reminded me of a half-grown wolf-bear I had once seen staring down a larger animal. "The princess is dead."

"I'm not dead. I'm right here. Come out. Please."

A scrawny, dirty youth edged out into the sun. His clothes were torn and stained. I've never witnessed such suspicion in someone so young. Except, possibly, the silent little girl with eyes as hard as agates, whose knife hadn't wavered.

"You're really her?" the boy asked.

"I am." I looked over at Lorcan and saw his pity and anger. For everything he and I have been through, we were adults. Not children left to fend for themselves.

"You look..." He trailed off. "The princess had long hair."

"I cut it. Impractical to maintain." I bent on one knee, slowly. The girl's knife never wavered. Nor did her eyes. She tracked my movement with her sharp, sharp stone blade. I saw myself in her, coming out of the castle. Brittle. One more blow away from shattering completely. "You may recognize my companions?"

"The Auralian Hero?" the boy said, glancing warily at Lorcan. I saw the hero worship blossom when my knight nodded once. "And the Leader of the Mountain Folk?"

"Yes," Keryn said, bowing. "At your service, child. Where are your parents?"

"Dead. Palla's, too."

"Who are they?" The boy gestured at our friends, and then to the girl, Palla. She dropped her hand to her side, but her knuckles were white beneath the grime, clenched around the hilt.

"Tahra and Tovian." I didn't bother to try and explain that the Ansi were not, in fact, a myth. We've already stretched these children's imagination by having the Princess and the Hero show up on a random day in August. "How long have you been here, alone?"

"Since the snowfalls in spring. Pirates killed everyone as they moved through. We escaped."

"They're gone," Lorcan said. He offered his hand. The boy warily placed his palm in the center, nearly as large, but thin. Starved, like me.

The children's families almost survived. I can see the self-recrimination writ on Lorcan's face. Had he worked a little faster, been more ruthless...

He was one person. A legend, yes, but one person against an army.

"You couldn't be everywhere," I told him softly, squeezing his shoulder. Lorcan glanced quickly at me, then at Palla. Scanning for any sign of danger, even from a child.

"We didn't know if it was safe to leave. You're the first people to stop here in months."

The girl's hard eyes closed briefly. When they opened again, there was a sheen of tears, but nothing fell. My heart broke.

"It's all right now. You're safe." I opened my arms. Palla shook her head slowly, but a smaller girl burst out of the shadows and ran into them, sobbing. She was so light I could pick her up easily.

"Yenita, get back," the boy barked, but it was too late. The child in my arms clung tightly to me. Her hair and clothing were pungent with filth but I didn't care. All that mattered was that this little girl had been through a trial no one should ever have to endure, and it was over.

THERE WERE four children in the encampment. Bennet, the eldest boy, was fourteen. The youngest was a boy around five named Filo. Palla, twelve, hadn't spoken a single word in months, though she was an adept hunter. Yenita, nine, was the chattiest of the group. She clung to me like a burr, and when I needed to disentangle myself for a few minutes, latched onto Keryn like a tiny monkey scaling a large tree.

All of them were malnourished and dirty. We had no appropriately-sized clothes to give them, so after we set up camp for the evening, Tovian and Tahra went to search the dwellings. Keryn hauled water to heat over the fire for a bath, and Lorcan, of course, cooked.

The children had a few plantains in their stores. The starchy fruits, what edible plants they could harvest, and any small game Palla and Bennet could kill were all they had subsisted upon for months.

Lorcan's apprehension radiated off him. Mindful of how feeding me made me sick. But the children aren't as far gone as I was. They ate and kept it down without incident.

Filo was particularly resistant to the bath Tahra tried to give him. The rest of the children obediently scrubbed until the warm water turned a mucky grayish brown with filth.

But they were clean, safe and fed for the first time in months. The three youngest ones slept in a pile on Lorcan's bedroll. He would share mine. Bennet had his own pallet, though he insisted upon staying up, sitting near Tahra and clearly enthralled with Lorcan, listening to Keryn and Tovian exchange stories of fighting during the war.

"We can't leave them here," I told him, when the fire had died low and Lorcan and I were the only ones left awake.

"The horses are already carrying too much weight."

"I *won't* leave them here."

He kissed my temple. The dying fire popped.

"I know, Princess. I won't either. We'll look for a wagon in the morning."

There was no wagon. We searched the burned-out remnants of the village for anything that might suffice, with no luck. So, Palla rode pillion behind me on my horse, Tovian took Bennet, Lorcan took Filo, and Yenita sat in front of Tahra. Keryn's huge mount carried a disproportionate amount of gear, though we had to leave much of it behind. Slowly, we trudged up the incline of rocky, arid land abuzz with insects in the grass. It cost us a day of travel, but it was worth it to rescue these abandoned children.

Three days later, we arrived in Cannavale, on the southern edge of Central Auralia. The town had been occupied for a time, before Lorcan freed it. Here, he was truly a legend, and greeted accordingly.

Of all the villages that had been occupied and burned, Cannavale has made the biggest comeback. Its citizens were rebuilding using rubble from the destroyed town, salvaging timber where they could, and mostly restoring the center of the city. The city's location as a waypoint between the castle, the Sun Temple, and the southern districts made it a strategic and economic stronghold.

We took lodgings in the local inn. Lorcan and I took one room, while Tahra, Palla and Yenita shared another, Tovian, Bennet and Filo another, and Keryn had one all to themselves.

Even with our own room, privacy was scarce. Here, Lorcan was greeted as a revered folk hero, with demands upon his time that took him away from my side. I had asked him to build up a new guard, which meant finding suitable recruits. I couldn't fault him for taking it seriously.

I donned my green checked dress from Tenáho over a linen shift. I know, from some reactions we've encountered, that my appearance has come as a shock to people who were familiar with seeing me before the war. Not just Bennet.

Here in Cannavale, I heard whispers that I wasn't really the princess, that I was an impostor. I already felt like a fraud. I know I'll never again look like I did in that green dress I wore in Paris. Lorcan isn't blind; he can see the difference. Feel it, too, when we are alone.

The fawning over my fiancé therefore stung, on several levels, though I told myself I was being petty. I hated having to think about how many of the women in the crowd had been with him—when I haven't. It's the same source of my frustration when everyone used to tell me he *really is something special.*

He belonged among these people in a way I could only pretend to. It wasn't like when we were in Tenáho, where I felt as though he was welcoming me into his life. Cannavale was a preview of our future.

Worse, I felt as though he's placed me on a pedestal, like I'm one of the statutes of my supposed ancestor. All I ever wanted was to be treated as a normal person. Doesn't he know that, by now?

Are you imagining there's any daylight between who you are and what you are? he asked me, back in his kitchen.

No, there isn't—and that's the problem. It always has been. I still feel isolated and alone. I'm still standing on Saskaya's deck watching through the window.

He takes his role seriously. I'll grant him that. While Lorcan was busy meeting with the newly-formed Cannavale Security Council—where I can provide little practical advice—Tovian escorted me to meet with Ifran's niece, Reba, at her atelier. Before the war, she'd been apprenticed to one of the court's tailors, and since renting this huge, sunny warehouse, she'd stockpiled a large quantity of fine fabrics at low cost. There's little demand for extravagance now, but she was betting on a brighter future.

I admired her optimism and hustle, along with her workshop filled with rolls and bolts of linen, wool, ivory spidersilk and dyed velvet. Some of the velvet had been damaged during the war, the purple a few shades too light, due to exposure to the elements. She hadn't decided what to do with all the fabric yet.

She showed me sketches of potential wedding gowns. The trick was to create one that would serve for both my coronation and wedding, as they were planned to be held on a single day.

"I suppose we'll have to have clothes made for Lorcan, too," I mused, not meaning for anyone to overhear.

"Only if you intend to see it through," Tovian replied.

He is too astute.

"I do mean to," I said briskly. "I was thinking out loud, that's all. He could wear his royal guardsman uniform. It wouldn't be unusual. My father did, for his wedding."

"But he was coronated later."

"How do you know that, Ansi?" I smiled, and my friend returned it.

"I told you. You couldn't find us, but we always knew where to find you."

I inclined my head. I've said something similar about Auralia on many occasions.

Reba took my measurements and promised to bring a rough version of the gown to the castle in a few weeks for fitting. Before we left, I agreed to send Lorcan in for a consultation, too.

We strode down the cobblestone street in companionable silence.

"Zosia."

When I looked over, Tovian's dark eyes were serious. "Yes?"

"If you still harbor doubts about him, wait."

I inhaled sharply. "It isn't him I doubt. It's myself."

I doubt that I will be enough to hold Lorcan's interest. Which means, by default, that I still doubt Lorcan's fidelity.

Worse, I doubt my sway over these people. I'm too young and overly serious by nature. I don't spark the imagination like my knight does, and I worry that he would use his legendary status to undermine my authority. It's a danger unique to Lorcan—Sorhab would have been viewed as an outsider. I might have had to fight my own husband for control of my country, but I'd have won. I'm not certain that would be the case with Lorcan, now that I've seen first-hand how universally adored he is.

"Is that why you only wanted one dress? In case the betrothal falls through?"

"There is my bankrupt Treasury to consider. It's practical to combine the events, and there won't be time to change clothes in between ceremonies. I sincerely doubt people would wish to travel twice, once for my coronation and again for a wedding. And then for Midwinter."

I avoided his eye.

"People would travel as far and as often as necessary to honor the occasion."

"Would they, Tovian?"

We paused, leaning against a stone wall to converse in low tones.

"You will be their Queen, Zosia. Why wouldn't they come?"

I tried to breathe through the tight, hot pressure in my lungs. The old familiar feeling of failure and anxiety, of not being good enough to please anyone. It was back. "I suppose. I wouldn't want to put anyone out. They have enough work to contend with."

Tovian regarded me thoughtfully.

"You are to be their Queen," he repeated.

"Which means I must put the needs of my people above my own. You know this. Your mother does. Raina does."

"When Raina and I married, there was opposition. Especially from the Myseči. We knew we could weather it because we were both committed to the union. I see your hesitation, and I worry that this will end in heartbreak. You both deserve happiness with everything you've been through. Not more pain."

You deserve better than a sham marriage, Kenton told me that night he refused me. What I deserve generally has little relation to what I get. Perhaps I don't deserve good things, because of what I am.

Everyone thinks being a princess is an easy life. Instant respect, beautiful gowns, a castle to live in forever. But it's a trap. You can't escape, and it costs you everything that matters. Love. Independence. Privacy. Autonomy. Your entire self-worth becomes wrapped up in the title. Everything you are becomes worthless.

Your life in service to the crown.

Here in Cannavale, it is obvious that Lorcan still has his pick of any woman he might want. I find it impossible to believe that, without my title, he would voluntarily shun them in favor of me. No one ever puts me first. He didn't. My father didn't. Cata certainly didn't, though she tried to soften my father's harshness. I thought I could get past the depth of that wound by ignoring it, and I have tried to, but I'm not fooling Tovian.

Every time I've tried to speak about my fears, though, people have brushed them off. Told me that I was silly to worry, or stupid to have them. That I was privileged to live this life and loneliness was my lot. I therefore said nothing, now.

"Do you ever think about quitting?" I asked, in a rush of breath.

"Quitting what?" Tovian asked, his brows knitting.

"Royalty. Giving it all up. Just walking away from leadership and everything that comes with it."

"No. But I know I could, at any time."

"I think about it every day. Every hour. I never asked for

this life." I scuffed the dirty stone with the toe of my slipper. Sunlight beat down on the back of my neck. I shivered in spite of the warm day. "But I can't. There isn't anyone else. The stakes of this marriage are so very high, Tovi, both for me, personally, and for the entire country. It would shake the people's confidence in me, if a second wedding were to fall apart at the last minute."

It would be a devastating blow to my own small crumb of confidence. It already is. What seemed like a reasonable thing to do in Oceanside feels more and more like a mistake.

Tovian seemed to understand the unspoken part. He squeezed my arm.

"I told him he should have been firmer with Tahra. Someone had to say something about her behavior and it should have been him. I think Keryn and I made the situation worse. Now, she feels like Lorcan is the only one who truly understands her, and vice versa, because they've become friends. Tahra thinks that if you weren't a princess, you wouldn't have such a hold on Lorcan's heart."

"I wouldn't," I said flatly. "I try not to think about it."

He has an unbreakable grip on mine.

We spotted Lorcan and Tahra coming down the street, trailed by Bennet and Palla. Speaking of hero worship, Bennet had gone from surly skeptic to dogging my knight's heels. It's darkly amusing, how quickly he latched onto the Hero of Auralia. Lorcan has that effect on people.

Palla, however, came to stand beside me. The one female person in the entire country to choose me over my knight. She still hasn't spoken a single word to anyone. As far as I can tell, she hangs by me because she thinks I can protect her. I will. As best I can. She goes nowhere without Bennet or me, or without her trusty weapon.

It puts my worries into perspective. Fretting over one dress or two is an absurd luxury. The pressure in my chest eased. I smiled.

"Reba wants to see you, Lorcan."

I saw him glance between Tovian and me, as though he knew we'd been talking about him before he came upon us. Almost as though he didn't like the idea of me confiding in anyone other than him. He wants me to himself. I don't think he understands that, being a princess, I can never be his alone.

I wonder what he will do when he finally comprehends that he will always share me with the history he reveres.

CHAPTER TWENTY-FIVE

Upon arriving back at the castle, I was astonished by how much progress Ifran and his crews had made. The rickety drawbridge had been replaced by a sturdier version, complete with rails. He had plans drawn up to salvage the rocks from the destroyed gatehouses and build a proper stone bridge instead. All it needed was my approval.

Lorcan disliked this plan. He wanted to be able to close off the castle from future threats. When I pointed out how that had backfired last time, he relented, but not without an argument. I could have asserted my status, but what kind of marriage would we have if I went around overruling him constantly? The way I've done before, and made him bristle?

We hadn't even made it to the royal apartments without a disagreement.

Word spread quickly. There was no reason for me to be surprised. Castle life is always gossipy, even when your castle is a marginally habitable ruin with a skeleton crew of staff. After dinner, from the privacy of our balcony, I called Raina to unload my frustrations while Lorcan showered.

"Did Tovian arrive safely?" I asked.

"Yes, and we are looking forward to reunion sex, so I need to keep this conversation short."

"You can have sex while pregnant?" I asked. I really hadn't thought about it before.

"Fucking hell, Zosia, don't joke about it. I feel like a whale already."

I apologized quickly. I wasn't about to confess that I had very little idea about what was and was not normal, much less possible, in sex, as I had so little experience with it. The disconnect between public perception and reality was grating when Lorcan and I were mostly out of view. Now, we were thrust into the unforgiving lens of public scrutiny, and I had no one to confide in about my deepest shame. My own betrothed would share a bed with me but spurned me, physically.

"I have a new maid," I told my friend, to change the subject and ease into the other source of my frustrations. "Norah."

"Is she good?"

"Seems to be. I only met her this afternoon."

I hadn't taken an immediate liking to Norah, but then again, I had never given much thought to any of my maids. They showed up, managed my clothing and styled my hair, and seldom made any overtures of friendship. Sometimes I tried to converse with them about their families, but that was as far as anything had ever gone.

"I think Norah might be a bit of a gossip." I am afraid she might be worse, but I have been known to be overly suspicious in these matters, so I kept my private doubts to myself.

"Fire her. That's my advice."

"I can't fire her over nothing."

"It's not nothing! I don't care how competent they are; servants who can't exercise discretion don't belong in the royal chambers. Let them work in the laundries or the kitchens or send them to the stables, where they can't spread secrets."

Raina has always been practical in this sense. She knows her place at River Bend, and has little patience for anyone who doesn't. I could stand to take notes.

"I'm not sure it was her," I hedged. "Lorcan and I had a minor disagreement, over the design of the drawbridge to the castle. Specifically, I want it to be a proper bridge instead of a retractable wooden slab."

"He had security concerns?"

"Yes. But I pointed out that last time, the drawbridge rather backfired."

"Zosia. You were the one who blew up the gatehouses."

"True."

"I know you would have done the same to a bridge."

"Yes, also true."

"So, whether it's a bridge or a gatehouse, who fucking cares? Right? The drawbridge won't keep anyone out who's determined to get in, and the bridge is expendable in an emergency anyway."

"I—" Had no response to that. Raina was right. It was a stupid argument, and I'm glad I didn't assert my authority because what a dumb waste of influence that would have been. It was the kind of minor disagreement that shouldn't have mattered, and wouldn't have, if I hadn't heard the servants whispering in the hallways afterward that the future queen and her chosen knight weren't happily engaged, after all. That our marriage was a sham.

Which it was, until very recently.

How could there be any real feeling behind the match, when a scant few months ago he made a habit of taking any woman to bed who offered?

It was like being smacked on an open wound. I knew that coming back here would mean facing scrutiny. I didn't know it would so quickly turn caustic. I wasn't a popular princess. Everyone had to put up with me because I was the last one. That is still the case, but now I have something other people want: an engagement to the Auralian Hero.

One I wouldn't have, were I not a princess, and he didn't desire a crown.

Lorcan came out onto the balcony, his hair damp from bathing. My breath caught. I wanted him so badly. It is a constant raw ache that he doesn't feel the same desperate way about me.

Lorcan bent over me where I was sitting at the rough wooden table Ifran had brought for us to dine privately. He brushed his thumb over my cheek.

"Good call with Raina?"

"Mostly. She thought our argument about the draw-bridge was silly. I have to say I agree."

It's not quite an apology. I don't feel as though one is warranted, on either side. We had a discussion and worked it out. Had it not been for all the eyes and ears upon us, we wouldn't need to revisit the matter now.

"I shouldn't have contradicted you."

"You're my head of security, Lorcan. I always want you to speak your mind. Please." We will weather this small setback. If we can't, what does it say about our prospects for happiness together?

"Of course. Anything for you, Princess." Lorcan dropped into the other chair.

"Except sex," I pointed out, dryly.

"Temporarily." He poured wine into my glass. Two fingers' worth. I can't handle much more. "Is it so bad to wait a few more weeks?"

"Two and a half months. I am counting every minute of every day." I raised it for a toast. He touched it with his, a soft ping. "I have been disappointed too many times to believe waiting isn't a risk, Knight."

"I trust I am not a disappointment to you, Princess."

I stared out over the cracked balcony rail, trying to decide how to respond. "No," I lied, knowing full well that if I couldn't bring myself to be honest with him now, I had no right to expect him to be honest with me later. "Not you."

I sighed. What if I let go? Stopped worrying that he will betray me again?

I keep trying to.

I couldn't fool Tovian. I wonder who else sees through my efforts to maintain appearances. Does Lorcan?

Reaching over, I took his hand and squeezed. Lorcan kissed my knuckles right above the ring he gave me in Oceanside.

"Did you get enough to eat?" he asked.

"I'm finished." It's an evasive response because I've decided to give up trying to get back to where I was before the war. To being the person I was, then. I'm physically recovered enough to fulfill my duties, and that will have to suffice. But I haven't told Saskaya, Raina or even Lorcan. I'm tired of thinking about food, and I have run out of time to rest. This is who I am, now. The sooner I own it, the sooner people will move on to criticizing me for other things.

Maybe the fact that no one has ever had much use for me, Zosia, will finally work in my favor.

We were in bed, Lorcan with his shirt off and his hand under my nightdress, together this way for the first time since Oceanside when a frantic knocking at the bedroom door startled us apart. One minute he was pressed against me; the next, his warmth replaced by cool air.

Norah, her blond hair in a loose braid down her back, a simple robe knotted at her waist, entered without waiting for a signal from either of us. Her gaze lingered on Lorcan's naked chest and skimmed lower, to where he was unmistakably aroused. I swallowed my annoyance.

"It's Palla," she said. "She won't stop screaming." My maid's eyes found mine. "She keeps screaming 'princess'."

I hurried toward the door. Lorcan stopped me.

"It could be a ruse."

"Lorcan, I can hear the poor girl." Faint, echoing shrieks accompanied Norah's intrusion.

He tensed. "Let me go first. Just in case."

I nodded, and fell back. He yanked on trousers and a shirt, while I grabbed my own robe. Then I followed him down the hall to the small rooms Palla and Bennet had been given until more permanent housing could be found. The two younger children had been temporarily placed with the family who was running the castle kitchens. Permanently, if it works out for them.

Palla's single bed took up most of the chamber. She sat straight up, eyes wide and unseeing, screaming. The sight of her hands clenched around fistfuls of the blanket was unsettling.

"A night terror," Lorcan whispered. "She's not really awake."

"What do we do?"

"Wait until it's over. If you try to awaken her while she's screaming, it will only frighten her."

I perched on the edge. She didn't react. I winced as she screamed again, "Princess!"

"Why do you think she's calling for me?"

Lorcan sat beside me. "Maybe you're the first person she's felt safe with since she lost her parents. Or could be a dream. There's not necessarily a rhyme or reason to it."

"Hm." I clapped my hands over my ears when Palla released a particularly loud wail. We both inched away when her legs began thrashing. Tears streamed down her cheeks, but her eyes, though open, were blank. "How do you know this?"

"Arya used to get them. Sethi was starting to." He kissed my shoulder. "Happens to kids that age."

I was again reminded of how little I know about children. I must have been desperate for love to delude myself that I could raise a daughter on my own. I would've been completely adrift. I could hire nursemaids and governesses but I'd have hated it, wanting to keep her for myself. I'd have been just as bad a parent as my own father was to me.

All at once, Palla collapsed, still and silent. A moment later, she moaned and pushed up to sitting with shaking arms. Her eyes were barely open, but seeing me, she lurched into my lap, trembling.

"Oh, you poor thing," I murmured.

Lorcan chuckled softly and ran his hand down her curls. "Congratulations."

"Hm?"

"It looks like you've been adopted."

"Isn't it usually the other way around? We would choose to take in a child?"

Lorcan's smile was soft. "Sometimes. Other times, you get chosen."

He carried Palla back to our room and placed her small body on the child's bed in the corner of our bedroom. I sighed. Finding time to be alone in the castle is going to be nigh impossible—not that I would dream of sending my new foster daughter away.

THE WEEK after our return passed in a blur. Lorcan was busy recruiting candidates to join the new royal guard, setting up a training facility, and trying them out. Bennet wanted to join, but he was too young. Tahra volunteered immediately, though it wasn't out of loyalty to me.

My days were consumed with preparing for our foreign visitors and straightening out the Treasury situation. Thanks to Lorcan's generosity, we had enough funds to plan a proper ceremony. Tovian's warning haunted me, though. I did have doubts, and no safe place to voice them.

I was haunted by the whispers, too. As if echoes of Bashir, and my father's constant criticism, didn't chase me down every hallway, I also heard the rumors about Lorcan and me.

He barely tolerates the princess. Spends all his time training the new guards to avoid her.

Princess Zosia is cold and aloof. Unfeeling. I don't think she cares about him at all; she only wants him because he's popular with the people, and she isn't.

Hasn't led a religious service since she's been back. All but neglected Midsummer, too.

I ignored them. But I heard them, all the same.

I told myself it should be enough that I was focused on shoring up the economy. But it wasn't. I might not care about religion, but they did, and they noticed how I wasn't prioritizing it.

Lorcan, sweaty from training, found me in my father's old study. When I was trapped in the castle with Bashir, I used to come here just to feel close to someone. Now, I come here because I hate hearing the way they whisper about me. It's the only place I can shut them out. I know Norah is feeding the rumors. Small details only a maid would know occasionally make the rounds, like the fact that Palla refuses to sleep anywhere but the children's bed in our room, and we've relocated to the cramped guard's bed just to get a bit of privacy.

But according to the rumors, it's Lorcan avoiding me. Honestly, it might be easier if he did. Being near one another with no outlet has been hard, at least for me.

I was, therefore, exceptionally pleased to see him now.

"How was practice?" I asked, setting aside the account books. My heart squeezed at the way a shaft of sunlight from the high, slitted windows cast a golden hue on his damp hair. I was reminded of that day at the Colosseum, when he boldly held my gaze and it felt unsettlingly like fate. My seventeenth birthday.

"Hard."

"Mm." I put my arms around his waist, heedless of the sweat, inhaling his scent. Lorcan chuckled.

"You don't want to do that, Zosh. I'm a mess."

"I don't care. I like you like this."

He kissed my hair, then my lips.

"Have you eaten?"

"Not yet." I'd been fretting over how much grain to buy for the winter. Prices are too high. The economy is running hot, with too few goods and too little money but a huge spike in demand. My economics class lessons seem too remote to help me get a handle on it. Probably wouldn't hurt to review the material, though, if only I could find the time.

"I'll call for lunch."

He ducked out into the hallway to hail the waiting guard. I go nowhere unaccompanied, not even within my own home. Again. I mind it less than before, having ghosted these halls for an entire year by myself, but it's been an adjustment.

"Will you be able to meet Scarlett when she arrives next week?" I asked.

"Of course. Tahra can cover the training while I'm away." I looped my arm through his as we meandered back to our quarters. "If it's all right with you, I'd like to name her as temporary captain during my absence."

"Captain of the guard at seventeen?" Tahra's age was only one of my objections, but it was the only one I felt comfortable voicing.

Lorcan smiled.

"Eighteen, soon. Not that it matters; she's an adult and wants to stay on. I'll be the real captain, of course. She's a good fighter, and there's no other obvious choice. It's only for a few days."

He was trying to be accommodating. I knew that, yet I couldn't overcome my hesitation. I regularly drop in to watch him train, mostly because seeing Lorcan in action is such a pleasure—but partly because I'm still haunted by the vague suspicion that I might catch them kissing. Or worse. I can't get past it.

Perhaps there's more truth to Norah's rumors than I want to admit.

He pressed a kiss to my forehead. "Bennet asked to be part of the guard, too."

"He's too young," I protested.

Lorcan frowned. "He wants to train with us. The way I did at his age."

Sixteen when he was sent out to be a spy-assassin. "We asked too much of you, Lorcan. I won't do that to my foster son, no matter how eagerly he volunteers. Bennet has already seen enough violence."

Lorcan's brows knit thoughtfully. "He'll be upset."

"No recruits under seventeen, even if they volunteer." I braced for an argument. But Lorcan surprised me when he nodded in agreement.

"Understood, Princess. They can work in the barns and train. But they can't join the knighthood, much less the royal guard, until they're of age."

"And only if they study. I want the focus to be education, not using children to fill our labor gap, as dire as it is."

"You're okay with Tahra, though? I don't have any other choices. I know she's been a source of tension, Zosia, but Čovari-trained fighters are hard to come by. Her complaint about guarding you came from a history of always being told to stay behind, not resentment toward you."

I don't quite believe it. But I'm the one who's been clinging to suspicion and resentment all summer, not her.

"Can you send her to meet Scarlett?"

"I could. But I think our friend would rather meet a familiar face upon arriving at an active volcano." He squeezed my shoulder.

"True."

Tahra is keen to prove herself, and perhaps giving her the opportunity to do so will help matters.

"If she wants to stay, then Tahra is a good choice. The only thing I know about guarding and fighting is that I have no talent for it."

"That's why you have me." Lorcan squeezed my shoulder.

We entered our living quarters and found Norah in our bedroom, putting away laundry.

"Shall I set out new clothes for you, Sir?" she called after him, watching as he stripped the dirty set off and over his head. Her eyes followed him into the bathing room, even if her body did not.

When she turned to me, I held her eye. Norah didn't blink, didn't look away. Instead, her mouth curved faintly upward at the corners before she said, "I shall leave fresh clothing on the bed for him. Your lunch is on the balcony. Is there anything further you require, Highness?"

"Dismissed," I snapped. But Norah took her time leaving. Placing clean tunic and trousers on the bedspread. Running her hand down the center of the underwear she placed on top, where his cock would be when he put them on. I observed this silently, and noted the way she did not curtsey to me when she left.

I closed my eyes. Whether she meant to seduce him or already had didn't matter; I only wanted this nightmare to end. Like Palla, I didn't know how to wake up.

CHAPTER TWENTY-SIX

For the next several days, I tried not to see it. I didn't want to. Yet there was no ignoring the way Norah's gaze lingered on Lorcan every time she was in our quarters, which was hourly. She barged in on the thinnest of pretexts—trying to catch him alone, was my guess.

He didn't respond the first time, nor the second, but as Norah became bolder and more flirtatious, I saw him meet her eye with wary unease.

He said nothing.

No reprimand. Lorcan simply ignored her, in silence.

I tried to do the same.

It didn't work.

Then I walked in on Norah waiting outside the bathing chamber with a pile of fresh clothes. She knew when Lorcan came back to clean up for lunch after training all morning with the new royal guards. She knew that I spent the mornings in my study until he was free to escort me into The Walled City or on other errands, that the guards' bed was always rumpled no matter how we tried to make it neat, and that I awoke alone in the double bed each morning because we always moved back to the main bed when Lorcan rose for training, so our foster daughter wouldn't find herself alone.

So did the entire castle.

I couldn't stop seeing the way Norah stroked Lorcan's underwear. I know—*I know*—that it's only a bit of fabric, that labor is not easy to find right now, and that to fire her would insult Ifran. That my mind needs to be focused on more important things. I need a castle manager to handle such matters, but until I have one, Norah knows the only one who can check her is me—and she has planted exactly the right rumors to prevent me from taking her to task.

If I speak up, I will look jealous, because I am. Weak, because I can be so easily manipulated. She's been devious in how she goes about it, too. How would I explain firing her?

Norah handled his clothes inappropriately, I would say.

Inappropriately, how, Zosia? Handling clothes is what maids do, would be the response.

She comes into my rooms all the time.

Yes, Zosia, it's her job to be in and out of our chambers. You of all people ought to know that.

When Lorcan came out a moment later and she still hadn't left to give us privacy, as a proper maid would have done, I glared. She cast me a smug, sidelong glance before saying to Lorcan, "The blue brings out the color of your eyes, if I may say so, Sir."

"Norah."

"Highness?" She curtsied as though she hadn't been attempting to flirt with my fiancé right under my nose.

"You are dismissed."

Norah tossed a haughty little glance over her shoulder

at Lorcan. He did nothing. After an uneasy look at her, then at me, as he tugged the hem down over his abdomen.

"Norah, you are dismissed from my service. Leave the castle and don't return."

Shocked silence echoed through the empty stone chamber.

"Highness, I—"

"Get out."

When she was gone, Lorcan turned to me with consternation. "Was that necessary? Help is hard enough to find right now—"

"You didn't do anything," I cut him off icily, furious with him for inviting this into my life, and feeling no responsibility for managing its impact on me.

"Exactly. Nor was I going to." I saw, then, that Lorcan was angry, too. He's trying to control it, but it's simmering there in his eyes. "What does it take to convince you, Zosia?"

"A little effort on your part would go a long way, Lorcan." I picked up my brush and drew it through my hair. Soothing. I remember my mother doing this when I was small. Cata when I was a bit older. Maids like Norah, too. How do I make him see? I don't want to argue but we need to have this out. The wedding is still two months away.

If it happens at all.

"Effort? Seriously, Zosia?" He inserted himself between me and my mirror, blocking my view, leaning his butt on the edge of my vanity, arms crossed and glowering. "Every day, all day, I am devoted to you. Only to you. But it's never enough to convince you to trust me. I don't know what more I can do—"

"You could have sent her away the first time she tried to

flirt with you." *You could at least acknowledge that it's happening, that I'm not making it up.*

"I ignored her. She would have given up when she saw I wasn't interested."

I set the brush down on the vanity next to his ass, not gently. We both jumped at the hard click of metal on polished wood. "And if she didn't?"

"It. Still. Wouldn't. Matter." His eyes were ice floes on an arctic sea. "It doesn't matter what she does. It matters what *I* do. I can't be responsible for other people's actions. Reassign her, but don't fire her over nothing."

"When she 'accidentally' comes in while you're dressing and insists on helping you? Would you say something then? Do something to deter her?" Mine are hard like emeralds. In the part of my reflection I can see in the mirror, they are as unyielding as sprouts of hope, daring him to let them grow for once. "Anything? Tell her to leave? Or would you sit idly by while she fondles your—"

"Enough. You've made your point."

He pushed off the vanity hard enough to rattle the mirror and everything on it. The brush toppled to the floor. "Clearly, it's too much to ask you to trust me. I fought for you. I risked my life for you. I nearly died for you. I made one mistake—a serious mistake, I grant you—"

"It wasn't one mistake, Lorcan. It was enough to set the expectation that any woman who wants to can have a night with the Auralian Hero—"

"I fucked up! I can't unfuck it!"

I've never heard him yell before. I didn't know he *could* roar like that. His curses rang from the stone walls.

"I can't undo what I did, Zosia. If you can't forgive me for it, then we cannot..."

He doesn't want to say it. Even now, when he knows it

would be a disaster for us, he has a taste for kingship and he wants it badly. Badly enough to destroy us. Me. He would be just as bad as the husband he saved me from marrying a few months ago.

Worse.

"You're right, Lorcan. We cannot." I rose and gathered my robe around my body. Regal despite my short hair and stick-thin body, despite the fact that every cell of my being quakes with rage and despair. Outwardly, I am calm. I hate the reflection of myself I see in the mirror. A perfect queen. I despise this version of myself.

Queen or not, I deserve better than to be humiliated by my own maid. Zosia, me, I deserve Lorcan's whole love and if I am only to have a fraction of it, then I'm better off not having it at all.

I can put myself first, even if no one else will.

But I wasn't the only one with pent-up grievances to air.

"There is nothing I can do to defend you from your own bitterness, Princess. Send away all your servants if you want to. This is not about me and what I would or would not do."

He opens a pack and starts throwing clothes into it. My heart fractured into shards of glass. The pieces shred my insides.

"You never even tried to defend us."

I said it softly, but it rang from the stone as loudly as Lorcan's shout.

"Don't you understand that in marrying me, you, too, will be living in a gilded cage, Lorcan? You have to stand apart from your people. Always. I believed you would come inside this castle and make a nest with me. But you didn't understand that a cage isn't only confinement. It's also protection. You left it open to any predator that wants to come in."

Lorcan didn't meet my eye.

"I'm not talking about Skía. I know you can spot those. You don't know how to say no to women. You didn't when Raina was in love with you. When she essentially proposed marriage, you accepted her dagger and pretended nothing had happened. Afterward, she felt embarrassed and devastated that you barely acknowledged the importance of her gift. That's no way to treat a friend."

He has no more practice in these matters than I do. We are so achingly alike. None of this should be happening.

"I need you to protect *yourself*. It's not right that you use me as a shield. Undoubtedly, Norah is painting me as jealous and unfair, poisoning the entire castle against me. I did this once as an example of what you should have been doing all summer, if you wanted to win my trust."

He slung the pack over his shoulder.

"Where are you going?" I asked, panicking.

"I couldn't win your trust. So, I'm making good on our agreement, and leaving." He strode toward the doorway. "Willingly."

At the door, he flung over his shoulder, "I should have known better than to think you, of all people, might have a little faith."

I CRIED ALONE in our rooms—mine alone, now—until Palla came in for bed. She looked around and asked, "Where is your knight?"

Not Lorcan. My knight. There is one person in all of

Auralia who holds me in higher esteem than the man I will not be marrying, and I love her as my own.

"He's gone away for a while, sweetheart."

She looked at me for a long time. I had no reserves, could do nothing but wait while she took in my red-rimmed eyes and red-tipped nose. Palla got her stone knife out from beneath her pillow and brought it to my bed. Then she crawled into the covers and said, "I will guard you, Princess."

I took her knife and set it on the bedside table. "No, Palla. I guard you."

My foster daughter slept soundly in the bed I'd shared with Lorcan the night before. A comfort to me in his absence. I lay beside her and didn't sleep at all.

In the morning, I rose early and donned a plain white dress that had been hanging in the wardrobe upon my return, without explanation. I don't know who acquired it. Probably Norah. I went to the sanctuary with its empty reflecting pool and pockmarked statute of the Goddess. I stood in the center. I did not kneel.

I studied the statue's features in silence for a quarter-hour. Then I turned on my heel and left without uttering a single syllable of prayer.

The priests and priestesses, who'd assembled at the castle to reestablish order, gaped after me, aghast.

Let them.

CHAPTER TWENTY-SEVEN

With Lorcan gone, I asked Tahra to accompany me to the Mountain Folk's territory to welcome Scarlett. I was surprised she'd stayed behind, after Lorcan left, though I didn't have the energy to consider why.

The trip was a welcome excuse to avoid answering phone calls from Raina and Saskaya. I could plausibly claim poor signal as an excuse not to call them back. Both knew the outline of what had happened and wanted to discuss it, but I couldn't. Not with them.

I was apprehensive about seeing Scarlett again. For one thing, she hasn't seen me since Scotland. I didn't want to have to explain my physical state. For another, Kenton's death loomed between us like a canyon I didn't know how to bridge.

It wound up being nothing.

"You look great! When did you get muscles?" Scarlett squealed when she leaped off the bow of the boat that had brought her to the northern beachhead. "Also, your homeland is fucking terrifying, Zosia. Is that lava?"

"The Mountain of Fire is an active volcano." I shrugged. "The elevation is high enough that it's usually surrounded by cloud cover, and yeah, seeing the lava flow is intimidating."

"Quite honestly, it looks like the entrance to hell."

"Okay, sure, I guess I could see that from a Christian perspective. We don't really do underworlds and damnation here. Your soul not ascending to the firmament with your ancestors is the worst fate we can dish out. Auralians tend not to be big on punishment."

"No, seriously. This place is scary."

I laughed for the first time in days. "It's not. Wait until you see the interior. Hope you're up for a good hike."

The entire island is a protective cage around the welcoming interior, the rock rising like menacing ribs from the sea to protect Auralia's vulnerable heart.

"Zosia?" Scarlett asked hesitantly. "Where's Lorcan?"

I swallowed past the lump in my throat. "Gone."

She was quiet. "Shit."

"We both went through a lot. We're in different places, now." Mustering my atrophied diplomacy skills was like trying to remember how to walk. Nobody knows how to talk circles around the truth better than a trained princess, though.

Except...I'm sick of deflecting. I'm tired of never being myself.

"I'll tell you the whole story when we get home," I promised.

Scarlett was enthralled by every single rock, tree, shrub and person she met during our journey. The stone and metal alloy doors to the domain of the Mountain Folk inspired comparisons to The Lord of the Rings, which made me laugh.

"This place is going to scare the shit out of those rich arseholes who bought themselves a pleasure trip to Auralia," she chortled as we walked along the underground passageway alongside the mining trolleys filled with boxes of our old life.

"It will certainly be an unforgettable experience."

"Have you thought about inviting a reporter along? Maybe National Geographic would send a photographer?"

It's a good suggestion. One of many details that slipped by me in the avalanche of everyday work. I need an assistant. Palla isn't old enough. Tahra is busy keeping the new guard on track now that Lorcan has flounced off to Goddess knows where. (Masika, most likely.) After Norah, I've been wary of being assigned a new chambermaid, much less one who would have access to the details of our Treasury, the condescending indifference and rejection from international aid agencies, or my own personal struggles. I let maids come in once a day to clean, but apart from that, it's just Palla and me.

I urgently need a proper Treasurer and castle manager. Rya would be ideal, but having broken with her son for good, I can't see her accepting my hastily made offer to come and work with me from last summer. Still. I should call her. Try to find out if she's seen Lorcan. Part of me dreads to ask, but not knowing isn't any easier. Did he go back to Tenáho and marry Masika, or not?

No longer my concern, but I'm preoccupied with the question anyway.

It was late when we arrived back at the castle. Scarlett was knackered, so I let her settle into the prepared guest quarters while porters brought our boxes from school into my parents' royal apartments for safekeeping. Apart from airing them out, my father's rooms are untouched. Located at the back of the castle for maximum privacy and security, not far from the adapted nursery I'm living in, they were relatively undamaged from the year of Sentinel blasts. I simply haven't had the heart, or the time, to confront what I might find in there.

The next day, Scarlett toured the castle with me in the morning. In the afternoon, we went into The Walled City to inspect the new piping system. New buildings were rising rapidly on the worker's chosen plots. Several enterprising souls had decided to build inns with taverns to house the workers and their families. It was starting to look like a proper town again.

Ifran showed Scarlett how, in the absence of having any stonecutters to work the quarry, he had repurposed the broken rocks from the destroyed buildings to rebuild the exterior wall, the foundations of new houses and shops, and pave the main streets. I translated.

"Here, we are building a new bridge to replace the previous, retractable one."

My heart pinched, remembering our disagreement. One Norah easily exploited, because Lorcan and I were trying to build on such shaky foundations. She sensed my lack of confidence before I even made it over the threshold of our living quarters, and ruthlessly went after what she wanted in a way that only I would see. Had I listened to Raina, Lorcan might still be here with me, but we would still be trying to shore up a relationship built on sand.

Scarlett pretended fascination with the design of the new bridge, currently being constructed with a scaffold over the once-raging moat. With the hydroelectric system functioning again, the churning turbines siphoned off enough of the waterfall and river's energy to return it to a gentle roar.

He'd even found a way to lift the dragon statues out of the moat. They will grace the entrance to my castle for another few centuries, at least.

The past, made new. Not forgotten, never the same again, but in some ways, better. Like me.

Like him.

But not us. Some things broken in the war can't be mended or remade.

Scarlett and I shared our midday meal on the broken balcony outside my rooms, with Palla and her ever-present knife.

"Is everyone here this fierce?" Scarlett asked, eyeing the grave-faced little girl who stared at her across a table laden with baked fish, wild rice, and greens. The threat in Palla's eyes was unmistakable in any language: hurt the princess, and I'll slit your throat.

"The survivors are." I patted the girl's hand reassuringly. She scowled. "If you look up on the broken tower there, you'll see her foster brother, Bennet, hanging around the guards."

Scarlett craned her neck. "He looks so young."

"Fourteen. Desperate to join the guard as soon as he's old enough." I smiled. "Education, first."

Palla, spying Bennet, waved. For a moment, she looked like an ordinary child.

"Oh! Before I forget. You asked me to bring you these." Scarlett brought out a bag with three boxes inside. "Converse. Size 36, in red, blue, and black."

I felt as though I'd been punched in the solar plexus. My gift for Arya. Tears made my vision swim.

"Zosh? Are you okay?"

I shook my head. Palla's chair scraped on stone. She put her thin arms around my neck from behind, and it was what I needed to get control of the sudden burst of emotion.

"I'm sorry. It's been a hard summer." I pulled Palla into my lap and began feeding her.

"Want to talk about it?"

Scarlett's gentle invitation had the same effect that Dr. Wen's had, months ago in Trissau. I spoke for a long time, letting it all out—every sordid detail about Bashir, the devastating loss when Lorcan pretended he didn't remember me, my fleeting happiness when he did, and my profound sense of betrayal when I found out Lorcan had been lying about everything. How we both tried to find a way forward together, only to fall apart under the slightest pressure when we returned to the castle.

"If I'd presented myself with more confidence, Scarlett, Norah's gossip wouldn't have found such an eager audience. She was only able to rattle me because...because in trying to prove his loyalty to me, Lorcan made me feel as though the only thing he wanted from me was the title. To be made king."

I sniffed and rubbed tears away. "In retrospect, maybe I misunderstood his purpose in refusing me. He was trying to demonstrate respect, but I didn't want that. I mean, I do want that, of course, but when he did nothing to manage all the adoration coming at him, I felt neither respected nor desired." I shifted and pulled a plate of food closer to Palla. "He had me up on a pedestal when all I wanted was to be a normal woman with him, but Lorcan never treated me like one."

"Oh, Zosh. That man has wanted you so badly and for so long." Scarlett patted my hand. "I can't imagine him ever treating you like some random girl he'd fu—" She cast a worried glance at Palla.

"She doesn't speak English. It's fine. We'll have to be more careful at River Bend, though."

"I still can't believe you kidnapped Hallie and her sister."

"I didn't. They, and their cousin, Cyrus, asked to come with us." I tried for a smile, which came out watery. "It was probably foolish, but you know how Lorcan is when people need help."

She smiled fondly into the distance. "A knight through and through. God, this stuff is so fascinating. You're all like living fairy tales."

"Without the happy ending." I sighed. I stroked Palla's thin back through her shirt. Her bony bottom was digging painfully into my even bonier legs.

"The story isn't over yet."

Which, I supposed was true enough. It hadn't worked out with Lorcan, but that didn't mean I had to continue concealing my true self from the world. I had my cage, and I could lock the world out when I needed to protect myself.

Or, I could leave it and venture out into the world, alone. If I died while out and about conducting my business, living my life, then at least I would join my ancestors having *lived*.

AFTER LUNCH, we went into my parents' apartments to sort through the contents of the boxes in privacy.

"Are you sure you don't want to send this to his family?" Scarlett asked, her palm flat on Kenton's cardboard crate, her pale face a shade paler than usual. I hope she brought sunscreen. Auralian sun will fry her the way it does Raina.

I shook my head. "Can't. They're dead."

"All of them?"

"Kenton's family led the last stand at Nansier. If not for them, the pirates would have made it all the way to the Mountain Folk, and if Keryn's people hadn't been able to turn them back, they'd have controlled both access points into the country. The province was essentially depopulated that night, but they did it. They sacrificed everything." A smile ghosted over my mouth. "The few remaining residents are charging a fortune for lumber. I can't blame them. It's our only source of wood. Ifran, as you saw, is having to get creative about repurposing—"

"Zosia?" Scarlett interrupted. It's her turn to cry.

"Yes?"

"I don't care about Ifran's tree problem."

I squeezed her shoulders and stood with her as she took a deep breath and opened Kenton's box. All she would ever have of the life they planned together, the one they weren't quite ready to claim. Silently, Scarlett removed his backpack, his books, the folded stacks of clothing. The archery set tucked along the side. She chuckled sadly and tried to put the string on the bow.

"He was so strong." Sniffling, Scarlett wiped her nose with a sleeve. "I always laugh now, when I read about skinny fantasy heroines with their bows. It takes so much upper body strength to shoot one of these."

She lowered the weapon and crumpled. Fell apart. I stood there trying to figure out what I should do, until it occurred to me, I could embrace her.

"Keep it. All of it," I whispered when her sobs subsided. "He would have wanted you to have it."

"I have nowhere to keep a bow and arrows. I don't even have a permanent home. I sold everything before I took the internship in New York. I was kind of hoping that maybe...if you needed a diplomat with a few connections and not a lot of experience, maybe you'd consider letting me stay here. I'll do anything I can to help."

I needed an assistant I trusted, and it seemed one had just volunteered.

"If you don't mind getting paid in the worst-performing currency in the world, I'd love it if you stayed on, Scarlett."

"Thanks. Kenton always promised to show me his home when it was safe to visit. Being here makes me feel as though I'm still close to him."

We went through the rest of the boxes, setting two aside. Raina's and Lorcan's sat untouched. Raina's will travel to River Bend with Scarlett and our foreign visitors, when they arrived, while Lorcan's...I didn't know whether he would ever come and claim it. In leaving me, has he walked away from his entire past?

My heart ached. I missed him. I knew I didn't deserve to ask him to come back, and that even if he did, we would probably confront the same disharmony that drove us apart this time. But I hadn't stopped loving him just because he wasn't here. Even death couldn't change that bedrock.

What was he doing, now?

I had no way to know, but there was one person I could ask—assuming I could summon the courage to call Rya.

FLOWER

CHAPTER TWENTY-EIGHT

The German tech billionaire and his Canadian wife arrived with three children in tow. Despite the fact that our auction had only included four tickets and a week, I didn't balk when they asked to bring their youngest child, age thirteen. I also invited them to stay an extra week, so they could complete a full circuit of the island's interior, similar to the route Lorcan and I took earlier in the summer.

The one sticking point wound up being a silly detail I never once considered until Mr. Knauss asked when they had to go through customs. By then, we were already having dinner at the castle.

"I was looking forward to showing off my Auralian stamp," his wife pouted. We'd defaulted to English, the one language we all shared.

"I, uh, will have to see if I can find one. Our passport office burned down during the war, and we haven't had a chance to reorder supplies."

Reorder supplies, from where? Arya's paper shop? I wasn't born, the first time my parents went abroad. I don't know how they jumped through all the hoops to get that set up. A passport was just something I had, from birth, unlike most of my people. Until it was lost the night of the invasion.

The next morning, after my new daily ritual of staring down the goddess statue for a quarter of an hour, I ransacked my father's study and then his private rooms in search of anything that might function as a passport stamp. I eventually found a prototype in a locked drawer.

We never opened to outsiders, and thus the stamp never made it to the official passport office that burned. Triumphantly, I went to mark their booklets, only to realize that I had no ink pad.

Shit. Now, what?

I texted Saskaya for advice.

You have one of those vials of energy liquid, right? The dark blue kind that glows, not the diluted version? It works as ink, in a pinch.

After searching through the few items Lorcan had left behind, I found one. The Knauss family posed with me while I stamped their passports with the faintly-glowing substance, imprinting a deep violet celestia symbol on paper.

It soaked through to three sheets. Oops.

"Dramatic," Mrs. Knauss said tightly.

"Sorry. We're still working out the formula." I tried to spin it. "You're the only five people in the world with a stamp like that."

"Six," Scarlett seized the stamp and pressed a symbol into her own. The Knauss family did not look best pleased with having to share their unique stamps, but since she was acting as one of their translators for the trip, they chose the better part of valor and didn't complain.

"Do cell phones not work here? I keep trying to text pictures to my boyfriend, and he's not getting anything I send," the eldest Knauss child said.

"There isn't a single tower in the entire country. You'll be issued a satellite phone, but you'll have to share it. We don't have very many."

"Share?" Mrs. Knauss said, almost comically put out. This is clearly not the multimillion-euro luxury visit with princesses she'd envisioned.

"You can still take pictures with your own phones and send them once you get home," I answered, firmly. Lorcan still had one. I could have called him any time during the past couple of weeks. I wouldn't have known what to say.

I'm sorry I never gave you a chance? Gave *us* a chance?

That wasn't the kind of thing you just picked up a phone to chat about. If he would even answer a call from me.

The night before the Knauss family, and Scarlett, were set to depart for River Bend, Tahra came to visit while Palla and I were on the terrace reading stories. The girl still didn't say much, but she liked to listen when I read to her, mostly histories of Auralia. They made my heart squeeze to think of how Lorcan loved this lore. Would have liked reading to her.

"Highness."

Tahra dropped to one knee. It was, frankly, a ridiculous gesture. I was dressed in loose Čovari trousers and a stained white shirt, barefoot, looking anything but regal. The Knauss family is disappointed by my lack of formality. They wanted the beautiful girl in the jade gown.

She doesn't exist anymore. They get me. Zosia. Reluctant princess, soon-to-be-queen slowly getting a handle on ruling. I'm all that's left.

"There's no need for that, Tahra." I motioned for her to rise. She did, fluidly, in that Čovari way that reminded me so much of Cata and Lorcan. Ever since he flounced, Tahra has led the new guards. There wasn't anyone else ready to take it on. I'm surprised, and gratified, that she stayed on. She chose me over him, which I wouldn't have expected.

"Are you ready to leave tomorrow with the tour?" I asked.

It's become a huge undertaking. Mrs. Knauss doesn't ride horses, so my one functional coach has been pressed into service to convey her and their luggage. Hallie, Laila, and Cyrus have decided to join the tour, along with Scarlett and Arya, serving as official documentarians using a fancy digital camera I found in Cata's box of belongings. My last-minute request for reporters yielded an invitation to submit photos we'd taken ourselves. DIY press, I suppose.

Honestly, I was looking forward to getting all these guests out of my castle, and out of my hair, so I could focus on my newest idea: building a greenhouse to supplement the castle kitchens through the winter. We could use old horse troughs to make raised beds, since the horses are still mostly running wild.

"I'm packed. The route is planned; Bennet will manage the guards remaining at the castle." She smiled tightly. A joke; she deputized him to watch over me and Palla in her absence, but he was not to get in the real guards' way. "We are ready, Highness."

"Excellent. I have the satellite phones ready for you."

Tahra nodded, seemed about to speak, then glanced at the little girl on my lap. I sighed. She wanted a private word, probably to ask whether I had heard from Lorcan. Not a subject I wished to discuss with her, or anyone else, for that matter. I missed him terribly, but that heartbreak was mine to nurse as I saw fit. No one else got a say.

"Palla, time to wash up for bed," I said, nudging her off my thighs. She slipped her stone dagger off the table and glared at my new head guard as she went inside. My fierce little foster daughter. "Is there something else, Tahra?"

"I came to apologize."

"For what?" I asked, confused.

"I never meant to come between you and Lorcan, Highness. I thought I could make him want me if I could make him see that you didn't care about him as much as I do. But I was wrong."

"Have you heard from him, since he left?" I asked quietly. Holding my breath.

"No. Not one word. He didn't even say goodbye." Her blue eyes welled with tears. The poor girl's had her heart broken, too. "I never meant any disrespect toward you, Highness. I know I wasn't...I didn't cover myself in glory this summer." She swallowed. "Lorcan was almost this mythical person. Saskaya was gone for nearly half a year, looking after him and helping him recover. She left her own son to tend to him. He was Lady Cata's chosen protégé, even though he wasn't Čovari."

Lorcan was always *something special*.

Tahra dashed tears from her cheeks. I can't think of a time when I've ever seen a Čovari weep. I learned my own stoicism from Cata. I waited, listening.

"Raghnall needed help with the baby, and I wasn't old enough to go fight yet, so they told me to hang back and guard the village if needed. For months, I heard all about his adventures. His victories. He was cunning, quick and strong, while I was stuck at home changing diapers." She sighed. "I'll never forget when he first came back. It was like meeting a legend."

Tahra's romantic reminiscing was starting to grate on my nerves.

"Yes, he earned his reputation," I said, evenly, wondering whether she would catch the hint of sourness in my tone. "You fell in love with him."

Along with half the women in Auralia.

As though she'd heard my unspoken thought, Tahra inhaled and stood straighter. "Like everyone did. I wanted to be special to him, and I didn't want to see that his heart already belonged to you. I've been as bad as that gossipy Norah was. I heard her spreading rumors about you being unhappy together. I knew it wasn't true, but I didn't say anything because I hoped that if the engagement failed, Lorcan would finally see me. But he didn't. He left without even saying goodbye."

I held her eye. I know he was aware that she had her heart set on him. But he breezed out of the castle like a shadow in the night, as if he'd never been here at all, taking half of the castle's hearts with him. Including mine.

She gave a shuddery sigh. Like that, her tears were gone.

"I've been a fool, though. If I'd gotten what I wanted, I would have to leave behind everything that makes me Čovari. We don't allow anyone to marry into the tribe. The elders won't change the rule. Not even for him," Tahra inhaled before continuing. "Which makes my resentment this summer even more childish. What I understand now is that he didn't want you because you were a princess. He wanted you despite it."

A lovely sentiment, if only it were true.

If it is true... then I threw away the thing I wanted most, with both hands.

"It's all right, Tahra." I couldn't keep the weariness out of my voice. The fucktangular love pentagram might be history, but there will always be opportunities to construct a new one. "You're hardly the first. It's not your fault. I'm sorry he was callous about your feelings."

"He seems to have a habit of that," she said, darkly. I suppressed a smile, recognizing the sound of a bruised heart. I wondered what rumors haunted Lorcan's name now that he's walked out on the last Auralian princess. Left her heartbroken, the way he left so many other women. Public opinion shifts like a flock of starlings in flight.

Right then, I decided I didn't care. I knew the truth about Lorcan's devotion to me. There will always be rumors, and would-be seducers, and naysayers. The only reason Norah got a wedge between us in a matter of days, is that doubt and suspicion had fractured our relationship before we even arrived. All she did was exploit cracks that were already there.

"It's all right, Tahra," I repeated. Her chin bobbed once. She took her leave.

Out of nowhere, I remembered that day when my mother was still alive and I saw him from her coach. Climbing onto the seat to look back at him. I'm sure he doesn't, anymore. We were only children, then.

I remember the feeling as clearly as I remember his eyes. An electric awareness, a compulsion, like fate whispering in my ear. *You are meant to know this person.*

He was there to help me through this life of leadership I never wanted.

I don't believe in omens, or fate. I am a scientist. If a phenomenon exists and you can document it, there is a rational explanation. You might not have found it yet, but it's there.

Lorcan has been a cornerstone of my life ever since I was a child. His father protecting my mother. Cata protecting him; protecting me. Concealing him until she felt the time was right for us to meet. Him protecting me to the brink of death; me returning the favor.

He is a phenomenon that has existed in my life for as long as I can remember. There doesn't have to be a rational explanation for the way I need him. It simply is.

Tahra's bruised heart will heal with time.

I have to find out whether there's still a chance to mend my own.

"Princess?"

Palla's voice called me into the castle, away from the soft rush of waterfall and river, birdsong and the faint noises of The Walled City below.

CHAPTER TWENTY-NINE

It was edging into mid-September, about six weeks before my coronation, when I rode out from the castle alone. I've never been outside the gates unaccompanied before, unless you count the night I led the Sentinels away from Marsh Hollow.

I didn't need to go far. Coming over the gentle rise of a hill, I found Lorcan waiting for me at the top near a rock ledge and a stand of trees.

"What are you doing outside the castle without an escort?" he called, appearing out of nowhere on a rocky outcropping. His voice soothed my every ragged nerve. I halted my mount, staring. Drinking in the sight of him.

"Looking for you."

Lorcan's hair was longer than ever, tied back in a messy queue. His eyes were flinty gray-blue under the bright sky. His simple traveler's clothes are clean, though I suspect he's been out here in the wild these many weeks, wandering and living rough. Watching over me from afar, clearly, or he wouldn't have found me so quickly. There's a haunted aspect to him in the gray beneath his eyes and the hard set to his mouth.

I don't know if we can move past the mistakes we've both made since our reunion. I know I have to try one last time.

If I don't, I'm consigning both of us to a lifetime of loneliness. We'll be forever trapped in the past. It's worth one last attempt at reconciliation, and even if it doesn't work out, I can make peace with myself knowing I tried. It remains to be seen whether he welcomes one more chance to work things out with me. I can't fault him for being done for good.

"Well?" he said when I didn't elaborate. "You found me."

"And now I have an escort." I smiled. I can't be sad about seeing him again. He remained stone-faced. "Ride with me for a while?"

I know he'll have a horse somewhere close by. I waited. Sure enough, after a tense stare-down, he disappeared behind the rocks, returning with his saddled gray mare.

We continued in silence down the road, past the fork leading to Čovari Village, without stopping. I might still be underweight, but after a summer of physical exertion, I'm stronger now than I ever was before. My endurance is better than ever.

We stayed the night at an inn in a small hamlet and pressed onward at daybreak. The innkeeper and the other guests noted us and undoubtedly set the local tongues wagging. Let them. There is nothing either of us can do to stop it.

Like the last time we made this trek together, we avoided towns where possible, choosing the harder, direct path up to the meadow, where the snows pile high in winter. We took the same route, now, only without pausing to examine every creature that crossed our path. Lorcan didn't ask questions, and I didn't make conversation either. There will be time for that later.

We reached the snowfield at dusk on the second day. I found a little spot near the creek for the horses to drink from and set about making a fire nearby. I got pretty good at this during my year in the Gaol, though it's been some time since I needed to stack kindling and strike sparks from flint and steel. Soon there was a small blaze. I set out my bedroll not far from the fire and dragged a log closer, to use as a seat. Lorcan watched me do this without interfering.

"What are we doing here, Princess?"

I slanted a look at him. "Annual pilgrimage."

That was all I needed to say. His jaw tightened. The last time we were here, I nearly froze to death.

"I don't intend to go into the water this time. The Goddess can hear my prayers from land." I ducked my head and stared into the dancing flames. "If she hears them at all."

"She—" He bit off the argument mid-syllable and jerked his gaze away.

I raised one eyebrow at him, but said nothing. I'm never going to believe in the goddess I supposedly represent, and that's fine. I don't have to. My people need their faith to get through this period of darkness; I am humbled to be the one bearing that light for them. It doesn't matter what I, personally, believe. It's enough that I respect theirs. His. It's enough that he respects my disbelief.

We can work from a place of mutual respect.

Is it enough, though?

I can't even begin to broach that question. I thought I

could, but every time I've tried to start a discussion during this journey, I choked on the words. I look at him and freeze up. I'm ashamed of the way I clung to my bitterness. He was right about that. I don't know how to convince him to trust me again, now that I'm working hard to let it go.

To my surprise, he's the one that initiates the conversation. He set up a small pot of rice, dried, salted fish and peas to steam over the fire, then added—from where, I don't know—butter and herbs. Lorcan and food. I can't stop the small smile, nor do I want to.

"I don't know how to begin apologizing," he said to the fire.

"You've apologized enough. You lost your memory, and when you woke up, we pushed you into fighting before you were ready. We were desperate. It's not an excuse for how we treated you."

I said we even though I wasn't there, because I know Raina and Saskaya did it to save me. I'd have made the same decision. The country was in desperate straits and we needed him on any terms we could get him. Making difficult choices is what it means to be queen.

Difficult choices are just part of being human. The stakes are a bit higher for me, but that aspect of my life is completely normal.

"We all did things we never thought we were capable of. I certainly did."

"Not that, Zosia." He made a face. "I mean the rest. What I did this summer. The way I tried to back you into a corner to get the outcome I wanted. I knew better. You warned me it wasn't going to work."

The fire popped. I poked at it with a stick, waiting.

"I didn't back down, because I've gotten away with

being an overconfident little shit for most of my life. The way I've acted this summer..."

He trailed off for a moment before continuing.

"I've had a degree of freedom you were never granted. You were right to resent me for the unfairness of that. You were right to resent all of us for how we treated you in the name of preserving the crown. Everyone who should have helped you let you down. Including me.

"I thought I was being so clever by using your desires to press you into marrying me." He sighed. "I, of all people, know perfectly well that the one thing guaranteed to make you resist tooth and nail, is to limit your choices instead of trusting to decide for yourself. I used to get so angry with your father every time he did that to you. Yet I was so terrified of losing you for good that I made the same stupid mistake. I couldn't have chosen a surer way to set us up for failure if I'd tried."

"It almost worked," I pointed out.

"It would have been a disaster if it had," Lorcan extended one leg toward the fire, his back to a rock. Relaxed, yet alert.

"True. I doubt we would have lasted the year if we'd gone through with it." We've always fought hard, both with and for one another. Whether in silence or with words, Lorcan and I have sparked from the moment we met. Cata knew it. The question was always how to direct it, how to tamp down the volatility lest we scorch everything around us. That was something we could only figure out for ourselves. We did, for a while. But we couldn't make it last beyond Tenáho.

"Zosia. I tried to coerce you into giving me what I wanted without giving you what you needed. Fuck." When

I glance over, Lorcan scrubs his face with one hand. I've never seen him look this defeated and remorseful. "No wonder you didn't believe me when I swore there would never be anyone else. I treated you like a prize to be won, a challenge to conquer. Not as a person I loved as an equal. I can't blame you for believing that once we married, I would feel entitled to carry on however I wished, because that's exactly what I'd been doing for months. I've had weeks to think about where I went wrong, and the answer is, everywhere."

It's finally the apology I needed to hear from him.

"Which is why I ask, Princess, what the fuck we're doing out here together."

I inhaled deeply and let it out. Now I have to figure out how to make my own. I don't know if I have the courage to let go of the past, but I'm trying to, because I do not want to live there anymore. "An annual pilgrimage seems like a good way to reset, don't you think? Together?"

I held out my hand. Lorcan took it, squeezed, and brought it to his lips. He pressed a kiss to the center of my palm. He didn't let go.

WE SLEPT SEPARATELY but near one another. In the early dawn I awakened to find Lorcan's arm heavy around my waist and his breath ghosting over my neck. I smiled and went back to sleep.

When I awoke again, there was daylight and he had breakfast on the fire. Baked apples with butter on hard bread. It's the best thing I've tasted in a long time.

After we broke camp, we climbed. Up and up and up, scrambling over rocks. The air grew thin and cold. September is late to be doing this. The sun is warm overhead. I peel off layers. Jacket rolled and put into my pack. Wool tunic tied around my waist until we paused for lunch and I started to shiver.

"Promise you won't go in?" Lorcan asks uneasily when the ice spikes come into view around noon. His words came out in puffs of white.

"I won't go in. I'm done freezing myself half to death for a deity that doesn't" —I caught myself in time— "listen." To Lorcan, she exists, although I think our last visit here tested his belief.

Once again, I went behind a rock to change into a warm white gown, gold jewelry, and sandals. Lorcan started a fire in the same spot as last time. Again, I can't figure out how he found fuel so quickly. Perhaps he packed it in, knowing our destination. He's resourceful that way.

I started down the narrow path to the shrine. When he didn't immediately follow, I looked back at him. "Well? Aren't you coming?"

"Me?"

Gods, he's adorable. I couldn't hide my grin. "Yes, you. Did you think I was the only one who needed to atone?"

"No, of course not... I—" He glanced down at his rough clothing.

"She doesn't care how you're dressed. It's a formality for me. Just come." I held out my hand. Lorcan took it without hesitation.

Inside the shrine, we stepped out onto the platform with the steps leading down into the freezing pool. Her effigy rose above us, tall and sparkling in the bright light reflected from the pond below.

"What now?" he asked.

"I usually recite the prayers I was taught when I was young."

Lorcan seemed to be entranced by the statue. "Have you ever tried talking to her?"

I resisted the urge to respond with a snarky, *it's a statue; it can't hear me*. "No."

"Auralia looks friendly enough. She is, after all, supposed to be your ancestor."

"I always thought so. Until I had to go into the water." I'm shivering now, despite the lined woolen gown I chose and the soft linen shift beneath. "Then she seemed more like a frigid bitch, if I may be perfectly honest."

Laughter crinkled the corners of his eyes. "She's a statue, Zosia."

I bit my lower lip to keep from grinning. We are the same in so many ways. His gaze locked on my mouth for a moment, and suddenly, I was no longer cold.

Lorcan's restless gaze skimmed the horseshoe of the ice-enclosed shrine. "Go on. What would you say to her? If you believed in her?" I rolled my eyes. His mouth quirked up. "Humor me, Princess."

"Fine." It is, after all, why we came here. I studied the effigy. Her perfect features are a study in fierce kindness. I see in her my mother. My aunts. My grandmother. This is a woman who is not afraid to love deeply. A warrior who would fight to the death to protect the land that's borne her name for five millennia.

She is me.

"I've been a pretty shitty living vessel for the past eleven years," I began. Lorcan groaned. I elbowed him in the ribs. "Hey, this was your idea."

He tried to contain his laughter, with little success. Barely suppressed chuckles keep erupting out of him.

"Anyway, moving on." I mock-glared at him from the corner of my eye. "It's not as though you've given me a lot to work with. You freeze my ass off every time I come here; you don't exactly deliver in our time of crisis, so forgive me if I'm a bit of a skeptic where you're concerned."

"A bit of a skeptic?"

"Shh. You'll get your turn."

"This is probably the worst prayer she's heard in five thousand years—"

"I'm going to push you into the damn pond if you interrupt me again." I pretended to push him. Lorcan indulged me by pretending I moved him an inch forward.

"Isn't swearing in front of the Goddess considered blasphemy?"

"It's not if it's the Goddesses' living avatar on earth doing the cussing," I said in a sweet, singsong voice, through clenched teeth, trying very hard not to let him see my smile. Failing. "Are you going to let me finish?"

He sobered. Barely. "Continue, Highness."

I cast him the haughtiest look I could summon. "As I was saying, Auralia, we have a rocky relationship. But I'm here. I will always be here. Every year. Except for last year, I think we can all agree those were exceptional circumstances."

"Agreed."

"Will you shut up?"

He was laughing again.

"Moving on. Again. I will say there's one thing you've done for me, for which I am profoundly grateful." Finally, Lorcan sobered for real. "You did send me the most annoying, if talented, knight protector in the history of Auralia. Without him, the country wouldn't exist today. I wouldn't be alive. For all his faults—and he has a few, the worst being how obnoxiously perfect he was before we broke his head—"

"You didn't break me."

"Let. Me. Finish." I addressed the statue again. "As I was saying, my knight protector was the most irritatingly perfect man ever to exist before he got bashed in the head while defending me, and while I regret breaking your perfect gift, I actually like him a bit better this way. It's like that Japanese art where you put broken pottery back together with gold—"

"Kintsugi," Lorcan supplied.

"That's it. Thank you. He's like that. Broken in places, but mended, and more beautiful for it. His imperfections make me feel a little less like a failure myself."

A sharp inhalation beside me. My ears and my cheeks burned, either from the cold and wind or embarrassment. That swooping sensation in my stomach. "I'm hoping, Auralia, that you can perform a similar trick with us. Because he and I have made a hash of this on every level. I mostly blame you for making us both such bullheaded, stubborn individuals who never want to compromise. You should have made one of us more inclined to settle. Preferably him, of course."

I was rewarded with an elbow to my ribs. I giggled.

"The one upside of us both being mulish and as contrary as the day is long is that we are both still here. Cracks and all. If there's a way to mend us, I'm hoping we get one more chance to figure this out."

All summer, we've been trying to rebuild gatehouses, instead of using the pieces to construct a new bridge between our past and future selves. I've been as guilty as he in this.

A moment of silence passed.

"Are you done?"

"I'm done. Your turn."

I waited with bated breath to hear what Lorcan would say.

CHAPTER THIRTY

He's quiet for a moment, gazing reverently up to the effigy's beneficent face. His brown traveler's tunic makes his eyes as blue as the sky above.

"I think your vessel is perfect in every way. I always have. You couldn't have asked for a more devoted living avatar. Even though she doubts you, Zosia shows up. She does everything you ask her to, and more. She's an excellent princess, and will be a great queen."

Oh, shit, I think I'm going to cry. Damn him. Every time I come to this place, my eyelashes wind up stuck together for one blasted reason or another. So uncomfortable.

"I have no right to ask for another chance, yet here I am, because I am arrogant enough to want her even though I don't deserve her. I failed her on every conceivable level. When I awoke after my injury, I should have spent every moment working to free her. I didn't. I left her to starve. Others tried to warn me. I didn't listen. It took me too long to remember her. Worse, I let others take what should have been rightfully hers, because I'd forgotten who I was. I still pursued her because there is no one else for me, even though I'd debased myself beyond being worthy of her." He swallowed.

"What I wanted to show Zosia this summer, was that I didn't want to clip her wings. I wanted to help her fly. But she doesn't need that. She'll do whatever she needs to for this country, with or without me. I need her to feel whole. Living without her these past few weeks has been awful. I didn't know where to go or how to get back to her, when I truly didn't deserve her forgiveness. The thought of losing her made me cling tighter than I should have.

"I worry that she'll shortchange herself in service to the crown, the way she would have done with Prince Sohrab. I couldn't stand by and let it happen, though I knew I didn't deserve her, and I couldn't figure out how to tell her what I'd done without losing her all over again."

I flashed him a grin and got a lopsided one in return. "I should have known she was too smart for me to fool her." He faced the statue again, studying her.

"Saying yes to Zosia meant nothing when I couldn't say no to anyone else. Rather than look in a mirror, I stormed out when I didn't get what I wanted. I tried to dictate terms to a queen, and she was right not to let me get away with it."

I know there's more to it than that. He left because in staying, he was hurting other people. Norah unwittingly stomped on the wounded part of him that will always feel guilty for getting a maid fired. We'll both have to get better at managing our emotions, especially since it's hard to tell where my trauma stops and his begins. But we can be gentle with one another. That's why we work so much better in private, away from public pressure. It was why

Norah's intrusion into our privacy cracked us apart so easily.

I squeezed his hand lightly.

"If we do get a chance to fix this, I will do everything in my power to protect her, encourage her, and keep her safe. Including protecting myself. I will never leave Zosia's side."

I squeezed his hand. We looked at one another, then at the pool.

"I'm not going in there," I said.

"Yeah, that's a bad idea. We'd both freeze to death."

"Guess we're done here, then."

Lorcan cocked his head. "Have you ever explored this area?"

"A little. Killing time while my father and the priests left me to freeze. Why?"

He scanned the shrine without responding. Inscrutable as ever. Auralia doesn't work miracles; I can say that with certainty.

"I want to check something out." Lorcan strode around the edge of the pool and nimbly leaped over the meter-wide gap between the main platform and the rivulet feeding out of the pond. He reached back to help me over it as well. "It looks like there might have been a bridge here, once. See the marks?"

Once he showed me where to look, I can't understand how I missed seeing them before. "Yes. Like small pylons for an ice bridge that melted or was washed away."

He nodded. "Let's see what's back here."

We edged forward. Lorcan got ahead of me and slipped between the ice splinters. A passageway opened.

"No fucking way." I exhaled in a cloud of pure astonishment. An optical illusion. Auralia's favorite trick on this island.

From where we stood before, it appeared to be a solid wall. Lorcan spotted the nearly invisible crevice that led to a larger passageway. We pressed on, hand in hand, shielded from the wind by the ice towers. Ice became rock. I can barely make out the marks from axes, worn smooth with time and weather, as we venture carefully down the passageway. My eyes tried to adjust to the rapidly increasing gloom. I stumbled into Lorcan's back. He kept me close as we inched forward.

The passageway curved and opened. Heat blasted my face. I gasped.

"What is this place?"

"No idea." Lorcan stopped, so I pressed close to him. "Am I imagining it, or do the rocks glow?"

"They're glowing." Faint blue light emanated from the solid surface. As my eyes adjust to the dimness, I slowly released Lorcan's arm and move in front of him. He doesn't like this, taking my elbow and trying to hold me back.

"It's okay. Listen." Water. Bubbling water. Steam on our faces. The skin on my hands ached from the sudden heat. "I think this is a hot spring?"

Lorcan exhales with relief. I can hear him trying to restrain his laughter.

"The water is warm...if you believe..."

I can't take it in, I'm so awed by the sight of the glowing rock grotto with impossibly blue water fizzing in a deep pool. "This is what they meant. It was a secret. My mother died before she had a chance to tell me. My father...he..."

"Didn't know. Couldn't have known."

Tears on my cheeks. My mother came here, spent a few hours in a natural spa, thinking and decompressing. Then she came home refreshed and ready to face the world again.

I'm laughing, but I'm crying for the horrors my father put me through in his ignorance. Ten years of near-death experiences in that stupid frozen pond nobody was ever supposed to set foot in. It's a decoy. To protect this.

It's easy to imagine my sisters and aunts and grandmothers making this trek once a year. A reunion of wise women meeting to share knowledge and friendship in secret, handing it down through the ages. To outsiders, they looked like tough women who could withstand hours in a frozen pond and come out beaming. In reality, they were having a spa day together.

In my imagination I hear voices. Laughter echoing from rocks. Women strategizing and parceling out the burdens of leadership so it doesn't fall too heavily on any one individual.

Until me. I didn't get lucky. No aunts. No grandmother. No mother to show me the way. No sisters to share the load. Only I went into the frozen pond. Because I was a child who didn't know better, trying to do her best with what little information she'd been given.

"Oh, Zosia. I'm so fucking sorry."

So much history and knowledge have been lost. Lorcan held me while I cried. I've missed my mother on every level, every day, for so long, but never more than in this moment. What a loss, for all of us.

"You're probably the only man who's set foot here in thousands of years," I observed, once I'd calmed.

He grinned lopsidedly. "The Goddess likes me."

I know he means me. He wouldn't be here without me, nor would I have found this without him—that jump is a big gap even for me as an adult; I never would have tried to cross it on my own as a child who simply wanted the misery of being cold to end. It's still an arrogant thing to say, so I smacked his shoulder lightly and was rewarded with a kiss. Our first kiss since this whole reunion started. I sank into it, wrapping my arm around his neck, opening to him without prompting. When we pulled back, both a little breathless, Lorcan tilted his head and asked, "Shall we go in?"

"I guess that's what we're supposed to do."

We stripped down. I removed my woolen outer gown and sandals, leaving the linen shift in place. Though it will turn transparent in the water, I don't feel ready to be naked in Lorcan's presence quite yet. Lorcan has never been self-conscious about his body, so he went down to his underwear. They hug his ass as lovingly as I'd like to. I was not remotely insulted to note that his semi-hard cock pointed to his hip bone.

Warm water caresses me like five thousand years of love.

I kicked across the pool in delight.

Violet blue. The color is unmistakable. The same as the diluted version that filled Lorcan's tank while he healed. The color of Saskaya's energy ink, only brighter.

Whatever bubbles up from the depths below is tinted with the same stuff that powered the Sentinels, that powers Saskaya's adapted dirt bike engines, and creates the blast from that gun prototype Keryn was testing. It heals. It is power. It is the essence of the Goddess Auralia. It has the potential to save the world, if enough of it exists.

The Sentinels were a warning from the past. *Be careful of how much you rely on technology. Trust in your people first.* One I didn't know how to heed, because I had neither the knowledge nor the power to make a difference.

I do now.

I laughed.

"You were the key."

"What key?" Lorcan, an Olympic-level swimmer, cut through the water toward me. His shoulders are defined by water and archery and the thrust of blades into flesh. I want to run my hands over them. I will, but for now, I was content to observe.

"The key to the gilded cage." How do I explain this? I tried once before, the night we fought and he left.

Lorcan paused beside me, one hand on the stone, legs churning to keep himself afloat. My shift floats around me; if he is a shark, then I am a jellyfish. I kicked away into the center of the pool. I am not an Olympic swimmer. I am merely average in all things physical, but I can accept that. My greatest ambition, after all, has always been to be normal.

"The castle is both a nest and a cage. I can't leave it safely without you. I'll be killed. I want you to live there with me, and I want to be out here, among my people, as much as possible. But to do that, Lorcan, I need you to understand what it is to be a public figure."

He listened, holding onto the side of the pool. I find an outcropping to perch on, submerged from the neck down.

"If you still want that life, Lorcan—and I would not blame you if you turned it down—you need to understand that you'll always have to stand a bit apart from the world. It can be very lonely. You'll have me, of course, but..."

"I can't be as accessible to everyone the way I was this summer," Lorcan finished for me. "Letting Tahra follow me around the way I did, for starters. I set an expectation. If the person closest to you doesn't put you first, why should anyone else?" He shook his head. Water drips down his neck. Droplets traced paths down his chest that I would like to follow with my tongue, but we aren't there yet. "I under-mined you without intending to. Again, no wonder you didn't trust me."

"I did in most ways." Aimlessly, I kicked my feet in the blue water, not paddling, just to feel it.

"Not with anything related to sex." Lorcan's gaze slides to my shoulder and the strap of my linen shift.

"No. I wanted to." Tears burned my eyelids again, but I'm done crying, at least for now. "In fairness, my issues long predate our being together. I've never felt like I get to live in my own body. I belong to everyone but myself. Espe-cially being the last of Auralia's line."

"It's a lot of pressure." Lorcan waited for me to continue. "I know that feeling, a little bit. Of belonging to everyone but yourself."

I shot him a look, and relented when I saw his sincere regret.

"Back in Scotland, when I still thought the only future available to me was to marry for political reasons, I was desperate to claim some positive experience for myself. My mother did. My grandmother was notorious for putting off marriage for years." I smiled faintly. "It's sort of expected, on the theory that young princesses will be more inclined to choose wisely if they're permitted to make a few mistakes first."

"But I got in your way."

I nudged Lorcan's knee with my toe. "You certainly did. And I resented you for it, as you know, especially at first. Not that the few experiences I did get were very positive. It was so frustrating, a feeling worsened by the fact that you kept turning me down."

He nudged me back. "I had my reasons."

"I know. I think I do, anyway." I sucked in a breath and ducked under the water. Putting distance between us. When I popped up a few feet away, Lorcan was watching me. "The first day you were assigned to be my guard. I was furious. You came into my room while I was packing to leave for Royals University." I smile at the memory. "My wardrobe was open. The only things left inside were the white gowns I was obligated to wear—before I had a choice about it. I wanted nothing more than to leave them all behind."

"'See something you like?'" Lorcan smirked. "I remember. That was the day I swore to myself I was going to marry you in a white dress."

"I thought that happened when you were ten," I teased, splashing him.

"True. But that was the day I felt it within my reach."

He lunged at me. I shrieked when he caught me around the waist, my cry bouncing off the rock as he carried me back to the side of the pool.

"That was also the day I swore an oath not to touch you," he said, quietly.

"To a dead king. I still don't understand why you held to it this summer." Actually, I think I do, but I want to hear it from him.

"It was the only leverage I had to get you to say yes. I want this life with you, Zosia." He curls one arm around me and speaks softly against my ear. "I meant it when I said I didn't want to be on the outside looking in. I've had that for years." Pulling back, he adds, "Of course, that's where I went wrong. Trying to coerce you into marriage."

"You're not the only one who got things wrong this summer." I smoothed his hair away from his forehead and traced the line of his scar. "I had this...idea. Not a very good one, I admit. Terrible, if I'm being honest. I briefly thought about getting pregnant—"

Lorcan's arm tightened around me. "Oh gods, yes, Zosia. I love that idea. I've envied Tovian and Raina so much." He exhaled into the crook of my neck. "To have the whole world know I was the one who made you round and happy like that—" His cock bumped my stomach.

I have to tell him; there's no way for us to move forward honestly if I don't. I took his face between my palms.

"I wasn't going to tell you. It was a purely selfish motivation. I was so tired of always feeling alone. I wanted someone for myself. Like Sethi, but a family member I can acknowledge publicly."

He went very still beneath my hands. For a moment, I don't think he breathed. "Did you think I wouldn't figure it out?"

"That was what gave me pause. I couldn't think of a way to conceal it from you, and to do so felt wrong. But then you kept turning me down for sex. It was maddening. By the time we were in Oceanside I realized that I wanted to keep a part of you for myself and the only way to do it was to marry you."

"The real reason she said yes," he laughed lightly, but there's hurt behind his joking.

"There's more, Lorcan." I wriggle out of his grasp and swim away, needing the distance. I don't know how he'll react to this. "Before this summer, I never entertained the idea of having a baby at all. I wouldn't have chosen to be a princess. Being put on a pedestal, always watched, never free to be myself. I don't know if I'll ever want to do that to a little girl."

He took it better than he did my first confession. "I'd

still choose to spend this life with you, Zosia. Even if you decide to let Auralia's line end with you."

Then I was crying again, but not noticeably, thanks to the water and the dim light. I ducked under the water again to get control over my emotions. When I popped up, he was right beside me.

"Zosia," he whispered against my ear. "Let's go home."

CHAPTER THIRTY-ONE

O ur return to the castle went unremarked—to our faces. Whispers along corridors. So many eyes upon us. I exchanged a glance with Lorcan and ignored them.

"You never called off the wedding," he said when we were alone in our temporary apartments. I still haven't been able to bring myself to sort through my parents' belongings in the royal chambers proper. We have a bedroom, a living area, a guards' nook, and a washroom. There's access to a balcony, though only half of it is usable. It's more than enough space for two people.

"Not officially. People knew you'd left. There were rumors you'd gone back to Tenáho to be with Masika." I tried to keep my tone neutral. Rya told me they'd been in touch, but nothing more.

I stripped off my travel-worn clothes. Stacks of paper sat on the table next to the laptop Scarlett had returned to me. Five days away, the work has piled up. Literally. There are account statements and expenses to approve. I can't wait until Rya can come and help me get a handle on the financial situation. I'm good at math—that isn't the issue —the problem is that there is so much money flying out of accounts that I'm worried I'll lose track of the record-keeping and create a mess. I sigh, take a seat at the table and start sorting through them.

Lorcan kissed the top of my head. "I did go back to Tenáho. To sell the cottage."

I glanced up at him. "Sell it?"

"To Masika. She wanted it before I came through and bought the place, but she didn't have enough money and it needed more repairs than she could make. Now that I've fixed the place up, I'm selling it to her at a loss."

"So that's what she was contacting you about. You could have told me."

"It wasn't all she wanted. She proposed to me, before I came to get you from the castle."

My instincts were right. But at least Lorcan appears to have handled it, instead of using me as a shield.

"I'll miss the cottage," I sighed.

"I didn't want to spend time there without you. We could buy a larger house. Or build one, eventually." He stroked the curve of my shoulder. "A summer cottage, to escape from the castle."

A blending of our lives, to the extent possible. "I'd like that."

"I should go and check in with the new guards."

"Go on. I know they'll be glad to have you back. Bennet especially. Tahra's been humoring him by giving him a role, which he earns by doing his lessons." I gestured to the pile before me. "I have plenty to keep me occupied."

"Don't work too hard, Princess." Lorcan kissed my cheek and left me to my paperwork.

For the first time, I didn't feel the impulse to follow him.

Fledgling trust. Wings stretching. I've weighed the potential for a fall against the lure of the sky for long enough.

I lost myself in work for a few hours. The way my father used to, avoiding his lonely, grieving daughter because he didn't know what to do with me. Both of us were locked in our grief, and we both leaned hard on Cata for support, putting her in an impossible position.

One of these days, I'm going to have to go through my father's belongings.

By the time Lorcan returned, I'd changed into soft clothes and was sprawled out on the bed, stomach down, trying to wrestle sums into submission. He was a beaming, sweat-stained wreck.

"Good session?" I asked, chin in hand.

"Tahra's newest recruit has a vicious streak," he explained, rolling up his sleeve to reveal a bruise blooming over his bicep. "I'm out of practice, a bit."

After he cleaned up and changed into loose pants and a threadbare shirt, Lorcan confiscated my computer and relocated it from the bed to the table.

"Hey!"

"Take a break, Princess." He rolled me to my back, pinned my wrists against the counterpane and kissed me breathless, crushing all my papers in the process. I laughed and twisted, but it's useless to resist.

I got one leg around his waist, my heel to his knee. Bucking against him as he pretends to torture me brought my center into contact with his hard length. My laughter faded into a moan. Lorcan's hot breath skimmed over the hollow of my throat. Despite the layers of fabric in between, it feels *so* good.

Slowly, I disengaged, sliding my heel down the back of his and inching up the bed. Lorcan released my wrists, though he didn't get up. We lay there, with him propped on his elbows above me, the question hanging in the air between us.

"I would. If you wanted to."

Have sex with me, he means. That elusive experience I've wanted for so long and with such disastrous results.

But that means asking Lorcan to violate one of his deepest-held values: no knight worthy of the name would deflower a princess without marrying her first. He's walked right up to the edge, yet in the end? It was the one shred of his former honor that he could hold onto, having so thoroughly debased himself.

I hated it, thinking it was a rejection of me. I can't fault him for not being specific about his reasons, though, considering the way I reacted to his honesty with me in Tenáho. Using the truth as a bludgeon when he was vulnerable with me was a cruel thing to do. No wonder he was reluctant to speak truthfully.

"I can wait." I sat up enough to take his face between my palms. "It's only six more weeks." I kissed his forehead, and let him go. There is a risk in waiting. It's one worth taking. "Consider it a wedding gift. Since I have no idea what else to give you."

"You are giving me yourself, Zosia. I don't need anything else." He squeezed me so tight I could hardly breathe. "You're already giving me a literal kingdom."

"Yes, well, be careful what you ask for. Kingdoms are a lot of work. Sort of like giving someone a puppy, only it never grows out of the peeing-on-the-rug stage."

I touched his nose. Joking again, though I'm terrified this will fail yet again.

My pulse picked up as he kissed me, soft and slow like it's the first time all over again. As if we're back in Cata's kitchen. Warm hands skimmed up my ribs beneath my shirt. I wasn't shy when he pulled me into his lap, and his shirt off. Then mine.

Well...that's not completely truthful, but I didn't shy away fearing that I can't compete with women long forgotten. That I'll never be enough to keep him. I always was, even when I couldn't see it.

No, Lorcan's blue eyes were downright worshipful. His hands trembled slightly as he brought them to my breasts, circling the peaks with rough thumbs.

"We can do as much or as little as you want, Zosia," he murmurs against my ear. I felt him buck beneath me.

"I don't know how," I whispered.

He brought me close for an embrace. Skin on skin. I tucked my face into the crook of his neck. Soothing strokes down my back. "You do, Zosia."

I shook my head, dismayed by my own shyness.

"You give amazing hand jobs," Lorcan whispered, "I've been on the receiving end of a few."

I laughed nervously. "I barely know what I'm doing."

"You have a few weeks to get comfortable, Princess. After that, you're on notice." He laid me down and covered me with his body. Letting me take his weight. "We have a lot of wasted time to make up for."

I reminded myself that it's okay to enjoy this; safe to explore. He's not going to leave me feeling more like an object than a person. I'm still more comfortable where he can't see me, though. That isn't going to change overnight.

But we'll keep trying until it does.

SEPTEMBER SLID INTO OCTOBER. Upon their return, the Knauss family spent a few extra days at the castle, beyond the time I had already granted them. I showed them my new indoor garden, though I omitted any mention of its prototype: the mushrooms I cultivated when food began to run out last spring. That phytology class I took in Scotland kept me alive.

They loved meeting Lorcan. It was hard to say who had the biggest crush on him, Mrs. Knauss or the daughter with the boyfriend, who seemed to be abruptly and conveniently out of the picture.

During my absence, Palla returned to her sleeping quarters with Bennet. Tahra treated Lorcan with frosty disdain, which he took in stride.

He began a new habit of cornering me at unexpected moments. It's the way we might have started if there hadn't been princess and knight, watched and bound on all sides by tradition and gossip, if Raina hadn't been a factor at the beginning of our forced proximity. If people hadn't been getting in our way for the entirety of our relationship.

Lorcan seemed determined to block any further interference.

Within a week, it got to the point where I couldn't pass him in the castle halls without my face flaming. Often, he would catch me around the waist and pull me in for a kiss until I tried to wriggle away—his favorite attack if I happen upon him when he's sweaty from training. If I'm busy, he'll glide past me with a light touch on my arm or back. Sometimes, he lets me pass by with little more than a heated exchange of glances that sets my every nerve on high alert. I know he's plotting to pull me into a darkened corner and kiss me—unless I manage to sneak up on him first.

My knowledge of every secret passageway and hidden

nook in this old ruin once saved my life. Now, it gave me a slight advantage over my competitive fiancé. Occasionally, I managed to sneak up on him. A dangerous game; twice, he came close to stabbing me when I caught him off-guard. Quick reflexes had one disadvantage.

Our game of pin-the-princess-to-the-nearest-hard-surface quickly put an end to any lingering rumors that the wedding was only for show.

Otherwise, the days passed in a blur of work. There are priests and priestesses to corral—not many, but someone has to do the honors of conducting our wedding and coronation ceremonies. With no living relative to perform the vows, I asked Rya and Saskaya to share the responsibility.

There were provisions to secure, not only for the annual harvest festival and wedding feast, but for winter, too. Staff to hire. Orphans to try and connect with any remaining family, or provide for if we couldn't locate living relatives. There were a heartbreaking number of the latter.

Scarlett took on an increasing share of administrative work, including everything outward facing. There were a frightening few days when Humayun managed to get our foreign accounts frozen, but that was quickly walked back after the Knauss family posted a zillion photos of themselves with Hallie, Laila, and Cyrus having the time of their lives in Oceanside. It's hard to argue that your daughter has been kidnapped when she's posting selfies about how this place would be paradise, if not for all the sharks.

Lorcan came in one evening to find me falling asleep while trying to rebalance the ledgers. Again. Everything is pinched and stretched. I can only hope Rya's plan to tax vendors and sell licenses at the Autumn Harvest Festival will put enough daels in our coffers to get through the next few months.

"If you're going to work this hard, Zosia, you should at least be working on something that matters."

"Auralia matters, Lorcan. Something you should keep in mind, considering you'll have a new title soon." The one he'll start using soon: King Protector, our equivalent to Prince Consort. It will take getting used to, for both of us.

He kisses me and plucks the ledger from my hands. "Do your schoolwork."

I *pfft*. "I'm never getting that damn degree."

"I will, if you will."

The mattress dipped as he crawled into the bed beside me.

"You don't care about finishing your degree." I did, for I saw it as a means of gaining a measure of respect I didn't have at home. An education was something I would earn on my own merits, as Zosia, not the princess. Me.

What do my personal ambitions matter, now?

"No. But you do." Lorcan smiled gently and brushed a strand of hair away from my face. "We were a team then. If you still want your degree, you should have it. Passing the last few tests wouldn't take much effort."

"Unlike a certain gifted knight, I don't have an eidetic memory. It'll take me longer than it would you. A lot longer." I yawned.

"My memory doesn't really work like that anymore," he conceded.

"Poor baby, having to learn like us mere mortals," I teased, though it's a serious subject. He'll be dealing with the trauma from his head wound for the rest of his life. For someone who spent years pushing away his feelings, not being able to fully control them must be so upsetting. "It would be smarter to focus on finishing the article. At least other people will read it. All ten scholars who might pay attention."

"You know there's a lot more interest in Auralia than there was before the war." He pressed a warm kiss to my forehead. "Come on. I'll help you study."

The thought of returning to political science and comparative religion was not exactly enticing. I hated those subjects. Economics class was all right. Might not be a bad idea to revisit the section on inflationary pressures since my country is facing them right now. Biology and ecology, though—he suffered through those subjects for me.

"You don't want to go back to studying plants. Be honest."

Lorcan pulled a pillow up to rest against. He handed me a marked-up textbook from the bedside table, where it's been sitting, untouched, next to my framed picture of mossy frogs, ever since I unpacked the items Scarlett brought from Scotland. "I don't mind. Seriously. I'll help you."

"We have more important things to think about than my useless academic credentials."

"You never know, Princess, when it might come in handy. We're close. Let's finish what we started?"

This is how, when I should have been courting the international press and arranging for carefully selected journalists to cover our wedding, I ended up re-reading textbooks last cracked when my father and Cata were still alive. Before I knew I had a brother.

My notes are a time capsule. Barely history, yet so far in the past that reading them makes me feel ancient. Not necessarily wise, though. I still have a long way to go before I live up to my name's meaning.

CHAPTER THIRTY-TWO

The night before our wedding, I tried and failed to take my political science exam, twice. The second time the satellite signal dropped out and booted me out of the system, I cursed and threw a pencil at the wall.

My frustration was enough to draw Lorcan's attention.

"Everything okay?" He'd been in the library killing time, waiting for me. This is the last assignment to complete. He's been done for days.

"No. It crashed again."

We have got to get a better internet system in Auralia.

"Is this really how I want to spend the night before my wedding?" I pouted, twining my arms around his neck. "Come on. Don't make me do this again. It's pointless."

Lorcan chuckles. "It's the last step. You can do this."

"I *could* do this, if the internet connection weren't so spotty and I weren't neglecting a thousand other things to take a test for a class that ended a year and a half ago."

He picked me up, which, admittedly, isn't hard for him to do. It puts us at eye level.

"Come upstairs and finish the test. One more time, Zosia."

"Why?"

"Because you want to."

"I don't, actually. Right now, I want to throw the computer out the window."

Lorcan sets me down, brings me in close and strokes my hair. "Finish the test. This is a night to leave the past in the past."

Grumpily, I collected my books and followed him out. Lorcan took the laptop from me. He also scooped up his notebook and pencil case from the table outside the office where he was guarding my time against interference. I assumed he was reading, because Palla had been with him for a while, until Lorcan sent her off with a maid for bedtime. Ever since he's come back, Palla has been more willing to leave her knife under her pillow.

"What have you been working on?" I admit I'm curious. Lorcan hasn't shown me a single drawing since I gave him those pencils. Not one. He's almost as shy about showing off his sketches as I've been about showing my body.

"I'll show you if you take the test."

"For a third time," I sigh.

"How badly do you want to see what I've been working on?" He smirked. I side-eyed my fiancé. "The connection will be better outside of your study. One more time. I won't make you do it again."

"You cannot make me do anything, knight," I reminded him, loftily. "I am your queen."

"Not until tomorrow, you aren't," Lorcan teased.

"Keeping me humble."

"Someone has to." Unlocking our apartment, he dumped the things he was carrying onto the unused guard's bed in the alcove. "I'll make it worth your while, Zosia."

"Fine," I sighed, genuinely frustrated. "One last try." I took my notes and computer out onto the balcony, wrapped in a loose sweater against the evening chill. My fingers were cold by the time I finished and submitted my responses, but it's done, for what it's worth. Assuming I pass, I will have earned my degree, though there's no way for Royals University to mail it to me here in Auralia, and no real reason to want it anymore. I slammed the laptop closed.

Honestly, this is a reminder of everything I once wanted from life and how impossible it has been to attain it. Why did I let Lorcan cajole me into doing this?

I'll never have the time to focus on researching Auralia's unique flora and fauna. Never get to work on isolating the chemical compounds in our medicinal plants. I might have cured cancer. Instead, I'm saddled with the Sisyphean task of keeping this island solvent and independent.

It's easier when I don't focus on what I can't have. Finishing my coursework has been the equivalent of picking a scab off a wound that hasn't healed, and never will. Like so much else in my life.

Lorcan picked up on my mood and took my computer away, again. This time, he put it away and sent me to wash up.

I was still out of sorts when I came to bed a few minutes later to find him sitting against the headboard, with his notebook open on his lap. His hair was damp from the shower he took while I was finishing my test, and he wore a loose, thin shirt. Devastatingly handsome.

"What's this?" I asked, climbing in beside him. I'm in

my usual nightshirt, one I stole from him a few weeks ago, and nothing else.

"Something I've been working on." Lorcan flips open the notebook to an image several pages in.

It's me, in formal regalia, sitting in the box section at the Colosseum that day when I was just seventeen. Five years ago. The first time we ever met, unless you count that moment in my mother's carriage. I stared at his drawing for a long moment. I look like a child, though technically I was of age.

"I've been trying harder to remember," he said, softly. "All of it. Not just the good and bad parts. Everything that's brought us here."

My heart skipped a beat. I edged closer to him, leaning my head on his shoulder. Lorcan turned the page. I gasped, then burst out laughing.

"I got that shirt from Raina, I'll have you know." It's a sketch of me the night we sneaked out in Beijing. My entire back is bare from shoulder to waist except for a long fall of hair, and I'm sliding through a crowd of dancers while half-turning back to him with a come-hither expression. I know full well it was more of a furious glare. "You didn't get my face right, though."

Lorcan chuckled. "I think this version is closer to the truth." He passes me what was apparently an earlier draft. Indeed, I am glaring properly. "But I like this one better."

He tucks it away.

"You must have hated me that evening." I sighed.

"Not at all. The opposite."

"That makes no sense, Lorcan."

He reached over to stroke my cheek. "That was the night I fell head over heels in love with you, Zosia. You were so much more than the stoic princess I thought you were.

Ambitious, brave and unconventional. I hoped that meant, eventually, you might want me. An unconventional choice for a knight protector, much less a king."

"Flatterer." I leaned into his touch, despite my self-consciousness.

"It's been an honor to be your knight, Zosh."

Our lips met softly, sweetly, but far from chastely. There was a hunger to our kiss, barely reined impatience, knowing what tomorrow will bring.

"Show me the rest?" I asked when we parted for breath.

He did. There's me sitting on my balcony in a nightshirt, feet on the railing, bare legs crossed at the ankle. Me on the airplane, gazing idly out the window. Pictures of my back, sitting attentively as I took notes in class. He always sat behind me.

There are sketches of me in Cata's kitchen, and in his kitchen in Tenáho. One of me in the green dress I wore in France, which Lorcan clearly spent some time on. There's me in Ansi clothes with a dragon on my shoulder, her tail looped around my neck for balance, looking properly furious this time. We both laughed. Me on horseback the day I came looking for him.

"They get a lot more explicit after this one," he said. A faint pink tinge creeps over his cheeks.

"Now you have to show me," I curled closer to his side. Lorcan looped one arm around me. My cheeks went from heated to steaming as he showed me the rest of his sketches. They start with us kissing, clothed, and quickly escalated to me, naked, beneath him, on top of him, my breasts exposed.

"You've really got the bedroom eyes technique down pat in this second section," I murmured, trying to think of when I've ever been so embarrassed.

"I had a lot of time to think when I was out in the wild alone," he said, closing the book and handing it to me. "About you. About us. About how I've acted this summer, and since waking up."

Lorcan inches down the bed and rolls onto his side, head propped on one hand. "Zosia, I'm so grateful you gave me one more chance."

As if I weren't embarrassed enough already.

"You were really thinking that about me?" I blurt out, meaning the sex sketches, because of course that's what I would focus on. The corners of his eyes crinkle.

"Constantly."

The heat crawled down my neck and across my chest. Lorcan chased the telltale pink flush with the tip of his finger, trailing down between my breasts. It's not as though we haven't been sharing a bed—not chastely—for the past six weeks, and well before that, too. I still turn shy at the thought of tomorrow night's significance.

"I think about you that way too," I whispered, then instantly wished I could take it back. I don't know why; it's not a secret. When you've had to hold everything in since you were a young child, talking about feelings becomes harder than it should be.

Easier to show than tell.

I scooted down and rolled half on top of him, pushing Lorcan to his back. He didn't hesitate to strip me of my nightshirt. I relieved him of his, too, admiring the play of muscles beneath marked skin. The story of a journey undertaken without fully understanding the import, etched onto his body forever.

To get here, to me.

I love every healed wound. I am humbled by the way my hands catch wherever I touch him. Everywhere except the hard ridge beneath me. I rocked my hips against him. A single layer of fabric between us. I brushed back his hair and bent to kiss the mark left by the wound that came so close to taking him away from me forever.

"One more night, knight," I whispered.

He groaned, clutching my hips and rolling me along his erection. I grabbed the headboard and sucked in a harsh breath as he did it again, harder, nearly hard enough to make me come. I followed the motion. Pressing hard. Not letting up. Lorcan's blue eyes bored into mine, bright slivers beneath a cage of lashes.

The last thing I saw before he flicked his thumb over my clit and brought me down mercilessly. Using my body, racing toward completion, as a tight pulse of pleasure forced a strained moan out of me. My movements would have stuttered had he not kept driving me hard until wetness soaked the cloth between us and we came to a slow, shuddering halt.

Lorcan urged me aside and kicked out of his soiled pants. He pulled me into his arms. Naked, we pressed close together, sharing kisses, sharing breath.

"One more night," I said, again. "You're on notice."

He chuckled sleepily.

"Don't worry, Princess, I'm more than ready."

FRUIT

CHAPTER THIRTY-THREE

I was still mostly asleep when Lorcan rolled out of bed, kissed my cheek and whispered, "See you at the Temple, Princess."

I fell back to sleep. Never been a morning person, not even on the day of my own wedding.

Eventually, one of my new maids ventured into the bedroom to rouse me. From there, the day was a blur of activity with an inordinate amount of time devoted to the grooming processes I tend to neglect when left to my own devices.

"Clever of you to tap Arya and Scarlett as reporters," Rya complimented me during the carriage ride to the Temple Plateau. "Gives my daughter something productive to do."

"That reminds me. Make sure we get pictures of her new Converse. I have an idea." I tapped my lower lip with one finger and scanned the lengthy checklist lying on the vanity table. Ifran was kind enough to have one hauled up here into the vestibule behind the statue of the Goddess.

Right now, our newly minted royal guards were clearing the last of the mourners from the Hall of Ancestors, where a display has been posted for the past week for anyone to come and honor their lost loved ones. Flowers and sketches are piled higher than my head against the mausoleum wall. We finally moved Cata into the square with my parents, and carved all three names on the stone closure. Together for eternity.

I wished they could be with us today. In one sense, they are.

Lorcan and Tovian were using the secret laboratory below to prepare.

Raina didn't come. It's too close to her due date, and she hasn't quite forgiven Lorcan. Or me. Hallie and Laila are here, though.

Birdsong echoes through the nearly-empty Temple. Bright chirps bounce from stone.

Reba came to my chamber carrying a large bag. She hooked the loop over the mirror frame—another temporary installation in the tiny, crowded space. With a slight, nervous smile, she untied the knot and pulled the bag down to reveal the gown inside. I gasped.

"Do you like it?"

"It's beautiful." I gave her pictures and suggestions, but what she's crafted is a perfect blend of modern and traditional Auralian aesthetics. Tiny white pearl buttons trailed down the high back, a nod to Oceanside. Sheer, tight-sleeved lace sleeves ended in a slight bell shape at the wrist —reminiscent of my old white ceremonial gloves, one tradition I don't intend to resurrect. Gold embroidery at the hem and bodice reflected the celestia, as well as motifs from the other provinces. There were jeweled emerald and amethyst violets for my hair, to match the flowers decorating the Temple and my diadem.

Reba passed me a box. "Scarlett sent a wedding gift."

My face flamed when I saw what was inside. She helped me into the underpinnings and a robe, then my new maid, Norah's replacement, arrived to arrange my hair. Scarlett popped in to do my makeup, since I'm woefully out of practice, which gave me a chance to thank her for the lingerie set.

"No need for thanks. I figured you couldn't get La Perla in Auralia. Might be a little big. I had to guess the size."

Birdsong was slowly overtaken by the unmistakable sounds of people filing into the building. While the Temple is stable, the roof won't be fixed until next summer, and the section of broken stone benches had to be cleared out to make room for standing observers.

"Time to dress, Zosia."

I was buttoned into the pristine gown with its billowing skirt. When the diadem is placed on my forehead, I'm as ready as I'll ever be.

I felt strangely calm. Not quite joyful—yet—but not at all nervous. Somber as I contemplated the gravity and significance of the day. I wonder how Lorcan is holding up. I wonder if he, like me, misses Cata.

I wonder if Saskaya and Raghnall brought Sethi with them. I'll have to remember not to acknowledge my only living relative as anything more than a close friend's son.

The priests and priestesses begin to sing. Birds chirped in the background. Their voices swelled and rose on currents of warm air, but my flesh goosepimpled beneath my gown. I shivered. I have the strangest sensation that a thousand ghosts are watching. I don't believe in ghosts. But I do feel the full weight of history as if the hands of my foremothers are carrying me into the future; a lightness in place of crushing weight.

Never knew I had such a superstitious streak.

"It's time." Reba waved me forward.

I can't hide my smile as I come around the broken statue of the goddess. So many faces in a blur below the dais. Only one matters. He's there, on the other side, waiting for me.

Later, I remembered nothing of the ceremony apart from how calm he was and the sound of birds.

Not the blessing.

Not the vows.

Nothing but the way he surveys the crowd before turning to me. A thrill skitters up my spine. I'm handing him everything he ever dreamed of having. I've never felt more powerful in my life.

When he turns to me, Lorcan's eyes are the blue of the hottest fire. The kind that scorches and cleanses, that melts the iciest of hearts.

The kiss incinerates my core.

Applause sends startled wings beating the air above us. This time, I'm the one who's blushing. I don't need a mirror to know it.

One last task—two, if you include opening the wedding banquet and planned three-day bacchanal that will take place in the streets of The Walled City—and then we can go back to our unassuming domestic nest, where I've been happier than I ever imagined possible.

My heart took flight, along with dozens of birds, flapping up and out the open hole in the roof. Goldenwings and finches, even a magpie.

We knelt for the coronation ceremony. The priestess removed my diadem and, after the swearing of an oath to uphold the laws, rule wisely and compassionately, etcetera,

etcetera, replaced it with a more ornate, heavier version. It pressed coldly against my temples. When I rose, Lorcan remained on one knee.

The priestess repeated the oath, with a slight addition to protect the queen and her progeny (if they should happen, not that anyone says it out loud).

I was the one who placed the simple gold and sapphire crown on Lorcan's head. Did I once say I would never choose him? Famous last words.

When he looks up at me, the rest of the world falls away. This would have been so fraught if we'd come to this moment with mistrust. It would have been so much lonelier to confront this responsibility alone.

"Rise," I say. He does, fluidly, holding my gaze. My core clenches. *Finally, finally, finally.*

The corners of Lorcan's mouth curl up. He can read exactly what I'm thinking. Moreover, he's not inscrutable to me anymore. I can read him, too.

He took my hand, and we turned to face the crowd. I couldn't help but glance over at him again, wondering if he remembered that day a lifetime ago when we stood behind my father at Midwinter with hidden, clasped hands. Lorcan was already looking at me. He squeezed my hand.

He remembers.

Then we were sweeping down the steps and out the aisle. Even I, who have made this trek on at least a quarterly basis since I was old enough to walk, was taken aback by the sheer number of people who traveled to be here today. The ruined roof and damaged walls had the singular advantage of enabling people outside to see the ceremony. They've been through so much. This ceremony gave them closure on a painful past and hope for the future.

I'm almost proud of myself for making it happen. It's worth it to see so much joy.

We descended the carved stone staircase, down through the darkness, with knights stationed at each landing. This would be an ideal place for an attack. Lorcan's hand-picked guards were to follow us down and keep us safe during the ride back to the castle. He handed me into the waiting coach, hastily repainted after the trip with the Knauss family.

"How does it feel?" I asked Lorcan as soon as we were in motion. For an answer, he pulled me into a soft, lingering kiss. My fingers brushed the edge of his new crown.

"Humbling," he says. "It's a bit surreal."

"For me, too." I traced his lower lip, then sat up and pulled the curtain back from the window to look at the crowds along the roadside. "I can't believe how many people showed up."

"They believe in you, Zosia. In us." He edged closer to me.

I sensed the slightest change in him, from relaxed to tense, a split second before Lorcan yanked me down onto the seat. Glass shattered. Wood splinters rained down on us as a heavy object crashed through the coach where my head had been.

"Fuck," he muttered, rolling off me and throwing the carriage door open. "Stay here."

"Wait!" Damn them, the Skía ruin everything—but they will *not* ruin this hard-won day. I'll kill them myself.

Lorcan had a blade out, flashing in the sun. He was already halfway through the crowd, which parted for him like water. The perpetrator, a grim-faced young man in plain travelers' clothes, kicked at the newly-minted king. Not an hour wed, yet he's out here proving that no harm will ever come to his queen. I can't help but admire that, but Lorcan shouldn't have to fight on his wedding day. He's not meant to be a killer. That part of his life is behind him.

The skirmish was over almost before it began. The would-be gang member soon thrashed in the grip of two men. Lorcan slid Raina's Italian stiletto out of its sheath and pressed the point to the attacker's throat above his bobbing Adam's apple. Seconds ticked by.

Don't do it. I won't contradict his first call as my co-ruler, no matter how much I don't want him to do this. I'm done with all the death.

Lorcan sheathed his weapon and walked away. I released a long exhale of relief.

"Take him to the Gaol," he called back over his shoulder.

"Your first wise decision as king," I said teasingly. But it's no use. The attack set off every protective instinct he's ever honed. His expression was granite when he returned to my side and took my wrist the way he's only done on a few occasions. He dragged me toward a two-wheeled carriage ahead, glass shards shaking out of my gown with every step.

"Get in, Zosia."

I let him push me into the seat, wondering why he chose this small, open vehicle when there are other closed vehicles he could have commandeered. I had my answer when he took the reins from the driver and set the horses galloping alongside the rest of the parade vehicles. Mounted guards formed a wall ahead and behind us.

"Lorcan. Stop."

He barely glanced at me, too preoccupied with getting me to safety to listen. I was too busy trying to keep my skirt from blowing around to attempt reasoning with him. When he gets like this, nothing will stop him until the threat is gone.

There are likely other Skía recruits scattered amongst the crowd. It wasn't lost on me that the instant I peered out the window, a vicious circular blade came crashing toward my head.

He anticipated this, and prepared well, but no one, even an assassin as talented as he is, can account for every possibility. There are more people in attendance than anyone predicted.

My heart bled when he said, grimly, "I won't fail you the way my father failed your mother."

"I know you won't."

Why doesn't history ever stay in the past?

Because it lives with us, within us, shaping our lives from the moment we take our first breath. I was wrong to think I could run away from it. Lorcan always understood that better than I did.

But we are not powerless over our legacies.

People scattered and dove as we came roaring up the cobblestone streets of The Walled City.

"Lorcan. Don't kill anyone."

He hauled back on the reins. The foaming horses slowed. They barely stopped before we tumbled out of the vehicle and darted over the replacement drawbridge into the castle, my skirt a sail behind us. Lorcan led me into a secret passageway, turning so fast I tripped over my dress. He caught me, picked me up and carried me up the stairs.

"This is an interesting twist on tradition," I said, still not getting through to him. I'm not even sure he'll catch the reference, in his current state of distress. Forcing reluctant brides over the threshold isn't something that has ever been tolerated in our matriarchal society.

"How can you joke about this, Zosia?" Lorcan set me down in the guard's antechamber of our living quarters. He's hardly out of breath. Must be nice to be that physically fit; I'm the one who's panting, and I didn't run upstairs carrying another human being. "You could have died! On our wedding day!"

I took his face between my hands. "I'm still here. Alive." I moved in for a kiss but he pulled away, scowling, and set about slamming shutters and locking every conceivable entrance. Within sixty seconds, the bright, airy space went dark. Only faint late afternoon light seeped in around edges and through hairline cracks. A thin golden shaft fell over his eyes when he finally turned to face me.

The attack came at the worst possible moment. Fear clouded the clear blue of his eyes. His sculpted mouth was a flat line. I can see the tick of his pulse on the side of his throat.

I am not letting anything interfere with my wedding day. Not Skía. Not Lorcan's personal demons. Not my own, either.

Moving slowly, to indicate that I'm not afraid, I stood toe-to-toe with him. First, I removed his crown and tossed it onto the guard's bed. The reminder of how everything changed today can't be helping right now. Then I removed my own. I picked the amethyst flowers out of my short hair, one by one, dropping them onto the plain green bedspread. *Plink. Plink.* Lorcan's gaze darted to the growing pile, then back to me.

Progress.

I held his gaze and gave him one final, direct order.

"Get me out of this dress, Lorcan."

I turned my back to him in a swish of spidersilk. The weight of his gaze falls heavily between my shoulder blades as he examines the long row of tiny pearl buttons marching down my spine. A pulse of need in my abdomen; flutters in my stomach. *Come on, come on.*

I gripped my gown with sweaty palms and moved the fabric of my long skirt to one side. The scuff of leather on travertine as he closed in. I closed my eyes. Finally.

CHAPTER THIRTY-FOUR

S haking hands at my neck, brushing aside my hair. I inhaled. My knees threaten to buckle. *Get me naked already, Lorcan.*

"I can't." His hands fall away. "The buttons are so small, and I'm—they're not—" Lorcan broke off.

I closed my eyes, resting my forehead and palms against the carved oak door. *Auralia's great golden ass, what is it going to take to get laid?*

Twisting as much as I could within the confines of the beautiful gown I was desperate to be free of, I slipped the Italian dagger from his belt. Holding the hilt toward him, I repeated, "Get me out of this dress, Lorcan. Now."

"I don't want to hurt you." Hesitant hands at the base of my neck. Of course, he feels better with a blade in hand. Still a killer, if a reluctant one. A smile tugged at the corners of my mouth. A tiny tearing sound and a slight pull near the base of my neck. The fabric loosened fractionally. "Or ruin your dress."

"Ruin it, Lorcan. Cut the damn thing off if you have to; I can't reach the buttons either."

A harsh inhale from behind me. The atmosphere in the room shifted as he sliced another loop. Rising tension within me as the back of my gown slowly parts down my spine. Cool air interrupted by warm drafts as he worked.

Then he pressed a soft, open-mouthed kiss to the nape of my neck. I moaned quietly as my knees nearly buckled.

"Hands on the door, Princess."

"Queen," I reminded him, obeying instantly. Now, we're getting somewhere.

Lorcan chuckled. The air electrifies. He kissed the nape of my neck again, moving aside my hair. "Keep them there until I say you can move."

I could only nod. When he tells me what he wants me to do, I don't worry I'll get it wrong. I can relax.

If he gets a thrill from bossing me around, even better. We both win.

The rest of the buttons fell quickly until the top of Scarlett's gift from the outside world comes into view: bridal lingerie. Lorcan faltered briefly as he took in the elaborate embroidery and fine lace.

"What is this?" he murmured, low and wondering.

"Keep going and you'll find out." He can't see my shy smile. It's in my voice though. He kept going, faster now, until he reached the last few inches that followed the rise of my ass. Then he stopped. I moved fractionally, trying to turn, but Lorcan covered my hand with his, forcing me to face the wood again, and said gruffly, "I'm not done yet."

"The dress will come off now," I protested.

"I'm. Not. Done." He kissed my back between my shoulder blades. "Admiring you."

Oh. I swallowed and tried to rein in my impatience as another surge of damp warmth pooled between my thighs. Lorcan went back to work. The silk drooped and cool air wafted over my heated skin. He exhaled harshly. I smiled, knowing what he's discovering: sheer mesh held together with satin ribbon on either side of my hips.

"Now can I turn around?"

I didn't wait for permission. The lace peeled down my arms like a snake shedding its skin. I push it off until the heavy gown puddled around my ankles. I turned to face him and stepped out of it, advancing on him as he took in the full ensemble—strapless corset, garters, stockings with wide, disbelieving eyes. Until that moment, I was nervous, unsure he'd like it despite Scarlett's assurances. The blue of his eyes is a thin sapphire ring around his blown pupils.

Two steps, and he was on me, shoving me hard against the wall, bracing against the impact with one forearm behind my head. I clutched at him, trying to get beneath his jacket, locking his mouth to mine.

"Why are you wearing so much clothing?" I complained between kisses.

"Do you need the knife?" he taunted, pinning me to the door with his hips. His erection dug into my stomach. Not where I want it. I get my hands into the space between us and tug furiously at fastenings.

"You're not helping," I grumbled when he nipped and licked his way down my neck, exploring my waist and breasts through the sheer top with warm, deft hands. At last, I got the buttons on his placket open—no help from him—and shoved it down his shoulders. Lorcan reared back long enough to strip his shirt off over his head.

Hot hands stroked down my flanks, tracing the lines of the garters to the tops of my thigh-high stockings.

"Gods," Lorcan breathed into my neck. "Can you wear this every day?"

I huffed a laugh. "You're supposed to be taking them off. Remember?"

He brought his hand beneath me and slipped it inside the edge of my panties, dipping into the soaking wet silk.

"Fuck, Zosia."

"*Pleeease,*" I begged through gritted teeth, rocking my hips forward. He slid two fingers inside me to the knuckle. No resistance. A choked sob, whether from him or from me, I didn't know. Or care.

I clutched at his shoulders, his hair, scrabbling and panting as he worked me. The crest hit fast and hard. Lorcan breathed into the crook of my neck while I clenched around him, taking me through it, making it last.

When it's done, we both exhaled in a long, shuddering sigh. Lorcan withdrew his hand from my panties and sucked his fingers clean with half-closed eyes and a low groan. Shocked, I covered my mouth with one hand, then lunged at him for a kiss. We both stumbled, his back hitting bare stone, while I snaked my hand down between our fronts, unfastened his trousers and finally got inside to palm his cock.

Lorcan gently removed me. "Not against the wall. Not after you've been so patient, Princess. We do this properly."

"Queen," I reminded him, not that it matters. Princess has been my nickname for almost as long as it's been a title.

"Goddess."

"Am not."

"Face the wall, Zosia."

"Again?" I whined. He covers my hands with his and whispers, "Don't you dare move."

I stay where he's placed me when he moves away, tamping down my impatience.

The touch of cold steel high on the backs of my thighs

made me shiver. My mouth fell open as he sliced the stockings straight down my leg all the way to my ankle, first the left, then the right.

"I thought you liked the lingerie," I gasped, airlessly.

"I do. Wear it later. Tonight, I want all of you."

He tugged confidently at the tiny hooks of the garter. No longer unsteady with unspent adrenaline. They fell away, taking the damaged stockings down with them. The corset falls next.

Turning, I launched myself at him. Lorcan grinned against my mouth as he caught me. There's a bed right here, but of course he bypassed it. Always letting the perfect be the enemy of the good, this man.

"We can move the crowns," I pleaded when he tugged me toward the bedroom. Lorcan's grin was pure wickedness.

"Ten steps, Princess. You can make it."

I'm not sure, honestly.

We did, in a tangle of kisses and laughter, with Lorcan losing the rest of his clothes along the way. We landed on the bed. I scrambled back, urging him along until he's on top of me, propped on his elbows. He takes my face between his hands.

"Zosia, I just want to say—"

I groan. "Lorcan. I don't need speeches. I need you to fuck me. Immediately."

He drops his forehead to mine, his shoulders shaking with laughter. "I love you."

"Great. Same. Let's have sex."

He kisses my forehead. Then, finally, he pushed back, peeled down the last scrap of clothing and settled himself between my thighs. I tilted my hips up, seeking. My mouth fell open in a silent cry at the intrusion. In and in. Deeper than I thought possible. So right—despite my internal organs being rearranged—and so, so good.

"Okay?" he gasps against my temple. A tremor wracks his body.

"Yes."

I know this isn't all there is to it, but I wasn't sure what to do next. I lay beneath him, taking his weight, stroking him from neck to firm, tight buttocks, squeezing gently. Lorcan muttered an incoherent curse against my temple. A roll of muscle from neck to thighs as he withdrew. I whimpered in protest.

He comes in again, slow and relentless. I shifted my legs wider. Again. Taking him in from everywhere. His eyes are bright and slitted beneath dark lashes. It's too much, and not enough. My vision shuttered. He retreated again, and I whined in complaint, trying to pull him back—and then it clicked. On the next stroke, I moved with him. Lorcan grunted softly and pulled my leg higher on his waist.

Pressure builds with each slick slide. This is amazing. I can't believe he made me go without this for so long. It's the opposite of alone, a connection so intense it electrifies every nerve in my body. Lighting me up from the inside.

I caught another glimpse of him as we moved. Sweat sheened his skin, with a droplet collected at his temple. I licked and tasted salt. He shudders. His hips jerked hard, and I gasped. I can make him react, too.

He redoubled his efforts. Slow and gentle turned frantic and needy, until I swear he swelled even larger inside me. Pushing me to my very limits. I screwed my eyes closed, lost the rhythm, and stiffened, exhaling a ragged cry. Lorcan made a sound—half-curse, half groan, a fragment of my name—driving hard into me.

This was an entirely new feeling. My abdomen pulsed

in waves that rolled up through my stomach, down my thighs, crushing the air out of my lungs. It went on, and on, for what felt like forever, until it began to fade and it wasn't nearly long enough. I collapsed, limp, against the pillow.

I skimmed my thumb along Lorcan's cheek and felt the tear trickle down into my palm. His arms tightened around me. I tangled my fingers in his hair as he slumped, pressing me into the covers with all his weight. I'm too spent to do more than hold him to me and sink into this languorous sensation of complete togetherness, wondering how I ever lived without it.

CHAPTER THIRTY-FIVE

H ours later, after more sex and a long sleep in one another's arms, we awoke ravenous for something other than connection. Neither of us had eaten since the early morning. Lorcan sent me off to bathe while he called for a tray from the kitchens and took it out onto the balcony, moving the chairs to observe the revelry in the town below. We never opened the ceremony.

Make your people happy.

In choosing happiness for ourselves, we did.

I went to stand at the stone railing with Lorcan pressed behind me, arms around my waist.

"They started the party without us," I said, pretending to pout.

"As long as everyone has fun." He kissed my head. "I have." I squeezed his hand. My body aches sweetly in places I didn't know existed. His gaze scans the bright fires and lamp lights. "I had no idea what I was asking for all those years ago."

"Well, you were only ten."

"You know about that?" He shook his head. "I

remember—vividly—how small you were next to your mother. You kept turning to wave and smile at everyone. You were pure sunlight. I couldn't stop staring. The queen kept trying to get you to sit still, but you—"

"Wouldn't," I finished for him. I was a normal, wiggly little girl.

"You remember?" Lorcan's skepticism is warranted. I hardly ever talk about my childhood. The good parts were too painful to dwell upon. So much of what came after my mother's death was misery. My father tried. There was love, but there wasn't a lot of warmth between us.

"Seeing you that day? Yes. I didn't think you did. There was a boy in the crowd with bright blue eyes. I remember being fascinated by him as we drove by. My mother was so annoyed when I got onto the seat on my knees, facing backward, to wave at you."

Lorcan squeezed my arm.

"My mum pointed out my father, but I hardly saw him. I was looking at you. She asked what I was thinking, staring so rudely, and I foolishly told her, 'I'm going to marry Princess Zosia.' Got a severe reprimand for my impertinence." He grinned at the memory. "Deservedly."

"And here you are. Surveying your domain."

He turned me within the circle of his arms and took my face between his hands.

"It was never about that, Zosia." He stroked my cheek with his thumb. "It was always about you. From the first. You were wrong in Tenáho; if you'd been a girl from the village, I never would have left to chase after a princess. I should never have let you believe otherwise. I wish I'd told you from the beginning."

"You'd have been removed from my service if you had." I smiled gently. He traces my lower lip with his thumb. I rested my hands on his waist, admiring, as I always do. Running my thumb over the ridge of scar tissue on his abdomen.

"Not this summer, I wouldn't have." He pulls me into an embrace. "I should have told you everything."

"Neither of us is exactly accustomed to speaking openly, from the heart," I mumbled into his shoulder. "Let's both of us try to do that a bit more? At least here, when we're alone."

He runs his fingers through my hair. "Would you really have done it? Had a baby and not told me?"

I didn't want to say it, but there's no avoiding it. "Yes. I think so. Again, every idea I had to conceal a pregnancy from you seemed unlikely to work, and you weren't going to give me the opportunity anyway."

"True." He holds me hard. "But would you have done it? Hidden it from me, if you could have?"

That's a different question. "Probably. I wanted to keep some part of you so badly, and I was so tired of feeling alone in the world."

He went very still.

"I'm used to having to choose between bad options, Lorcan. I am rarely presented with good ones."

"I know." His arms tightened around my shoulders as he murmured against my temple, "I will never give you a reason to doubt me again, Zosia."

Of all the vows and oaths we've spoken today, this is the one that hits me hardest. I sighed into the crook of his neck. "Nor I, you."

OUR NEST of private bliss lasted for as long as the wedding feast—three days—and then it was back to work. In between lolling about in bed, we ventured into The Walled City to dance in the streets, me in the white embroidered dress from Tenáho, which Rya had brought with her when she and Arya moved to the castle.

But the honeymoon was far from over.

During one particularly heated discussion with Ifran and a woman insisting she is granted her family's lot prior to the war to build her new shop—hardly unreasonable, but that lot had already been doled out as part of Saskaya's payment plan last summer; none of the other solutions I offered would suffice—my patience hung by a thread.

Lorcan came over, took me by the arm, and said, "Excuse me, I need to fuck my wife."

Blood rushed to my face. My ears burned with embarrassment. Not that it's any great secret, how the royal newlyweds can't keep their hands off one another. Still, it was a bit much.

He pulled aside a tattered tapestry. The stairway behind it once led to my old room. Now there's a gaping hole midway up, covered with boards. The cloth hung over the entrance is partly to deter people from coming up here and partly to cut down on drafts as late fall sets in.

Conveniently, there's a window with a deep enough ledge to perch on while Lorcan pushes aside my skirt and takes me hard and fast. Cold from the thick glass seeped through the wool at my back, a welcome counterpoint to the sweaty heat and friction. My cries echoed from the stone.

"What brought this on?" I asked, breathless and teasing, when we were finished.

"I missed you."

"It's been five hours since you left." I can't stop giggling. I love these surprise attacks. He essentially spent the six weeks before our wedding training me to be aroused at the mere sight of him. Brilliant strategist, using his powers for (my) good. "You don't have to get up so early every day. Try sleeping in once in a while."

He touched his forehead to mine. "Too much to do."

"Tell me about it." We fixed our clothing. "I cannot believe you said that," I laughed in between kisses as we exited the stairway.

"What?"

I repeat his exact words.

"You misheard. I said 'I need to talk to my wife.'" Lorcan slung one arm around my shoulders. "You have one thing on your mind, Zosia."

"That makes two of us."

"True. We should plan a proper holiday. Back to Ocean-side, since we can't go off-island until we get our passport situation sorted out." We lingered, reluctant to part ways again, clinging to this stolen moment in the middle of the day. A vacation does sound nice. I still haven't recovered fully, though Saskaya and Raina aren't badgering me about it anymore. Lorcan and I have been working our asses off for months. The press from the Knauss family's trip was positively fawning. From my favorite clipping:

For a country on the brink of ruin only months ago, Auralia is rebounding fast. Led by a young princess whose initial missteps led to international condemnation, few believed the country could find its footing at all, much less re-establish gover- nance, jump-start its economy and provide for the many orphaned children from the year-long battle. Princess Zosia Auralian is wise beyond her years and down-to-earth in her approach to leadership. Meeting her feels like visiting an old

*friend who just happens to live in a tumbledown old castle in the
most beautiful country imaginable.*

Cata would be so proud.

"You just want to visit the Ansi again," I said loftily,
tilting my chin upward. "Play with paint."

Lorcan raised one eyebrow, and even though my body is
still soft and hot from being with him, I wouldn't mind
going again. He has that much of an effect on me. Always
has. I don't stand a chance of resisting him; I never did.

"And you don't?"

Surrender is much more rewarding, anyway.

I bit my lower lip. "After Midwinter? We can take Scarlett to see Raina and Tovian's baby, and head south from
there."

"Let's do it. Get you out of the castle." He kisses my
forehead. "A princess isn't meant to be caged; she needs to
stretch her wings."

"Queen," I reminded him, not that it matters. It's sweet.
My heart thrummed steadily in my chest as I inhaled his
scent, reluctant to let him go even for a few hours.

THE DOWNSIDE of being married to Lorcan was that it
became infinitely more difficult to make him blush,
whereas I found myself blushing constantly.

That icy demeanor I thought I had perfected? Gone. I
can only summon it with great effort, and never when he's
nearby.

"How are you this cute?" Scarlett asked, holding out her
phone. The images of our wedding and the interior of
Auralia have lit the outside world on fire with curiosity.

"Auraliaphilia" was the word of the year, which...I don't know how to feel about it.

I'm glad we have no plans to return to the outside world yet, and are limiting our entry visas for next year to fifty, half of which are reserved for scholars. One of our guests snapped a picture of Big Ada and now I'm fielding hundreds of requests every day begging me to issue a permit to study dragons, from every country in the world.

I really need to hire someone to manage the flood of supplicants. Scarlett is a capable diplomat and communications manager, but we're only two people. We sold the remaining visas at auction with the proceeds funding the Treasury; not a day goes by when some rich asshole isn't pinging my private email begging to be granted entry. (Thanks, Knauss family, for sharing that information.) Some have requested to become citizens. I doubt they'd be so keen on the idea if they knew I would tax the living shit out of billionaires for the privilege of moving here.

Other pressing matters include finalizing plans and permits for redeveloping The Walled City. Shopkeepers have eagerly petitioned for the right to build.

Where to put housing? A school? Where to put green space and community buildings? How best to encourage growth without creating a sprawling mess? What about the other cities and villages in need of repairs?

Ifran, already overworked, is trying to contract with woodcutters in the Timberlands to provide enough raw wood to start building more permanent structures beginning in the spring. Keryn's people are using the volcano's heat to make bricks. Transportation remains cumbersome and slow.

Decision after decision, all of it impacted by the tallied receipts from the wedding celebration. Under Rya's firm hand, the Treasury situation is starting to shape up. Still, it will be a great relief when our finances aren't a constantly shifting puzzle of competing priorities.

Hidden within the avalanche of emails was a brief one I nearly missed. A response from the head of branding at Converse. Reba's stockpile of damaged spidersilk velvet in Cannavale? Sold, to manufacture a limited-edition sneaker, with a cut of the sales coming to us.

Who could have predicted that when an eighteen-year-old princess's impulse purchase of cheap shoes in a shop in Beijing would eventually inspire a solution to my country's solvency problem?

It's a good reminder to me that Auralia has a great deal to offer the world. We do best when we don't discount our own value. The way I used to do to myself.

Now, I just have to do that same trick thousands of times with equal success, every day, until I die. But I don't have to do it all alone.

With so much activity to fill our days, months passed in the blink of an eye. Before I knew it, I was writing the Midwinter speech. Lorcan, sitting beside me in our now-shared study, wasn't drawing filthy pictures of me, for once. He likes to tuck them into my pocket for me to find during the day, so I know what to expect at night.

Mostly, though, he just likes passing me dirty notes and watching me blush.

Gods, I adore him.

"What are you working on?" I asked when I could no longer contain my curiosity.

"The article."

"Article..." I have to search my memory. "For the journal?"

He nodded. "It's the last bit of unfinished business from before. The editors are keen to capitalize on Auraliaphilia."

"I truly despise that word."

"What, you don't enjoy being a global celebrity?" Lorcan teased.

"It's not just me, my King." You can tell which part of the study is mine by the mess of papers, and which part is Lorcan's, with neatly piled stacks and well-organized books next to his laptop. I nudged a clipping over to him. It's a fawning profile of "the warrior king and his philosopher queen."

Not that they bothered to get our power structure right.

"Here's what I was thinking might work as a vision statement," he said, putting his computer on top of the clipping. A pink tinge touched his cheeks. Ha! Score one for Zosia. Finally. "An outline."

I quickly scanned through his ideas. "This is much better than anything I've come up with."

It isn't as though I haven't tried to finish the article. Last summer, we were still at odds and I didn't have much confidence in anything I was doing. Then, it fell to the wayside after our wedding. If Lorcan hadn't taken the initiative to finish it, no doubt it would still be languishing at the bottom of my to-do list. The pressure of putting all your hopes for the future down in print for the world to read and dissect is terrifying.

But he's never let fear hold him back.

I sat on his lap and started editing his document. Lorcan watched over my shoulder, gently working his hand under the hem of my loose sweater. I ignore him as best I can while typing a few paragraphs. Then I shifted my weight to give him a better view of the screen. He stroked my stomach and nuzzled my shoulder, reading what I had hastily composed from his outline.

"You're not making it easy to type," I complained as he moved lower, hands inside my waistband. "Or think."

My scheming husband chuckled. "It's good. I like the three-phase strategy."

"Yeah?"

"Breaking it down is helpful." He withdrew his hand from my clothing and hugged me around the waist as I sat crosswise on his thighs, reading what I added to his outline. "'We have three distinct populations to attend to: the elderly who have lost family members and will need support as they age, widows and single women, some of whom have or want families, and a sizable group of orphans. Plus, we desperately need laborers. We have to factor in the cultural differences between the different tribes and ensure that no one group is disadvantaged. There is fertile ground for discord, if not carefully managed.' Well done, Zosia."

"You're the one who came up with the framework," I pointed out, playing idly with the hair at the nape of his neck.

"We're a good team." His hand went back under my shirt, and the mood shifted. I slammed the laptop lid closed, then adjusted so I'm straddling him.

"Take a break?" I asked, looping my arms around his broad shoulders and bending down to kiss him. The bulge of his cock lengthens and rises beneath me. Lorcan had my shirt off in seconds. His hot, hot mouth devours me, licking the peaks of my nipples before sucking them between his teeth.

A knock at the door interrupted us. Lorcan pinned my

arms behind my back and kissed me hard, preventing me from calling out or getting up to answer.

They knocked again, then left us in peace.

"We're not done discussing the paper," he whispered.

"We're not discussing the paper," I pointed out. Lorcan's wicked grin did wonderful things to my insides. I forget, sometimes, that I can tell people to wait. My husband likes to remind me, usually by asking if I know what's even sexier than having a princess begging for him. (Answer: a queen.)

In other words, he guards my time as well as he guards my safety.

"You know, this is all I thought about the entire time we were writing the first draft." He nipped my throat and ground against me to demonstrate.

You're enjoying this, aren't you?

Yes.

The memory still incinerates me, three years later. I ruffled his hair, trying and failing to summon mock anger. "You tanked my grade as foreplay? Bold move, Lorcan."

"Hey, it worked," he laughed. "Eventually."

I couldn't really disagree.

CHAPTER THIRTY-SIX

My fingers were stiff around the reins and my breath puffed in huge clouds as we rode up the steep road toward River Bend.

"Are we there yet?" Scarlett called out.

"Are you five?" I yelled back.

She gestured at the frosty landscape. "Travel by horseback is not appealing this time of year."

"That's why we avoid it unless we're visiting newborn babies who can't travel." My horse tugged at the reins, trudging with his head hanging down in the vain hope of finding grass poking through the snowdrifts.

"Have you considered trains?" Scarlett asks. "Since you've made clear that cars are out of the question and dirt bikes aren't cutting it."

"Trains," I repeated, wondering why I didn't think of it myself. "Interesting idea." All the advantages of commodity transport without the inherent risks of cars. "The Mountain Folk have them. Small ones, in the mines. If Saskaya and Raghnall could consult designs from the rest of the world,

I'll bet they could develop a system for our complicated terrain…"

My imagination was off and running. More plans. More money. More knowledge needed. It never ends. I never want it to. The challenges are stimulating, and the opportunity to impact Auralian society for generations is both heady and terrifying.

I couldn't replicate my father's hands-off, administrative approach to ruling if I wanted to. Every decision we make is consequential.

Lorcan wasn't into the train idea. "You'd have to blast through some of the best parts of Auralia. Not worth it."

"What if we could devise a workaround, though?"

The train debate lasted the rest of our journey to River Bend. King Myseči was ecstatic to have an excuse to show off his new grandson.

"Look at you," Scarlett laughed on seeing Raina with her newborn, Ravian. We'd settled in and were gathered around the fireplace having tea. "Holding that baby like a natural. Never would have imagined it when we were together in Scotland."

"Indeed, we've come a very long way." Raina smiled, a little sadly, remembering our lost friends. A mournful twinge in my heart. I reminded myself that we carry them with us. Kenton, Cata. My father. History lives with us. Grief never really goes away. We just learn to live with it, over time.

Especially true for Scarlett. She laughs, but she stays because this country is the only part of Kenton she'll ever have, now.

"Are you getting any sleep?" Scarlett asked, reaching for Ravian and settling him into one arm.

"I am," Tovian shrugs. "Raina not so much. He's up every couple of hours wanting to be fed."

"That's how it goes," Lorcan murmured, which leaves me feeling like the only person who knows absolutely nothing about babies. I shot him a raised eyebrow. *Don't get any ideas.*

Raina caught me and bit back a smile. While the others were cooing over Ravian, she leaned over to me. "It's good to see you happy."

"Thank you. I am. I'm glad you and Lorcan have made up."

"Mostly. I accept that he was not acting like his true self when we argued. All of us have been through a lot in the past year, but the two of you, perhaps more than anyone." Raina inclines her head toward her son. "You're not planning to have one?"

"No."

Before the wedding, Lorcan and I both agreed to take contraceptive teas. That way we each have veto power over the issue. Plus, there's less of a chance of an accident happening—even Auralian herbs aren't one hundred percent reliable, and we've been testing their effectiveness for months.

"What are your plans for the winter? Not staying here, I assume?" Tovian asks.

"Heading south to Oceanside. Might stop in to visit Brenica," Lorcan squeezed my knee. My face burned. "We might combine it with bridge inspections, with an eye toward reinforcing them to support the weight of trains."

Since we're headed south, he agreed it would be prudent for me to do some basic, preliminary assessments, in case we change our minds later.

"Trains?" Raina perked up. "You'd have a tough time

getting all the way down to Oceanside, but if you could pull it off, it would be great for the interior. Grasslands District might really benefit."

"It's an idea we're exploring," I told her, reluctant to overcommit without Lorcan's buy-in. I can make an executive decision if I want to, but I try to avoid doing that. Especially around large issues. His reasons are always thoughtful even when I disagree with them.

"You want to hold him?" Scarlett asked Lorcan, who practically lunged at the opportunity, sitting forward with his arms held out. Raina and I exchanged smiles.

"Support his head," Raina reminded him when Ravian flopped a little during the transfer.

"I've got him." Lorcan settled back in his chair with the baby on his chest, stomach-down. Ravian made little gurgling noises and rocked his head back and forth before giving a shuddery sigh and going still.

"Unbelievable." Raina rolled her eyes. "How come his own dad can't put him to sleep that easily?"

Lorcan patted the child's back, smirking. "Babies like me."

"Babies, goddesses, horses—is there any creature on Earth that the Hero of Auralia can't tame?" I teased.

"Took him long enough to win you over," Scarlett observed. I made a vulgar gesture.

"Worth the effort," Lorcan said. His gaze burned through me until I had to look away. Blushing again, I'm sure. I do that a lot nowadays.

I went to crouch behind my husband's chair. Ravian's dark eyes popped open the instant I brushed a fingertip along his forehead.

"You have the longest eyelashes," I murmured. The baby sighed contentedly. Lorcan hiked him a bit higher, looking back at me over Ravian's round little head, his wheat-colored hair tickling Ravian's black curls. His mouth curled upward as his gaze locked on mine. "I think he smiled at me?"

"Probably." Tovian chuckled. "Or passed gas."

Ravian shoved most of his fist into his mouth and made an adorable cooing sound. I dared to stroke his soft little arm with my fingertip.

"Would you like to hold him?" Lorcan offered.

"Me? I don't know how." Sethi was already walking when I met him. I thought he was small, but in retrospect, he seems huge compared to this tiny two-month-old. When we stopped in Čovari Village, my brother was talking up a storm.

"Go on. Try it," Scarlett said, encouragingly.

"Um..." Despite my misgivings, I returned to my chair and let Lorcan pass me the surprisingly heavy, floppy bundle of baby. "I don't know how to do this."

"Support the head!" Raina exclaimed.

"Right!" Panicked, I tried to get him into the same position Scarlett had used. When that made him cry, I tried shifting him to his tummy the way Lorcan held him, nearly dropping him in the process. Lorcan bent over me, rearranging the baby at an angle so he was on his side with his head resting on my shoulder. Ravian calmed instantly.

"How is it that you've never held one before?" Scarlett asks, puzzled.

I shrugged with one shoulder. "Never met one before."

"No cousins?"

I shook my head, though I'm not looking at Scarlett. I was fascinated by the helplessness of the infant in my arms. I can't imagine ever being that blissfully trusting.

The piece I've been missing falls abruptly into place, landing with the weight of destiny.

I don't want a child out of duty.

I want a child because I am the last in a line of women who've loved their daughters since the founding of Auralia.

Whether or not the first queen was a goddess made mortal, is irrelevant. She was strong enough to lead a band of devoted people away from everything they knew, through hostile lands, picking up like-minded followers and leading them into a vast ocean of unknown danger. Her faith and optimism led them to the unlikeliest place imaginable: a rocky spit of land dominated by three mountains, one spitting fire.

A place where women could thrive alongside the men brave enough to work with us, instead of attempting to dominate us.

I am the inheritor of a love that's been handed down from mother to daughter in an unbroken line for five thousand years. Mine is a legacy worth passing on. I will love every bit as fiercely as Auralia herself loved that first princess—and so will her father.

I glanced over at Lorcan. He's watching me, intently, in the way that used to bother me. Gently, he held out one finger. Ravian wrapped tiny fingers around the tip, then attempted to drag it into his mouth.

My king smiles dreamily. The sight constricts my heart.

"He's getting hungry," Raina said, taking back her son. Lorcan stroked my shoulder.

"See? Babies are nice. I remember when Arya was born. I was so excited to have a little sister." He made a rueful face. "Had I known what a pain in the ass she'd turn out to be, I might have reconsidered."

We both laughed. Arya has thrown herself into learning

English, badgering both Scarlett and Hallie for conversational practice. She's determined to study journalism abroad and has even started distributing her own newspaper here at home. It's been surprisingly successful.

The next morning, I made my tea without contraceptive leaves.

Lorcan is still taking his. I can always change my mind.

SHORTLY AFTER OUR visit to the Ansi Village and arrival in Oceanside, I started feeling tired and my breasts ached at the slightest contact.

Lorcan was perplexed as to why I suddenly didn't want to be touched there. I was confused as to how this had happened so quickly. (I mean, I know how it happened—the Ansi painting ritual was definitely a factor.) There was no avoiding the fact that I was pregnant. Early stages, but the onset of nausea confirmed it. Knocked up.

I felt a lot of conflicting ways about it, and as usual, my instinct was to keep it all inside. It's a shock to find out that I could even *get* pregnant, considering my family history. There's a chance I'm still too underweight to carry a baby to term. What if I lose the pregnancy? Miscarriage is common. I knew that from my mother's struggles.

I don't want to get Lorcan's hopes up and then disappoint him. Speaking of whom, *he was supposed to be taking contraceptives.* When the hell did he stop?! Did he stop? Maybe our highly reliable brew conveniently failed?

But if I don't tell him and the worst happens, I would have to go through a miscarriage all alone. I don't want that, either. He'd be hurt if I didn't tell him. We agreed to be honest with one another.

Plus, the longer I try to keep this a secret, the longer I have to keep pretending I'm fine, when I'm too tired to do anything but lay on my back in the sun. Laying on my back is about the right amount of energy expenditure for me.

"You're going to get a sunburn," Lorcan told me, with an edge of annoyance, as his shadow fell over my face. I cracked one eyelid open. His blue eyes were barely visible in the overhang of his hair. They match the color of the sky.

"Mm." I brushed his hair away from my forehead and smiled up at him.

"What's going on with you, Zosia?"

"Tired."

The shadow moved away. He flopped down onto the blanket beside me. "You didn't get out of bed until late."

"Never been a morning person." I shrugged.

"Later than usual, Princess."

"Queen," I reminded him lazily. Lorcan snorted.

"Now you've made it as far as the beach, and you're barely moving. Are you feeling okay?"

"Did you get tired of rock climbing?" I asked sweetly.

"I got tired of rock climbing *alone*." He tugged my limp hand. "Come on, let's swim."

"With sharks?"

"They're not a problem this close to shore and you know it." He rolled up onto his side, propping his head with one hand and frowning at me. "Seriously, Zosh. You've been like this for days."

"Just relaxing."

I grinned. Lorcan wasn't amused.

"Are you sure you're not still sick from the fish?"

Another telltale sign: I developed a sudden reaction to

the taste of seafood. Which is a bit of a problem in a place where seafood is the primary source of sustenance. The night of our arrival, I took two bites of salted cod and threw up.

"No, it's not the fish."

"You just want to lay here with the sun on your face, doing nothing?" he asked, incredulously.

"Is that such a problem?"

"No. It's not like you, though." He reached out to touch my chest, stopped, and pulled back. Probably thinking about how I winced this morning when he tried the same thing.

"Come here." I pulled him down to whisper in his ear. Lorcan's body went stiff and still.

"I...you're sure?"

"As sure as I can be without medical confirmation." I don't try to conceal my grin. "Around next November, if all goes well, we'll have a daughter."

Lorcan rolled onto his back. He stared blankly, wide-eyed, up at the sky. "Holy shit. Why didn't you tell me you were stopping?"

"I was just sort of...testing the idea. I figured I could change my mind." I poked him in the ribs. He flinches. "It never occurred to me you weren't taking them."

He reddened. "I never started."

I groaned.

"You are such a liar!"

"I am not. We said either of us could quit taking them whenever we wanted. Both of us got veto power. Well, I didn't expect you to stop taking them ever, and if you did, I wanted to be ready." He covers me with a tight hug. "I can't believe it. I'm so happy."

"Me too, Lorcan." I wrapped my arms around his neck. "Me too."

EPILOGUE
EIGHT YEARS LATER

"Can I take off the blindfold yet?"

Lorcan's low chuckle was a promise. A shiver worked slowly down my spine. Silk slid away from my face. City lights flashed past our car window. New York City, to be precise. Arya was finishing her master's degree at Columbia University, in journalism. Not that she needs the credentials, having already established herself in the field, but she wanted them and it's our policy to fund education for any Auralian who wants one.

"Where are we going?" I asked. Lorcan put one arm around my shoulders and brought me in for a kiss.

"That, Princess, is a surprise."

I didn't correct him. I just smiled and kissed him again. "Is there a reason you requested the green dress?"

Every year, he plans an extravagant celebration for me, to make up for the two awful birthdays I spent in the castle. I'm sure months of effort went into making this night possible.

"I have fond memories of you in it." His hand trailed

down my bare arm. His mouth at my throat, nipping that spot that never fails to melt me from the inside. "You look great."

After three children, I'm surprised it still fits.

We stopped in front of an unassuming limestone building on a quiet block. Lamplight overhead turned Lorcan's hair—still an overlong mess, partially obscuring one eye—*never change, my love*—an unnatural shade of orange.

"This way." He made a show of folding up the silk blindfold and placing it into the pocket over his heart. My heels aren't made for narrow alleyways. This one is surprisingly clean.

"If you're planning to fuck me in an alleyway for my birthday, Lorcan, I will castrate you," I whispered.

He glanced over his shoulder at me with a bemused expression. "No, you wouldn't, and now I'm tempted to. Unfortunately, that's not why we're here. This is the back entrance. Avoiding paparazzi."

"Like your sister?" I asked sweetly.

"She's already inside."

Arya has made a name for herself as the official royal photographer of Auralia. Mostly, this involves taking pictures of her brother and me, hence my joke.

Lorcan knocked on an unassuming door. It opened instantly. A huge guard patted us down. My husband's scowl as I got frisked was hilarious. To this day, he does not like it when anyone is overly familiar with my person. I bit my lower lip and smiled.

"Keep that up and your birthday evening will be very short," he murmured.

"Mm, I doubt that."

We've earned our reputation for scandalous PDAs, but even I was thankful for the dark hallway when Lorcan pinned me against the wall and curled his tongue into my mouth. I held him there, wanting more, promising everything, for a long time.

"It's a good thing I haven't put on lipstick yet," I laughed when he released me.

"Go on. I'll mess it up again later." Lorcan skimmed his hand down my bare back and waited while I popped open a compact. Then he led me upstairs to the big reveal.

A nightclub. I clapped delightedly.

I outgrew the clubbing scene before I had a chance to really experience it, which is probably for the best. My few forays didn't go that well. This is a grown-up version, a fancy speakeasy-style club for the rich and famous. Which, these days, includes us.

We haven't exactly achieved world peace, but Auralia punches far above its weight in terms of global influence. Our mysterious violet liquid, which no one has yet chemically identified, has massively undercut the global use of fossil fuels. By selling it to the biggest polluters and the smallest developing nations alike, we more or less single-handedly took out the oil and gas industry. Climate goals are finally getting on track.

A lot of powerful people are *pissed*.

Humayun's petroleum fortunes declined precipitously, which threw Trissau into a bloody succession battle. Interestingly, Sohrab emerged victorious and became king in his own right. He modernized the country to the point that Hallie, Laila, their mother, and Cyrus are free to come and go as they wish. Cyrus moved back home, taking with him a Myseč husband. Trissau is now our closest trading partner.

Ours might not have been a disastrous union, though it

wouldn't have been a happy one. I would always have missed Lorcan, had I gone through with it. (Lorcan is less philosophical about it, barely tolerating Sohrab, and vice versa.)

We sell our energy liquid subject to certain conditions, pressuring countries large and small to invest in decarbonization, education and habitat preservation. Despite this, demand is higher than ever, and our Treasury is bursting at the seams.

The Sentinels were a warning about technology and how much we rely upon it. They were never meant to save us. But their power source has been a gift to all humanity.

"Our table is over there." Lorcan gestured to an alcove with teal velvet seats and a silver tin wall, the space ornamented with a sparkly glass chandelier. Raina waved.

"This is amazing." I clutched his forearm and followed closely behind him.

Tovian bussed my cheek in greeting, as did Arya, Scarlett, Hallie and her wife. Laila and Damir sat crushed together at the back of the huge booth, along with Palla and Bennet. Still inseparable.

"Happy birthday!" Arya called out.

Drinks. Cake. Laughter. It's a night of freedom in the outside world, made possible by the very man who curtailed my first attempted foray all those years ago in Beijing.

I squeezed his knee.

"Raina, you're not drinking?" Lorcan asked. Tovian smirked. Proud father, again, and the only man I've ever met who's as besotted with his wife as mine is. Raina and I are both incredibly lucky.

"Number five, due next Midwinter." She sighed. "Hoping for a girl this time."

Four boys. I can't even imagine. One is enough for me.

Our son's arrival was a complete shock. We were expecting a third girl, when out came a little boy instead. Lorcan loves our daughters without question, but he was delighted to have a son. It wasn't supposed to be possible; he, of course, took this as a sign that the Goddess has shown her favor.

Can't really argue that we've led her country into a golden age. Not that I believe in such nonsense, but the legends are clear. Auralia only sends sons to her progeny when her line is secure.

Ileana—Lili, for short—our eldest, inherited all of my studiousness and her father's devotion to our religion. She's likely to become the next High Priestess of Auralia as soon as she's old enough—a duty I am more than happy to surrender whenever she's ready.

Catrya, our middle child, is a warrior like her father—all scraped knees and elbows and playing with pointy objects. Palla adores her and Tahra is teaching her all the Čovari secrets, alongside Lorcan. He's also taken the lead in Sethi's training. Cata's protege is training her son. There's a symmetry to it that's both sad and wonderful. I wish she were here to see it. My father, too. He got a lot of things wrong, but he was still my dad. I like to think he would've been a better father to Sethi than he was to me.

I keep hoping Ronan will be a scientist after my own heart. At two, he certainly seems interested in testing concepts like gravity, velocity, and his nursemaid's patience. I love my children with my whole heart.

Lorcan swept back my hair and leaned in to whisper, "Would you like to dance?"

"Always."

I adore dancing, especially with him. We slide out of the

booth and make our way down to the seething mass of bodies. The song is one from the 90s, an era I wasn't around for, though I've heard it enough to know some of the words. I slink between people, leading him to the center of the floor.

A hand lands on my arm. Gentle. Firm. Lorcan spins me into his arms. We swayed in time with the music.

"Good birthday?"

"I'm still wondering what's in store for me later." Sliding my hand down his chest, I patted the pocket he tucked the blindfold into. Lorcan's hand glided down the smooth silk of my gown.

"And I'm wondering what this is." He traced the outline of the new lingerie I'm wearing. The nice thing about bits of lace and silk is how easy they are to conceal in your luggage.

"Something I picked up in Paris." I tapped his lower lip with my forefinger.

A flash burst nearby. We glanced over, saw Arya snapping pictures, and shrugged. She knows when to catch us at our best, and when to leave us alone. Her photographs are PR gold.

My lips brush against the rim of his ear. "What's in store for me, Lorcan?"

His arm tightens around my waist. "Thirty years old."

"Yes? And?"

He palmed my ass. "I'm going to make you come once for each year."

A tremor wracked me.

"That'll take you a while. Better get started, don't you think?"

Lorcan's chuckle vibrated through me. He might get one or two on the way back to our hotel.

"We can go now, if you want to, Princess."

He might get one before we get back to the car.

As much as we miss our children when we're away, it's nice not to hear the pad of little feet coming to our bed. It turns out that we are terribly lenient parents. Often, we wind up with two or three small bodies wedged between us. It'll be nice to get back, but...

Tonight is for freedom. For us. Together.

Get an exclusive sweet and steamy bonus scene with Zosia and Lorcan:

https://BookHip.com/XDSMMNR

THEN FIND out how Raina meets Tovian in *Crimson Throne:*

Excerpt:

Eighteen days after the invasion

I wish we'd left Zosia in Scotland, where she was safe.

There are so many regrets I don't have time for. Not if I want to outwit the men searching for me.

I'm marginally more familiar with this place than they are. Nobody sets foot in the Boscage if they can avoid it. Between the insects, the heat, the humidity, and the dragons—not to mention rumors of the mordecam—I'm not too pleased to be here myself, crouched in the under-brush, sweating and itchy, gritting my teeth against the *endless stinging gnats* so as not to betray my hiding place.

Rustling underbrush. I froze, heart pounding.

Something very large and decidedly not human slid through the trees. I glimpsed leathery scales the color of tree bark and rust, a slow movement as a very large animal made its way down the pathway minutes behind the men.

Reila save me, it's real.

I closed my eyes and tried not to panic.

The mordecam. The beast of legend. It cornered the Goddess Auralia and her sisters, Reila and Astra, and was about to eat them until the Hero Protector saved them, so the story goes. Auralia married him and founded the royal line of descendants of the goddess.

Zosia is the last of the goddess' line. It's kind of impor-tant that we find her.

It's also *so annoying* how so many of the legends omit that part about the other two goddesses when telling that legend, not that it's my biggest concern at the moment.

My biggest problem right now is getting the fuck out of the Boscage and away from that monster.

Never thought running *toward* war would be the better option. Yet here I am. Running toward danger. Again.

Auralia can afford to lose me. Unlike Zosia, I'm not essential. My tribe is the largest subgroup, and my family is huge and sprawling. I have two younger sisters, a multitude of cousins, and aunts galore.

Still, I'd rather not be lost. I'm looking forward to being coronated eventually. I've had a couple of years of fun, and I've been ready to settle down for a while. But Lorcan refused my marriage proposal, and then war broke out, and—

A hand encircled my waist at the same moment as its partner clamped around my mouth. My back hit a warm, solid wall before I could scream.

Even when you're not here I can't stop thinking about you. You're going to get me killed.

"Quiet," a man said, in English.

My heart raced. *Fuck, fuck, fuck.* Captured by one of the pirates? Shit, no. I've seen what they do to women. I'm not going out that way.

He dragged me backward several feet. There was a rush of movement in the trees. A large animal moving through the undergrowth. *Very* large.

The instant it was gone, I bit down hard on my captor's hand. I could only latch onto a scrap of the fleshy part, so I made it count.

He grunted and tightened his hold around my waist. Fortunately, Lorcan taught me how to fight hard and dirty —and I've had plenty of practice over the last several weeks. *Turn your weaknesses into strengths.* He's not the biggest guy in the world, and he has a lot of experience with winning when he's outmatched.

I pray he's alive.

I slammed my elbow into my attacker's ribs. He was ready for that move, but not for the way I stomped on his foot and threw my head back to hit his chin with the back of my skull. Double elbows to the ribs, a grunt, and I was free.

I made it five steps.

My assailant made a flying leap and tackled me to the ground. I rolled and kneed him in the stomach, kicking. He got a hold of my wrists and *flipped* over me, landing softly on his back, out of reach of my legs. Still gripping my forearms.

That's not a pirate move. They're agile and strong, but generally untrained.

"You fucking bastard," I hissed in English, twisting to look at him.

Our eyes met. I blinked. He's beautiful. Wide, dark eyes fringed with the longest lashes I've ever seen. Full lips and a sloped nose. Black hair cropped close around his head and smooth, umber skin.

I blinked again, then torqued up to kick him in the face.

He released me, so I continued rolling over and pushed up to standing. The world spun slightly as I regained my balance. Too late.

The pirate got ahold of my arm and yanked it high up behind my back. I yelped, then hooked his ankle and fell on purpose, taking him down with me. After a scuffle, I got on top of him and pinned him to the dirt with all my body weight. It's the only way a smaller opponent can subdue a larger one. How many times have I practiced this with Lorcan—

—except my friend never got a boner when we were sparring.

"Are you fucking kidding me?" I demanded in Auralian, panting hard. "You're turned on by this?"

"It's not every day I get my ass handed to me by a gorgeous stranger," he said, in my language. "Marry me?"

I growled, pulled back my arm and tried to deck him.

Read Crimson Throne now:
https://books2read.com/crimsonthrone

AUTHOR'S NOTE & ACKNOWLEDGEMENTS

This is the story of how Zosia and Lorcan stole my heart and refused to let me give up on writing.

In January of 2020, I wasn't in a good place, mentally. I'd suffered a setback with my primary pen name, Carrie Lomax. I was burned out. You know that state where you can barely function, feel like a failure—exhausted, anxious, and unable to meet the basic demands of life?

That was me.

I said I was done writing. I started a new day job in mid-February of 2020 that required me to be in an office 9-5 Monday-Friday. I walked away from being an author.

One month later, the pandemic hit.

I was *already* in burnout when I suddenly had to impress a new boss and team while working remotely, and supervise a kindergartener and 3rd grader doing Zoom school. My husband was also working from home. Tensions were high. Balance did not exist in those early weeks, when we were all just trying to survive.

I'll never forget the sense of dislocation. Before/after. One day, you think you have your life sorted out, and the next, everything is changed.

I coped by turning to comfort movies. Now, I am a die-hard romance fan and have been for my entire adult life. Romance has saved my sanity more times than I can count. But in movies, I like explosions. Action. Intrigue. I no longer had to commute, and I wasn't writing, so I sat in my basement rewatching *Jurassic Park, The Lord of the Rings,* and *The Bourne Identity* at night when my family was asleep. (As well as *Contagion*, to my husband's bafflement.)

Movies where the good guys win, and love triumphs.

Stories in which there's a before/after moment that changes how you view the whole world.

Okay, Joline, but what does this have to do with Auralia?

After a few months of watching movies and drinking wine on my couch, I slowly started to come back to life. Story ideas were pinging around in my head again.

This was my first foray into fantasy romance. I felt like I was re-learning how to write.

Then, in March 2021, my grandmother passed away.

I put away my stories—at that stage, it was in 2 parts—and spent the summer slowly acclimating back to real life, in a changed world. Parts were recognizable. My kids went to summer camp. They struggled to catch up in reading and math. We all adjusted to this new version of the life we'd known before.

I couldn't stop thinking about Zosia and Lorcan. About my own rocky relationship with my father when I was her age, and how, now that we're both older, we've learned to appreciate one another. As I write this, he is coping with Stage 4 cancer. It's terminal. I'm glad that didn't happen when I was 18 and trying to figure myself out. I'm sad it's happening now.

And I thought about how, as a parent, I try every day to do the right thing, even though I often fall short. I wanted my story to show how people who are trying their very best can fail despite their best efforts—and that our mistakes don't make us undeserving of love.

Along the way, I started reading about Vučedol culture,

a Serbo-Croatian people who flourished between 3000 and 2200 BCE. Some of their religious symbolism is associated with the cult of the Great Mother, which provided a jumping-off point for my concept of Auralia's dominant religion. They had their own astral calendar based on an Orion cycle. Little is known about their language, making it an ideal "source" I could use as a reference point, while making it up or borrowing from modern-day Croatian as I saw fit. Dr. Surrain, a specialist in bilingual education, gave me tips for making the invented words believable (and pronounceable).

All errors are my own. The biggest error I ended up keeping was the spelling of Auralia. "Aurelia" would have been ideal, but it turned out to be trademarked. I didn't want to get lawyered, so I changed it.

I also plotted out a journey for the original settlers of Auralia, through the Adriatic Sea to Greece, through Egypt —where Auralia picks up the "ra" sound in the middle— and out the Red Sea into the Indian Ocean, where they find their magical island. Radiant Horizons is a free download.

By November of 2021—National Novel Writing Month, or NaNoWriMo—I had a map, a history, a partial language, a religion, and a baseline draft. My planning document was 40 pages long, single-spaced. I rewrote all 125,000 words into a 200,000-word story split by the beginning of the invasion.

Before/after.

Zosia, already struggling to form her adult identity under crushing pressure, is forced to re-evaluate everything she once believed. I was sure I wanted to publish these two books, written solely in her voice.

Then I wrote a "companion novella" in Lorcan's voice.

Oops. That wasn't part of the plan, but the mission was to write things I loved, and I loved getting his view on events.

What does it mean for someone to lose their purpose in life? How would someone as driven as he is react? (Not well.)

At this point, I sent my lengthy story to Dr. Sarah Surrain and Eve Pendle, both of whom provided invaluable insights. Their feedback led me to combine Lorcan's book and the beginning of Zosia's second book, resulting in the trilogy you're reading now.

Thank you to both for the thoughtful and helpful comments. I'm sorry I killed off Cata—thus far, my most controversial decision as an author! (I also kept the apples. Sorry, Sarah!) I am so grateful to have you smart women as friends.

To Jackie Barbosa, your encouragement and friendship is invaluable. Thank you for telling me to go after what I loved instead of trying to push through burnout.

I have been so fortunate to find a community with authors Zoe York's wonderful author group. You keep me sane in this wild business! Loki is in charge, and I rely on Write All The Words to keep me on track. I also want to thank Lisette Marshall and Vela Roth from the FaRoFeb board for offering sound advice. We all grow and learn, and I my next book will be better thanks to all of your insights.

I'm also grateful to my husband, Michael, and my children, who've heard more about this series than they ever wanted to.

To Kelly Leone for providing detailed beta reading, and Charity Chimni for editing—this series wouldn't shine without you.

To my readers—if you've liked, commented, reviewed or simply enjoyed this story—a heartfelt thank you. I hope you loved Zosia and Lorcan as much as I do. If you'd like to learn more about what inspired them as characters, I encourage you to sign up for my newsletter at https://joline pearce.com/newsletter/

I hope you'll continue the *Fallen Realm* series with Raina's book, *Crimson Throne*, and Auralia's standalone origin story, *Radiant Horizons*, available when you sign up for my newsletter.

Life is full of before/after moments—the pandemic; Russia's invasion of Ukraine; a loved one dying. I hope this series resonates, whether by providing a distraction from things we can't control, an outlet for grief, or the realization that we all grow into our power with time.

Sometimes, the bravest thing we can do is sit with our sorrow and be a light in the darkness.

And sometimes, that light is a TV screen in your basement while the world falls apart around you.

-Joline

ABOUT THE AUTHOR

Joline Pearce writes dark and angsty fantasy romance with an irreverent streak. A librarian by day, she is obsessed with shadow royals, likes pink wine, Converse shoes, and doesn't function without a *lot* of coffee. She also writes bestselling, award-winning historical and contemporary romance as Carrie Lomax. Joline lives in Maryland with her husband, two kids, and a Boston Terrier/Beagle mix rescue dog.

- facebook.com/authorjolinepearce
- x.com/JolinePearce4
- instagram.com/jolinepearce
- bookbub.com/profile/joline-pearce
- tiktok.com/@jolinepearce

BOOKS BY JOLINE PEARCE

Awakened

Sweet Briar (Sleeping Beauty Retelling)
Midnight Deception (Cinderella Retelling)

Fallen Realm

The *Fallen Realm* series is meant to be read in order:
Main trilogy:

- *Falling Princess*
- *Eternal Knight*
- *Queen Rising* (happy ever after)

Crimson Throne can be read as a standalone.

Get all 5 books in a convenient box set exclusively on Amazon.